LOVE, BLOOD & FURY

STRINGS OF FATE: **BOOK ONE**

MELISSA J. KINCAID

LOTS OF LOVE CREATIONS

LOVE, BLOOD & FURY

STRINGS OF FATE **BOOK ONE**

MELISSA J. KINCAID

Love, Blood and Fury
A Strings of Fate Novel: Book One
By Melissa J. Kincaid

ISBN (Paperback): 9780645054804
ISBN (Hardback): 9780645054828
ISBN (eBook): 9780645054811
ISBN (Special Edition Paperback): 9781764048620

Published by Lots of Love Creations.

Edited by Carolyn Gilpin.

Commissioned art by @kalynne_art (Kalynne Pratt) consisting of characters Ariiaya, Lorch and Elijah.

Cover design, map and illustrations by Melissa J Kincaid.

To my family, friends and all who encouraged me to pursue my dream.

Enjoy this piece of my heart, hold it close and know that you helped
make it become possible.

The Land of Fythnar

Main Characters

Ariiaya Trillia:	Arr – ee – aya	Trill – ee – ah
Elijah Wolfe:	Ee – lie – jah	Wolf
Lorch Kruel:	Lor – k	Crew – el
Krepth Hallier:	Kre – p – th	Hal – ee – er
Nemesis Rion:	Ne – meh – sis	Ree – on
Tikkani Alinar:	Tik – an – i	
Emerson Alinar:	Em – er – son	
Quinn:	K – win	
Valdis:	Val – dis	
Lynnera:	Lin – era	
Sybell:	Si – bell	
Klotho:	Clo – tho	
Etropos:	E – tro – poss	
Lakhesis:	La – kes – is	
Devina:	Deh – veen – ah	

Court Families, Creatures and Towns

Freya:	Frey – ah	
Jero:	Jer – row	
Thogan:	Tho – gan	
Kadec Brolikian:	Kad – ek	Bro – li – kee – ann
Tyverus:	Tie – ver – us	
Hannera:	Han – eera	
Ghila:	Gill – ah	
Brohem:	Bro – hem	
Eliverus:	Ee – lie – ver – us	
Kryvern:	Cry – vern	
Fythnar:	Fi – th – nar	
Viridya:	Vir – id – ee – ya	

North Court
The Dragon's Teeth
Ayrith
West Court
Bonemire
East Court
School of Fate
Viridya
Evergrave
The Sapphire Depths
Colkirk
The Wastes
Amberbourne
The Slither
Traders Bay
Lilidale
Pendle
South Court
The Cove
The Ivory Plains
Fjoll
Mirfield
The Boundless Sea
Skaald
Erstonia

CHAPTER ONE

A hooded figure moved through the crowded street like a shadow.

Had anyone been paying attention, they would have noticed that the figure made no sound of footfalls, no reassuring tap of boots on the uneven pavement. They did not stop to look at any of the market stalls, piled high with taffeta and fine goods. The alleyway was cramped full of people, humans and elves alike, leisurely browsing the array of items on display.

Located on the western coast of Fythnar, Traders Bay was renowned for its after dark market stalls, offering everything from high quality silks and materials to meticulously crafted pieces such as vases and jewellery.

It was an unseasonably warm night, and the moon hung high in the midnight sky, the inky blackness sprinkled with winking stars.

The crowded alleyway sparkled with lanterns, strung from crumbling wall to wall across the alley, giving it an almost ethereal look – like glitter on shit. Traders Bay was not an attractive town, or the most well-kept. The air had a lingering stink of fish and salt, the lapping of waves against the moss riddled docks a constant melody. Many of the seamen who docked there came from far away lands, trading their goods for exorbitant prices, then moving on. The streets were filthy, the houses in shambles, but people did not come to Traders Bay for the sightseeing and real estate. The dark market also offered other things to sate the desires of more nefarious individuals, like prostitution and slavery.

These particular services were not so obvious, nor were they on display – they were only available to those who knew where to look and who to ask.

The hooded figure did not touch anyone as they moved, no accidental brushing of a shoulder, no gentle nudges to make their way through the crowd. They moved like water through gently parted fingers. The individual under the dark cloth hood was intent, unquestionably sure of where they were going.

Finally, pausing at a stall lined with crates of apples, the figure said nothing as they awaited the clerk's attention. The man, stout and balding, paused while waxing an apple to add to the array of meticulously shining fruits to gaze at his silent customer.

"Wha' can I get ye?" he drawled before looking up. The clerk, aged in his late forties, narrowed his eyes when the figure did not respond.

"If ye looking for cloth…" he trailed off, eyeing the figure's clothing – a black hood hid their face, the cloak trailing to their feet and ending a hand's length from the cobblestones. A leather corset was wrapped around their torso, adorned with gleaming buckles and hardened leather. Under the cloak, a belt flashed a hint of silver.

Daggers.

Boots to knee length encased their feet, intricate patterns pressed into the leather. This was no ordinary patron of the market, and the clerk felt heat begin to rise up his throat.

"Or if ye be after arms, there be an arms merchant two stalls down from 'ere," the clerk said quickly, placing the apple down on the others and proceeding to point down the market alley.

"I was told you would know where I could find ivory…"

The voice, undoubtedly female, slid like warm honey, a breathy cadence which caused ears to perk and legs to wobble. Mysterious, gentle, and deadly calm tinged with a promise of pain.

The clerk's brows narrowed, sweat beading on his forehead.

Was it oddly warm tonight, or was it his new cotton tunic?

He swiftly swiped the beads away with the back of his hand.

"I-Ivory? N-no… Miss? Only apples 'ere!" he choked out, throat bobbing, a cold sweat saturating the neckline of his tunic.

The figure, head ever so slightly inclined to the side, followed a tiny bead of sweat from the man's lip, down his chin to his neck. It did not take a magician to see the man was nervous, and the smell his fear was emanating was acrid in the air. The figure's nose wrinkled under the cloth.

"I'll ask again…" said the woman, voice firm. "Ivory… or do you require a jog of your memory?" she said as long nailed fingers emerged from her cloak.

In a flash, a dagger was buried in an apple, a hair's breadth from the clerk's groin.

An alarmed squeak left the man's lips and he inched back, eyes riveted to the dagger's ruby-encrusted hilt. "S-Seems I'm remembering something… erm… Ivory you say? Yes… I-I know a man by that name. Be it him you are after? Mr Ivory… hard man to find he is," the man spluttered, his words rushing from his lips in a torrent.

"Yes, he prefers crowded marketplaces where one cannot have a private word…" the figure drawled, retrieving the dagger from the apple and slipping it back into its sheath. The movement was fluid, swift, practiced.

"He needs to be given a message…"

As she spoke, she pulled a piece of golden string from the pouch at her hip. She held it out to the clerk, whose eyes widened as he absorbed what this meant. The string emanated a strange radiating light, as if it has been pulled from some sort of enchanted tapestry. It shimmered in the lanternlight.

Anyone who laid eyes on it knew that this was no ordinary string. It did not come from any of the stalls lined in the filthy, candlelit street. It did not come from a distant land, was not a rare piece of textile, nor did it come from a faraway place with an abundance of magic and wonder.

This string belonged to the Three Fates, woven from the Tapestry of Life, and this was a sign that someone's life was about to end.

It was then the clerk – with a cry like a crazed animal – grabbed the table and launched the carefully arranged display of apples at the messenger of his doom. With surprising physical ability, the stocky, overweight man vaulted over the side of his stall and ran like ravenous hounds were on his heels, knocking over his neighbour's array of hard cheeses in his craze to flee.

The hooded figure dodged the assault of apples with a twist of her body and sprinted down the market alley, dodging patrons like fish through water. Using the lip of a stall as a boost, she climbed up the side of the nearest building, finding purchase using jutted-out stones and wooden window frames. The stall owner below gasped and cursed, checking their display to see if anything had been touched by the figure's boots.

Not a single item had moved.

The apple stall clerk, in his frenzy to flee, pushed market patrons into the dirt and elbowed people out of the way. There were plenty of places to hide in this dark, dank town, but the man knew he would not get away easily. In a world of fight or flight, he was opting for flight. No-one stood against an assassin sent by the Three Fates, and he knew his chances were next to none if he were to fight.

The assassin flew across the rooftops, boots lightly thudding on thatched timbers as she leaped between buildings, keeping her target in sight. Below, the man's strained gasps were audible over the hustle and bustle of the market, the stench of his fear like a trail of crumbs to his pursuer. People moved out of his way, and those who did not were shoved violently aside.

The assassin's nose winkled as she launched herself from a roof just above where the man had begun to labour. The repugnant scent of the man's fear was a lingering taint upon the air she breathed.

Her hand shot out, wrist flicking with a flourish, and suddenly a nearby display of fruit and vegetables beside the fleeing man exploded. Shouts of alarm pursued, and the assassin flicked her wrist again, causing the next display of bread to explode. Normally she would not resort to causing destruction with her magic, but she was not about to let her target escape.

She had waited too long to sink her blade into this one.

The man screamed as he ran, assaulted from all sides by flying food, but his retreat did not slow. With a frustrated grunt, the assassin shot from the rooftop, landing on the next building and rolling to soften the impact. Without pause, she continued to sprint, eyes flicking up to see a clothesline overladen with clothing, just ahead of the running clerk.

She shot out a hand and snapped her fingers together.

Magic sparked in the air, and the clothing on the line burst into flame with an audible crack, before the assassin twisted her hand again, making a downward swipe.

The flaming materials dropped, right into the path of the fleeing man.

He skidded to a stop, toppling back onto the cobblestones before staring at the flaming barricade before him in terror.

Covered in juices and ash, the clerk jumped to his feet and glanced behind him, expecting to see a hooded figure of death hot on his heels. His gaze flew over the rooftops around him in rapt terror, eyes bulging and jowls wobbling. When all he could see were angry faces of market patrons and stall owners, he blew out a breath and quickly limped into a branch alley to his right.

The alley was scarcely lit and reeked of piss – the clerk felt the adrenaline coursing through him like hot fire.

Had he lost his pursuer?

That was unlikely.

The Fury had used magic! In front of innocent people! Had the Fates slackened their training over at the school for assassins?

His nefarious dealings had finally caught up with him, it seemed.

The clerk paused to catch his breath, hands on knees and inhaling in long gasping wheezes. Sweat dripped from the tip of his pink nose.

Suddenly a figure emerged from the shadows, as if it were one with the darkness. A blade pressed against the man's jugular, the steel to his skin so close to piercing. He cried out, but soon snapped his mouth shut for fear of his throat being opened to the night sky. Sweat cascaded down his forehead, breath hissing between clenched yellow teeth.

He was going to die, he knew that, and there was not a thing he could do about it. The Fates had finally drawn his string of life from the Tapestry, and his time was about to end in one of the worst ways possible.

By assassination.

"How did you find me?" the man hissed, sweat trickling into his eye. The assassin slowly smiled from beneath the hood of her cloak, a flash of white teeth behind red lips, canines slightly elongated. Her breath tickled his ear, lips brushing his lobe. Anyone looking into the alley may have mistaken the two entwined in an embrace, save for the dagger pressing against the trembling man's throat.

He had been so careful! Every track, every sliver of evidence that could point to him and his dark dealings had been efficiently swept under every rug possible. Every person sold had their papers burned, their origins a secret.

How had this assassin – a woman no less – found him?

"Once your thread of life is spun and measured..." her blade pressed deeper, and the man let out a low groan of terror. Blood beaded on the blade edge, as the skin broke. The assassin's voice was low, silky, like melted caramel over a decadent dessert.

A dark stain began to bloom on the man's breaches as he pissed himself.

"There is no escaping your final fate."

The line laced with a tone of finality that had been used hundreds of times before. This was the absolute truth, those who had dark dealings got what they deserved in the end, and it was her job to deliver this justice.

In a motion as quick as silver, the blade sliced through flesh, cleaving the man's windpipe open to the air. Blood sprayed the dank wall with a glitter of scarlet, a mural of vermilion droplets glistening in the moonlight.

The clerk made a gurgling sound and dropped to his knees. With a thump, his body hit the uneven, wet stones of the alley, his lifeblood pooling around his body in a slow expanding puddle of crimson.

The assassin wiped her blade across her elbow, a hiss of disgust sliding from her lips as she eyed the body. Con Ivory was more than just an apple stall clerk. He dealt primarily in trafficking elven slaves to the local brothels. This was not uncommon in Fythnar, not by a long shot, but Ivory dealt primarily with elves who were far too young to know what was happening to them.

She had been waiting for his thread to be pulled for a long, long time…

Ariiaya Trillia knew that the evidence of her work would soon be wiped away by beings employed as a clean-up crew by The School of Fate, but any scrap of this filth being dashed from the face of the kingdom could not come soon enough.

With a long sigh, Arii bent over the cooling body with her blade and set to collect her trophy.

♋

The head rolled across marble floor, stopping just shy of a pair of immaculate, diamond encrusted shoes. The man's face, slack in death with eyes rolled back, stared up at the shoes' wearer.

"Always one for theatrics, Ariiaya Trillia," the woman said as she clapped her hands together with obvious admiration. Grinning, she shot a look back at her two sisters on the dais.

Behind them stood a large draping tapestry. It was a remarkable sight, an onslaught of imagery all tangled up in a detailed scene of unexplained history. Castles, people and animals, all entwined in stories. Arii swore she could see a dragon's silhouette in there somewhere when she looked hard enough.

The Tapestry of Life glittered and glowed, enchanted with magic.

The room was lit with an array of haphazardly placed candles, wax littering the stone floor with puddles of white. The walls were dark stone, and some of the mortar had slowly began to flake away, green vines of ivy breaking through the weakest parts to splay across the stone. All around them were large stacks of books, ancient tomes with unreadable spines and discoloured pages that left a heady scent of old vanilla in the air. The School of Fate had a library, but the sisters kept their favourite and oldest tomes here in their weaving room, where they spent most of their time.

"That is why you are my favourite assassin!"

The red-headed woman clapped again with glee as the severed head seeped blood across the stone floor.

"Anyone else would provide a trinket as proof of their successful hunt, or perhaps a finger."

She bent over, grabbing the head by what little hair it had and lifting it for all in the room to see. Con Ivory's jaw wobbled in an eternal silent scream as Etropos shook the severed head.

"Brilliant work, my Violet Assassin," she crooned, a grin splitting her lips.

Arii rose from her crouch before the dais, her head lifting. Slowly she removed her hood, striking violet eyes revealed – the reason for her moniker. She was still young for a Fae at twenty-eight, her skin pale and flawless, a face that disarmed even the hardest of men – disarmed them even as their heads were removed from their shoulders before they could blink.

Ariiaya was a Fury, one of the Fae blessed with magic, and taken into service by the Three Fates as a young girl. All Fae had magic lying dormant within them, but it took a considerable event to unlock the awakening – emotional or physical. Some Fae lived their entire lives without their magic manifesting, such a thing was not unheard of. All of the Furies in service of the Fates were taken in at a young age when their magic awoke, trained to control their power and forfeit their emotions, turning them into the deadliest assassins in the land – weapons wielded in the name of the Gods.

Once the land of Fythnar was teeming with Fae – delicately

pointed eared beings with incredible strength, grace and magic unlike the other races they shared the land with.

Now, they were a dwindling species.

"I aim to please." Arii drawled, not a flicker of remorse or emotion on her face. "His string was long overdue to be cut…" she said, brushing a strand of hair from her face. Her hair was unique, a biproduct of her magic. Dark, thick brown tresses reaching to her breasts, slowly lightening to honey at the ends. All Furies tended to have unique hair which was a result of their magic, matching their incredible beauty.

All the better to draw in their prey.

Etropos snickered and wiggled the head again, making Mr Ivory's jaw waggle in time to her voice.

"Bad men always get what they deserve, isn't that right, Mr Ivory? No longer will you serve up elf children on silver platters."

The head jiggled in agreeance.

Arii suppressed a wince. Etropos loved to play with the remnants of her victims. From behind Etropos, two other women stood, all dressed immaculately in attire fit for a function at a royal castle. Etropos was the liveliest of the three sisters, the other two were more placid and stoic in comparison.

Klotho, a woman sporting midnight hair and pale lips, looked at the head of Con Ivory with slight disgust, her top lip twitching. Of the three sisters, she was the one who pulled and weaved the threads from the Tapestry. Each woman was beautiful, their eyes all a shade of gold that matched the shimmering tapestry beyond.

The other woman, Lakhesis, was donned all in white with silver hair and blood red lips. Lakhesis measured the strings of the Tapestry, determining the victims' span of life. She stared serenely at the scene and when she spoke, her voice was light and airy.

"Good, now take that vile thing away, if you are done playing with it, Etropos. We have the next assignment to deal with," she said, waving a carefully manicured hand dismissively before turning back to her work.

The last sister, Etropos, was the allotter of justice – the hander of the assignments to their assassins.

Beside Lakhesis, Klotho pinched a thread of the tapestry and began to pull. The string came free of the drapery, glowing much like that of Mr Ivory's string in the market.

The Three Fates handed down justice after being told by the seemingly non-sentient drapery who was to be ended. Normally the targets were criminals, individuals who evaded the regular justice of the royal guards. Those chosen were purely random and chosen by the Tapestry itself, and it was a continued debate of what the Tapestry was and where it had come from. The three sisters themselves did not know – it just was, and they were its messengers.

Many believed the Tapestry of Life was a link to the Gods, controlled by a higher power. Through methods inexplicable to anyone but them, the Fates had glimpses of who the string could belong to, the visions flowed from one sister to another – first Klotho, to Lakhesis and then Etropos, the latter being the one to deliver the message.

The visions were but fragments, they claimed – the exact target an educated guess.

Turning, Klotho passed the string to Lakhesis, who studied the thread intently. Slowly, her eyes lifted to Etropos, and the red-haired woman dropped the severed head to the floor with an audible *thump*. Rushing to her sisters, Etropos took the string between her fingers, handling it as if it were made of glass.

The string, unlike that of the previous one handed to Arii, appeared to be woven of pure glowing gold, so unlike that of the rest of the Tapestry.

The sisters looked at one another, as if a silent conversation were happening between them, before turning to Ariiaya in unison.

"Your next assignment…" Etropos murmured, her grey eyes glazed over as visions assaulted her mind. Her sisters had the same look as she held up the golden thread. "…will be located in the royal castle of Viridya."

Her voice took on a sound of distortion, as if someone or *something* were speaking through her lips.

"We see a crown, and a royal seat covered in blood…" Etropos' flippant smile was long gone, her hair lifting on a phantom wind as the message was passed through her from the Gods.

Arii felt her entire body tense, a spring coiling within her.

As long as she had been in service of the Fates, she had never heard of an assignment to take out a royal. Viridya Castle was a fortress made of gold, almost impossible to infiltrate, as discovered by countless previous assassins and shady persons hoping to either take out someone from the Court within or rob from the royal treasury.

Klotho was next to speak, her voice clipped and noxious. Her brows narrowed and her teeth bared. "Your next target sits upon the royal throne…" she confirmed, and the air in the large room was thick with magic.

Arii felt trepidation slither through her form, a fine tremor running down her spine as Etropos spoke.

"Your target, if the Gods speak true, is Lorch Kruel, the young King on the throne of Fythnar."

Arii felt her blood turn cold.

Well, shit…

⌘

"My next target is the King."

The air in the cluttered tavern was stifling, and even as the golden rays of dawn's light touched the rafters, the space was crammed with people drowning their sorrows.

Arii lifted a mug of mead to her lips, sipping the amber liquid before her violet eyes flicked to her two drinking companions. Sitting across from her was a dark-haired male with striking green eyes. His face was clean shaven, the straight black strands of his hair falling into his eyes. He was handsome, in a mysterious way, with sharp cheekbones and thick brows. Krepth Hallier was her oldest friend, their history starting before her magic's awakening and her service under the Fates.

His eyes roved Arii's face, as if scouting for the answer to a riddle.

With a sigh, the assassin lowered her cup to the wooden table. Her other companion, a slim female with straight silver hair to her chin, had been throwing darts at a board.

A perfect bullseye, every time.

Arii did not expect anything less from her long-term friend and fellow Fury, Nemesis Rion. But the woman's hand had paused in mid-air just as Arii delivered the news. Her aqua eyes slowly slid to the two at the table.

"Will you stop staring like I have a second head, Krepth, it is starting to piss me off," growled Arii as she lifted the mug to her lips once more.

They had the back of the tavern to themselves – their usual spot when they needed somewhere at short notice to meet but also hidden from prying eyes. The tavern, located in Colkirk – a little seaside village just south of the School of Fate – was a popular place for a careless social gathering.

It also featured the best mead in Fythnar, in Arii's opinion.

Nem's full lips pressed in a line as their male companion barked out a laugh, his smooth voice laced with amusement.

"Gods Arii, you are full of fantastical jokes tonight, I do suppose you get that way as the bloodlust wanes after a hunt," he chuckled again, taking a swig of his own mead.

"She isn't joking, Krepth..." said Nem as her arm lowered to her side, fingers clutching the dart. It was not like Ariiaya Trillia, the infamous Violet Assassin, to joke about a mark given to her by the Three Fates. The woman was emotionless and cool, not one to joke around with something so serious, so monumental within their small society.

Krepth lowered his mead to the table as he studied Arii's deadpan expression. "You're not jesting? Are the Sisters of Fate taking the *godsdamn* piss?"

His tone flipped from jovial to serious in a split second. It was unlike the shady spymaster to lose his cool, but this was unlike any news he had heard in a long time. Perhaps *ever*.

Arii's carefully composed expression faltered for a small moment and Nem was then beside the dark-haired assassin like a shadow.

"The images given to the Fates are undeniable..." Nem said, her gaze flicking up to her friend's face. "If what you described is exactly what they relayed, then I have no doubt that the King is your target."

"Viridya Castle is near impossible to infiltrate." Arii said, pausing as Krepth lifted a hand.

"You cannot sneak into the castle and slice off the head of the King," he said, brows pulling in a look of frustration.

'Quiet!' Nemesis was quick to jump in, her voice hushed.

They spoke of high treason after all.

"So, what do you suggest?" Nem barked, frowning. They all knew that the targets given by the Three Fates were final, and there was no point arguing.

A Fury should never question fate.

Arii absently wondered what the young King had done to draw the Gods' ire.

"Usually, you are full of good ideas, Krepth. Perhaps I should have approached you when you were sober," said Arii, one brow arching.

Krepth's mouth opened to retort, but Nem was quick to speak first.

"We will have to get you in under cover, ensure you have the closest access possible to the King." Nem's aqua eyes were pinned to her friends. "You will need to go in as a servant, get the King's attention somehow..." she trailed off, before lifting a finger. She hesitated, staring at her mercury-coloured nails, filed to long points. Nemesis was known for scraping them across surfaces before ending her targets, her nails enchanted with silver. It was a hell of an effect, causing the toughest men to loosen their bowels in fear as her swift shadow descended.

And the sisters called Arii theatrical.

With hand raised and fingers curled, Nem's gaze lifted to Krepth.

"What perfect timing," she breathed, a revelation coming to her.

Krepth's dark brows narrowed as his eyes lifted to the light-haired Fury.

"Explain," he snapped, impatient.

Elongated canines flashed as Nem grinned sardonically.

"It is the King's birthday tomorrow."

Arii felt something stir in her gut.

Was it excitement? Trepidation? Emotions were foreign to her, pressed into the deepest depths of her mind thanks to her training as an assassin.

Of course, the annual birthday party was a massive celebration in the golden behemoth of a castle, filled with fine food, festivities, and well-dressed rich people. It also required extra catering staff.

How old would the King be now, twenty-seven?

Krepth snapped Arii from her reverie, clicking his fingers together in front of her face as he said, "Perfect! Arii, I have connections that can get you into the castle as an extra hand. We–" he eyed Nem quickly, "–will create a diversion that will enable you to stand out to the King."

Arii's eyebrows creased as she stared at her friends. It was uncanny, how the two of them seemed to be on the same wavelength at times.

The remainder of the time, the two were normally at each other's throats.

Krepth inclined his mug at Arii, a dark grin splitting his handsome features. "It will be up to *you* to do the rest."

He lifted the mug to his lips, followed by with a wolfish grin over the rim, and Arii saw immediately the resemblance to his shifter form, an enormous black wolf with deep viridian eyes. Shifters were elven people who could take the forms of animals – some could even use magic for healing, but their magic stopped there.

"Fucking hell..." Arii muttered, such an unladylike curse to grace delicate lips, which in turn caused Nem to chuckle darkly.

Arii pinched the bridge of her nose as she said, "I knew cheating in that game of cards last week would come back to bite me on the arse."

"Cheaters never prosper," agreed Krepth, lifting his mead in a mock salute.

Arii tilted her head to him, both brows now raised as she said, "You were the one who suggested tampering with the cards!"

The Shifter offered her another wolfish grin. "Mhmm, that's the golden word, *suggested* – you did the rest."

"Fucking hell..." repeated Arii.

"We have much to do in little time," Krepth continued, tipping the remainder of the mead down his throat and slamming the mug to the table. Nemesis mirrored his action albeit a little more delicately and dropped a hand on Arii's shoulder in comfort as the pair stood, preparing to leave.

"Any hint of what to expect, perhaps?" snapped Arii. Krepth's trademark smirk spread across his face at the assassin's unimpressed expression.

"And ruin the birthday surprise? Come now, Arii."

Ariiaya's eyes turned dark in the candlelight, two pools of deep amethyst.

She hated surprises.

"Oh, Arii?" called Krepth, glancing over his shoulder as he headed for the tavern door. Dark hair shifted into his glittering green eyes, filled with amusement.

"Don't get killed," he said with a grin, pulling up his hood before disappearing into the night beyond.

Nemesis
Rion
Melissa Kincaid

CHAPTER TWO

Arii had learned the basics of their volatile land during her lessons at the School of Fate. When she was not wielding a blade, she had her head in one of the many textbooks from the sisters' library. Once a land united, Fythnar had been a prosperous place of allied nations, each bringing their own unique trades from all four points of the continent. Trade was teeming, and allegiances were strong. The land was brimming with magic, along with fantastical beasts of all kinds. Living in harmony with the creatures were Humans, Elves and the Fae. The Fae, a strong and proud elven race with powerful magic, had ruled all four Courts of the land.

Then things changed. In the North, the Fae living there held dominion with majestic, magic-bound dragons. Slowly the humans of the land began to fear the power of the Fae, so they began to rise up and form rebellions. Just over two hundred years ago the humans slowly began to wipe out the Fae – in particular the males of the species. It was believed by the humans that male Fae were becoming far too powerful, and that power was causing them to show signs of madness. The uprisings were swift, carefully planned and bloody, and before long there were only a handful of male Fae left, up until the last known males in a family ruling the North Court were killed in their beds on a cold Winter Solstice night twenty years ago.

The Courts at all points of the compass in the continent of Fythnar had families watching over them. The North Court consisted of the Kruel family, ruling over the vast majority of the map in their glittering castle of gold. The Kruel family had ascended to the throne once the last royal family were wiped from the board. With no one left of the bloodline, Valdis Kruel – Hand to the King in the North, had taken the throne of Fythnar, earning his son the title of King once the boy turned eighteen.

The East Court was submerged in the thick and dense forest of Evergrave, their homes built into the ancient trees headed by Freya Bloom. The folk there were the elves also known as Shifters, Krepth's people.

The South Court was seemingly in a constant state of Winter, ruled by Jero Vox and his twin brother Thogan, from their impressive castle overlooking a vast range of snow-capped mountains. Their people were harsh and barbarian-like, weathered and bred for battle.

Lastly, the West Court floated on an island just off the coast, the land littered in rainbows of flowers in an eternal Spring. In the middle sat a crystal castle housing Prince Kadec Brolikian, a party boy ruler who always seemed to be throwing a sparkling event.

Viridya Castle in the heart of the North Court was a sight to behold. A colossal structure built on the edge of a massive waterfall, the home of the royal family was made entirely of pure gold. Rumour had it that the original king who built the impressive structure was absolutely infatuated with himself, and demanded he be able to see his reflection wherever he went on the castle grounds. Those architects surely outdid themselves. With turrets reaching to incredible heights, the castle overlooked a mass of water called The Sapphire Depths with an impressive view of the sprawling land.

It was said that no one can sneak into the Viridya without immense difficulty, as it was surrounded by massive bodies of water. The only way to and from the structure and its pristine grounds and town was a bridge, only wide enough to allow horses dragging carts of supplies.

Arii's eyes were pinned to the glittering sapphire body of water, all that was in sight from her position on board a supply cart as it headed along the bridge towards the castle.

She lifted the canvas covering to catch a glimpse of the shimmering golden colossus and blew an impressed whistle.

"No matter how many times I see this damn place, it never fails to impress me." she said, awe slipping into her carefully masked tone.

Sitting across from her in the cramped supply cart, Krepth's teeth flashed in a grin from under his hood.

He tilted his head, forest green eyes on his friend. He studied her attire and pinched the dull cloth of her cotton pants. Arii battered his hand away, a grimace of annoyance fluttering over her features. Krepth's chuckle was dark and humorous.

"You are too used to being the 'golden castle' yourself in the towns you frequent, Arii. Look at you, I have never seen your skin look so dull," he said, canines flashing.

He was like a wolf, surveying his lunch. Nem had once asked her if she had ever tangled in the sheets with Krepth.

A roll in the hay with a Shifter? No, thank you...

Besides, Krepth was her oldest friend, and she would never go there no matter how incredibly handsome and charming he was.

"Well, I can't walk into the castle looking like a typical Fury, you know. I'll be recognised immediately." she waved her hand over her luminous face, and magic crackled in the air. Her eyes, naturally a vivid shade of purple, were now dulled to a dark blue. Her lips curled into a humourless clenched teeth grin, showing blunt human teeth – her elongated canines hidden under a veil of magic.

"Is the distraction ready?"

Krepth nodded and his eyes were suddenly serious, all laugh lines disappearing.

"Nem has everything under control. You need to ensure you catch the King's attention, and NOT give away your cover..." he gestured at her plain servant attire. "That means-" he held up a hand and began to count on his fingers. "One – no unnatural super Fae speed or magic, humans are freaked out by that kind of thing." he lifted another finger. "Two – No killing anyone at the party aside from your intended target."

When Arii's mouth popped open, Krepth held up a hand to stop her protest.

He continued, "Three – Do not, I repeat, do NOT blow your

cover! If this goes wrong, we will never get another chance."

Arii offered him a sly smile. "You said 'don't blow your cover' twice. I don't need to be reminded."

Krepth poked a finger to her nose, causing Arii to rear back and growl.

"Now now, little Fury. I know sometimes the thrill of the hunt gets to that sharp mind of yours and hazes your priorities."

Arii's brows narrowed and then she shrugged, finding no reason to argue. It was true, the thrill and bloodlust of a good hunt did sometimes fog her mind.

The thread had been pulled and it was ordained that King Lorch had to die. Everyone who had their string pulled from the Tapestry of Life had it cut eventually. No one in history had ever escaped this fate.

Again, Arii found herself wondering what this royal had done to piss off the Gods.

What Arii knew of the young King was that he was absentminded, negligent, entitled and a spoiled brat, distracted by the glitter of court life. He was known for his love of women and gave the West Court's party boy Prince Brolikian a run for his money, throwing fancy parties and spending the town's taxes on gold and jewels rather than fixing the run-down streets and assisting poverty-stricken families.

The cart rumbled to a halt at the castle checkpoint. A smattering of guards dressed in silver armour, adorned with red capes and a symbol of an open jawed reptile pressed to their breast of their attire, demanded the cart drivers present their identification. The horses snorted and stomped their hooves in agitation, eager to get to the stables and be fed after the journey.

"We are hired help for the King's birthday festivities." said the driver, a thin and tired man, as he supplied a roll of parchment to the guards. As one man studied the papers, another headed to the back of the carts.

A gloved hand threw back the shade and a guard stared into the back of the cart where Arii sat. For a heart stopping moment, the guard's eyes slid across her face to the space adjacent from her, and

Arii expected the guard to call a warning when he saw the hooded male occupying the space. Her eyes slid to the spot and was relieved to see the spymaster was gone. She would never understand how her friend did that, disappeared into the darkness like he had never been.

Sure, she was skilled at subterfuge but Krepth was a whole other level.

The guard's eyes lingered on Arii, but soon fluttered over her to survey the crates of supplies accompanying her in the cart.

To the guard, the assassin looked no more than a meek servant.

Her eyes remained low as the guard tossed the canvas closed and rapped his fist against the cart side, to signal the all clear. The cart jerked and began its lumbering roll through the gates, the thick mahogany doors slamming behind them with a boom of finality that had Arii's hairs rising on her arms.

She slowly sat forward, flipping her dagger from one hand to the other. Her eyes lifted from the weapon, her preferred choice of steel. It had tasted so much blood, and soon it would taste that of the King.

ঙ৪৪০

Ariiaya slipped deftly between two party goers as they chattered and laughed, their hands shooting out to take the offerings of the silver platter she held. The party was in full swing, the colossal high-ceilinged royal throne room was filled with the chatter of voices. Decadent furniture was covered in spreads of fine foods ranging from whole stuffed pigs roasted and propped with blood red apples in their mouths to elaborate spreads of desserts, glittering with sugar candy and carefully arranged displays of succulent canapes.

The walls of the room had been fixed with stone to offset the linings of gold, and the grand throne room was lined with windows – allowing the moonlight to filter through. Above the royal seating area stood floor-to-ceiling stained glass cathedral windows, the world beyond the intricate colours dark as pitch. Expertly carved wood candelabras adorned the walls, lit with flickering candles which caused the gold to glimmer in the candlelight.

It was an impressive room, one which took the palace staff the entire day to set up, dragging the heavy and expensive mahogany tables and chairs from the castle cellar. The castle cooks had outdone themselves, as well as those who has decorated the room in an array of lanterns filled with candles. Flowers lined the walls and various table settings, a natural display of whites, reds and yellows with thick green leaves. Hanging from the impossibly tall ceiling were glittering chandeliers, intricate metal masterpieces made of pure gold.

Arii's eyes skimmed across an expensive looking rug, large and round, in the middle of the array of dining tables. It sparkled, as if magic infused the strands of the fabric. It was not magic of course; magic was feared in Fythnar after all. Those with magic were either hunted, served the Fates or stayed hidden.

It had been many years, two hundred to be exact, since any kind of significant magic wielder was known to the land. Arii's magic was mild, useful – but not incredible. It was an advantage in a fight, and she could cast little tricks, heal minor wounds and flutter light veils, but nothing like the incredible Fae magicians of old. The power of one's magic came from within, and their abilities reflected their control and training.

History showed that male Fae were the strongest of all magic users, until the uprising. Humans, despite not having magic themselves, were strong in numbers and sheer fear induced persistence.

Her eyes roved the elaborately dressed royal guests as she drifted through the crowd, serving food and beverages. She felt like an old rag in amongst a pile of fresh laundry. Her garb was plain, her looks nullified with magic. She prayed to the Gods that no one here could sense magic.

Those Gods owed her for her service, surely.

At the end of the impressive space was an elevated dais, and there was placed an elaborate, high backed wooden carved throne, laced with gold detailing and jewels encrusted into the backing. A young man sat there, his posture no way that of a King. He slouched slightly, body angled to one side, arm resting and propping his head in a look of pure boredom. His light brown hair, tinged with copper, was short but thick, swept in a stylish wave which emphasised his high cheekbones and alluring, thickly lashed ocean blue eyes.

His eyes slowly swept the festivities. Anyone would have thought by the King's posture that his birthday celebration was a boring council meeting. What women, and some men, said in description of the young King in taverns across the Kingdom did not stray far from the truth. King Lorch Kruel was an incredibly attractive man and would be more so if he sat straight and with authority like a true King.

His eyes held a weight that would have any woman melt, their depths glimmering with mischief. He was young, twenty-seven exactly this day, and looked every bit the snot-nosed royal he was rumoured to be. He blew a breath between his teeth and watched the party held in his honour with the mildest of interest.

Beside his throne were two more chairs, pulled to the side like an afterthought. Perched on the one closest to Lorch was an older woman, her hair like spun silver tinged with gold, braided, and pulled into an elaborate knot on her head, adorned with jewels and a delicate golden headband. Her eyes, a lovely sky blue, surveyed the masses as they danced and celebrated. Her face was cool and calm, no sign that she was enjoying the celebrations either. There were hints of laugh lines on the skin around her eyes. Arii knew her to be King Lorch's mother, Lynnera Kruel. Dressed in a simple gown of moss green with silver trimmings, the older woman was elegant and beautiful.

Beside Lynnera sat a younger woman with golden spun hair, much like her mother. Sybell Kruel was the King's sister, an enchanting and beautiful woman of twenty-three. She was watching everyone down her petite nose, a look of distaste on her stunning features as she was approached by a servant who offered her glittering golden sweet wine in a glass goblet. She waved the servant away dismissively, boredom written plainly on her face as her dark brown eyes rolled in annoyance.

Beautiful she might be, but Sybell Kruel was said to be a surly bitch.

What a lively bunch... Arii thought as she swept up another tray of delicate edibles and moved through the throng, pausing to offer a canape to another party goer. Her dulled dark blue eyes inched over the man's shoulder to survey the royal family, and paused on a severe presence on the opposite side of Lorch's throne, where an older man stood straight, his armour freshly polished and a sight to behold.

Valdis Kruel, father of Lorch and Sybell and husband to Lynnera, was a formidable and severe looking man. He had the exact same coloured hair as his son, his face chiselled and weathered with a light copper-tinged beard. It was obvious that his son has inherited his eyes for they were the same deep blue. A scar ran down the right side of his face, obtained in battle long ago. Valdis's thick brows were narrowed over his hard face, a face which had probably only ever smiled once or twice in his life.

Then there was the mysterious figure to the far right of the royal family, standing like a shadow out of place. A hood hid his face, all that was visible was a strong, lightly bearded jaw. Arii wondered momentarily who he was, standing like a statue on the royal dais. He was clad in dark armour – a mix of lightweight, expensive leather and dark tinted silver plate. On his hip was a sword, a shimmering sphere of ruby encrusted into the pommel, the guard made of polished gold – the metal gleaming in the firelight.

A bodyguard?

Surveying his position on the dais – so close to the King – confirmed her thoughts.

There were a few more guards stationed on the bottom of the steps leading up to the dais, along with one more well-dressed and armoured man.

All stood straight backed, hands by their sides and eyes darting across the party.

Her brows narrowed as she swiftly avoided a party goer who almost collided with her as they danced by.

This she had not considered, there were sure to be many guards around and she hoped Nem's distraction would be something significant, and soon.

ⳝ

After a few hours, Arii flittered to the edge of the party to take a break, and her eyes drifted to the sounds of a man's singing across the room. The night's entertainment was a small musical band with acoustic instruments fronted by a young man dressed in dark blue tunic and pants, his voice echoing in the colossal throne room. He had quite the voice, and paired with the melody of the instruments, he belted out songs that had the room moving with abandon.

Whipping up another tray and balancing crystal goblets of sweet wine, Arii made another round of the room, past an elaborately decorated table where she paused in her tracks. Her magically dulled human-looking ears twitched as she heard a familiar voice.

A stunning burgundy haired woman sat on the lap of a very dazzled man, his eyes glittering as if he were watching a goddess.

At a glance, Devina Divine could indeed be mistaken for a goddess. Her body was voluminous, her skin creamy and flawless. Painted into a stunning gown of sky blue, she was almost too bright to look at without squinting, as if looking into the sun. Her ears were delicately pointed, her slightly elongated canines flashed as she threw her head back and laughed in a show of forced humour.

Gods above, she was in plain sight, utterly and unmistakeably a Fae Fury in all her undulled glory. Heads turned, particularly that of the male party goers, but some women too, more to slap their husbands as they threw longing glances at the Fae female.

Arii felt a bubble of anger ripple up from her stomach. If Devina blew her cover tonight, she would kill the female herself. It was likely the assassin had a mark in the castle and she pitied the man who bedded the stunning redhead tonight.

Devina threw her mass of wavy deep viridian hair over her shoulder and stared directly at Arii, canines flashing in a sultry grin, like a cat about to have at a bowl of cream. She was enjoying this immensely and her expression said *Why not have a little fun before getting to work?*

Arii met her stare with a heated one of her own, chin lifting and lip curling in clear warning.

Devina's answering chuckle was audible over the riot of sound in the room but her eyes were first to break the staring contest.

Ignoring the woman, Arii continued on, heading closer to the royal dais. Any moment now and Nem would deliver on her distraction.

Arii needed to be ready…

೦೩೮೦

The castle grounds were silent save the echoes of the music, voices from the party and the rumble of the waterfall that reached the dark area housing the carts of the extra hired help.

A leather-clad shadow nimbly leapt upon the cart without a sound.

Silver nails carefully peeled back the canvas of the cart, revealing an assortment of heavy sacks and crates.

With a wave of her hand and an exhaled breath, the air shimmered with a veil of magic as a spell lifted from the air, and Nemesis's moonlit eyes lay on a steel cage.

From it came the deep, heavy breathing of a large creature, followed by the stench of carrion. Nem lifted her hands, eyes riveted to the terrifying creature as it slept, a reptilian beast of nightmares.

Closely resembling a typical draconic wyvern, this creature was a twisted cousin, with a snout full of dagger sharp teeth and thick eyebrow ridges, a long neck and barrel chest running to long forelegs, tipped with menacing curved claws.

The beast had thin skin connecting its arms to its body, which could have assumed to gift the creature with flight, but the skin was far too thin for that. Powerfully muscled hind legs preceded a long tail. The entire creature was covered in black scales, riddled by a motley array of scars and dirt, possible remnants of its last meal in its teeth.

Swiftly, the Fury dashed her fingers through the air above the beasts' snout – a little bit of manipulative magic to the animals priorities, making it's target clear.

This was the most insane thing she had done to date, and Nem was a murderous, cold blooded killer.

Her lips split in a wicked smile as she flicked the latch on the cage.

 C3&8O

If there had been a clock nearby, Arii would have glanced at it not for the tenth time this night. She felt edgy, her eyes jerking to every clink of a glass, every bellow of a courtier as they spoke to one another in excitable tones.

What was taking Nemesis so long with her distraction? Perhaps she had been caught by the castle guards?

Unlikely.

The King's royal Red Guard were not the most honourable of men, made up primarily of ex criminals, murders and rapists. Ever since the uprisings against the Fae two hundred years ago, hardly any man would willingly go into service for the Kruel family, so they resulted to the dregs of the Kingdom to fill their army barracks. The family's selfishness and lack of care for their subjects was what had sealed the division of the North Court from the East, South and West Courts.

They had inherited the throne after mass murder after all-

Arii's thoughts were interrupted as a loud screech thundered from outside the throne room, like an animal in fright. It split from somewhere above the royal dais, causing the glass cathedral windows to shudder.

From beside the King, Valdis Kruel placed a hand on the hilt of his sword, stepping forward as the sound repeated, causing the guests to slowly pause their celebrating.

Arii felt her arm hairs stand on end, a flicker of anticipation rocketing through her body as she placed her tray on a nearby table, taking care to be inconspicuous. Swiftly her fingers shot out, swiping a nearby kitchen knife from a platter of roast mutton, adrenaline coating her tongue as her eyes darted to the dais.

She knew that sound.

Holy Mother of Darkness, Nemesis was truly insane.

Confusion lined each feature in the room, shadows playing across faces in the glowing candlelight. Some people continued to dance, oblivious to the noise of something crashing outside.

Suddenly a scaly mass shattered the towering windows above the royal dais with a thundering boom, causing shards to rain down like diamonds. The monstrous creature screamed down into the room, claws skidding and screeching as it scrabbled for purchase on the marble floors.

The beast righted itself, and slowly its head lifted, lips rippling back from a jaw of glinting serrated teeth as it bellowed a roar at the packed crowd. Muscles twitched beneath its thick hide of obsidian scales.

It took only a few seconds for pandemonium to hit the people as the shock wore off and panic set in.

Between the guests and the royal throne was a beast that haunted nightmares, a biproduct of failed attempts to replicate the proud and fearsome dragons of old.

A Kryvern.

From the mouth of the shattered window, Nem hung by a line of rope, cloaked in darkness and surveying the damage she had caused. Her eyes found Arii, and their gazes met.

Nem gestured in a salute to her friend, her face devoid of emotion. *Good luck.*

The sign was clear, and she swiftly disappeared into the darkness.

The creature bellowed again, causing glasses to rattle and people to scream in terror.

Arii's eyes snapped to the creature, its eyes like glowing pools of blood as it sprang upon the nearest guard. The man screamed as the massive jaws clamped around his middle and the beast shook him like a ragdoll, his cries of agony shrill and keening. Blood flecked the walls and splattered the polished marble floor as the Kryvern threw the body into the crowd, the man seemingly boneless and most certainly dead.

Utter terror took hold of the room as people fled, knocking one another out of the way as they ran for their lives.

Across the room, Devina stood from the man she had used like a settee and led him from the room, a drawn-out sigh escaping her lips as if she were pissed her night had been rudely interrupted.

Typical Devina.

The Kryvern's nostrils flared, and its massive head twisted to the dais where the royal family stood, guards hesitantly moving to protect them. The beast bellowed, glittering ruby saliva flicking from its bloody maw as the hooded bodyguard moved to shield King Lorch.

In a swift movement that should have been impossible for such a hulking monster, the Kryvern leaped with a screech towards the King.

It was as if Arii were moving through water at first, fighting the panicked crowd to reach the dais. Her eyes darted through the fleeing bodies as she shoved aside a screaming woman. She thought it best not to use her dagger for this, rather than give her profession away. For now, the ornate blade remained strapped to her thigh beneath her robes, the metal warm against her skin.

Suddenly she was free of the crowd, skidding across the marble, her fingers clutching the kitchen knife.

The royal women were screaming shrilly, the guards pulling them away as fear had the young King pressed against his throne, the hooded bodyguard shielding him with sword drawn. Claws flashed, swiping across the man as quick as lightening and hitting their mark. The hooded figure attempted to dodge but was clipped, the beast's claws raking his arm and flinging him out of the way of the Kryvern's intended prey thanks to Nem's magic.

Standing on hind legs, the beast's shriek was like nothing Arii had ever heard. A low, drawn out bellow, coalescing into a long, high pitched screech like iron claws raking down stone.

It was as if the world was in slow motion, she could see Lorch Kruel's petrified, wide eyes as he stared up at the bringer of his death, his body in the animal's shadow as the beast closed in.

Valdis was yelling, bellowing for his guards to save their King. The creature's tail whipped and slammed into oncoming men, its gaze never severing from its prey.

Lorch's eyes inched to the right and met hers over the beast's shaking hide as Arii sprinted up the dais – now metres from the monster.

She was going to be too late.

It was going to end him before she could.

She saw King Lorch's pure fear, just a boy who at that very moment regretted his entire entitled life. His eyes wide, teeth clenched in a grimace, he knew he was seconds from death.

Then she was leaping.

Arii flipped over the scaly mass like a circus act, body twirling.

Then the creature jerked as the woman landed gracefully between it and the King. She crouched before him on all fours, her head down and honey tipped hair slipping over her shoulder as the world slowly caught up.

Behind her, the light in the beast's eyes winked out and the huge body fell to the floor with a booming *crash,* the kitchen knife lodged in the back of the animal's skull.

Arii's head lifted slowly as her body followed suit, her eyes meeting those of the King. His were wide and glassy, sweat saturating his brow.

With intentional slowness, Arii's hands lifted to show she was no longer armed, predicting the guards' movements just before they sprang into action, grabbing her and shoving her back on her knees before the King.

Lorch was swift, moving with surprising surety considering he had nearly been in the jaws of death not a few seconds ago. His hand was raised, golden rings glittering.

"No, unhand her! That is an order!" he snapped, and the guards hesitantly let go of his saviour with obviously reluctance.

Lorch's eyes was fixed on the mysterious, plain serving girl, a girl who had just saved his life.

"Who are you?" he breathed, stepping towards her as his voice wavered. "You move like no one I have ever seen."

From the King's side, his father approached as guards began to converge on the dead beast.

"Answer your King, servant." Valdis growled, his hand still poised on his sword hilt as Arii remained silent. Her eyes slid to the King's father before returning to the King himself.

"Arii… my King." she added, before remembering to address royalty the correct way.

"Arii Clearwater," she said, her gaze dropping to his feet.

Submissive, meek, a low servant. Here, she was not to be an assassin, death delivered in a beautiful package. Here, she was just a slave, a servant who now had the King's full and undivided attention.

Krepth and Nem would be so proud.

"Commander Hawke, see to Elijah's wounds." Lorch said, his gaze never leaving the woman before him, expression composed but flecked with wonder.

To the side, an older man with dark grey salted hair and clad in royal armour helped the King's hooded bodyguard to his feet. The cloaked man, now sporting a bloody wound on his arm, shrugged his helper off and turned to leave the room for the infirmary, as if he were too proud to accept the offer.

"Miss Arii Clearwater will be assigned to guard training." Lorch said suddenly, and from his side Valdis began to protest.

"Son, that is preposterous!" he gestured with his hand in frustration at the meek girl before them. "She is a servant!" It was obvious this man had not a fleck of respect for anyone lower in class than he.

Arii kept her eyes down, but her jaw clenched.

"This woman saved my life, and for that I wish to repay her with an honour. She is wasted in the kitchens!"

His cerulean eyes speared his father like daggers, before turning to the slowly returning crowd.

"Good people, this woman saved my life, and for that she will be bestowed the honour of training with my royal guard!" The young King bellowed, as a mass of eyes stared up at the proceeding with a mix of fear, awe, and strange admiration.

His father seemed to back down, but only slightly. He remained silent as Lorch knelt before her, carefully placing a hand on Arii's chin, tilting her face to meet his.

Her eyes met pools of ocean blue, the young man's lips curling ever so slightly as he said.

"Welcome to the Red Guard, Arii Clearwater…"

CHAPTER THREE

King Lorch's party ended right after the commotion of the night.

What party goers were left were quickly ushered from the room as a group of guards and servants began the difficult task of removing the cooling, monstrous scaly mass, and set about repairing the cathedral window. Blood trickled down the beast's neck from the kitchen knife lodged in its brain, the ominous *drip, drip, drip* the only kind of music now in the emptying room.

The older man with grey flecked hair, Hawke, knelt by the beast and surveying the perfectly placed precision of the blade which had slid through soft tissue in perhaps the only part of the animal's skull without thick bone. He seemed the only one not to be repulsed, the expression on his weathered face was thoughtful, thick brows pulled together.

"Incredible…" he mused, as he stood to face Valdis Kruel.

The copper haired man's face was unreadable, but the air around him crackled with carefully suppressed anger.

"What is?" snapped Valdis, in a foul mood. Or perhaps that was his natural temperament. Arms were folded across his chest as he surveyed the Commander of the Red Guard. "That a plain serving girl knew the anatomy of a Kryvern enough to know how to bring the beast down with a single stroke?" he snarled, his form radiating disapproval.

Commander Hawke slowly stood and stared at the King's Hand. "I would like to speak to the girl if I may," he said, a statement and not a question. Valdis knew the Commander would question the girl with or without his permission.

With a curt, dismissive nod of approval, Valdis turned and stormed from the throne room, a procession of guards hot on his heels, leaving Hawke with the remaining castle staff to deal with the clean-up.

Hawke nodded to the guards and headed towards the castle hall, turning for the room where the woman had been taken while they organised a place for her at the training barracks.

As Hawke neared the room, he eyed the two guards posted at the door and nodded. The two men saluted before shifting aside to let him enter the room.

Inside, the woman stood by the window, surveying the dark night outside. The sound of a gale battered the windows, and torchlight flickering in the distant grounds. She could see the glittering lights of the homes connected to the castle grounds, little embers of light slowly flickering out one by one as the town nestled down for the night.

Her body slowly turned, her eyes lifting to watch as Commander Hawke entered the room, leaving the door open behind him. Silently the guards followed, taking up positions either side. He would not meet alone with this unknown woman, who had single-handedly just taken down one of the most feared beasts in the land. She stood like a slender shadow, the moonlight bathing her face in silver, her dark eyes fixed on the men.

Hawke lifted a hand, approaching her calmly.

"My name is Hawke Roe. I am the leading Commander of the Red Guard," he said, face crinkling in a smile.

Arii got a sense of kindness from this man, whose dark-bearded face had seen many Summers.

He did not radiate an air of hatred like his superior.

Arii dipped into a practiced courtesy, remembering her manners. It was not normal practice for an assassin to bow to anyone but the Fates, and she had to make a mental note on when to do so properly.

Rising, Arii offered the man a small smile.

"Arii Clearwater, Sir," she replied, and Hawke nodded gently.

"I know your name and believe the entire kingdom of Fythnar will too, soon. You are the King's saviour, after all," he paused before adding, "Very impressive, I must say. How does a mere serving girl manage to move with as much grace as an acrobat?"

His eyes were inquisitive, no air of malice, just pure curiosity.

Arii shrugged, before realising the gesture may come across as rude.

She lowered her gaze to the marble floor.

"I have not always been a maid. Before I was stuck scrubbing pots and pans, I was part of a traveling circus. My act was the trapeze."

Hawke's lips twitched, as if he would laugh but he was far too polite to do so now.

"Truly? Well that is not at all hard to believe," he said, the skin around his eyes crinkling. In his prime, Hawke Roe would have been a very handsome young man.

"Miss Clearwater, it seems your talents are being wasted in the kitchens, so if you'll come with me, I will show you to the barracks."

Turning, Hawke motioned for her to come.

Without pause, Arii followed the Commander as they moved through the candle-lit castle halls.

Arii's eyes roved the elaborate golden walls and watched as her dull, doe-eyed reflection tracked her movements. She wondered just how much gold had been used to create the castle – everywhere she looked featured the reflective material.

Soon they approached a small open space, and Arii's braid whipped behind her as a gust of fresh air pummelled them. The hallway to the barracks was open to the elements, the night air cool and crisp. Until that moment, Arii had not noticed how much she had needed to inhale fresh night air.

The sudden temperature change from warm to cool had her skin pebbling with gooseflesh, her lungs expanding in welcome of the cool, fresh air. It soothed her insides and caused a small shiver to skitter down her spine.

The rumbling crash of the colossal waterfall could be heard, a light spray of water fluttering up to coat the balustrades in a wet sheen.

If Arii was clumsy, she would have easily slipped on the wet floors, but she was a Fae, and Fae were not clumsy.

As the group entered the barracks, the guards stationed themselves around the entry and settled for the night. Hawke motioned to the room, filled with a line of beds on each side.

Already occupying most of the beds were a motley crew of young men and women, all of their attention shifting to the new addition to their group. Most expressions held curiosity, and some awe. They had all no doubt seen her slaying of the beast from their stations around the throne room during the celebrations.

Hawke motioned to the occupants of the room.

"This is Miss Arii Clearwater, the newest recruit to our contingent. Show her to the bathing rooms and ensure she is given a uniform. She will be joining you in training from tomorrow morning."

With a quick nod to Arii, Hawke turned on his heel and slipped from the room, leaving her before a small sea of curious eyes.

A young female was the first to approach, closely followed by the remainder of the room. Questions as well as some dazzling profanities erupted from their lips, a flurry of "How did you-" and "Nyx's arse that was amazing!" and "Holy hells a Kryvern!" and "How in the Gods did you get to the King so fast?!"

Arii remained silent, her eyes cataloguing each face in the room and burning them to memory.

The woman who approached first spun and waved her arms at the others in an attempt to calm their excitement.

"Shut up, all of you! Give the girl some room!" she bellowed.

Arii's eyes noted her pointed ears and delicately uptilted golden eyes. Her light brown hair was pulled into a knot atop her head, accentuating her high cheekbones and small nose. She was definitely of elven heritage.

Closest to her was a slender male, his face bearing a striking resemblance to the elven female. Most certainly a sibling, the two looked almost identical.

When Arii remained silent, the female tilted her head inquisitively as the remaining recruits quietened down.

"I'll bet you're tired, not every day you fight a Kryvern and survive without a scratch." She gave a reassuring smile. "Let us get you to the bathing rooms to wash up, then to a cot to rest, eh? There's one free by me." She took Arii's arm gently.

Arii's hairs stood on end at the contact, and she had to chant a mantra in her head that she was under cover. Any other day and she would have this female against the wall with a dagger in her throat for touching her.

Swallowing thickly, Arii pressed back the thought and forced her lips to twitch in a sorry attempt at a replying smile.

Kindness, this girl was showing kindness.

It seemed the gesture was so foreign to the Fury that she had to remind herself that not everyone was a cold, stone hearted killer, like those she spent most of her time with at the School of Fate.

"Thank you," she murmured and allowed the woman to lead her towards the bathing rooms, straight through the lines of beds.

"I'm Tikkani by the way, this-" she cocked her head at the boy trailing close behind, "-is my twin brother Emerson," she said, her tone conversational and light. Arii's eyes quickly surveyed the boy, his light brown hair cropped short with a fringe and his eyes tilted and gold in hue, a male replica of Tikkani.

Interesting. Twins were rare in this land.

Tikkani's eyes darted to her brother, and Arii swore for a few moments they spoke to each other without words. The boy, without a sound, rested a neatly folded pile of clothing by the door and slipped back out of the bathing rooms to where curious eyes still watched.

Arii eyed Tikkani and was met with a grin. "Oh, don't worry! I'll make sure none of those slack jawed lumps come snooping while you bathe." With a wink and a twist, Tikkani breezed from the room and closed the door behind her.

Arii's hand lifted to her chin as she stared at the back of the closed door, grazing the skin where not a short time ago King Lorch's fingers had lifted her face to meet his. His eyes, like deep pools of sapphire, had drunk her in with an intensity and intelligence she had not been expecting of the young man. She recalled his look of pure awe, his lips parting before he spoke.

In her stomach, a flame ignited, and she soon was ripping off her servant garb, desperate to be under the hot water and washing away the thoughts now racing through her mind.

Gods it had been too long… Stupid, basic desires.

She reprimanded her traitorous body before throwing her clothes to the floor, turning on the water and stepped into the piping hot stream as the room filled with steam.

∽ↄ

The golden light of dawn filtered through the windows of the barracks, closely followed by the rustling of blankets. Moans and groans filled the cool stone room as its occupants began to wake.

Tikkani lifted her head, a bird's nest where her carefully pulled knot was the night before, her golden eyes groggy with sleep. She stared over at the cot containing their newest recruit and snorted as she saw she was already up and dressed, the mass of her dark brown hair expertly weaved into a thick braid falling casually over her shoulder.

Ariiaya sat lightly slouched, legs parted as she leaned forward with a look of a hawk surveying a mouse, her dark eyes unreadable.

"Oh fuck me…" groaned Tikkani, pressing her face into the pillow. "Another early riser…"

Her brother Emerson began batting her with his pillow.

"Gods Emer, I'm getting there okay?!" she moaned, slowly sitting up and rubbing her eyes with the heels of her hands.

Emerson looked at Arii apologetically. "Apologies, Miss,

Tikkani is not a morning person, nor does she have a filter for her crude, disgusting mouth."

He ducked his head in a motion she took to be shy. Arii's brow quirked at this as the boy's cheeks blossomed with a tinge of pink, and he swiftly began making his cot, his eyes not meeting hers again.

Arii held back a smirk. Emerson seemed almost *scared* of her.

Good.

The heavy door to the barracks opened and Commander Hawke entered, clad in a dark and much more carefully tailored version of their recruit uniforms. Like theirs, his featured the Kruel family crest, a reptile. Except the open jaws of his insignia were smelted from gold. The pin glittered on his tunic.

"Good morning recruits, I trust you all slept well given last night's events," his eyes immediately finding Arii as the crew quickly lined up at the ends of their beds.

Some nodded, some replied with a curt *Yessir!*. Arii remained silent, feeling the weight of the Commander's gaze.

"I will be taking Miss Clearwater from you today, for a short stint in the training ring. I need to see what weapons sing best with our fresh blood here," he nodded at her.

Without delay, Arii moved towards him, and he called to the others. "Muck the stalls and help load the carts. There is much to tidy after the King's celebrations last night."

As Arii accompanied the Commander from the quarters, her keen hearing picked up the protests of the recruits at having to be on clean up duty. She suppressed a smile, knowing she would feel much the same. After a particularly bloody job, she left the dirty work to a cleaning crew of Shifters. They would converge on the scene as rats, cats and small inconspicuous animals, then shift to their true forms and carry out the cleaning without prying eyes.

Brilliant... That had been Krepth's idea.

The morning air was mild, the sky overcast with grey as Arii followed the Commander. The silence was heavy, and slightly uncomfortable – but Arii guessed the feeling was one sided. She felt on edge, eager to get away and fulfil her mission so that she could head home.

Servants bustled about nearby as they followed a neat path towards a structure with a gently pointed roof, the walls either side of the entrance hung with dark red drapery, stitched with gold lace, the family crest stitched into the heavy fabric.

They entered a stone-lined room with high ceilings and a centre marked with a ring of chalk. On the far right was an impressive array of weapons propped on a wooden board.

Arii's eyes found the daggers first, then slid to Hawke as he approached the stand. He picked out a polished sliver sword, lifting the weapon and surveying it with dark brown eyes. He turned and twisted his wrist, the sword whirring through the air before he pointed the tip at Arii.

"I figured you are already gifted with smaller blades, having studied the precision of the knife in the Kryvern's skull," he said without preamble, throwing the sword to her, hilt first. Arii caught the sword neatly, her brows narrowing as she curled her fingers around the smooth velvet hilt.

Keen eyed bastard, she thought, watching as Hawke drew his own sword and motioned to the ring in the centre of the room.

"Lucky shot," was all Arii replied, canines pressed into the flesh of her tongue behind her lips.

Too keen eyed.

Hawke brandished his sword and it whistled through the air as he dropped into a fighter's stance, hand raised to motion Arii forward. Arii stared, hesitant but not out of fear. Hawke was far too observant, and she knew she would have to act cautiously. From the round shells of his ears, Arii knew the man was human, perhaps aged in his mid-fifties.

It would be a shame to have to kill him...

When Arii entered the ring, Hawke wasted no time to begin his assault. His sword cut the air and headed directly towards her side. Her own sword jerked and met his with a metallic *clang*, and was soon defending her left side, then middle. She met him blow for blow, and the Commander twisted with a swiftness belied by his age, skill moulded from years of service. His strikes were like that of a cobra, aimed at her thigh and causing her to angle her sword to avoid the metal slicing her leg.

He was talented, she gave him that. Hence his title she supposed.

With a few more parries, the sound of metal on metal echoed throughout the training room to the beat of a silent rhythm.

After ten minutes of solid swordplay, Hawke slowed his advance and stepped back.

A slow smirk slid across his weathered features.

"Just as I thought," he said, "Prior training with arms. Impressive." He lifted the sword. "Where did you learn to fight like that?" he demanded, his tone serious but not unkind.

Breathing hard, Arii was surprised at the old man's forwardness. She was not winded by any means, but she was not expecting the attack.

"Sword thrower at the circus…" she panted in response, her teeth flashing in a cocky grin. "Taught me the way of the sword every day, before swallowing them down his gullet for entertainment."

She lifted a brow as the Commander blanched at her.

Cool it Arii, he is already suspicious of you… her mind hissed, and her grin vanished.

"Sir," she finished, straightening her stance and lowering the sword.

"Truly impressive…" said Hawke, his chocolate eyes regarding her with a respect and curiosity he had not felt in a long while. "I don't suppose you'd like to tell me a little more about your time before you were a servant?"

When he was met with a cool glare and a stoic expression, Hawke's teeth flashed in a quick smile as he chuckled. "A woman of few words, I see. Well, more will be revealed in good time. Something tells me you are not the deep conversational type."

Again, he was spot on, sharp and eagle eyed like his namesake.

He turned and surveyed the weapon stand, plucking out four

daggers and turning to her.

"Show me again how you are with daggers, Miss Clearwater."

ೞ

The sun reached its zenith in the sky and was soon retreating to the tip of the hulking mountain range in the distance, bathing the land in the beginnings of a sunset before Arii and Hawke's training was over. They had sparred for the majority of the day, having only paused for a break at midday for a bite to eat. Hawke's keen eyes missing nothing as they tested each weapon on the rack, from daggers to a heavy headed mace, to a nasty looking club with spikes on the tip.

Arii performed best with the daggers of course, but also took well to a bow. She stared down the length of an arrow, eyes narrowed in concentration as the feathers from the fletching tickled her cheek. Hawke stood close by, his expression calm and patient. The duration of the training, Arii had held back her full potential lest the Commander become more suspicious than he already was.

Being a Fae had its perks – incredible reflexes, abnormal strength, hypnotic looks and the gift of magic – paired with years of vigorous training and discipline, she was the perfect killing machine.

Never in a million years would they allow a Fury within metres of the King. She had been so close last night, enough that she could smell the sweet wine on his breath, see the thickness of his lashes, the tiny dip in between the bow of his perfect lips.

The arrow loosed with a *thwang* and embedded itself in the hay target at the end of the training room. The arrow wobbled, having pierced the painted space just to the right of the blood red bullseye.

Arii's eyes darkened. She *hated* holding back.

She was The Fate's top assassin.

She *never* held back…

"Close," murmured Hawke from the sideline, his arms crossed against his chest. "I think that is enough for today, recruit." Slowly he approached her, his fingers twisting around the grip of the bow.

"I trust you remember the way back to the barracks while I tidy up here?" he said, eyeing her. Hawke knew she was distracted, seeing her movements deliberately held back.

Arii's eyes lifted to the Commander, nodding curtly.

"Yes, thank you," she said as she passed him the basket of arrows.

"Sir," she added swiftly before bowing at the waist.

Manners... her mind chastised.

Eager to be anywhere but under his prying gaze any longer, Arii was swift to escape.

She made her way from the training arena towards the barracks, her eyes sweeping over the golden bathed castle grounds. The gardens were immaculate, filled with thick, lush green trees. The walls encircling the area were tall and solid, gold metal plating causing the sun to reflect across the trees nearby. Itching to explore, Arii wondered – if she were to slip to the King's rooms and await sundown with a dagger in hand – one deftly stolen from Hawke's weapon trove and now snug against her thigh – would anyone notice? The few soldiers she had seen were busy marching about, their eyes more preoccupied with the castle walls and beyond than what was inside.

Arii's keen eyes narrowed in on a black tuft of fur, just visible from behind a nearby stone wall.

Her brows shot up in curiousity. Did the royal family have animals on the grounds? She made a beeline towards it, then slowed as the tail was replaced with a long black muzzle. Following the muzzle was a large lupine head, mischievous green eyes fixed on her as the massive black wolf seemed to smile, white teeth flashing.

Krepth.

No normal wolf would grin at her that way.

Quickly she followed, the wolf slipping back behind the wall and out of sight. As she approached, she was greeted by the shadowy form of a man leaning casually against the masonry.

"Colour me impressed, little Fury!" Krepth said, his face splitting in a grin. "Your story will be told in taverns for ages! A meek serving girl single-handedly taking down a Kryvern. Brilliant!"

He chuckled, sweeping his body into a low, mocking bow.

"The King's saviour, they are calling you. Who would have thought you'd ever be called such a thing?" He snorted a laugh. "You?!"

Arii's lips twitched to a smirk.

"You're lucky, Krepth. That Kryvern almost finished the job for me. The Fates would have been furious."

Krepth winked slyly. "I never had a doubt, not even for a second." He flicked her nose with his finger affectionately.

Growling and batting his hand away, Arii's cheeks heated as Krepth pushed away from the wall. Despite her cold and withdrawn persona, he had always insisted on treating her like the little sister he'd never had. Krepth was only two years older than her – but this did not stop her from attempting to kick his arse from time to time.

The damn wolf was slippery, always evading her frustrated fists.

Now, those fists remained balled at her side, her lips pursing as he drawled on.

"I just came to check in, little Fury, and to remind you that time is of the essence."

He slipped past her – to where, she had not a clue. Krepth went wherever he pleased, pacing casually with hands slipped in the pockets of his pants.

"He has a shadow," Arii said to his back, and Krepth turned to face her. "The King, he has a bodyguard. I would suspect he will be a constant presence; one I was not counting on."

Her friend's lips parted in his usual charming, cocky smile.

"So… figure out a way to get the King alone." His eyes roved over her plain recruit's garb as he added, "Let a bit of that Fae magic shine through. He won't be able to resist."

Grinning slyly, the Shifter turned and sauntered off into the growing afternoon shadows, whistling a merry tune.

"Mutt…" Arii growled, before heading for the barracks.

She knew Krepth was right, she had to get the King alone, then bury her dagger in his heart.

In her pocket she fingered the golden string of the Tapestry and twisted it around her finger, so tight it began to cut off her circulation.

HAWKE
ROE
Melissa J Kincaid

CHAPTER FOUR

"Fuuuck, I hate horses!" groaned Tikkani as Emerson, Arii and a boy named Quinn headed towards the stables the next morning.

Emerson's cheeks were scarlet, his eyes avoiding Arii's as they walked. He proceeded to be incredibly shy around her, never striking up conversation or making any sort of eye contact. He also seemed embarrassed by his brute-mouthed sister, glancing at everyone apologetically every time a profanity erupted from her mouth. The twin siblings were opposite sides to a coin personality wise, but identical in appearance.

Quinn chuckled next to Arii. She had recognised him as the singer at the King's celebrations. He was lanky in stature, dark tan skin and a mop of curly hair on his head. He radiated a calmness that put most of the other recruits at ease.

He was also a shameless flirt.

Arii had given not a single scrap of invitation, but the young man had not needed any as he dropped his arm over her shoulders and chuckled.

"Newest recruit gets to muck the stalls!" he hollered, and Tikkani clapped her hands in agreeance.

"Gods yes! That is the tradition, Arii. Like it or lump it," she cackled madly, and Arii silently feared for the girl's sanity.

Arii wondered if any of them had actually seen any sort of battle, ever felt the warm spray of a dying man's blood on their face and the chorus of screams on a battlefield.

She thought probably not, if they screwed their noses up at horse shit.

As the group approached the stables, Arii felt a shift in the air.

Two guards exited the stables, closely followed by Valdis Kruel. He was clad in his usual fine attire, house crest pinned to the breast of his immaculate doublet. His eyes were like two emeralds as they narrowed at the recruits, obviously hearing their commotion on their way down the gravel road.

The group fell dead silent and stared, before the bodies around Arii bowed respectfully.

She followed suit, albeit a second later.

Valdis' eyes were on her, and she felt the peculiar sensation of ants crawling over her skin as the man's lips curled.

"His Highness the King is in the stables today. Return when he is done."

But a moment later, a voice called from within the stables.

"Father, do not be rude! The recruits have a job to do. Allow them entry," called King Lorch, which caused his father's eyes to cloud.

"As you wish…" he growled and nodded to the recruits before swiftly stepping by them and heading towards the castle.

That man surely has a sword up his-

"Please enter, recruits," called the King, and Tikkani's eyes met Arii's.

She saw fear in their depths.

Arii felt something foreign to her, the need to shield these naïve soldiers in training. She briefly wondered at what would light fear in the girl's eyes, but it slid to the back of her mind as she thought it best to not leave the King waiting.

She was the first to move, leading the small group into the stalls.

They were quaint, so unlike the picture she had in her head prior to entering. She had imagined grand ceilings, gold laced mahogany stall doors and polished floors. Instead, she was faced with a cosy room with ten stalls leading to another wide-open door, covered by a low ceiling.

She blinked, surprised. She assumed everything in Viridya Castle was grand, gold and compensating for something.

Realising this may be a private building for the King and his family's horses, she paused just within the doorway. The other recruits slipped past her to the racks to retrieve rakes and hoes, obviously knowing exactly where to begin.

Straight ahead stood King Lorch. He was dressed in a fine doublet of dark green stitched with gold thread and trousers of dark brown. The sun backlit his lean form in a golden halo of light, his thick copper hair swept up at the front, his blue eyes wrinkled at the edges.

Their eyes met and his teeth flashed in a cocky smile.

She had been staring… and he had noticed.

"Miss Arii Clearwater! What a surprise! Please join me, won't you?" he said, motioning for her to follow as he paced into a nearby stall. Momentarily stunned, Arii kicked herself internally and followed. She entered the stall after the King and watched as Lorch lifted a brush and began stroking the coat of a caramel mare. Arii admired horses, and this one was indeed of incredible stock.

Its glossy wheat coloured mane shimmered in the morning light filtering through from the open doors. Muscles rippled beneath the animal's silk coat as the beast huffed gently. Arii paused by the mare's neck to stroke the animal's soft, velvet muzzle as it turned its head to her inquisitively.

"She likes you," pointed out Lorch, his voice smooth and clear.

Arii's eyes shifted from the mare to the young man as he drifted to her side, brushing the animal's neck with care.

"Day Dancer is a good judge of character," he said, head tilting towards her, lips quirking in a smile. "Besides, I told her all about my saviour… so that may have swayed her decision."

He leaned towards her, his breath tickling her cheek. "I don't suppose you would enlighten me on who you are, Miss Clearwater?"

Arii's eyes drifted to his, one elongated canine pressing against her tongue. She knew she should speak; his expression was expectant.

So, she spun her carefully thought-out story with confidence, keeping her voice gentle as she said, "Before I was a servant, I grew up with a traveling circus…"

The King's brows lowered over his eyes, their depths swimming with curiosity. "Truly? How did you end up catering at events from something as exciting as a circus?"

She worried her bottom lip between her teeth as she watched his long fingers continue to brush Day Dancer's mane. "I would say the pay, but that would be a lie."

Lorch huffed a laugh, causing her eyes to dart to his face. Their shoulders brushed, and she suddenly noticed how close he was.

So *very* close.

How easy it would be to pull him near, slide the dagger from her thigh and across his throat in one fluid motion…

Arii felt the air sizzle between them, and suddenly the moment was interrupted by a throat clearing from across the stall. Lorch went still, his eyes drifting closed. He blew out a sigh and tilted his head to the shadow lingering in the corner of the room.

The hooded bodyguard was standing with his arms folded across his broad chest, a frown of disapproval visible from under the fabric.

Of course, he was here.

Elijah… that was his name, was it not?

Lorch's lips twitched and he stepped back from Arii, but his eyes were glittering with mischief. "Elijah here is a royal buzz kill," he chuckled, continuing to brush the mare's flank as if the little moment of electricity between them never happened.

Arii's eyes made their way from Lorch to the hooded stranger. His attire was the same as the last time she had seen him, dark hues and tinted black armour. He had a dangerous air about him, dense and radiating – or perhaps that was because she could not see his face. Just like the night before, Elijah wore a hooded cloak which left all but the bottom of his face in shadow.

Arii's head tilted and she watched as, impressively, Elijah's mouth frowned even further. She felt a weight on her shoulders, a crackle of energy across her skin.

"We have business in the castle, my King. Do not forget your meeting with the council today," Elijah warned, his voice deep and smooth like silk.

Huh, she had presumed his voice would sound like a dull blade.

Lorch sighed long and hard, and when Arii's attention slipped back to him, the King had the end of her braid in his fingers. He smoothed his thumb over the honey tip of her dark tresses as he said, "Too bad, I was hoping to get to know my saviour."

The King pouted, letting her hair fall before offering her a wink.

Her voice was barely a whisper as she said, "There really isn't much to know, Your Highness."

Lorch grinned, white teeth flashing. "Now I'm sure that isn't true. I will seek an audience with you later, Miss Clearwater." He smiled before adding, "Accept, lest I make it an order."

Placing the brush into a basket nearby, the King inclined his head before turning to leave. Arii stood motionless as Lorch, with one last glance, exited the stall.

Elijah followed, his long cloak sweeping the hay as he paused just beside her, hood keeping his features in shadow. That weight she had felt earlier pressed on her now, the hairs on her body lifting on end, a fire ricocheting through her veins. This man, whoever he was, pulled a feeling of fight or flight from within her that was usually next to non-existent.

He was looking at her, but she was unable to see his eyes.

"You'll do well to keep your distance from the King..." he drawled, his voice like melted chocolate, laced with warning. She felt that voice drift over her senses, and she swore for just a second, she could taste the light sheen of magic on her tongue.

Peculiar indeed.

With that, the man named Elijah swept past her and was soon gone from sight.

It was only a few moments later that Arii realised her hand was twisted in Day Dancer's mane, the silk strands pulled taut enough that it almost hurt.

With a drawn-out breath, she slowly retrieved the brush, moving to busy her own hands and preoccupy her mind from the blur of thoughts beginning to coalesce.

"Gods, that guy gives me the creeps," whispered Tikkani as she joined Arii in the stall. Her voice was low, as if she were afraid the bodyguard would reappear at any moment.

"Who is he?" breathed Arii, her eyes finding Tikkani's as the girl began to brush Day Dancer's other side. She paused, peering over the horse's quivering rump, a look of carefully veiled uneasiness on her features.

"The scary hooded guy? That is Elijah Wolfe, the King's personal bodyguard. I heard his bark *is* as bad as his bite. Hardly anyone has seen his face, save for the King and a handful of other people, and he is said to be a total badass in combat."

Arii continued to brush, her eyes preoccupied with the horse's coat, her mind lost in thought. She knew the King would have guards, but a personal bodyguard with the air of an assassin had not crossed her mind. Tikkani sighed loudly and slid the brush back in the holder nearby.

"Alright, that'll do for now. This place is pretty spotless. Let's head back to the training arena and let off some steam. You look like you need it, Arii," she said, spinning on her heel and marching from the stall – as if she could not get away fast enough. Arii vaguely wondered why Tikkani had such an aversion to horses.

Perhaps – to get her mind off the mysterious cloaked man and the honey-lipped King – she would ask her once they got to the training ring.

Arii chewed her lip in thought as she exited the stall.

⋈

A crisp breeze fluttered through the trees, picking up a gathering of fallen leaves and passing them across the castle gardens in a gentle dance. In the distance, the ever-constant rumble of the waterfall could be heard.

Lynnera Kruel sat at an elaborate dining setting on an elevated balcony overlooking the gardens. She lifted a cup to her lips, blowing out a breath to cool the tea before sipping delicately. In the distance, a hint of the thatched roofs of the small town could be seen, peaks of well-maintained homes owned by the wealthy people of the North Court.

The sun bathed her spun gold hair as her head tilted to the warm rays.

Across from the King's mother sat Arii, her back rigid against the chair, her eyes fixed on her lap where her fingers were twined.

The invitation to have tea with the King's mother was unexpected and received by messenger moments after Arii had returned to the barracks to wash the day's work off her body, not to mention the pool of sweat on her lower back as a reminder of her close encounter with the King and his shadowy bodyguard.

Now the woman's eyes were drifting serenely from the gardens to her guest, lips pursing in a smile.

"My dear, you are awfully quiet. Please, be at ease," she said, setting the cup down on its accompanying saucer with a clink.

Arii's eyes lifted ever so slightly to meet Lynnera's, taken aback by the hue resembling her son's. The man's sapphire depths had been burned into her memory, it seemed.

Arii cleared her throat and spoke. "Apologies, My Lady. I…" She paused, hoping her tone was meek and dull, devoid enough of its usual bravado. Acting was difficult. Killing without mercy was far easier to her.

"I am not used to being in the presence of royalty," she finished weakly.

Lynnera's eyes were gentle. "Of course not. Please do not fret, you can be assured that you are safe here." She motioned to the simply dressed handmaidens drifting around them. "I am sure there are many people wishing to speak with you, my dear. What you did two nights ago is a hot topic of discussion right now." The older woman leaned forward and placed a lightly wrinkled hand over Arii's.

Arii suppressed an internal shudder at the contact.

"You saved my son's life." Lynnera said, her tone heavy with meaning. "Such a thing cannot be easily repaid. Tell me, what can I give you that could begin paying this enormous debt I owe you?" She squeezed Arii's fingers. "Gold, jewels, an estate? Whatever you want, I will gladly give it."

Arii had no doubt that the King's mother was speaking true.

Her gaze lifted to meet Lynnera's oceanic one. "All I want are some questions answered, My Lady." She paused, allowing the woman a moment to object.

With a smile, the King's mother leaned back and motioned with her head, her brows rising. "Is that true? Not riches beyond your wildest dreams? Well, of course my dear. Please, speak your questions. I do insist though about the gold." She smiled encouragingly. "I have already arranged an account set up for you. Anything you want, you will have."

Arii swallowed thickly. She had no need of gold, but she knew many who would gladly take her donation. A poverty-stricken orphanage in Amberbourne, or the little farms on the edge of The Sapphire Depths which had been razed naught three weeks ago by rogue Red Guard soldiers.

"It's about King Lorch, My Lady." She paused, formulating her question as not to seem too prying. "He is young, he doesn't seem the Kingly type?"

Lynnera leaned back in her chair and smiled. "Ah yes, my son unfortunately did not choose to ascend to the throne. He was placed there by his father. Much to his dismay." She brushed away a stray lock of hair that had come loose from its carefully crafted knot. "The King would much prefer the benefits that being King brings. Wealth… Women…" She eyed Arii. "When my son sets his eyes on something, he is relentless until he gets what he wants.

Unfortunately…" She sighed. "Matters of royal significance have no importance to him. His father takes care of all matters of the Crown. Lorch is incredibly intelligent; despite the appearance he holds in front of his courtiers. But it seems my son much prefers to leave the hard work to my husband."

Arii paused, then said, "When you say he was placed on the throne…" She trailed off, and Lynnera continued.

"When the last royal family – Gods rest their souls – left this earth before their time twenty-two years ago, my husband was Hand to King Tyverus Herington." She smiled gently. "With no surviving members of the Herington line, my husband held the throne until Lorch came of age at eighteen."

Arii thought of what little she knew of the Herington family. She was only young when news crashed through the Kingdom of the royal family's murder. Tyverus, his wife Hannera, daughter Ghila and sons Brohem and Eliverus were slaughtered in their beds by rogue soldiers.

It was rumoured the killers were human rebels, a carefully planned uprising of people who feared magic, a traitorous weaving from within the castle itself. Some said they secretly wanted the riches of the kingdom for their own. Others seemed to be of the thought that the group who carried out the murders still had the same beliefs of usurpers who had initialised the killings of male Fae, the fear still strong, believing the males of the family to be in possession of powerful magic.

"The Herington family were Fae?" asked Arii, watching as Lynnera nodded in confirmation. As far as Arii knew, there had been no evidence of magic in the family's line, and they were slaughtered out of pre-emptive fear.

"So sad what happened to them, so unnecessary. Fear is a powerful thing, my dear, it brings forth an ugliness from within that makes people do unspeakable things."

Lynnera turned as a maid approached and curtseyed by their table.

"My Lady, your husband requests your presence in the council chambers," the woman said, unsure eyes drifting to Lynnera's guest.

Arii withheld the urge to bare her canines unnecessarily at the girl.

Lynnera nodded and turned back to Arii. "Should you have any further requests, my girl, do not hesitate to come to me." The woman placed her hand atop Arii's again before saying gently, "And do not mind my son. He can be an insufferable, cocky young fool but his heart is unlike any I have ever known. As gold as these castle walls."

With that, Arii was left alone to ponder her words.

ᙢᙣ

Swords clashed in the early morning light filtering through the windows of the training area as two figures sparred.

The taller, larger figure of the two dropped and swept a leg out in attempt to trip his opponent, and the move hit home. The second figure, with a grunt, landed on his backside with a muted thud and an obscene curse.

The man on the floor speared a hand through his copper hair, muttering another colourful curse under his breath and lifting his gaze to the shadow above him.

"You are lucky, Elijah, that you are my friend," said Lorch, standing and rubbing his bottom. "I would have your head for that if you were anyone else."

Elijah was clad in a lighter version of his usual armour. The metal plates were gone, leaving him in dark, lightweight leather and cloth. The larger man flipped the sword in his hand, his movements fluid and practiced.

"And I would chide you for your foul mouth were you not my King," said Elijah, his tone light. His lips twitched in the closest thing to a smile he would offer from beneath his hood. He held out a hand, helping the King to his feet.

Lorch waved his hand dismissively at Elijah's tone and sauntered to the weapons rack nearby, slotting his practice sword back into place.

From the ring came Elijah's soft voice. "You are improving," he said simply, moving to return his own sword.

"Nyx's arse I am…" laughed Lorch, hand on his tender rump again. "I hate that you make me train, Elijah. Again, it is a good thing you are my friend." Watching his companion place his sword on the rack with care, Lorch peered to where Elijah's eyes would be if he were not wearing the hood. For a long time, Elijah had worn the hood to keep his face in shadow. It had not always been that way though; it was only as the boys matured that Elijah began to withdraw into himself. Memory fluttered across Lorch's eyes – memories of a simpler time…

Lorch, aged around eleven, held out his hand to a boy who had fallen in the dirt. The boy stared up at the copper haired Prince with a look of caution, his face masked with a guarded expression. After a moment, he took Lorch's offer of help and stood, brushing mud from his breeches in an attempt to clean himself.

"You alright?" chimed Lorch, his round face painted with a smile. He had seen this boy around the castle grounds before. He was skinny, almost malnourished, and he was often mucking stalls and carrying vegetables to the castle kitchens from the nearby crops. He was a few years older than Lorch, but it was hard to tell due to the boy's skinny body and slumped shoulders.

He nodded and his eyes quickly dropped to the ground. He knew that he was standing before the Crown Prince, and it was clear the boy had not a clue how to react.

"I'm Lorch. You have been here at the castle for a little while, haven't you? What's your name?" Lorch chirped, his tone friendly.

The boy hesitated, knowing you must always answer royalty when spoken to. He cleared his throat before answering.

"Elijah, my prince," he said, his voice timid and eyes downcast. "Elijah Wolfe."

Lorch grinned and lightly tapped the scrawny boy on the shoulder.

"Tag, you're it!" he suddenly cried, and Elijah's eyes lifted quickly to the Prince with a look of guarded dismay.

"C'mon!" giggled Lorch as he turned to face the castle grounds. "Race you to the kitchens. Last one there has to lick Cook's toes!"

With that, the light-haired boy was running.

Elijah's lips twitched, the corners curling. The offer of some fun was too hard to ignore when you were a child.

Soon, the boy was sprinting after his Prince.

Lorch would always remember when he had helped his friend out of the mud, and the events leading to their tight bond. They had grown up in the castle together, and it did not take long for Elijah's body to fill out with access to proper food and warm lodging. As they matured, he gained height on Lorch and soon he was enrolling with the Red Guard as a soldier.

Elijah had always been guarded and stoic, even as a child, but he did let a little of that guard drop when Lorch was nearby. Lorch was like light to his hesitant darkness.

Lorch was not a soldier by any means, having no interest in combat. He found that when he held a sword, he became like a fish out of The Sapphire Depths. His friend insisted he know the basics of a sword, if it ever came to defending himself. Elijah warned he may not always be there to protect him, which Lorch would brush off with a dismissive hand.

In his mind, Elijah was always in the shadows watching over him.

"I think I'll set an audience with my saviour," Lorch said lightly. He could feel the air around them become dense with Elijah's disapproval as the man turned to him, lips set in a frown.

Typical Elijah.

"I do not think that is wise, my King. I do not trust her," he said, his tone careful.

Lorch's head tilted, hand slipping into his pocket, proceeding to return his rings back to his fingers one by one. "Nonsense… I am merely curious about her, that is all." His lips parted in his usual grin. If Lorch could see Elijah's eyes, he knew they would be rolling behind his cloak. "Besides, you will be close by. I do not have anything to worry about."

Elijah's frown remained as he said, "The way she felled the beast in the throne room, she moved like someone with intense combat training… I do not believe her to be just a mere servant…"

Lorch's lips curled. "I quake to imagine her talents elsewhere!"

Elijah huffed with disapproval, causing Lorch to chuckle. He was always trying to get a rise out of Elijah, like prodding a bear. It was thrilling and terrifying, the man was stoic like a disapproving statue but to get a reaction from him showed Lorch his friend was not turning to stone completely.

Lorch was fascinated by the young woman. *The King's Saviour.* There was something about her that had him drawn to her, like a gold-laced moth to a flame. Perhaps it was just the fact she had saved his life, but he was determined to know more about her. How had she gotten to him so quickly on the dais? Had she no fear? Even his guards and his father had shown fear before the creature. He recalled her dull, pretty features and dark eyes, her thick brown hair tipped in gold. Her expression was guarded, and he wondered what her smile would look like…

Lorch shook away his thoughts.

"Let us break our fast, I heard Cook is preparing sweet cakes," he said, and the two men exited the training room.

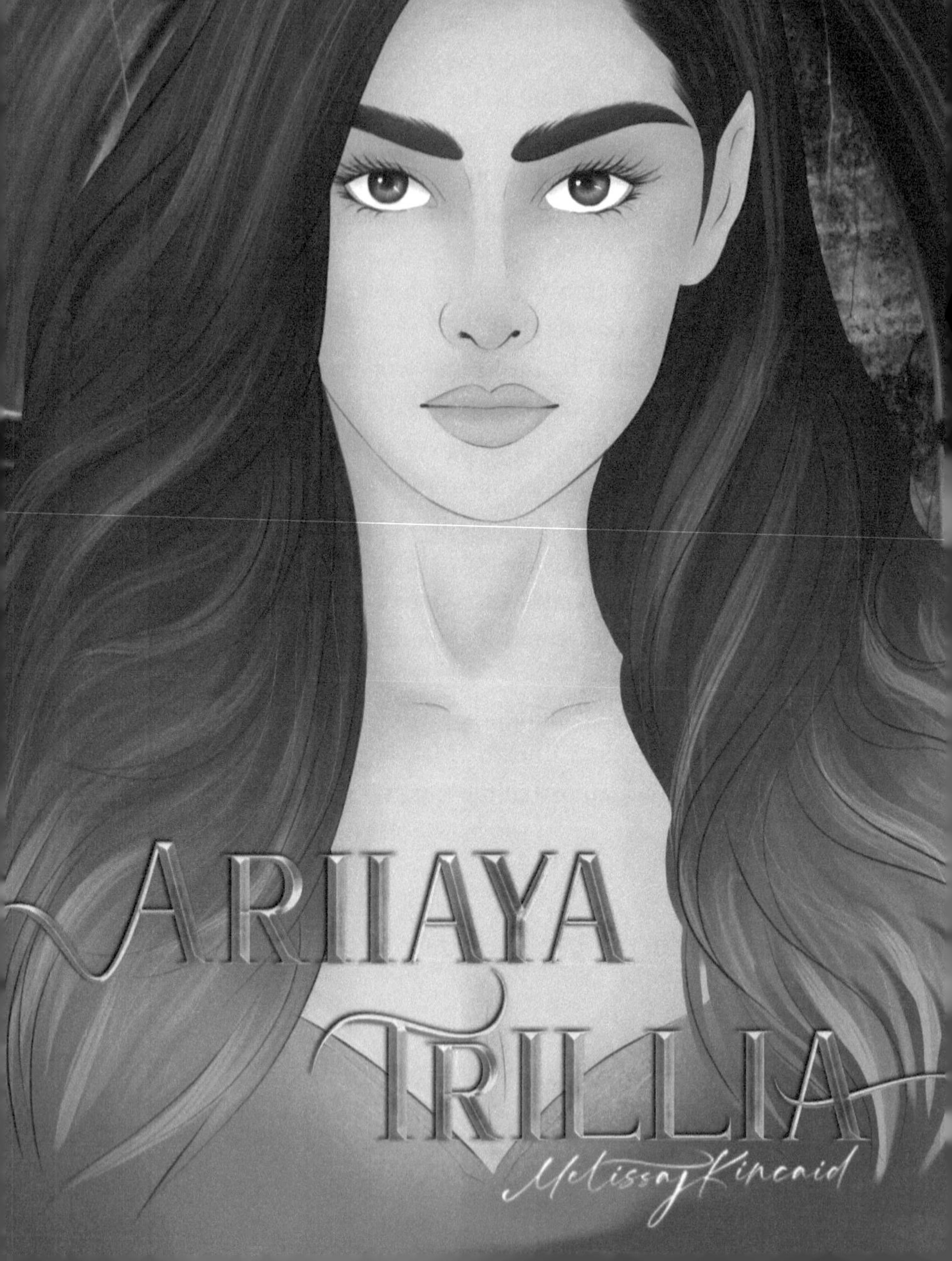

Ariiaya
Trillia
Melissa Kincaid

CHAPTER FIVE

Black mist drifted over her boots, the moist, thick air speckled with stardust as she inhaled – eyes raking the glittering, endless expanse of night ahead.

Arii's tongue coated with the sweet taste of magic, her hair rising around her shoulders as her lips parted to exhale a cloud of white smoke. Around her the world was dark as pitch, the void above a twinkling galaxy of diamonds.

Where was she? Was this a dream?

Ahead, a tall, broad shouldered figure cloaked in a hood stood with his back to her, cloth billowing in a breeze she could not feel. Her fingers lifted, gliding through the thick dark mist as she began moving towards the figure.

Her ears began to ring as she approached, her eyes drifting to her boots as she heard the gentle sound of running water. Head dipping, she saw the floor beneath her feet was like a crystalline lake, the surface reflecting the inky cosmic sky above like a smattering of fireflies. As her feet moved, the stars danced around her boots.

Chin rising, Arii's eyes widened as the figure began to walk away, his body shrouding in black, glittering mist as she lifted a hand.

"Wait!"

Her chest constricted, her heart stepping up in panic at the prospect of the stranger's escape.

Who was he?

She had to know.

"Who are you?" she called, her voice echoing across the starlit void as the figure paused. Arii moved forward a step, pausing hesitantly when the stranger halted. The space between them shortened as she stopped an arm's length away, her nose twitching to the scent of woodsmoke and pine.

Slowly, the figure turned, and she felt her breath hitch as gloved hands lifted to the edges of the hood, removing the covering.

Staring back at her, the face was her own.

"Do you not know your own heart, Ariiaya Trillia?" whispered her reflection, gloved hand spearing towards her with the swiftness of a striking snake. It smashed through her chest, punching into her ribs with a violence that stole her breath with a snap. Pain caused a supernova to burst before her eyes as Arii dropped to her knees, her own blood cascading into the inky blackness of the shadow lake. Where her blood flowed, pearlescence reacted upon the water – her life fluid turning to moonlight against the darkness.

Startled, speechless and dying – Arii's head tilted to gaze up at her hooded reflection, watching her own beating heart jerk in her hand, blood oozing down the woman's clutched fist as her teeth flashed in a smirk.

"I don't think you need this."

Then, her heart slowly coated with ice, the muscle ceasing its beating as blackness clouded Arii's vision.

"A Fury should never feel emotion."

The heart turned crystalline.

"A Fury should never love."

A fissure began to form down the middle.

"A Fury should never question fate."

Then, her heart shattered completely, shimmering shards of dust slipping through parted fingers and dancing upon a silent breeze, into the night beyond as her world exploded into white light.

 CB BO

Her strange dream had caused her to wake and clutch her chest in a silent scream, her nails digging into the fabric of her bed clothes. When Arii had felt the violent thrum of the muscle beneath her palms – very solidly within the cage of her chest, she had sighed heavily and fallen back upon the cot – letting the sound of the sleeping recruits sooth her thunderous heart.

What in Fythnar had *that* been about?

She had lain awake for what felt like hours, watching the dark room slowly turn light as the morning rays reached through the windows above, all the while clutching her breast for fear her heart would punch through her chest.

⊰⊱

Soon after Lorch and Elijah departed the training ring, the space was again occupied with bodies as the recruits entered their afternoon training.

Arii clashed wooden swords with Tikkani, welcoming the action as a distraction from her tumultuous thoughts as the *clack clack clack* of the colliding wood echoed about the room,.

To their right, Emerson notched an arrow in the bow he held and eyed the target on the far end of the room, letting the arrow loose. It whistled through the air and smacked into the chest of a wooden dummy. Emerson slowly lowered his bow, surveying his target as Hawke stopped by him.

"Good. Your skills with the bow are improving, Mr Alinar," he praised, turning to survey the other recruits.

Arii was impressed with her opponent's prowess. Tikkani was swift, her movements matching her own blow for blow, albeit Arii was still holding back her Fae strength. So far the days had been packed with training and small tasks around the castle, and Arii itched to survey the insides of the castle itself, to begin planning the best places to lie in wait for the King – and perhaps learn where his bedchambers were. She imagined the hooded guard would not accompany him into personal quarters, surely.

Had Elijah been the cause of her strange dream? She could have sworn it had been him standing in the black lake of starlight.

There was a split second where Tikkani's eyes darted to an opening caused by Arii's wandering thoughts, striking like a cobra and slashing the sword towards Arii's right leg mid parry.

Crack! The wood of the training sword hit Arii's thigh with an audible sound.

Tikkani paused, motionless, her golden eyes widening with shock. She was surprised she had gotten in a hit, perhaps having doubted her abilities up until that point.

"Hah!" A laugh broke from Arii's lips, her mouth splitting in a grin of surprise. The sound was strange and not heard before. Heads swivelled and lifted at the foreign sound.

Even Hawke was watching now, surprise colouring his weathered face as the group watched Arii, the girl who had not smiled once since she had arrived, had not shown a glimmer of emotion.

Now her lips were wide with a grin, her dark eyes glimmering, her brows raised in surprise.

Tikkani was hesitant, obviously having expected a curse or a rebuke, but soon her own lips mirrored her opponent.

"Nice shot," Arii said, watching Tikkani rise from her crouch, fold her arm across her stomach and sweep into a theatrical bow.

"Thank you, thank you," Tikkani laughed, twisting to bow at their audience.

Hawke's smile was genuine as he approached the ring. "Alright, that's enough," he nodded to Tikkani, then to Arii. "Perhaps you've found a match in the ring, King's Saviour?" he said with a small laugh.

"Unlikely, it was a lucky shot." Arii said, her gaze shifting from the Commander to Tikkani with humour.

"Perhaps the King's Saviour could put her sword where her mouth is…"

The attention of the room shifted to a figure dressed in cream as she stepped into the afternoon rays of light cascading through the windows.

It was Sybell Kruel.

Hawke's expression was guarded as the young woman, her lips pulled into a scowl, approached the ring. Following in the Princess' wake was a maid with shoulder length burgundy hair, her posture meek, shoulders curled inward slightly.

"I'll bet with a little training, I could wipe that cocky smile off her pretty little face," said the Princess, her hand gesturing to the group. "Surely, how hard is it to poke each other with sticks all day?"

Poke each other with sticks, huh? Arii supposed the Princess would feel differently when one of those *sticks* ran her through the belly and spilled her entrails like a stuck pig.

Hawke's voice was soft as he responded to the Princess after bowing respectfully.

"My Lady, it takes years of practice and a great amount of skill-"

Sybell cut him off. "Teach me," she said, lifting her chin. "I wish to learn."

Hawke lifted his hands in surrender, his voice gentle as he reasoned. The recruits all shifted behind him uneasily, all but Arii who studied the Princess with mild curiosity over the Commander's shoulder.

"My Lady, that would be impractical. A Princess does not-"

"You refuse me? I demand to be taught." Sybell's hands were balled at her sides now and Arii imagined she was two breaths away from stomping her foot like a spoiled child who was used to getting her way.

How interesting that the young woman wanted to learn. She would have thought she would prefer drinking tea and gossiping in the royal wing.

"I beg your pardon, my Lady, but training is wrapping up for the day." Hawke approached Sybell and Arii swore the Commander began to reach for the Princess' hand, but his own paused and dropped as if he realised what he was doing just in time. His voice was very gentle now, as if trying to please her but not wanting to be obvious. "Perhaps on the 'morrow?"

"Sybell, do not be ridiculous!"

Lynnera's voice came from the right. The woman stepped into sight and her expression was apologetic. "Excuse the interruption, Lord Commander," she said, her smile hesitant.

The Commander, who was unusually speechless for a moment, shook himself and replied, "It is not a problem, not at all, my Lady."

Hawke was quick to bow, deeper this time.

Arii noticed this with curiosity. Her nose wrinkled as a smell of perspiration added to the thick mix in the air that was not there before.

Was Commander Hawke sweating?

Ah yes, there was now a light sheen on the man's forehead. Did the woman make him nervous? Or perhaps he fancied her? Arii added the suspicion into her mental bank.

Sybell huffed and twisted on her heel before storming from the room, golden locks flying behind her. She most certainly was used to getting her way. The handmaid trailed after her quickly without a backward glance.

Lynnera offered Commander Hawke a resigned smile, before dipping into a slow curtsey. Arii swore the two shared a longer than necessary glance, and Lynnera's eyes held a look of longing, before the older woman went after her daughter.

Interesting indeed.

○ 8 ○

Life as a recruit was picked up quickly, and Arii felt herself sliding into a daily routine that mainly consisted of training at dawn, running the castle grounds, followed by general duties like cleaning the stalls and standing guard as carriages entered and exited the castle gates. It was monotonous, but she was slowly learning the layout of the castle grounds, and the people who inhabited it.

Swiping cheese from Quinn's hand, Tikkani chuckled as she popped the stolen morsel into her mouth before grinning at the boy beside her. His mouth was wide, his brows narrowed, and a look of mock outrage painted his face.

"You little she-devil!" he exclaimed and punched her in the arm.

Before long the two were wrestling on the stone floor where the group sat to eat lunch, flinging insults and fists in their scramble to best each other.

Emerson looked at Arii apologetically and spoke over the grunts and curses of the flailing pair.

"Do not mind them, they often get like this."

Emerson was still incredibly shy, but over the last few days he had begun to show a slither of confidence around her.

Arii plucked a grape from the wooden tray in the middle of their group, popping it into her mouth and chewing thoughtfully.

"Perhaps they should fuck and get it over with?" she observed as the two recruits in question broke apart suddenly, their faces scarlet with embarrassment. They slid as far from each other as possible, Tikkani shooting an outraged look at Arii.

"Goddess of darkness *no!*" she exclaimed, her voice rising as Arii saw from the corner of her eye that Quinn's face flickered with hurt. She felt a pang of sympathy but dashed it away, refusing to become attached to the odd group. She had a job to do, and once it was done, she would not see them ever again, unless it was under her blades in her escape from the castle.

Tikkani's cheeks remained red as she said, "No offense, Quinn, but you aren't my type."

Quinn waved his hand dismissively, seemingly nonplussed.

"It's alright, you're not my type either. I prefer my women strong and deadly. Preferably with flaming burgundy hair…" he trailed off, eyes glazing and expression becoming distant, lips curling in a grin. He sighed dreamily, and Arii knew exactly who Quinn was referring to, so she withheld comment.

Devina Devine was known throughout the Kingdom for her

drop-dead beauty – pun intended. Her profession as a Fury was well known and feared yet the fiery woman was still the idol of young men's dreams. She did not hide her identity like most others of their troupe did. She revelled in the attention she was given by men, right up until she gutted them with a knife – or her nails – whichever she fancied in the moment, grinning sardonically as their life faded from their eyes. Most of the time it was mid-lovemaking.

If you wanted to call it that of course – Devina had never loved in her life.

Feeling emotion was something that the Fates belted from the mind and bodies of all of their recruits, until all that remained were cold, unattached killing machines.

Such was the life of a Fury.

Such was *her* life.

"Nyx's arse, Quinn, how many times have I told you that Devina Divine would never look at you twice! She's a Fury assassin, a weapon-wielding bitch of death. They all are." Tikkani shoved a small slice of cheese into her mouth and chewed.

Quinn was not deterred, his face wistful. "Gods she is as her name suggests… divine…"

Arii snorted a laugh. Tikkani was not wrong about Furies. If only she knew she was sitting next to and dining with one at that moment.

It was odd, Arii felt at ease with the three recruits. She did not trust easily, and she never had, but she felt light, almost – dare she say – happy around them. She refused to think much more on the strange feeling as her eyes danced over the group, her expression becoming closed once more.

Quinn was a typical young man, thinking with the head in his pants more often than not. The boy ogled every pretty female in the castle, and he was often found sweet-talking the castle maids. Now, he chucked a grape at Tikkani's head and Arii was sure they were seconds away from another wrestling match.

Her dark eyes slid to the view just beyond them, the sky clear and cloudless. The air was crisp, and the sunny day was perhaps one of the few they were to experience before Winter swept the land.

They sat on a flat pad of stone, situated at the front of the castle and above the roaring waterfall. The large expanse of stone ended with a short wall to ensure no one fell to the raging white depths below. The best way Arii could describe the odd area was a sort of landing pad, perhaps used as a launch point for the dragons that once lived with the royal Fae families of old. History told that the Fae who once ruled the North rode on the back of fearsome dragons. Since the killing began, resulting in the disappearance of powerful magic wielders, the dragons too had disappeared.

Arii wondered if the goliath beasts truly were extinct.

The crashing of the waterfall rumbled on, filling the silence as a light spray of water fluttered over them, dampening the stone. In the short time she had known the recruits, it had not taken much to glean their histories.

Tikkani and Emerson were born on a farm close to Mirfield, a small establishment of fisherman and sheep farmers, west of the South Court. The people there were quiet and honest. After their mother had died giving birth to them, their father had raised the two elves until they entered their twenties. Craving new scenery other than grey skies and raging waves (and the stink of fish guts – Tikkani's least favourite memory) the twins set off the join the Royal Guard. They enjoyed the labour to an extent, but they really did it to pursue their love of archery. Tikkani had revealed that her brother had a long-term partner who currently resided in Evergrave – a young man who was quite the opposite to Emerson, cheeky, loud mouthed and always spouting stories. Luc and Emerson were a perfect match, balancing each other completely. It was hard on Emerson – being away from his love, and when Arii enquired as to why Luc did not join them at the castle, Tikkani smiled sadly and said, "Evergrave is the safest place for people like them to be themselves. The only reason they aren't together there now is purely because Emerson did not wish to be parted from me. They'll see each other again soon – we have plans to visit Evergrave next spring! You should see the difference in my brother when he is with Luc. It's vomit inducing… Gods they are crazy about one another."

Arii smiled, having knowledge of how accepting the Shifters of the East and people of the other Courts were of couples of the same sex, and could think of no better place for them to happily reside together in the future.

Quinn's history was a little murkier. An orphan, he was raised in Amberbourne and worked for a blacksmith – using his talented hands to mould fancy steel candelabras. At night he sang at the local tavern for extra coin. He had never known his parents, having been abandoned on the blacksmith's doorstep when he was just a babe.

Emerson was the first to speak as the group ate in silence, picking from meat, bread and cheese from a board rimmed with green and red grapes in a simple yet satisfying selection for the mid-afternoon.

"It's almost full moon soon. I hate this time of year," Emerson said, his voice wavering.

Arii tilted her head to him, curious. "Why?"

Tikkani was the one to reply. "Once a year, with the full moon, there is a night where the Water Nymphs of The Sapphire Depths rise to hunt." She placed two fingers on either side of her lips, resembling fangs. "Any man not locked away during the hunt may just become their dinner. The Nymphs only seem to venture to the towns closest to the lake, lest they wither from being in the open air too long."

Arii's brows shot up, not having heard of this particular event before.

"The Nymphs are said to be insanely beautiful, full bosomed and irresistible to men, their preferred meal," continued Tikkani. "They lure them in with their songs and bodies. Having said that though, if the pickings are slim and they happen across a woman, they won't hesitate to drain her dry."

Tikkani swallowed. "So they say, anyway…" she finished. "I have not seen one myself as the castle is normally locked up tight so that they cannot enter. We will be posted to guard duty that night as back-up should anything go wrong."

Arii felt a thrill at the prospect of a fight on the horizon. She was sick of holding back her strength, tired of pretending to be someone she was not.

Quinn chuckled sardonically. "If it were not for the fact that the Nymphs sucked the blood from your body, I'd willingly let them suck my-" He was interrupted with a slice of bread to the face, before Tikkani again tangled with him on the stones, raining punches to his gut.

Quinn's warbled laughter rang in the air.

Arii and Emerson both rolled their eyes in unison and watched as Tikkani shoved the same slice of bread into Quinn's filthy mouth as he gurgled laughter.

ೞ೮

"Up now, rise recruits!" called Hawke as he smacked his sword against the solid stone wall of the barracks, causing many of the bodies inside to jerk and arise quickly from their beds.

Having been in the castle for four days now, Arii knew this was not the usual waking routine.

She felt a layer of urgency in the air as the Commander clapped the sword against the leg of Tikkani's bed.

"Rise! There have been reports of Kryvern sightings in neighbouring Amberbourne." He sheathed his sword and spun on his heel, facing the bleary-eyed recruits as they flailed around the room, preparing to depart.

It was still dark outside as the recruits hurried about the room, readying themselves to set out.

Soon the group was mounted on horses, their recruit clothes replaced with leather and armour as they followed a procession of soldiers, headed by Commander Hawke. Passing through the colossal gates to the bridge leading from the castle across the water, Arii peered from under her silver helmet at Tikkani riding beside her. The girl looked nervous, and Arii did not blame her.

"Argh, I hate Kryverns," muttered the girl.

Arii glanced at the elf sideways as she stated, "You'd have a tough time finding anyone who likes them."

Tikkani offered a weak chuckle as she clutched the reins, knuckles white against the dark leather.

Kryverns were fierce, feral creatures and they were hard to take down. Arii had made it look easy in the throne room, but she had taken the beast by surprise. Without that, they would have a real challenge on their hands.

The ride to the town would take hours, hours that Arii knew would raise the group's anxiety to high levels. She could smell it on the air, laced with the earthy scent of the horses they rode.

Fear.

The forest grew thicker as they snaked along the dirt road, the sky lightening with spearing rays of orange as the sun rose from behind the jagged mountain peaks. Amberbourne, a large town to the east of Viridya, was roughly three hours' ride on horseback. The houses were small, but there were many, with cream walls and dark wooden frames, the roads paved with stones. Not many of the towns featured stone roads, most had dirt and mud – poorly maintained and neglected by the current government.

Situated south of The Dragon's Teeth mountains, Arii was not surprised that a Kryvern had made its way into the town. They were said to inhabit the old caves and tunnels there which were once home to wild dragons, sometimes venturing out further in search of food.

"This is becoming far too often an occurrence for my liking," said an older man as he rode at the head of the procession with Hawke. His words had Arii's ears twitching.

"The beasts are hungry. The people need funding to better protect their stock. Perhaps if the livestock were not so easily accessible, the beasts would be deterred," said another as the group moved at a steady pace.

Arii was not a stranger to the fact that the towns of the North Court were slowly declining, their taxes high and their wages slim due to lack of trade with the other courts.

As their procession neared the town, the thatched roofs became visible. Rising above the area was a thick, dark spiral of smoke.

Commander Hawke nudged his steed's sides with his heels and broke into a gallop. The procession followed suit, and soon they were entering the town to sounds of screaming.

People were running for their lives, women and children and men.

Ahead, a resonating roar sounded, and a mass of black scales flashed into view as a full grown Kryvern leaped upon a fleeing townsperson. Its jaws teared into flesh and sinew as it ripped the poor man's leg from his body. Red ruby eyes lifted as the guard's horses skidded to a halt in the street, the beast's lips rippling over jaws of flashing silver teeth.

Many of the horses whinnied and reared as the Kryvern's long neck lifted, nostrils flaring as though inhaling the fear in the air. It dropped the man's leg with a sickening *thump* and turned its massive reptilian form towards the newcomers. The thin skin from its legs to torso shuddered as a growl rippled within its barrel chest.

About the size of a large horse, the beast was the largest Arii had seen, bigger than the one she had slayed at the celebration days earlier.

Commander Hawke was quick to dismount, slapping the rump of his stallion and causing it to flee. His cloak whipped about his form as he unsheathed his sword, facing the beast without a sliver of fear. His jaw was set, his eyes hard.

The guards around him followed, as did the recruits.

Arii could hear the low whispering of fearful curses beside her as Tikkani drew her bow and notched an arrow. Quinn drew a sword, as did Emerson. Arii could smell the overwhelming stench of fear in the air as she drew her own weapon, eyes narrowing.

Quinn whispered beside her, "Come on, Kryvern slayer, you're up."

His attempt to lighten the situation fell flat.

The beast's eyes ran across the small party and it stepped forward, eyes alight with blood lust, long black tail whipping back and forth. Ruby droplets tapped the stone as saliva mixed with blood dribbled from its maw.

Suddenly its neck snapped forward and the beast's jaws widened as a screech assaulted the air, the only warning before two more massive forms smashed over the houses either side of them.

Three Kryverns. Three *goddamn* Kryverns!

Chaos erupted as the party split, leaping out from under the two beasts as they came crashing down.

Commander Hawke was sprinting at the first Kryvern, slashing with his sword. It screeched in fury as the two forms danced, Hawke parrying the swiping claws as best he could with nothing but a sword.

Arii was swift in pushing Quinn through a nearby doorway, and soon after she grabbed the twins by the scruffs of their uniforms and dove into the opposite abandoned house just as the guards before them were set upon by the two beasts.

"Fuck!" screamed Tikkani, amber eyes wide with panic and breath rasping in terror, hyperventilation apparent. Arii grabbed her tunic and yelled in her face.

"Get somewhere high! Load your bow and aim for the eyes!" she bellowed, pulling the girl to her feet and shoving her towards the back door of the house.

Emerson was not stupid, he nodded and pushed Tikkani towards the door. His face was white with fear, but his movements were surer than his sister's.

Arii pressed her back against the wall and twisted to peer out and down the alley. The Kryverns were preoccupied with their prey, two of the four guards who had accompanied them from the castle. Blood sprayed across the cream sandstone walls of the alley; the sound of bone being crunched audible over the snarling.

Arii's eyes met Quinn's over the space. His were lucid with fear, his arms shaking violently as he struggled to keep hold of his sword.

Arii cocked her head, indicating to run.

"Go!" she mouthed.

She was surprised to see the boy shake his head in response.

Not without you.

Arii wanted to snarl at his recklessness.

Blowing out a breath, she slid into the alley and flourished a kitchen knife in her right hand, retrieved from the house, her sword in the other. She could smell the coppery tang of blood on the air.

"Hey!" she yelled, causing the two beasts to lift their heads and stare in her direction.

Quinn decided then to do as he was told and slipped into the street before sprinting the opposite way.

Ari's lips curled, adrenaline shooting through her veins as she prepared herself under two sets of blood red eyes.

The beasts roared and crashed towards her, almost fighting one another to get to their new prey. Arii let her magic drop, the veil over her eyes fading and their violet depths brightening, her Fae vision becoming crystal clear and homing in on her target.

Her body turned slightly before her right arm struck out, and the knife was flying. It whistled through the air before lodging in the eye socket of the far-left beast.

The Kryvern screamed, losing its footing and crashing to the stone in mid momentum, causing the beast beside it to trip and fall.

Using the lip of a nearby window, Arii dashed up the side of the house and pulled herself onto the rooftop, narrowly avoiding the crashing beasts.

It was highly likely they were both still alive and very pissed off.

She sprinted across the rooftops, screeching roars reverberating from the alley in her wake.

"Arii!" came Tikkani's voice from the top of a nearby two storey house.

Arii's head snapped up to see the twins notching arrows in their bows. Close behind her, one of the Kryvern was in hot pursuit, its massive bulk causing the rooftops to crack and splinter as it leaped across the structures.

Arrows whistled past her head as she sprinted, lodging themselves in the beasts' shoulder, ricocheting off its chest. The beast bellowed, enraged.

"The eyes!" screamed Arii as she leapt over a narrow opening between rooftops. Arrows whistled past again, and one hit its mark, spearing through the beast's eye and into its brain. The Kryvern roared, crashing with a resounding *boom* through the wood and tile, its dying cry echoing across the town as wooden stakes from the ceiling pierced its belly.

From the rooftop above, Arii heard Emerson's cry of triumph, and felt a strange flicker of pride.

Gods, she was growing soft.

Her breath whistled through her lips as she sprinted the rooftops, heading for where she had last seen the Commander. As if the thought brought him forth, she heard a yell and a roar in the distance. She had grown strangely fond of the old man; it would be a shame for him to become a Kryvern's meal.

Flying across rooftops, she saw now two Kryverns facing off against the Commander and his men in what looked to be the town square. A fountain bubbled in the middle, blood and debris strewn across the stones, a cart left in tatters.

Arii saw the torn-up bodies of townspeople, counting at least three.

They had not stood a chance.

One of the beasts still had the knife lodged in its eye socket, blood dribbling from the wound.

The men looked worse for wear, covered in crimson and scratches. The Commander was in front, attempting to shield his guards. Arii felt her chest compress as she neared the scene.

He was so selfless, such a different man compared to Lorch's father.

Arii felt a flicker of memory for her own father, a tall man with delicate pointed ears, strong features and blue eyes, dressed in fine councilman's clothing.

The image faded as quickly as it had appeared.

Arii leapt from the roof and rolled on impact as she hit the stone street, continuing her sprint as she slashed her sword along the nearest beast's flank. It twisted, one good eye now on her as she spun and severed the tip of the animal's tail. It screeched, jaws snapping as Arii danced away, her bloody sword striking out and attempting to lodge her blade in the Kryvern's remaining eye. The blade glanced off its thick scales and she felt the impact reverberate up her arms.

Arrows whistled through the air again, some flying off the beast's thick scaled hide, and one lodging in the soft skin between its neck and shoulder. Arii's head snapped up to see Tikkani, Emerson and Quinn all hurrying to reload, firing arrows as fast as they could. The beast roared and reared its head at the distraction, and Arii took that split second to glide underneath, sliding her blade across the soft skin of its throat. Blood poured like a red waterfall, drenching the stone as the creature gurgled, its bulk flopping to the ground like a sack of bones.

Two down, one to go.

Arii turned, and her eyes met Hawke's. In their depths she saw awe, mixed with pride, and she swore she also saw confusion.

Before she could wonder where the confusion came from, the Kryvern's shadow drifted over the Commander, soon followed by massive jaws opening wide.

It was if the world moved in slow motion as the beast clamped its jaws around Commander Hawke's middle and lifted the man from the ground.

Arii felt her body move before thoughts entered her head.

She swore she could hear screaming nearby. Furious, gut-wrenching screaming, which she realised was ripping from her own lips.

The recruits above were yelling, the firing of arrows lessening as they ran out of ammunition.

Arii flew at the beast, leaping on its back and gripping the raised scales protruding from its spine. Grasping a dagger from her boot, she stabbed into the beast's neck with a yell, aiming between its scales and holding on as the animal bellowed, causing its jaws to let go of the Commander.

The man was tossed across the square, his body landing in a crumpled heap.

The world was chaos around her, voices yelling amongst the screeching of the beast as she held on. The Kryvern attempted to clamp her in its jaws, but its neck was just shy of reaching her as she dodged its teeth.

Suddenly she felt fire across her thigh and saw a flash of foreclaws raking her flesh, cleaving through her armour like butter. She screamed in pain as the claws caught and she was thrown from the beast's back, tossed to the street, the breath punched from her lungs as her back hit stone.

Fire erupted and ignited her veins, agony rippling throughout her entire body. Her vision suddenly dulled as her magic fled her, and at that moment Arii realised that the Kryvern had claws made of iron.

Iron was almost deadly to the Fae, caused their magic to flee them for a short time and if the metal touched their skin, it burned them as if the material had been sitting in a burning hot forge.

Just my damn luck.

With an agonising groan, she attempted to rise. The beast was close now, jaws dripping with saliva, its iron claws glittering with blood. Its eyes were alight with ravenous hunger. How had she not noticed the claws before? It was not natural; these beasts had been modified to have iron where normally dark bone sprouted.

Who would do such a thing?

Arii grabbed the base of her helmet and yanked it off, her hair flying in a wild, sweaty mass, before throwing the protection away.

The Kryvern roared, saliva flicking over her face as she bared her teeth in response. If anyone were close enough to see, they would have glimpsed elongated canines flashing in defiance.

A Fury greeted death with a snarl and a baring of teeth, defiant until their last breath.

Then the beast paused, and suddenly its head dropped from its body, severed where the skull met the spine. The head thumped to the stone, soon followed by the body as the beast fell, lifeless.

Standing over the twitching corpse stood Commander Hawke, sword raised, his face speckled with the beast's blood. Breathing hard, he swept to her side and surveyed her wound with dark eyes.

As he reached for her leg, she hissed savagely.

"How did you – arghh!"

"Let's get you back to the castle, Miss Clearwater," he said and lifted her into his arms as her vision turned black.

KLOTHO
Melissa Kincaid

CHAPTER SIX

"Get up, Miss Trillia. Get up and for the love of the Gods try again."

Dashing her sleeve across her split lip, Arii slowly pushed to her feet, eyes narrowing at the woman above her as Klotho stepped back, golden eyes luminous in the moonlight.

Arii slid her tongue over her lips, wincing as salt from the air touched the wound, a result of the blow delivered with the intention of teaching her a lesson.

Waves crashed like thunder against the bluffs, the purple night sky sprinkled with a handful of stars.

The courtyard was haloed with flickering torchlight casting dancing shadows along the ancient, crumbling stone walls. Salt gathered within the cracks, the moist ocean air causing the grey walls to glisten with tiny droplets.

The School of Fates was a crumbling shell of its former self – once a towering, solid and proud structure that held generations of proud Fae families.

Now, it was home to killers and a magical, sentient Tapestry.

Weeks had passed since her arrival, yet the pain still thrummed in her heart like a cancer. She missed her family, their absence like a hole in her chest.

It had taken Arii this long to get used to the sound of crashing waves, the cawing of seabirds and distant boom of storms offshore. Her clothes stank of sulphur and the meals tasted strange on her tongue – as if just a little too much salt had been used in the cooking process.

Then, there was the magic.

That she had not gotten used to yet, but so far she was finding it much easier than the unfamiliar sounds and smells of the old castle. The magic filtered through her veins like starlight, tingled her fingertips with a feeling of cold that had nothing to do with the night air. The magic had entered her life like a hurricane, awakening a beast inside that had scared her at first. Yet, as much as she feared the beast, she also could not imagine her life without it. Knowing it was there – even though she was not entirely familiar with how to use it – brought a mild sense of tenacity to an otherwise crippling situation.

Arii's amethyst eyes drifted across the small gathering of women around her, a rainbow of odd coloured irises watching.

Klotho turned on the spot, her dark robes billowing as she spoke.

"You will quickly learn that to feel emotion will lead to failure. The Gods do not take kindly to failure – especially when they choose you to mete out their justice." Her golden eyes danced over the small sea of young women, then back to Arii once more.

Her face was smooth like a pearl canvas – the only physical sign of anger was a tiny twitch in her top lip.

"Fear is naught but an emotion. Banish emotion, and you will banish fear. What you will learn here is the ability to press back what you do not need. You do not need fear and you do not need emotion. You do not need anything but a solid weapon in your palm and clear mind."

She lifted a hand before her, fingers splayed and palm up to the sky as thunder boomed above, a sound so deep that the ground shook beneath their feet.

"The less you fear, the more you can face. Banish fear completely – and you can face anything."

Suddenly, lightning snapped from the sky – a fork of sizzling electricity slamming into the stone, just a few feet from Arii's boots, sending sparks flying over the bodies standing nearby. Arii jerked back, eyes wide in the blue light.

Klotho's midnight hair whipped around her face, her eyes glowing as she pointed her finger in Arii's direction.

Fear coiled her gut and turned her insides to jelly as Arii scooted back on her backside, narrowly avoiding a strike of lightning that cracked against the stones between her feet.

"Grab that fear in your hands and press it back into the deepest, darkest reaches of your mind, young sister. Fear should have no place in the heart of a Fury, for fear has the ability to cloud your judgement and compromise your mission."

A second hand joined the first, the wind around them picking up. The others stood still, yet Arii saw fear and a flickering of uncertainty, particularly in those her own age. All of them knew what true fear and pain felt like, it had been one of those emotions that had awoken their magic and lit them like a beacon for the Sisters of Fate to find.

To take that fear and will it away... just like that? Arii thought it impossible.

From the moment a trainee arrived, the Sisters of Fate were ruthless. There was no reprieve, no time to mourn the lives they were plucked from or their families – if they had any left. Straight away they were thrust into classes about the land and its histories, then they were thrown into intense physical training. Arii had only spoken in short to some of the other young girls but she had gathered that many of them had been swept away from lives that were dark and grey anyway.

Magic awoke with a significant emotional event, ironic really that they were then told that the emotions which had awoken their gift were now to be forfeited.

Her young mind had trouble understanding, but what she did know was that the pain she had experienced at her magic's awakening was something she never wished to feel again.

Klotho continued. "Nothing else matters now but your service to the Gods, and what you do with the gift bestowed upon you."

Thunder boomed, the sky fluttering with silver light behind a film of dark clouds. The air was charged, static skimming across Arii's skin as she staggered to her feet, just as a crackling spear of lightning dropped from the sky.

The energy met with Klotho's outstretched palms before she spun around and thrust out her hands – electricity and magic melding as the woman threw the sparking ball of energy directly at the girl in front of her.

Arii heard sharp intakes of breath, her only warning before the magic came her way. She only had seconds to react, and within those seconds she grasped her fear, forcing it back alongside images she'd much rather forget.

Her mother's waxen face, her father's cries for them to flee.

The pain of her magic's awakening.

She fixed them behind remnants of a broken heart as she slammed up barriers...

And welcomed darkness.

Throwing her hands up, Arii thought of nothing but a dark sky sprinkled with purple stars, taking those stars and moulding them into a glittering shield of jagged shards before her. The magic heeded her call, tingling her palms and heating her blood as the shield snapped up before her, just as Klotho's attack slammed against it. The young girl skidded back from the force.

Energy snapped along her arms as the magic dissipated, and Arii's eyes lifted to her teacher, meeting golden depths that glittered with a tiny hint of triumph.

"Good," Klotho said simply, the storm above seeming to dissipate almost instantly as she added, "That will be all for today. Dismissed."

The raven-haired woman exited the courtyard in a flurry of cloak and mist.

Exhaling a cloud of white, Arii's eyes searched the backs of her retreating classmates.

A girl with silver hair stared back, the straight silky strands cut perfectly to her angular chin, her large aqua eyes luminous in the moonlight. Arii had seen her in her classes. The skinny girl always wore a frown, her chin down and shoulders turned inward as if awaiting an invisible blow. Arii had felt sorry for her, wondering what had happened to land her here.

After some time, she discovered her name was Nemesis, and Arii wondered what kind of parent would call their child such a bizarre name.

That was until the girl opened her mouth and spoke.

"How did you do that?" the girl asked, her voice monotone and unwavering – a no-nonsense tinge to her words that had Arii feeling that she would not get away without answering.

Arii's eyes dropped to her palms as she lifted her hands and murmured, "I just... imagined pulling the stars in the sky into my hands and–"

"That is stupid!"

Arii's eyes shot up, narrowing as she snapped, "What?"

The girl balled her fists, little canines flashing as she repeated, "That is stupid! You can't pull stars into your hands."

Arii tilted her head, unsure where the girl's anger was coming from.

"You asked how I did it, so I'm telling you," she snapped tiredly.

Fatigue slithered through her body suddenly, as if she had sprinted the castle grounds without a break. Some of their first lessons were to teach them about their magic, and the repercussions of using too much too quickly. She imagined this to be the result.

As Arii moved to pass the silver haired girl, her sleeve was grabbed. She turned her head to angry eyes of blue, teeth baring as the girl snarled, "You think you're better than everyone else, but just you wait."

Then, the girl shoved past, making for the archway leading back to their dorms.

Arii was left blinking, cheeks flushed pink and lips parted in surprise.

What in Nyx's name was wrong with her?

Mind tinged with unease, Arii trailed the others from the night and into the damp halls of the School – all the while swallowing against a thick taste of sugar on the back of her tongue.

଼୍ଷ୭

Waves crashed against the western bluffs as Valdis headed a procession of guards towards the crumbling castle atop the hill. The wind whipped their cloaks, causing the banners bearing the Kruel family crest to flap wildly as they neared the School of Fate.

The front gates opened slowly, old gears screeching as the battalion entered the castle grounds. Valdis lifted his chin, copper hair windswept and hard eyes roving the area as a few young, cloaked women attended to his troops and their horses. He slid from the saddle, his face a permanent scowl as a woman with dark locks approached and dipped into a curtsy.

"My Lord Kruel, the sisters are expecting you," she said, and without pause turned to lead him towards the castle. Valdis was not surprised; the sisters knew things many did not. He had not needed to send ahead a messenger.

Entering the structure, Valdis followed the woman through familiar hallways and soon entered the chamber where the immense woven Tapestry was draped. Held by pure gold bars and ended with ornate bindings, the Tapestry glowed with energy.

Valdis felt a sense of longing, a clench in his gut at the sight of the thing, the magical energy surrounding him in the room. His sapphire eyes speared to the three women atop the dais as they turned to their guest.

He bowed at the waist as one of the women approached, her raven hair swaying about her hips.

"Ah, Lord Valdis, what a pleasure it is to see you," Klotho mewed, lips curling in a smile.

In all the years he had known them, the Three Fates never aged. Their skin was smooth, incredibly beautiful and they looked to be forever frozen in their late twenties.

"To what do we owe this pleasure?" called Lakhesis from the dais as she handed a freshly woven thread from the Tapestry to her light-haired sister, Etropos, who had a wicked grin splitting her features.

The thread, unlike the one given to Ariiaya just days before – glowed only dully with magic.

"He just cannot get enough of us lately, hah!" cackled the red-haired woman.

His visits had become more frequent of late. With the division of the Courts becoming increasingly clear, Valdis sought an alliance with anyone he possibly could. The sisters – situated just west of Viridya, were his strongest allies. What they asked was simple – if he or any of his people discovered a Fae, they would be turned over to the sisters. If that Fae was male however, Valdis carefully kept his mouth shut upon discovery. Male Fae were increasingly rare – he had his forefathers to thank for that.

In return, the sisters offered the services of their assassins. Those that the King ordered be put to death were normally clear threats to the Crown – or perhaps someone who had just gotten under Valdis's skin.

It did not take much.

Just last week he had ordered the death of a man in the small lakeside town of Pendle – a man who had spoken freely in the local tavern about how the North Court was spiralling into ruin, all thanks to the brainless boy with his arse on the throne, before proceeding to call for a coup, and storming the castle just like the events of twenty years ago.

That sort of talk was illegal in their court. Valdis had eyes almost everywhere in the North, and news travelled to him fast, soon resulting in the man's head stuck on a pike in the town square.

There were no second chances for traitorous talk.

The Hand to the King believed ruling with fear was the best strategy, despite Lorch's weak protests. The boy however did not question his father's methods – preferring to be preoccupied by something shiny as it drifted past his vision. How his son had not turned out more like him – Valdis blamed the gentle hand of his wife. *If only the boy were more like his sister*, thought Valdis. It was too bad he could not place a woman upon the throne. Unlike the East Court, the North had *never* had a female ruler, and it seemed Valdis was a stickler for holding old traditions.

Valdis eyed Klotho as she sauntered around him, her dark gaze cool and assessing. She ran a finger along his chest, her long nails skimming the metal of his armour as she paused at his side. Valdis felt the hair on his arms raise, a taste gliding over his tongue like he had just consumed a lick of honey.

Magic.

It made his stomach clench uncomfortably.

"You sent a Fury into my home," he demanded, gaze hard and unforgiving on the woman beside him. His jaw clenched. "Why?"

Lakhesis, from atop the dais, was first to reply.

"Are you not relieved? That Fury saved your son's life. Had it not been for her, your son would be naught but a smear atop that throne you love so much."

Valdis's hands clenched at his sides as he snarled, "Answer me, *why* is there a Fury in my castle?"

The sisters exchanged glances before Klotho spoke. "Our reasons are known only between us and the Gods." When Valdis remained silent, Klotho whispered. "Fate has been decided, it is not for you to intervene."

Valdis' eyes darkened considerably as he breathed a frustrated sigh. He supposed if that fate referred to his son – the boy would be dead already.

"Have we not worked together for many years? You have allies in the North Court, and I would expect you to be with us, not against us," he said.

"It is not our place to question the Gods, Lord Kruel. Those who do often draw their gaze," Klotho said simply, picking a speck of lint from his shoulder. "We are sorry," she added.

Valdis knew that she was not. The words were forced and false on her tongue.

"It has not escaped our notice that there are transports carrying Nexus Crystals to Bonemire," said Etropos suddenly, changing the subject. Valdis was like a dog with a bone – the man would latch on and not let go unless distracted with a juicy chunk of meat. Bonemire was a dark stone fortress just north of Viridya castle, housing the armies and soldiers of the North Court.

"My Lord, all of the male Fae magicians were wiped away two hundred years ago. Magic is just a gentle flutter in the veins of a few now. Hardly worth using the crystals to absorb any magic. Anyone who were to notice may think you were building an army," she paused, eyes sparkling. "Do you fear a return of strong magic, Valdis Kruel?"

Valdis felt the hairs rise on the back of his neck. "Nonsense, the crystals are inactive. They were found by miners in The Dragon's Teeth. Nothing more," he said, his words clipped.

Etropos' eyes narrowed at this as she surveyed the man. "Are funds so dry that you must resort to selling fancy crystal paperweights, My Lord? Or shall we be worried for more nefarious reasons for your harvest?"

Valdis's lips twitched – but he kept his sneer at bay. "The North believes it is best to destroy the crystals – save anyone else getting ideas about them. We all know what happens when one consumes the shavings of the stones, and we believe it best to remove the temptation as best we can."

"Your reasonable foresight is to be admired, My Lord."

"I am not just about keeping order in my court, ladies. I am also determined to ensure our people are safe."

"Safe? We heard of more sightings of Kryvern venturing from the mountains – falling unchecked upon your towns and livestock."

"We are taking care of that. More men are being stationed in the towns, in case the beasts come sniffing around again."

"Good," said Klotho, just to his left. He had almost forgotten the woman was there – watching him with a heavy, golden gaze.

"What the people of your Court need now is to know that their rulers care for their wellbeing." Her head tilted slightly, lips curling before she added, "Even if they do not."

His eyes slid to her.

Feelings and caring were not words normally used for Valdis Kruel. The man did nothing without personal gain – the sisters knew this. Now, they surveyed the man as he swept his hard gaze over them, lingering on the glowing Tapestry behind them before breaking away.

Klotho spoke, her words gentle.

"Long ago, the assassins trained here were once used to guard your castle of gold, Valdis. Furies were revered and respected, their talents used for far more than dealing with the evil that slips the notice of your authorities. It is a shame that it has to be this way."

Valdis eyed Klotho briefly before swiping her words aside.

Perhaps hundreds of years ago Furies were more than shadowy assassins, but like his forefathers, Valdis did not trust the Fae as far as he could throw them.

After a pause, Valdis spoke – his words clipped.

"Although my questions were not answered as I would have wished – I thank you for seeing me at such short notice. Winter is near, and as always I expect should any news emerge from the other Courts – you will be sure to send word." The anger in his voice was hardly hidden.

Etropos glanced at her sisters, sharing a look before she spoke. "And the same goes for you, my Lord. May the Gods watch over you."

Valdis knew he would not get anything more this visit, and he lacked the patience. He had much to do.

With that, the King's Hand bowed, cloak sweeping, before he turned to exit the room.

ଔଚ

Lorch sat by Ariiaya's bedside in the castle's medical ward while Elijah stood nearby. As soon as the group had returned from Amberbourne, Lorch had been found in the library by a messenger, carrying the news of their return.

When he had seen Commander Hawke, covered in blood and sweat, with an unconscious Arii in his arms, he had felt his stomach drop. The group was fewer, and they all looked exhausted.

Once she had been patched up and settled to rest in the infirmary, he felt compelled to sit by her bed to make sure her eyes opened again. It was only with the steady persistence of Elijah at his side that he took breaks and ate.

Three wild Kryverns in Amberbourne. Such a thing was almost unheard of. The beasts were becoming bolder, or perhaps just hungrier.

Lorch leaned forward in his chair, pinching the bridge of his nose before swiping his hands through his hair. This was not normal, the feelings created within him by this woman he barely knew. In the past, he had merely had some fun with the women presented to him and left it at that. What people said about him regarding that was true.

For the first time he wanted to get to know a woman. She was fierce and strong, a mystery he wished to solve.

She captivated him.

When her dark eyes surveyed him, he could see a carefully concealed curiosity within their depths – and unlike other women she had not yet showed any signs of throwing herself at him. Strangely, he liked that about her – a challenge he had not known he wanted.

Now he catalogued her face. The thick, dark lashes creating crescent moons against her soft cheeks. Her lips were pink and lightly parted in sleep, her left cheek marred by a bruise. His eyes swept the waves of her dark hair, fading to light gold at the ends. Her hair was down, framing her face and he wished she would wear it that way more often; it made her look softer... less angry.

He was not used to seeing her without a scowl, and her relaxed face was beautiful.

From over his right shoulder, Hawke's gentle voice broke the simple sounds of Arii's breathing.

"Your Highness…" he said, his hand coming to rest on the young man's shoulder. "Miss Clearwater is perhaps the most resilient woman I have ever witnessed; she will be fine."

Lorch sighed and stood. He had not bathed in two days and thought it best to clean up before she woke.

He gazed at Hawke. "You'll send her to me when she is well enough to walk." That was not a request, and the authority in Lorch's voice was a rarity. Hawke bowed gingerly in answer as Lorch touched a hand to the Commander's arm.

"I'm glad you came back alive, Commander," he said, and Hawke's gruff face flickered to a smile, his chocolate eyes skipping to the woman on the bed.

"Without her I would not be here, my King."
Lorch's sapphire eyes glittered. "You and I both, Commander."

KRYVERN
Melissa Kincaid

CHAPTER SEVEN

Memories flashed behind Arii's closed eyelids. The feeling of her leg being feasted upon by a million fire ants; the constant reassuring presence of magic fleeing her body, leaving her drained.

The Kryvern's talons glinting in the sun as it stalked towards her, the clicking of metal on stone, the agony of iron cleaving through her flesh.

Slowly her eyes opened, and her tongue darted across dry lips, her mouth as parched as if she had trekked across an entire desert. She felt the warm tingle of magic returned to her veins and almost groaned with relief.

She thanked the goddess of darkness and applied her dulling magic just as Commander Hawke entered the infirmary.

The room was large, light and quiet. Beds lined the walls, separated by curtains of white silk, fluttering in the breeze from a nearby open window. Her nose twitched at the soothing scent of lavender – a small bunch propped in a delicate vase nearby.

Hawke lowered himself to the chair closest to her bedside, his face holding a gentle smile.

"Welcome back, Miss Clearwater," he said softly, and she noticed the bandage around his middle.

Her eyes lifted from his patched wounds. "I thought…" she cleared her dry throat and tried again. "I thought you were dead," she said, attempting to sit up slowly. Her leg ached but her Fae healing would be kicking in by now, knitting the damage together twice as quickly as a human could heal.

Hawke handed her a crystal glass of water from her bedstand and she took it gratefully.

"I could well have been, but luckily my armour prevented the teeth from piercing anything vital. I must praise you for your swift work, your actions saved many lives." He shifted gingerly before nodding at her leg under the white sheets. "That was a very nasty wound you sustained, Miss Clearwater. Having said that though, your wound is healing nicely. You'll be back and sparring in no time." The handsome old man's lips twitched. "And you will be able to show the King that you are recovering. He visited you many times while you slept, you know."

Arii paused with the glass to her lips and narrowed her eyes. She lowered the glass carefully, tapping the rim with her nail as she said, "He did? How long was I out?"

Hawke shrugged, before wincing lightly. "Two days," he confirmed, and Arii cringed. Two days without reporting anything to the Three Fates, and two additional days that the King was still breathing. She was surely running out of time to fulfil her assignment.

"Thank you, Commander," she offered. "I will see the King as soon as I am dressed."

Hawke looked as if he were about to say something more, but the look dispersed and he rose from his seat slowly, offering a smile. Whatever he was going to say did not matter anymore.

"He is in the library. Down the hall and to the left."

With a small, ginger bow he exited the infirmary.

Arii threw the sheets back and slipped off the bed, dressing in her novice uniform, neatly laid out on a chair nearby. Brushing her hands through her hair swiftly and weaving it into a long braid, Arii exited the infirmary, heading for the library.

ᘔ

As Arii approached the large doors to the library, she noticed the entry was occupied by guards. The two armour-clad men straightened and nodded as she approached, sliding aside so she could enter. Without a second glance, she pushed the doors open and entered the room.

Never before had she seen such a breathtaking sight.

The high ceiling was domed over by a stunning metal structure of stained-glass windows, the glass panes catching in the sun and causing a glittering rainbow kaleidoscope of colours to splash across the room. The walls were lined with bookshelves, separated occasionally by a long window connecting with the glass structure above. In the middle of the room was a large pool filled with crystal clear water, the beautiful, tiled artwork beneath the surface distorted by the ripples.

Any free space in the room was occupied by tables with red padded velvet chairs. Gold candelabras were fixed on the ends of the bookshelves, and Arii noticed that every space that could be was covered with more shelves. Books, old and new, filled every shelf, seemingly endless titles filling the room with the scent of vanilla. The room was magnificent, but also had a sense of comfort with the warm wooden furniture and light rays of sunshine.

Standing by the pool was Lorch, his dark blue outfit immaculate and without a thread out of place. He turned, the copper in his hair catching the glittering rays from the stained glass above as he smiled.

"Ah! My Kryvern slayer has returned, and with two more notches under her belt!" His expression was delighted, a hand smacking against his thigh. "Gods I wish I could have seen that!"

Had the King been displaying worry for her wellbeing, none seemed to be obvious now.

Arii's lips twitched in a wry smile. "It is lucky you were not there, Your Highness. I don't think I could have saved you again from three of the beasts."

Lorch was chuckling, his eyes alight with mirth. "I absolutely have no doubt you could have kept me protected, My Lady. The men say you move like a whirlwind, and they now call you Kryvern Rider."

She pressed her tongue to the inner wall of her mouth at that. Her repertoire of names was growing.

Lorch motioned for her to approach, gesturing to a table nearby laid out with tea, cakes and fruit.

"Please, join us for breakfast."

At the mention of 'us', Arii's eyes drifted to the dark figure of a man by a nearby window. His hood shifted slightly but he remained staring out the glass, seemingly ignoring them. With a moment more of pause, Arii's eyes glided back to Lorch.

"Thank you," she replied and approached.

Looking up at her through light brown lashes, Lorch leaned towards the table and pinched a little white cube and lifted it for her to see. "Sugar?" he offered, and Arii's brows rose in surprise as the King poured the steaming amber liquid from a gold teapot into a delicate, gold-trimmed teacup.

"Should it not be me serving you the tea, my King?"

Lorch chuckled and placed the sugar down.

"Miss Clearwater, you saved my life. As we stand here now, I want you to see me as a potential friend, rather than your King," he said, blue eyes glimmering.

This was perfect. The King wanted to trust her, and her to trust him – offering a sort of hand in *friendship*.

All the better for her to get close and strike.

"How is your leg, Miss Clearwater?" the King asked, a flicker of concern on his face. She remembered Hawke telling her that he had visited her many times while she slept. Again, she felt her mind drifting to question why he would do so.

What had he to gain?

"It is healed enough. I barely feel pain now," she replied, watching as Lorch gestured in Elijah's direction.

"It took Elijah about two days to heal from his wounds inflicted by the Kryvern too."

Arii threw a look over Lorch's shoulder to Elijah's dark form. He almost seemed to absorb the shadows around him, despite his position against the window.

"It was lucky that Commander Hawke was not killed," she said, gaze returning to the King, noticing his eyes were fixed on her. Under his gaze, she tried not to twitch.

"And thanks to you, he lives to fight another day," Lorch said, leaning to swipe a grape from the platter, popping the fruit into his mouth.

"Alright, if we are to be friends then I feel I can speak freely while we are here," Arii said boldly, her chin lifting.

Lorch's teeth flashed in a smile. "Of course," he replied lightly.

"The Kryverns we faced in Amberbourne, they were modified to have iron claws," she said, and she could feel the shift in Elijah's direction, the air becoming strangely heavy.

She dismissed it before continuing. "I think someone has been modifying the Kryverns, but for what purpose I do not know."

She knew this was something she should be confiding to anyone but the King, but she believed he may know something, and after her injury she wanted to know.

Better yet, she wanted to find out if they were preparing the beasts to attack Fae specifically. Iron was a Fae's kryptonite. If whoever was doing this was targeting Fae, then why modify the already deadly creatures? Fae numbers were so little now, and male Fae were non-existent. All she could think was that someone was preparing for something, but for what she had not a clue.

Lorch's brows shot up and he looked stunned. He surveyed her with questions swimming in his eyes, his lips pursing as he mulled over her words. He lifted a hand to take the end of her braid in his fingers, pinching it and surveying the lightened ends. Such peculiar hair, like the ends had been lightened in the sun. After a pause, he spoke, his voice seemingly distant in thought.

"The Kryverns come down from the mountains sometimes, they are starving, and food is scarce in the Dragon's Teeth. I have men in hunting parties clearing the land of as many as possible, but they are incredibly difficult to take down. I lose many men with each encounter, and it takes at least fifteen per beast."

His eyes met hers and she let out her breath. Gods, he smelled good, like sweet soap and honey. Her Fae side, kept carefully suppressed, wanted to grab the man by his finely tailored tunic and inhale deeply.

Get a grip, Ariiaya.

Lorch did not seem to notice her inner turmoil and continued. "I have had no reports of iron claws on the beasts, but if what you say is true, I could make some enquiries." He tilted his head, eyes smouldering, and she could feel the heat of his breath brush her face.

She also noticed the slow lowering of his tone, the nonchalant and almost uninterested cadence of his words. Her gut simmered with the beginnings of persistence, but suddenly she realised just how close he had become.

Far too close.

Smiling gently, Arii slipped past him, moving around the table of food in a swift motion – eager to put distance between them. She could feel the burn of Elijah's gaze on the back of her head, and she supposed their talk of modified beasts was done – for now.

"I'm famished," she said, and she heard Lorch's breathy laugh behind her. She plopped down on the padded chair and swiped a cake from the colourful display, choosing one with white sugar frosting.

Lorch soon joined her, and Arii watched as he sat on the red padded settee and leaned back, swinging one leg up over the other. The King bounced his leg on his knee, eyeing her openly and curiously.

"Of course you would be famished, you have not eaten in two days. Once we part, I will have a full meal brought to you, and of course you will not be required to participate in guard duties today."

Arii spoke around a mouthful of sweets. "Sthanks," she said, covering her mouth with her hand, startled. Gods it was hard to remain formal around him, he made her feel casual.

It was dangerous.

From her left, she heard a *tsk* from Elijah. She had almost forgotten he was there, save the heavy weight of his gaze which had not left them while they spoke.

"It is the least I can offer for you saving Commander Hawke," he said, and his tone was honest. Resting his arm on the shoulder of the seat, fingers lifting to his clean-shaven jaw in a gesture of thought, Lorch seemed on the verge of speaking again when the doors to the library opened.

A man entered, his brow covered with a sheen of sweat, as if he were nervous. Elijah pushed from the wall to stand straight, alert and ready for anything.

The man bowed quickly and deeply.

"My King, I am sorry to interrupt but we have an unexpected guest to the castle." As the man spoke, a new figure entered the room.

Arii felt her lips quirk in an unexpected smile.

Standing in the doorway was a woman in all of her undulled Fae glory. Ash blonde bob wavering around her sharp face, aqua eyes glittering, lithe figure draped in a raven black gown.

Nemesis entered the room with chin lifted and lips curling in confidence, and her eyes were fixed on Arii.

෬෮

King Lorch's eyes settled on the new addition to their gathering, before bowing lightly to the woman in the doorway as the guards clicked the door closed behind them.

"To what do we owe this pleasure, erm…"

Lorch paused and Arii was surprised to see a slight hesitation in his normally quick and gracious manner. Nem's eyes were on Arii as she spoke, their aqua depths a riot of questions; and Arii felt that she was in for an absolute tongue lashing later.

"Nemesis Rion," Nem replied, breaking her gaze from her friend as she swept into a curtsy. "I am here on behalf of the Three Fates." Her piercing gaze was on the King now. "They feel it is about time an official Emissary was required in the castle. They are aware of the rise in sightings of Kryverns from the mountains in the North."

With a cool, stoic look, Nem said "I am here to offer my assistance and through me, the Fates council."

Lorch was quick to smile and approach the woman, taking her hand in his and placing his lips to the back of her palm.

"It is my pleasure to accommodate you, my Lady, and I gladly accept the Sister's offer of assistance."

Well, he would be stupid not to accept anything from the Three Fates, thought Arii. They were the most powerful in the land next to the King's forces and the heads of the Courts. They held mass influence and the most magic since the male Fae magicians had been wiped out.

Arii spared a quick glance in Elijah's direction, and saw the man was rigid, arms either side of his body, one hovering close to his sword. He did not trust anyone around the King, and it showed. When she let her eyes drift back the King's exchange with Nem, she saw her friend's eyes were on her again.

"The Fates heard of her involvement with the Kryverns in Amberbourne," she paused, tilting her head in Arii's direction as she added, "I would like to speak to the King's Saviour."

Her expression did not leave any room for argument, even for the King.

"Alone," she finished.

Arii felt the hair on her neck stand on end.

Nyx's arse she was in trouble...

Lorch paused before glancing at Arii, and she swore she saw nervousness in his eyes.

The King was nervous for her?

He was a bloody fool without knowing it.

"Who am I to deny the Sister's request?" He shrugged, and then Elijah spoke, his voice low and deadly.

"You are the King, you can refuse whatever you see fit."

Arii felt tension in the air that she could almost taste if she only opened her mouth. She blew out her breath inconspicuously.

The bodyguard had balls.

Nem' brows were arching high on her narrow face, and Arii knew that if the King were not an audience at that moment, the Fury would be sliding her knife between Elijah's ribs and into his heart in a flash.

Lorch lifted a hand in Elijah's direction, placating. He could feel the thickness in the air also and offered a wide smile and a laugh to ease the tension. Arii was noticing more and more that Lorch was a peacekeeper rather than an instigator. He seemed inclined to avoid conflict, rather than seething for it like his father.

"Elijah, it is fine. Let us leave the ladies to talk," he said and directed his smile to Nem.

"Miss Clearwater has become especially important within my guards. I think the Fates will like her." He shot Arii a smile before motioning for a very unimpressed Elijah to leave the room. They exited, albeit the bodyguard a tad slower, and Arii swore he paused for a split second at Nem's side. From beneath his hood, she knew he was glaring at Nem with mistrust.

If only he knew whom he stood beside.

Nemesis Rion would gut him like a fish and use his skull as a paperweight.

The door clicked shut behind them, and Nem was rounding on Arii a few moments later. With a smooth wave of her hand, the silver haired Fury placed a veil of magic around the room to prevent eavesdroppers, and Arii tasted the magic on her tongue. She imagined Lorch Kruel and Elijah Wolfe pressing their ears against the door in an attempt to listen to their conversation – the image causing a bubble of laughter to rise in her throat.

Nem's lips curled back over her teeth.

Oh, she was royally *fucked.*

"What in Nyx's name are you *doing*?" Nem snarled, storming

towards her like an enraged Kryvern. Arii stood quickly, her usual bravado smattering across her features.

The two stood nose to nose.

"You have no idea what has been happening here, or what I have had to endure!" Arii flicked a hand at her novice's uniform. "Do you think I *want* to be here, working for the man I am meant to have assassinated by now?" she snarled into her friend's face. "I have not had a moment with him alone thanks to the man who shadows him everywhere he goes!"

Slowly Nem inched away from Arii, the fire in her eyes lessening as she spoke. "Had I not witnessed his bodyguard just now, I would be far angrier with you, Arii," she said, placing a hand on her shoulder. "The Fates are wondering what is taking you so long. They almost resorted to sending Devina, but I offered to come instead – also planting the idea of a second set of eyes. You owe me." Her lips twitched in a small smile, and Arii felt her muscles relax.

"There are Kryverns, Nem, and they have iron claws and teeth."

Nem's brows narrowed at this as she responded, "Impossible."

"It's true, one swiped me naught a few days ago and my magic fled my body. Someone is modifying the beasts." Arii blew out a breath. "I feel something is at work here, and something big is coming."

"And you feel it's up to you to get to the bottom of it?"

"Well, I feel after almost having my leg ripped off, it has become personal."

Nem slipped to the table bearing the cakes, swiping one up in her silver nails. She paced, taking a bite of the cake as a look of contemplation graced her features.

"Iron, you say?" She chewed thoughtfully. "Do you think someone could be preparing to hunt Fae once again?"

Arii bit her lip. "There are hardly any Fae left, Nem. Unless whoever is doing this is preparing to oppose the Fates? Furies are the only Fae left." She paused. "Unless there have been reports of Fae in the other Courts? But I have not heard."

Nem shook her head. "If there were signs of males in the other Courts, Krepth would have heard and reported it to the Fates."

"Well, there have been more frequent sightings of the Kryverns, and people are bound to notice their modifications sooner or later."

"It's possible," said Nem, swallowing the cake. Her striking eyes lifted to Arii. "Are the other Courts aware?"

The other Courts.

Arii recalled a mark she had in the West Court a few years ago, a young spring lord who had found a fondness for a forbidden substance called Crystal Ice, and set about selling the stuff for exorbitant amounts of gold. The drug, if taken for a small amount of time, caused paranoia and violence along with an incredible high. It was said to be created from the shavings of Nexus Crystals, a mineral mined from the Dragon's Teeth mountains that were once used as a sort of conduit for magic, and the stones could store magic like electricity in a glass jar. The crystals were fabled nowadays – with the absence of powerful magic there was no longer a way to fill them with power.

Unpowered, the stones were naught but crystal paperweights, except for their drug factor.

So, Arii had been sent by the Gods to end the young lord's thread of life. It was a shame, the boy had found riches at the expense of ruining the lives of others, and as the light left his eyes, she saw regret there.

The image remained in her mind for months afterward.

She was reminded of the young man when she looked at Lorch Kruel – they were of the same age.

Arii's eyes met Nem's briefly, before sliding to the window.

"I'm not sure, but the King will send word to the other Courts, right?"

"There seems to be more discord between the four Courts now than ever before. The events of the past and the fear of another uprising seems to be keeping them from coming together," Nem replied.

"Does that surprise you?"

"Not at all, the relationships between the Courts have been rocky since the slaughter of the Herington family."

Arii bit her lip, feeling a chill run down her spine. The family had been killed in this very castle. She briefly wondered where the events had taken place and made a mental note to dig out some tomes and read up on the history.

Who knows, she could learn something that could shed a little light on her current questions.

It was rumoured that the rebels who stormed the castle had set loose a Kryvern as a distraction before falling upon the family. The irony was not lost on Arii after Nem's similar use of the Kryvern at Lorch's birthday party.

"Alright, fulfil your assignment soon but find out as much as you can before you do," Nem stood before turning to her friend.

Arii broke from her reverie, glancing at the silver haired Fury.

"Oh, and Arii, don't get yourself killed."

Arii nodded and smirked at her friend.

"Welcome to the North Court, Nem."

< 80;

Arii was greeted at the barracks by a hot meal on a wooden serving tray as she returned from her time in the library, and she gladly set to downing the hot beef soup and a side of bread.

Sitting in the gardens close to the barracks, the air was becoming cool as it reached half afternoon. Part way through her meal, she suddenly noticed Quinn, who was watching her intently. She had not even heard his approach, her mind so unusually preoccupied.

Her hand paused halfway to her mouth, a chunk of the bread dripping with mopped up soup, and she did not need to speak for Quinn to answer her questioning gaze.

"Thank you, Arii." he said simply, and she felt a mass of weight behind his words. She knew he was talking about their Kryvern encounter.

She placed the bread down and looked at him, his mop of brown hair to his dark brown eyes – wide in his tanned, boyish face. She noticed that he had the tiniest shadow of hair beginning to grow on his chin, and she imagined he would grow to be a dashing young man. She suddenly thought of Tikkani, her lively face and foul mouth, and then Emerson, his gentle disposition and shy smile. She imagined them heading off to battle and their short lives getting cut short on the end of some stranger's blade, or by the jaws of a Kryvern. She suddenly felt her own beast within begin to rise at the thought.

These people, they did not deserve to die.

She felt a stirring within herself that she had only ever felt once before, the feeling she once held for her mother long ago. She smacked the feelings down and swallowed, before answering Quinn, her voice but a whisper.

"Don't mention it, Quinn." she said, offering him a small smile.

The boy returned it with his own, before it lifted into his usual lopsided grin.

"Would you believe Emerson is bragging! Actually *bragging* about his perfectly placed arrow that felled one of the Kryverns, the one – I may add, that was nipping at your arse on the rooftops. I thought you'd want to come witnesses this rare moment of confidence; our boy is becoming a man!"

With a grin, Arii stood and retrieved the tray of half-eaten food.

Quinn draped an arm over her shoulders as they headed together towards the barracks.

Arii did not push him away this time.

QUINN RYDER
Melissa Kincaid

CHAPTER EIGHT

A boy of around nine years dashed through the golden halls of the castle, laughing merrily and clutching a worn blanket in his slim hand. He flew down the candlelit hall heading to his parents' bedroom. It was early, and the boy knew he should still be in bed, but excitement filled his belly, his little body humming with energy. He could not sleep, for it was the morning of Winter Solstice, and he imagined the array of colourful gifts riddling the pine trees brought in from the forest and decorated with those little glittering hanging lanterns he loved so much.

Winter Solstice was his favourite time of the year.

Slapping his hands against the wood, he chuckled and pressed open the door to his parents' bedroom.

"Mama! Papa! Wake up, it's Winter Solstice!" he cried as he entered the dark room, candlelight flooding into the room from the hall beyond.

There was no candles lit inside, no fire in the hearth. Why were his parents not up and awake yet? They normally rose just before he did, preparing the gifts for their family.

The boy's eyes slowly made their way to his parents' bed, and he felt his hands begin to quake, the blanket rising to press against his chest.

There upon the bed lay two bodies, vermillion stained sheets around them, glassy eyes wide to the ceiling and throats cut open to the air. Hovering above the bodies of his parents was a dark shadow, and it tilted its head towards the boy as a wail began to rise from his throat.

The shadow's eyes flashed, jagged teeth yawning wide in a terrifying half-moon shaped smile.

The boy sobbed in fear, blinking as the scene slowly melted into something else.

Suddenly on the bed lay Lorch Kruel, sapphire eyes normally full of life glazed with death. Hovering above him now was a lithe, dark figure, violet eyes flashing, and elongated teeth pulled into a sardonic grin.

Elijah shot up in bed, sweat drenching his bare skin, chest rising and falling rapidly as he speared a hand through his mussed hair.

Outside, lightning streaked across the sky, followed by the deafening boom of thunder.

CB&CO

The next morning, castle staff flitted about the grounds, hauling furniture and crates towards the main building with haste.

Arii lifted the bow and notched an arrow, resting the thatch to her cheek as she narrowed her gaze at the target across the grass. Her attention was grabbed by some maidservants fluttering by with tablecloths, the white material catching the sun's rays like they were flagging down an army in surrender.

Arii slowly lowered the bow and looked at Tikkani in question. Tikkani's gaze was returning to her from watching the maids also.

"Oh, that's right!" she clicked her fingers. "Tonight, is the biannual *stick our wealthy noses up each other's wealthy arses* soiree!"

"The… what?" said Arii, resting the bow by her side.

Tikkani waved her hand in the air dismissively.

"The royal family hold a party twice a year for all of the wealthy people of their Kingdom. Don't ask me why, an excuse for royal fuckwits to wine, dine and be merry," Tikkani said and jogged towards the target, proceeding to gather the arrows littering the grass.

Emerson groaned from a few metres away at his sister's boorish language.

Arii briefly wondered if Lorch put out invitations to the leaders of the other Courts. Could this be an attempt at the extension of an olive branch?

"We will be required to be on guard duty during the party. It is pretty chilled, honestly. We stand around, make sure no drunken brawls break out and no uninvited guests try to barge their way in," Quinn said, taking the arrows from Tikkani and shoving them into a leather satchel as he grinned.

Arii could feel excitement radiating from the boy, enough for her to ask.

"And?"

Quinn was practically vibrating now as he said, "And there is a very good chance *she* is going to be there."

Arii knew exactly who Quinn was talking about.

The flame haired bombshell, Devina Divine.

The boy practically drooled on his tunic when he spoke of her.

Ah puppy love.

"Oh, please Quinn!" moaned Tikkani as she poked him in the butt cheek with an arrow tip. Quinn squeaked and the group began to chuckle.

"A boy can dream," Quinn said meekly, rubbing his backside.

"Wet dream!" said Tikkani with a mad cackle, and soon Quinn was sprinting after her as she retreated, swinging his bow above his head and calling curses at the top of his lungs in a comical display of anger.

Arii and Emerson once again found they were rolling their eyes in unison, retrieving their training weapons, and trailing in their friends' wake.

CS ⬥ SO

The King's throne room was once again dressed in an array of fine furniture, tables covered with carefully arranged floral centrepieces and lanterns flickering with candles inside. Moonlight glimmered through the cathedral windows over the throne.

People from all over the North Court, dressed in fine clothing and gowns, feasted and knocked back sweet wine as if it were going out of fashion.

Arii was almost upset she was on duty tonight. Even her uptight arse would loosen at a party like this. The music was quick and jovial, people danced with abandon on the free space in front of the raised dais, as well as standing and conversing in groups around the tables.

She stood on the outskirts, evenly spaced from Tikkani and Emerson. She was closest to the royal dais, the others spaced at the middle and entry to the room, along with other guards and Commander Hawke. They were all dressed in their armour, having been cleaned up after their time in Amberbourne, save for their helmets. The King had requested they keep the head armour off, allowing them a little bit of comfort in the stifling room. Another hint at the unusual kindness that Lorch Kruel was not widely known for.

Her eyes met with Tikkani – who grinned widely back at her, causing Arii's lips to twitch into a small smile in reply. The girl was growing on her, despite her defences.

Arii's gaze slid to Emerson, and her smile lifted slightly. This morning she had caught him grinning so widely over a piece of parchment that she thought his face may split in two. The handwriting upon the letter was neat and sloping – and she knew by the pink tinge on the boy's cheeks and the shimmer in his eyes that it was a letter from Luc. Despite her best efforts, her heart squeezed at the undiluted joy on his face.

Gods, she was softening.

Quinn was once again with the brass band, his melodious voice echoing about the room. That boy had a set of lungs, Arii gave him that.

She watched without expression as Lorch – looking glorious in an immaculately tailored suit of dark grey stitched with silver thread – meandered about the packed room. His simple gold crown was perched on his russet hair as he chatted with an older man and his young wife, the King's face plastered with a smile. Arii found herself surveying his smile, watching the way he ensured his attention was solely on his courtier as the man rumbled on about his business selling antiques.

That smile though, was not like the ones he had given her.

Nyx's arse, was she getting to know his smiles? Arii bit her tongue as punishment, almost tempted to draw blood.

Lorch's shadow, Elijah, was also visible and not far away from the King. Always nearby and watching. Arii's eyes narrowed, she could practically feel his moodiness from across the room.

So far, she was not the man's biggest fan. He seemed dark, brooding and unapproachable; someone almost as severely guarded as herself.

Across the room was a flash of glittering red, and Arii spotted Devina on the arm of a middle-aged man. She was clad in a floor length gown of shimmering blood red, her burgundy hair pulled into an elegant knot. Loose tendrils fell about her neck and face, striking against her pale skin. The man looked stunned, his lips wide in a grin as if he could not believe how lucky he was.

Arii knew he was, in fact, the *unluckiest* man in the room, soon to be a corpse on Devina's bedroom floor. Devina's blood red lips cracked in a smile at her prey as the man handed her a crystal goblet of sweet wine.

Arii slid her eyes from the Fury back to Lorch, passing Quinn on her way. She paused on Quinn as the boy's voice hitched in the middle of his song, and Arii forced her eyes not to roll.

Who knew who was watching?

At the thought, she glanced to where Elijah stood, and weight pressed in on her as she saw his hooded head was inclined her way.

Bloody uncanny! Was he a mind reader now?

Across the room, Nem was conversing with a woman. The courtier's hair was the colour of raven's feathers and she spoke animatedly with her hands, her carefully manicured fingers dancing as she delved into her story. Nem looked bored, her light eyes sliding from the woman to the party, and then to Arii.

The silver haired Fury's eyebrows twitched ever so slightly, and Arii knew that internally Nem was laughing at her.

How ridiculous that *The Violet Assassin* was on guard duty at a party, protecting the man she had to kill? Nem knew now why Arii was stalling but it did not make it any less absurd. If they were back at the School of Fate, they would be engrossed in a battle of banter that would shake the stone castle walls.

Suddenly Devina was swiping a small pastry roll from the table nearest to Arii, and her amber eyes were alight with amusement.

"Oh, my dear Ariiaya! Guard armour really becomes you!" she chuckled. "Fitting, really."

Arii pursed her lips and stifled a hiss.

"Fuck off, Devina."

Devina's lips pouted in a mock pout as she said, "Coming up with the best comebacks – as usual."

"Flutter away now, peacock. I'm on duty," snapped Arii.

"Duty!?" breathed Devina around her full mouth, only replying after swallowing the last of the pastry and licking her nails. "You're taking this far too seriously, Violet Assassin," she drawled. "Why have you not killed him yet?"

Arii wanted to catch the woman's smirking head and slam it into the tray of cream cakes between them.

The temptation made her fingertips tingle.

If anyone overheard Devina's words – the mention of the Violet Assassin – her cover could be blown. Arii and Devina had never truly gotten along, the woman was insufferable, self-absorbed and wicked, and not wicked in a good way. She would stab a fellow assassin in the back if they were in threat of taking her glory. Arii did not trust her, and never had.

Besides, Elijah was already suspicious, and she could feel it in his weighted gaze, colourless eyes staring their way.

"I'm working on it." Arii snarled, eyes breaking from Devina to survey the room. Did every Fury in the school know of her assignment? Were anyone watching, it would look as if the redhead were surveying the table of delights beside where Arii was stationed.

Eyes lifting, lips curling – Devina plucked a blood red strawberry, lifting it to her lips in a very unsubtle display of flirtation as she flicked her tongue across the tip of the fruit and said, "Well, if you are not going to get on with it tonight, allow me a chance to roll in the silk sheets with the handsome King first."

Arii felt her gaze slide to Devina, and bile rose in her throat as she was met with a sultry gaze.

"Why not, if he is fated to die soon anyway?" cooed Devina, turning to begin a beeline to the King.

Arii felt strange heat begin to rise in her cheeks and an odd feeling bubbled within her.

What on earth was that?

What did she care what Lorch did behind closed bedroom doors? She swallowed the feeling back and locked it away within a vault of steel.

Ignoring Devina's words, Arii continued to survey the room of radiating bodies, the air thick with heat, sweat, body odour and laced with lust.

She could feel the untamed Fae in her rise and whimper.

Gods it had been so long…

Her attention snapped to an angry female voice across the room.

Sybell Kruel was sitting on her seat up on the dais a few feet away, glaring at a young maid who was dipping her head in submission.

"I asked for sweet cakes and cream, not wine!" the golden-haired Princess bellowed.

Holding a silver tray topped with glass goblets, the maid looked a lot like Tikkani, thin, brown haired and sporting the pointed ears of an elf. Arii was not sure what brought on the rise of anger, perhaps the fact the girl was elven and reminded her of her fellow recruit, or the unfamiliar feeling warring within her after Devina's detour, but she felt her hand begin to rise, waving subtly in the Princess' direction.

Her hand twitched, and the goblets of wine were suddenly spilling over Sybell's glorious cream ball gown with just a small flick of magic. The Princess' sound of outrage was audible, and some patrons of the party stopped to stare.

The young maid looked mortified.

Arii felt satisfaction sizzle in her veins.

"My Lady… I… I…" the girl spluttered as the Princess' ire was turned directly on her, eyes like daggers as the girl quaked in her shadow.

Lorch was by the maid's side in an instant, and Arii blinked in surprise. The King took the maid by the arm and made her rise.

"Please, take a break, young lady," he said, and the girl was swift to flee from the dais.

He turned to his sister and straightened. At her side, Lynnera was pinching the bridge of her nose as if this were a common occurrence at their royal parties.

"Calm yourself, sister…" he said gently.

The Princess was radiating anger like a storm, and Arii wondered if Lorch would require backup soon.

She looked like she was about to breathe fire like the dragons of old.

"Calm myself? Calm myself?! I hate these stupid parties; they are such a bore! Why must I sit here, hour after hour, and watch people frolic and grind against one another," she growled, and Arii swore she saw Lorch wince.

Gods, she was a little brat.

Lorch's back straightened, and Arii noticed the air of authority in his voice. She was making a fool of him in front of his subjects.

Gesturing to her bodice, covered in golden liquid, Lorch's voice radiated with authority.

"Go get cleaned up before that stains," he said, shifting to look at Hawke. "Commander, take the Princess to her rooms to change."

Commander Hawke did not need to be ordered twice. He approached the dais, but before he could lend the Princess a hand, Sybell barrelled past him, bumping the man with her shoulder roughly as she passed.

Hawke's face was almost hurt as he glanced after the young woman, before looking back at the King and bowing, then pacing quickly after her.

"I am sorry for your sister's disrespect, my son," said Lynnera, her blue eyes watching Hawke's retreating back with an unreadable look. Lorch sighed and slid into his chair, rubbing his fingers over his jaw.

"Gods she is impossible! Every Gods damn party…"

"She is restless," said his mother, her eyes sliding to him. "She requires a distraction. Perhaps it's time we send out letters for a potential husband?"

This made Lorch chuckle and slap a hand against his knee. When his laughing eyes met with his mother, he noticed her face did not share his humour.

His smiled faded. "Oh, you are serious," he breathed, and then his grin returned. "Can we add to the letter 'Dragon tamer required'? Or will that be seen in poor taste?"

Lynnera's lips quirked at her son and she shook her head. "Lorch…" Her expression softened. "Perhaps it is also time for *you* to seek a bride? The throne requires heirs."

Lorch groaned long and hard, waving his hand dismissively, as if this were the hundredth time they had discussed the topic.

"Mother, please…"

Arii swore that Lorch's eyes sought her out and their gazes locked.

She was first to look away.

Before she did, she saw a glimmer of longing in the King's gaze.

Across the dais and opposite to where Arii stood, Elijah pressed his tongue to the roof of his mouth and catalogued the scene to memory with keen eyes, seeing the flick of Arii's hand, the spilling of the wine on the Princess' gown, and then tasting the veil of sweetness on his tongue.

Elijah knew then that Arii Clearwater was a user of magic.

CB&O

The party continued well past midnight, and Arii saw across the room that Tikkani was fighting back a yawn, pressing her hand against her mouth as her eyes watered. Arii almost felt sorry for her, but knew the party was nearing a close as the last of the partygoers stumbled off to either head home, or lodge in a spare room for the night. She could hear the distant sound of rain tapping the glass windows above.

She loved the rain.

Or perhaps she just enjoyed the sound.

Love of anything was supposed to be an impossibility for a Fury.

There had not been any further interruptions to the party save for the little spat with Sybell on the dais, and Arii had kept her eye out for any strange people from the other Courts attending the party.

There had been none but snotty nosed North courtiers. It disappointed her. For a little while she had hoped to see a golden skinned Westerner, or a gentle faced Eastern Shifter.

Hell, she would not have minded seeing a tall, rugged Southerner.

Lorch said his farewells to the last couple of people dwelling the room, and Arii noticed Commander Hawke approaching her side.

"At ease, recruit. You're dismissed," he said, his tired eyes softening. "Some left-over food from the party has been taken to the barracks for you and the others to enjoy. Good work tonight, Miss Clearwater."

Arii offered the Commander a small smile. "Thank you, Commander."

"Miss Clearwater, may I have a word?"

Arii turned to see Lorch, standing nearby with his hands in the pockets of his pants. Her insides churned as Hawke bowed to the King and spared her a quick glance before he paced quickly from the room.

It was then that Arii realised Lorch, Elijah and herself were the last to remain.

Her tongue darted to wet her lips before she bowed to him.

"Did you enjoy the party, Your Highness?" she said lightly. She could feel Elijah standing a few feet away, face hooded in shadow, his hands by his side, always in reach of his sword.

"I would have pulled my own fingernails out than let it go on all night," Lorch sighed, running a hand down his face to pinch his chin.

Arii paused at this. She thought he liked the random, glittering parties he held in this room. She had watched him enough throughout the night to know that he had not enjoyed the party like she thought he would, turning courtier women away – albeit politely.

Despite this though, she noticed that whenever a story or concern of royal importance was brought to his attention, he deflected them smoothly to speak to his father. It was strange, and it confused her. One moment she felt he may care enough to hear out one of his subjects, then he was brushing them aside like he found it difficult to listen. Her head told her he perhaps did not know how to handle the pressure, her gut told her that perhaps he thought he was doing the best thing by referring them to his father, the King's Hand.

Lorch had a charming and smooth manner when it came to the people, so different from the stories she had once heard, despite his unsurety in dealing with his duty.

The best moment – burned into her brain – had been when King Lorch Kruel had turned away Devina Divine.

That had caused Arii's lips to curl and her chest to compress with barely contained laughter. She had seen Devina's glare, and her ugly grimace as she stormed away and into the thrumming mash of dancing partygoers.

Oh, how she wished she had a painting of that exact moment, strung up in her room in the grey dorms of the School of Fate. It would hold a prized place above her mantle – perhaps doubling as a dartboard.

Lorch inclined his head towards some nearby doors.

"Care for some fresh air? It's stifling in here."

Before she could reply, he was moving towards the doors.

Arii glanced at Elijah, but realised the motion was a waste, she could not see his eyes – only a hint of his constant frown. Her eyes narrowed at him, and she had no doubt under his cloak he was giving her the same dirty glare.

With a small sneer, she followed after the King.

The night-time air cooled her clammy skin as Arii exited the throne room onto the small balcony, her dark eyes adjusting from the light of inside to out. She paused, her gaze dropping to a shiny golden object on the marble floor.

A crown.

Lorch's crown.

She felt her hair stand on end, and her lips pull back over her teeth as a light gust of rainy air whipped her braid over her shoulder and she spun to the sounds of struggle.

In the moonlight stood Devina, holding Lorch to her chest like a lover, her wine-red hair tinged with glittering beads of rain. Her hand was cupping his cheek, nails pressing into his skin, the other held a knife to his throat. Though her lips were curled into a smirk, her eyes were livid with anger.

Arii's hand flew to the sword at her hip, drawing it slowly.

"Devina." she hissed, and Lorch's eyes darted. She knew he wanted to speak but was wise and remained silent lest the blade press harder into his windpipe.

Devina's eyes widened with sudden dawning.

"Well, well… what do we have here?" she said, and her slightly unhinged laughter fluttered into the night air as the Fury nodded in Arii's direction. "Is *she* the reason you refused to share my bed tonight, Your Highness? Do you have any idea who she is?"

That flame haired *bitch.*

She was going to blow her cover, all because Lorch refused her advances.

Devina Divine *did not* like to be refused.

Lorch's eyes were hard now, half of his face illumined by the moonlight. She could see the fight building, the anger igniting. Rain puddled on the marble, glittering like jewels spilled across the floor.

Her eyes locked with his and she shook her head ever so slightly.

Don't you dare try it.

"Come on!" called Devina. "A mere maid servant who felled a Kryvern with nothing but a kitchen knife?" She shifted and the blade caused blood to well and trickle down Lorch's neck.

His lips quivered in a silent snarl.

What could Devina gain from taking Arii's target? Was her pride so wounded from being refused, enough to anger the Three Fates? She knew this was Ariiaya's assignment, she knew the Fates had chosen her. It was an unsaid rule that one Fury did not overstep another where their assignments were concerned.

Arii took a step forward, sword raised, and Devina took one step back, pulling Lorch with her.

Arii's expression was stone.

"Let him go, Devina, before you make a big mistake."

Devina's look was perplexed, her fingers pressing Lorch's face closer to her own. She brushed her lips along his ear and inhaled before whispering, "His fate has been decided, his death is near."

The shadows behind Devina rippled, and Arii felt her heart stutter as Elijah's deep voice cut the night air.

"But not before yours."

Like a viper his hand speared the darkness and clasped hers which held the dagger. His other hand shot his own blade at her kidney, and like a flash the Fury was twisting on the spot.

Lorch ducked at that moment, narrowly avoiding her blade, and sliding to his knees. In a move Arii has never expected of him, Lorch twisted and swept his leg out in an attempt to take the woman's feet out from beneath her.

The fire-haired Fury was a blur, dodging Lorch's attempt at sweeping her feet from beneath her while parring Elijah's blade as it sheared the material of her gown. Metal against metal rang in the air as Lorch rolled out of the way.

Elijah rained blows on the assassin, his blade whistling in a blur of stabs and parries. The man's movements were quick and precise, giving the Fury a sure run for her money.

Arii sprinted and skidded across the marble to Lorch, grabbing his arm as he stared at the two fighters as if entranced.

"Your Highness!" she growled, and when he did not look at her, Arii said more forcefully, "Lorch!"

His eyes skipped to hers at that moment and he stared.

A line of blood trailed down his neck from a shallow cut, and Arii felt anger – gut churning, *confusing* anger as the ruby colour trailed below the neckline of his tunic.

Lorch gripped her hand and she stilled as he whispered, "Elijah!"

She saw in his face fear for his bodyguard.

How odd.

He had countless guards, countless men who could replace the hooded figure by his side, but he looked to be concerned for the man.

War raged inside her, and she stared at Lorch's face for what felt like an eternity. With a nod, she rose and faced the battling duo, the sword spinning in her hand.

When she surveyed the two fighters, she realised she was not needed. Elijah had forced Devina back and the Fury's eyes were wide with surprise and anger. Her hair was coming loose from its binds, burgundy strands fluttering as she ducked and narrowly avoided Elijah's singing blade.

Elijah's hand snapped out, silver whistling in the moonlight. His blade nicked Devina's exposed flesh, leaving a line of red in its wake. Even from her position a few paces away, Arii could see how close the man's blows were to gutting the woman. Red mixed with black as they danced in the moonlight – their movements almost beautiful if it were not a fight to the death.

Devina parried a jab at her gut before sparing a swift glance over her shoulder as she sensed Arii's approach, and her expression was dark.

"So, you've chosen," the Fury hissed.

It was not a question.

Arii and Devina hated one another, had for majority of their time training in the School of Fate, but they were fellow Furies. If only Arii could explain, could tell her what she had told Nem. She tried to convey this with her eyes, but before Devina could read her expression, the woman was twisting away and pressing her back to the balustrade. Her features were set in a feral snarl as she turned, vaulted the railing, and leaped into the darkness.

Arii knew the leap would not kill the assassin. She would surely be back, but not by invitation.

Elijah was barely winded as he sheathed his blade and went quickly to Lorch, helping him from the floor.

"Are you alright?" the guard said, and Arii noticed his voice was laced with genuine concern.

Lorch brushed it off and rose.

The fear written on his face earlier was gone.

He turned to Arii and stepped forward, taking her hand in his. A shiver tingled up her spine. Suddenly he was pulling her towards him, and his lips were pressed to her cheek, warm and gentle.

Arii's eyes widened in surprise as he pulled away slowly. His eyes met hers and he smiled.

"Thank you, once again, Miss Clearwater," he whispered, and she saw genuine gratitude in his eyes.

She felt uncharacteristically speechless. She had hardly done a thing. Had she not seen it with her own eyes, she would not have known how incredibly talented with daggers Elijah was.

His talent rivalled her own.

Her beast rose its head, tilting and surveying the dark man curiously. She would not admit it, but his prowess had left her hot under the collar.

Not in a bad way it seemed, if the heat slowly pooling in her core were any indication.

Soon Lorch was turning from her, his hand lifting to his throat.

"Let's get back inside, I've had enough excitement for one night."

His hand touched the cut as he headed for the door.

Elijah's head turned to Arii, and she felt like he was waiting for her to say something. To *confess* to something.

When she stared back at him in silence, her chin rising in a look of defiance, he growled – actually *growled*.

That heat in her core began to fizzle out as cool night air dashed about them, teasing her hair with invisible fingers.

What was eating him?

His dark hood glittering with rain in the moonlight, Elijah turned to follow his King in from the night.

DEVINA
DEVINE
Melissa Kincaid

CHAPTER NINE

"And where in the Gods name were you last night when Devina poked her nose into my business?!"

Arii rounded on Nem the next day as they met in the library. The morning was overcast, calling for more lanterns to be lit along with the wall candelabras in the domed space, the pool in the centre of the room reflecting the grey sky above.

Nem lounged on a padded settee and tapped her long silver nail against her bottom lip, her legs crossed.

"Devina is a bitch, you know that. The woman hates to be refused."

Arii groaned and was about to proceed with some other profanities that matched her thoughts when Nem lifted a finger.

"Why not have just let her slit the King's throat? It would have saved you a whole lot of trouble."

Arii's fists balled at her sides. Nem was right. Why had she not just let Devina take the kill? She could be headed home by now, back to the School to continue with her work. No more strange feelings foreign to her. No more sapphire eyes watching her from across the room. No more static in the air under a hooded man's unimpressed, eyeless glare.

Why did the thought of leaving confuse her more?

Arii swallowed before responding.

"Having the King alive will give me a better chance of finding out who is tampering with the Kryverns."

Nem sighed and stood slowly. "Why do you care? Why does that bother you so much, Ariiaya?"

Arii paused as she envisioned a woman then, with features almost identical to her own. The angle at which she saw her mother was from below, warm hands cupping her cheeks as her mother's face lowered to hers. Her eyes were violet, just like Arii's, and they were also filled with fear as her blood-streaked face hovered above her own.

"We must go!" cried her mother, grabbing Arii's arm and dragging the six-year-old girl through the forest. In the distance, there was the drone of alarm bells in the direction from where they were fleeing.

"But what about Papa!" wailed Arii, clinging to her mother as the woman pulled her into her arms and ran – ran as quickly as she could over the damp terrain. Her breaths were laboured, and Arii remembered it was raining.

Water was in her eyes, drenching her clothing, and that of her mother. Her eyes lifted, watching the clawing fingers of the trees sway against a darkening sky.

She did not understand what was happening, why they could not go back for Papa.

"I'll explain soon, little Violet. I promise," her mother gasped and continued their escape through the forest.

In the distance, thunder boomed like a war drum.

Arii gazed out the window, and Nem seemed to register where her friend's mind had faded to.

"Whatever this is, Arii, you know you cannot prevent it. If the past is to repeat, who are we to interfere with fate?"

Arii turned to her friend. Thankfully, she had not read the additional feelings smattered across her face.

It was not just the Kryverns which kept her here.

Lorch was not who she had believed him to be.

Never before had Ariiaya Trillia questioned fate.

ॐ

Water gently lapped against the banks of the lake as skin glittered in the moonlight. A woman emerged from The Sapphire Depths, completely and utterly naked. Her silver hair rippled in waves to her lower back, modestly covering her breasts; from hips to toes she was covered in iridescent fish scales.

She rolled her head as if she had just awoken, stretching the soreness from her neck and wiggling her toes in the grass.

Her eyes, as dark as onyx, slid languidly to gaze at the golden castle above. Colourless lips lazily pulled into a smile and teeth flashed as she turned to the water to watch the shadows of other women emerge in her wake. Behind them, a full moon hung in the midnight sky.

She spoke, her voice like the hiss of a snake, rough as if she had not spoken in a year.

"It is time, sisters. Let us hope for a better harvest this year."

Behind her, a small sea of smiles began to appear, excited and hungry.

The castle grounds were silent save the murmuring of the waterfall and the gentle swish of trees swaying in a steady midnight breeze.

A soldier stationed just behind the main castle doors yawned long and wide before rubbing the heels of his hands on his eyes. It had just ticked past midnight, and the full moon loomed in the dark inky sky.

The man sighed dramatically and hitched his belt uncomfortably, tired and aching from watching the castle gate for hours. He had only slept for a short while prior to his shift, having spent time in the local tavern drinking mead with other soldiers off duty. He was paying for it now, it seemed, as his eyes drooped and his face split in another wide yawn.

Out of habit, the soldier slid open the metal slat on the window, peering out to the bridge beyond the castle gate. Not expecting any movement on the stone pavement that stretched into the distance, the man's expression remained bored as he surveyed the moonlit night.

He turned away to shift his belt again then peered back through the window. A shift of movement caught his eye.

Blinking, the man straightened and squinted, wondering if his eyes were playing tricks. He swore he could hear a woman singing, a gentle, sweet melody that made a warm feeling course through his body.

"Chay!" the man called.

Another soldier joined him as he gestured to the window.

"What?" the second man barked, his expression just as tired as his companion.

"Can you hear that?"

Their eyes fixed on the stone bridge beyond, the melody became louder in the night air as a figure came into view. Hips swaying, the woman stepped into the golden firelight of the torches along the castle walls. She was draped in a long traveling coat, silver hair shimmering in the dim light as the song washed over the men again.

Stunned, they looked at one another before turning back to the woman.

"Excuse me, miss? Are you lost?" called the first man, watching as the women paused just before the window. Her eyes were as dark as pitch, her lips in a gentle smile. Her manner was meek as she dipped in a quick curtsy.

"Sirs, I have been traveling all day and most of this night. Might I not come in to warm by the fire?" Her voice was alluring, thick lashes fluttering as she tilted her head to gaze up at the men.

Silent for a few moments, their heads disappeared as they ducked behind the mahogany gate.

"What do you think? It is the middle of th' night, the woman just wants a place to stay."

"You got to be kidding me, Chay, ya' know what night this is!

What if she is one of those… Water Nymphs?"

The man named Chay blew a dismissive breath.

"Nah mate, look at her, she is so slight and not a fin in sight! Beautiful, innshe? Perhaps she'd like some company, warm her bed? Eh?" The man smiled slyly and began to straighten, heading for the lock on the smaller door connected to the colossal gate. The first man was quick to follow Chay as he began unfastening the lock.

"I don't feel this is wise, Chay, you know our orders!"

"C'mon, mate!" hissed Chay as he pulled on the door, opening it to the moonlight beyond. "What's the worst that could happe-"

A shadow flashed, and the man named Chay was suddenly on his back on the stones, a ray of moonlight illuminating the man's glassy eyes and torn out throat. The cobblestones where he lay bloomed in a pool of blood. The first soldier screamed before stepping back, eyes locked on the slain man. His legs quaked, but he soon snapped into action, fleeing for the emergency bell nearby.

Stumbling, the man grasped the rope, pulling with fumbling fingers, causing a shrill ring to echo through the silent courtyard.

A shadow leaped upon him, and the piercing toll of a bell was soon replaced by shrill, dreadful screaming.

"So, what do you think, Miss Clearwater? King's Head or Dragon's Tail?"

The throne room flickered with candlelight as Lorch turned to gaze at Arii, who stood against the far wall in her guards' uniform. Arii's expression was lightly stunned at being directed a question as the King and his father sat at a table, a chessboard before them.

To progress in the game of King's Chess, a coin had to be tossed. For reasons unknown to Arii, Lorch seemed to be asking her what side she believed the coin would land on. She had always loved the embossed imagery on the royal coins. One side had the impression of a man's face – his features not resembling anyone she knew. The other side held a symbol of a dragon, wings splayed and tail curling around the circle of the coin.

Across the table, Valdis sat with his hands pressed together in contemplation, elbows resting on the wood and knuckles pressed lightly to his lips. His blue eyes flickered to his son, and then to the guard who had his son's attention.

Nearby, Hawke lingered by the window, gazing out into the night.

Arii was surprised that Lorch was not tucked away in his rooms, guarded and secure. Instead, he insisted they play King's Chess in the throne room. It seemed the King preferred they all be awake and alert. Arii found that she agreed with him.

"Erm…" murmured Arii.

"Just toss the coin, son," hissed Valdis, the word *son* almost sounding like a curse on his lips.

Arii's mouth snapped shut, almost thankful to Valdis that she had not needed to reply. Lorch chuckled gently, his attention back on his father and the game. The air in the room felt tense tonight, as if everyone were waiting for something to happen. Arii knew the significance of the night, but she could not deny the heaviness in the air.

Or perhaps that was the dark cloaked figure of Elijah, standing across the room from her.

The air constantly felt weighted, charged, as if a current of electricity lingered wherever he stood. It was peculiar, the tension around the bodyguard. Arii often found herself gazing his way, drawn to him, and wondering what he looked like beneath the hood, and what history had moulded him into the deadly man she had witnessed on the balcony.

Lorch placed a white marble figurine on the chessboard with a light tap, breaking her reverie and drawing her attention back to the game.

"Fine, Father. Gods you are impatient."

Valdis's brows twitched, the only expression on his scarred face. With a sly grin, Lorch moved his figurine towards one of his father's on the board, just as a bell began to toll.

Lorch paused, as did the entire room.

Soon after, a soldier burst through the doors and Arii recognised Quinn's eyes through the helmet, perspiration visible on his brow. He breathed heavily, as if he had just run the length of the castle.

Lorch stood quickly, his chair scraping against the marble.

Quinn entered the room and dropped to a bow.

Commander Hawke stiffened to attention by the window.

"My King, the alarm bells by the west gate have been rung. There has been a breach."

Arii felt her stomach drop. A breach? How?

Valdis was standing and moving to retrieve his sword, propped against a wall nearby as Elijah moved to the King, his voice a swift murmur.

"We must get you somewhere safe."

"You and Miss Clearwater go and find out what is happening, I will go with my father and Commander Hawke to the royal quarters. I need to make sure my mother and sister are safe."

Lorch slapped a hand on his bodyguard's shoulder, offering a smile as he said, "If the Nymphs have indeed breached the castle, you have my full permission to let loose on them, Elijah. Send them scurrying back to The Sapphire Depths."

Arii felt a shiver.

If the night Devina had threatened the King was any indication of Elijah's combat prowess, she was eager to see him in full action. Without the King to worry about, she imagined he would be a sight to behold.

She almost felt sorry for the Nymphs… *Almost.*

Elijah's hood bobbed as he bowed to the King, before turning to face her.

"Let's go."

Quinn led the way through the castle halls, heading for the courtyard where he claimed there had been fatalities. Luckily, it had been sealed off, but the soldiers there needed backup. They passed other soldiers as they hurried to their posts, the scent of fear tangible in the air.

As they entered the courtyard, Arii realised she had never seen a Water Nymph before. When she saw the array of bodies strewn on the stones of the inner courtyard, their skin ashen and throats torn out, she realised she really did not care to.

Drawing his sword, Elijah surveyed the carnage. Ahead, a cloaked figure leaned over one of the bodies as if in mourning. Arii drew her own sword, feeling adrenaline begin to rise within her.

Something felt terribly wrong.

The woman – for the figure was slim and feminine – slowly began to rise and turn to them. Beside Arii, Quinn began to shake, his own sword wobbling in his hands.

She was stunning. Her skin was pale like milk, her eyes large and dark. Her hair fell in thick silver curtains as she pulled back her hood. Her lips curled as she unclipped her cloak, allowing it to fall and pool around her feet.

Oh shit.

Standing before them, scales glittering across her breasts and down her legs, her body was like an hourglass. Fins sprouted from her sides, fanning out like wings as the Water Nymph's lips pulled back to reveal jagged teeth.

Her entire expression changed from serene to that of a nightmare as the woman shrieked. "Finish them, my sisters! Break through the doors and feast upon the castle!"

Suddenly shadows were upon them from all sides, their small group breaking apart as chaos erupted.

Quinn screamed as a shape slammed into him and knocked him to the stones. His attacker had black hair, her scales catching the moonlight as her teeth headed for his throat. He screamed again, flailing with his sword in panic.

Suddenly a dagger was lodged in the woman's back, and she turned to shriek as Arii lopped her head off with her sword.

Dark blue blood flecked Quinn's helmet, some beading on his eyelashes as he blinked rapidly. Swiftly, Arii grabbed Quinn's plate armour and forced him to stand. "Don't let them near the doors!" she growled, grabbing Quinn's hand and pulling his sword into position before him. Her fingers curled around his, tightening his grip. "You can do this, Quinn!"

Quinn's terrified eyes hardened as he nodded.

"Right," he said, heading for the doors to defend them with other soldiers. Arii briefly watched him go, hoping to the Gods that he survived the night. Strangely, she had grown to like the boy.

Her gaze snapped to the courtyard, and she felt her blood run cold.

Elijah was surrounded.

His sword lifted, and suddenly she found herself fixed to the spot as she watched in utter awe of what unfolded. The air crackled, and she swore she heard thunder in the far distance. White light strobed behind the dark, clouded sky – flashes of light illuminating the hooded figure as shimmering bodies closed in.

The first Nymph launched herself at the man with a scream, face contorted in ravenous hunger. With a fluid motion, Elijah's sword took her head from her shoulders in one swift swipe. The other Nymphs screamed in anger and pain at their fallen sister, launching with looks of revenge. Elijah dodged and slashed his sword, movements fluid and controlled, each attack precisely aimed to deliver death. He danced, rather than moved, his body twisting to meet each attacker, one after the other.

One Nymph flew at him after another. Elijah slashed one across the chest, dipping down to swiftly pull a dagger from his boot, tossing the weapon as quick as lightning, burying it in the second Nymph's chest before she had even come close. His fist flew, snapping another's head to the side, before following through with a swift stroke of his sword, dark blood spurting like a violent fountain as he opened the creature from groin to neck – her entrails spilling upon the stones. Elijah stood and spun, meeting each flash of scales with his sword.

Gods he moved like a Fury.

Before Arii could think any longer on how his movements had her blood aflame, she twisted to slash an attacking Nymph. The silver haired beauty stepped back in the nick of time, her face alight with fury.

"You will do well to give up now, girl!" she hissed. "The castle will run red and we will feast."

"Not if we can help it," Arii grunted, pressing forward.

"Hah! Why do you aid these men? Place down your sword and we will let you live. Men's blood tastes all the sweeter than women's, anyway."

Arii's lips quirked. "It seems I need these men alive, sorry to burst your dirty bubble."

With that, Arii advanced on the woman, her sword flying in a blur to take off her head. The Nymph dodged and snarled, her glittering form spearing in Elijah's direction. She had no doubt Elijah could handle himself, but these foes were swift and fierce.

Arii found herself pausing.

If the Nymphs took down the bodyguard, she would have better access to the King. The thought was followed by the memory of Lorch's eyes, filled with fear for Elijah the night Devina attacked on the balcony.

That look had Arii backtracking in her thoughts. An unfamiliar feeling fluttered in her chest at the memory.

Nyx's arse, this place was making her gentle, pulling at the strings of feelings she kept buried deep, deep within.

Perhaps part of her wanted to be the one to end the bodyguard's life.

Yes, that was it.

He looked to be a challenge, and a Fury liked a challenge. He had been nothing but a hindrance to her, and it was obvious that the man disliked her. She knew his suspicion was warranted, and he was doing his job.

But still…

With a frustrated growl, she sprinted in Elijah's direction.

He was a flurry of black cloth and steel. Where he moved, blood sprayed, and Nymph heads rolled. He was a whirlwind of death, and the creatures began to fall back. The dark eyes of the silver haired Water Nymph glimmered with uncertainty, with shimmering moonlit bodies beginning to hesitate in their advance.

All the while, Elijah's hood did not fall, keeping his mysterious face in shadow – all that was visible was his lightly downturned frown.

Even as he dealt death, Elijah still managed to look unimpressed.

Arii slashed one of the Nymphs, making a path to Elijah. The air reeked of blood, the metallic taste tangible on her tongue, filling her nostrils. Any other day, this would have set her Fae blood alight with the lust of battle, but this blood smelled wrong, as if tinged with dirty lake water.

"What are you doing? Kill them!" the silver haired Nymph screeched, pointing at Elijah and Arii who now stood back to back.

The two guards circled, weapons raised as they eyed the remaining women. Arii felt the heat of Elijah at her back and could hear the steady sound of his breathing.

"Are you alright?" he murmured unexpectedly, giving her pause.

"Just dandy, I think some of their blood went in my mouth," she whispered back, spitting on the stones.

She swore she heard a hint of a smile as he retorted, "I thought you'd left me to defend the castle on my own. Your movements are sloppy, recruit."

She dared a swift glance over her shoulder, face incredulous.

The nerve!

Before she could tell him where he could shove his sword, the silver haired Nymph let out a shriek of frustration – ripping Arii's gaze back to the creature.

When the Nymphs did not move further, Silver Hair screeched again.

"Leave now, return to the depths with what is left of your sisters," growled Elijah, his breath hardly winded.

The silver haired woman moaned in anger again as her sisters began to flee through the gates. Her head whipped back to the two soldiers, her onyx eyes alight with rabid frustration.

"I'll drain you myself!" She flew at Elijah with an enraged screech.

The man flipped his sword to clasp the grip and slammed it into the woman's throat. She staggered, before he was grabbing her skull and smashing it against his knee. She wailed, and soon found herself with her face pressed against the bloody cobblestones.

Arii was on the Nymph's back, dagger pressed to her throat and shoving the woman to the floor.

The Nymph spat, the blood of her sisters wetting her face. "Wait!"

The woman cried out, just as Arii pulled her head back by the hair, dagger poised to slit her throat.

"Wait! I have information!"

Arii paused, knife pressed into the woman's jugular. Elijah was swiftly kneeling before the woman, cloak billowing around him. Arii was not sure what information the creature could possibly provide to them that was worth her life. Her head tilted to Elijah, and without a word between them, they decided it was worth hearing her out.

"Speak," he ordered.

The woman twitched and Arii pressed her blade deeper into her skin. This seemed to spur her on. "Some of my people have been disappearing from the lake," she rasped.

Elijah's growl was low and dangerous as he snapped, "And this matters to us how?"

"They have been disappearing over the last few weeks. Prior to the full moon. My spies have told me that they have been fished from the depths by small groups of Red Guard soldiers."

This caused Elijah to jerk. "You utter lies."

The woman's laugh was light but pained. "It is the truth! Someone is ordering my people to be plucked from the depths like common fish and flung into containers filled with water – aboard wagons bound for Bonemire. For what purpose I do not know."

Arii's brows drew in confusion.

What would Red Guard soldiers want with Water Nymphs? She wondered briefly if Nem knew what this could be about.

"Perhaps it is to thin your numbers before the next full moon," spat Elijah. Were it not for him, the castle and all of its men would have been drained of blood tonight.

The Nymph gurgled a laugh, the dark blue puddle rippling as she spoke. "Something is happening in the North. My sisters living in the pools in The Dragon's Teeth Mountains claim more sightings of Kryverns. The beasts are being disturbed from the dens and some are even being captured and transported in the same wagons as my sisters."

Arii felt her stomach bubble with dread. Why would the royal guard be transporting the beasts to their training base and prison in the North?

"Why would you tell us this?" said Elijah. The Nymph chuckled darkly, causing Arii to press her face into the bloody stones once more.

"Perhaps one expects some mercy to be given?" murmured the creature, her voice wet.

"And why would we do such a thing? You slaughtered a dozen of our men!"

"It is our nature to become ravenous every full moon when the Gods above allow us to have legs rather than fins for one night. Please, my Lord," the woman begged. "If you spare me, I will ensure word of your mercy is taken to the depths with me. Perhaps it will sway my sisters to leave the castle alone next full moon."

Arii pressed the dagger to the woman's neck, harder this time.

She had enough. It was time to end this.

Before she could split the scaled woman's windpipe to the air,

Elijah moved a hand to her arm, halting her. Arii's dark eyes flicked up to see his hood angled her way.

"Let her go."

"Wha–"

"Arii, let her go."

Elijah must have known she would take convincing. He had *never* addressed her by her first name before. The brief words they had exchanged up until this point could be counted on two hands.

The sound of her name from his lips caused a warm shiver to shoot down her spine. She did not need to see his eyes to know he was staring her down, a hair's breadth from giving an order.

With a last shove in the Nymph's back, Arii removed the dagger from her neck and stepped away. The woman slowly stood, eyes wide and fixed on Elijah, her expression disbelieving.

"Go now before I change my mind," he growled, not sheathing his sword. He was ready if the Nymph decided to attack again.

Lucky for her, the woman was not so stupid.

"Your mercy will not be forgotten," she said, her tone meaningful and soft. She turned and fled in a blur, out the gate and into the night.

⊰∘⊱

"Why did you not kill her?"

Their swords clashed in the training arena the next morning. Steel kissing steel, Arii pressed her attack on Elijah as she spoke. He met her stroke for stroke and was not even winded after a solid thirty minutes of consistent sparring.

To say she was impressed was an understatement. He moved like he was made of water, each stroke of his weapon landed in a precise spot to cause the most damage, or the quickest kill.

It caused fire to rocket through her veins.

How in the Gods name was she to fulfil her assignment with him shadowing the King at every step? She had not been expecting someone of such skill to be by his side.

As they sparred, Elijah spoke.

"Sometimes one must show mercy."

Clang.

"Mercy may just sway fate in your favour at a later date."

Clang.

What did this man know of fate?

Swords clashed again and her blade ran down his, causing their bodies to come closer. She could feel the heat of him through her leathers, a tingling in her fingertips. Perhaps he was a tad winded? Her eyes narrowed as she attempted a peek below his hood.

He shoved her back, and she grinned slyly.

Dropping suddenly, she swept her leg out to trip him.

Elijah anticipated her move and jumped, then they were once again dancing in a flurry of fluid swipes, jabs and twists.

After the attack on the castle, Elijah and Arii had reported the Nymph's words to the King. They were all unsure what to make of the information, and Lorch had agreed to ask questions of his council. Lorch seemed unsure – even unbelieving that anything but imprisonment of criminals and training was happening at the fortress to the North, but he agreed to do some digging after a firm word from Elijah.

Now Arii and Elijah were alone in the training arena, the morning rays bathing them in golden light. Arii was not sure about the man, but she had not been able to get a lick of sleep after the events of the full moon. Adrenaline from the fight kept her awake, twisting in the sheets as she replayed the beautiful death dance she had witnessed. Her mind was a flurry, questions belting her from all angles.

Who was Elijah Wolfe?

Why were creatures being transported to Bonemire like cattle?

Who was tampering with the Kryverns?

She wondered if what the Water Nymph had said was true, and not just a ruse to be set free. Either Elijah was a fool or had incredible foresight that could aid them later on.

Gods, was she going to *help* them with whatever event was on the horizon? If the feeling in her gut was correct, she knew something was coming that would throw all of her plans into disarray. Surely the Gods would allow her a brief reprieve from her duties? Besides, she would fulfil them, it was to just take a little longer than expected.

When she had come to the training arena in the early hours of the morning to begin some exercises, she was not expecting to see the hooded figure of Elijah, sparring in the ring on his own. She had lingered in the shadows, watching his broad shoulders and practiced steps of his feet as he dipped and turned.

He had paused to watch her, his lips pulled in a frown.

She wordlessly grabbed a sword and joined him in the ring.

There was a weighted silence between them, but it was no longer so uncomfortable. Every now and then, she attempted a sneak glance under his hood. He knew what she was doing, and so far, she was unsuccessful.

Now, Arii was tired of holding back. She finally had someone who matched her own skills, and she was eager to work up a sweat. Eyes narrowing and smile vanishing, her veil of magic dropped, and her vision flashed into crystal clarity, eyes dancing over her target. The threads in the material of his cloak, the fine hairs of dark stubble on his chin, the smoothness of his lips.

Her Fae eyes saw it all with crystal clarity – as if peering through a telescope. She felt a shock of electricity sizzle through her veins as the magic danced through her body like starlight, and suddenly she was a blur of steel, raining down on him.

He blocked her swift attacks, and they danced to a silent song.

She could have sworn she heard a suck of breath under the cloak before her sword slammed against his, and with a swift twist and a jerk of her wrist – the weapon was sent flying from his hands.

Grinning in triumph, she dipped into a fluid crouch as the crash of the sword hitting the floor rang through the arena. She stood, sword flipping in her hand as she pointed it in Elijah's direction.

Her sword pointed at air, for the space before her was empty.

Cool steel pressed against the side of her neck, and Ariiaya – the deadly Fury assassin – was completely floored.

"How the fu-"

"You are far too full of yourself…" His breath was a warm caress against her cheek, its cadence deep and gentle. He held her upper arm, his body pressed close behind hers. A scent of leather and sandalwood drifted across her senses, causing her toes to curl in her boots. He smelled like the forest – deep, woody and surprisingly complex, as he murmured, "When you become cocky…"

She began to struggle, and he held her tight in an impossibly strong grip. "…you begin to lose sight of important details."

Arii's lips pulled back in a snarl as her magic veil slowly lifted once more.

"Where did you learn to move like that?" she hissed.

His laugh was like a dark melody. "Many, many years of training." He paused, before adding, "And years of discipline – discipline which *you* lack."

Arii gnashed her teeth together in fury.

Bested by some… human male.

Elijah mistook her silence for shock. "I must admit, you are incredibly talented yourself. With some fine tuning, you will be a force to reckon with on the battlefield."

Arii felt his chest against her back, solid and unmoving. Gods he was strong. The air sizzled between them, and her lips began to quirk as she dared to slowly turn her head.

He was so dark, dangerous and mysterious.

She very subtly leaned back into him, pressing her bottom against him, and for a small moment their breath mingled.

She swore she heard his breath hitch.

Ever so slightly.

He made her blood boil, and not in the bad way which she was expecting. She felt the dangerous fingers of attraction claw at her stomach. How could she be attracted to a man when she had never seen his face? It surely was not his *stunning* personality…

Arii's lips quirked in a smirk as she turned her head once more.

Suddenly the knife was gone, and he shoved her away – just before she could peek beneath his hood. She rubbed her neck where the ghost of the blade lingered.

The knife twirled in Elijah's hands as he barked, "Again."

From the shadows of the training arena, eyes watched the pair spar. Lips curled as the thing smirked, and it glided a tongue along dagger sharp teeth.

The thing in the shadows was growing hungry.

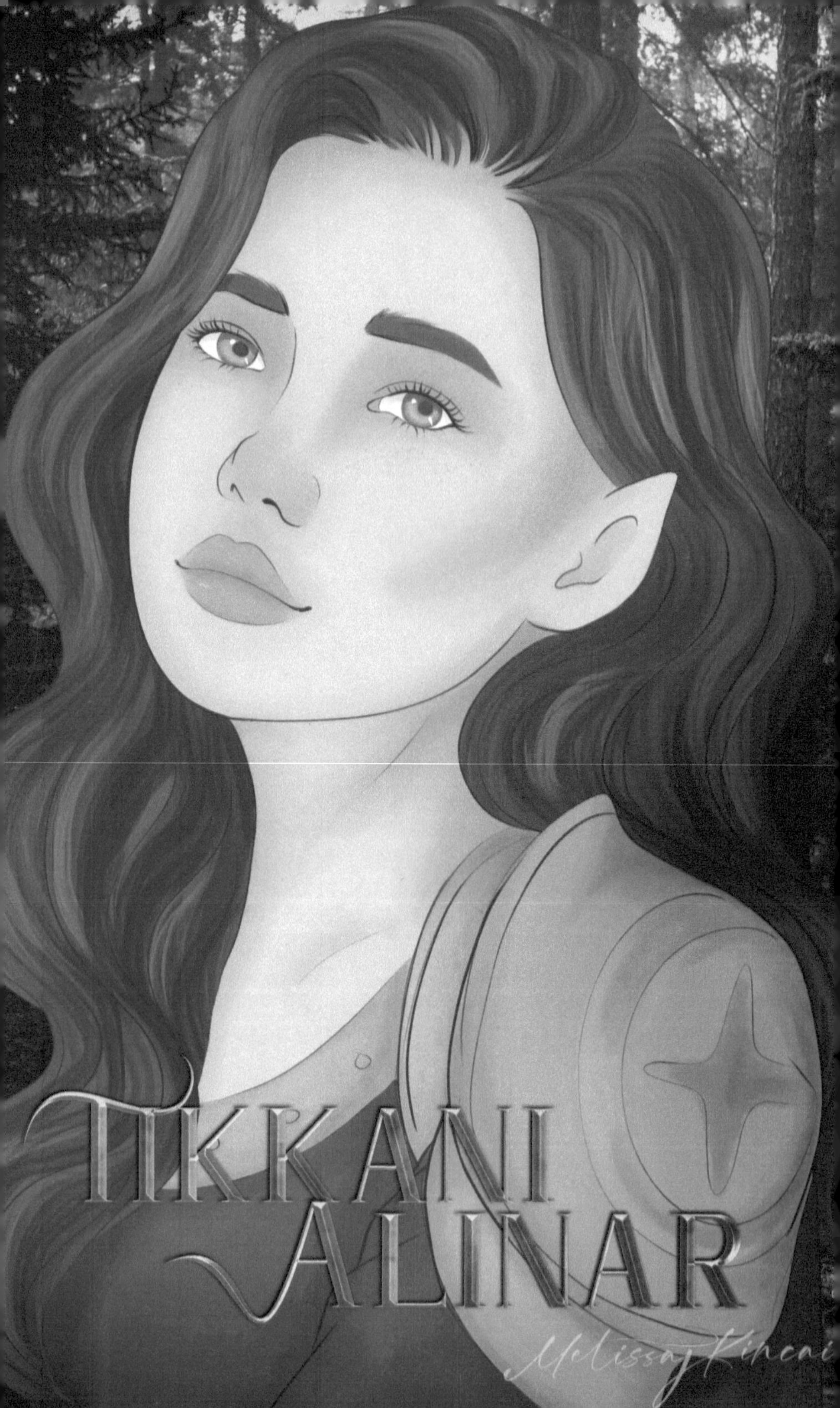

TIKKANI
ALINAR
MelissaJKincai

Chapter Ten

Another night of twisted sheets, another night of waking with a light sheen of sweat on her brow.

Calloused, battle hardened hands roved her body, dark stubble tickled her in places that she had not been touched in a long time. The man was hooded and faceless, a cloak draped across their bodies as she writhed in the moonlight. His touch was like fire, his tongue a wicked thing that had her back arching and her fingers gripping the sheets as pleasure sheared through her body.

Her heart was a riot in her chest, a tornado of whirling confusion. Part of her wanted to tell him to stop, to grip the cloak and yank him away – yet part of her wanted to beg him to *never* stop.

The face beneath the hood lifted and slowly came into focus, dark blue eyes lifting to meet hers as a seductive smirk tugged at Lorch Kruel's swollen, ravaged lips…

Arii shot up in her cot, pawing at the sweat forming on her brow, her chest rising and falling as if her body could not get enough air.

Gods these men, they were getting beneath her skin.

Now, they were both entering her dreams.

Arii was sure she was the first Fury to be kept awake at night by the thoughts of two men. She wondered if there was something in the water here, something causing her mind to run away with itself into dark fantasies of desire. If Nem knew what haunted her dreams of late, she would surely laugh in Arii's face. She would call her a stupid fool, and she would slap the thoughts from her head.

Perhaps that was what she needed, a good slap to the face.

A Fury does not think.

A Fury does not feel.

Arii pulled on dark brown pants and boots before heading to the bathing room, brushing sleep-mussed hair quickly before slipping a white tunic over her body. Splashing water over her face and pausing to look at her reflection, she blinked at the wide-eyed woman staring back at her before sighing heavily and pushing from the basin.

Today was her day to be off duty, and her dress was casual and comfortable. She slid a knife into her boot, along with the efficient strap of a dagger to her hip.

Casual did not mean unarmed.

After the night of the full moon, Arii had been relieved to see all three of the recruits alive and unscathed. Swiftly passing the beds where Tikkani, Emerson and Quinn still snored, she headed for the door and entered the cool morning air.

She then ran smack bang into the King.

Stunned, she dropped to one knee, causing Lorch to laugh gently.

"Please stand, Miss Clearwater. I was just coming to see you."

Blinking, she stood. Her eyes found the lingering shadow of Elijah nearby, causing her to swallow heavily.

"Me?" she asked.

Lorch was dressed in a light tunic of moss green, sporting dark brown pants and dark boots.

He looked… just as casual as herself.

She was not used to seeing him look so… not like a King. His light brown hair was swept in its usual style, the copper highlights glinting in the morning light. His face was lit with a smile.

"Yes, you." he confirmed, grinning. "Care for a tour of the gardens?"

Lorch insisted Arii loop her arm with his as they strolled the vast expanse of the castle gardens. It was strange, the North Court was close to the Winter months, but still the grounds were bathed with sunlight, the air warm and mild as if Summer insisted on lingering.

Lorch spoke of his mother, and how amazed he was at the patience the woman showed for his stuck up, ill-mannered sister. He spoke of his father and of the councilmen he had dealings with. Words left him like a waterfall, and eventually Arii felt a kind of peace wash over her at the sound of his voice. She knew she should be gathering valuable information and finding out more about what the Water Nymph had said, but after a short time she realised that Lorch in fact knew hardly anything about the fortress to the north. Lorch, despite being the King of the North Court, knew little of the workings of running a kingdom. It was incredibly strange, yet Arii got the distinct impression once again that Lorch heavily relied on his father when it came to his job.

She did not know much about Valdis, but she did not get good vibes when in his presence. When Arii asked about specifics on the fortress to the North, Lorch tilted his head to her. "Bonemire? That is all run by my father," he said as they paced below a hanging willow tree.

Arii chewed her lip as they walked. She sensed Elijah was nearby and listening. Surprisingly though, the man cloaked in shadow did not add to their conversation.

It was also a surprise that Valdis did not sit on the throne himself.

His control of everything to do with the Crown explained the ravenous poverty striking the smaller towns, the small bands of rogue guards causing trouble in the inns and flaunting their royal pins to get special treatment where businesses desperately needed coin.

Surely Lorch could see what was happening right beneath his nose?

There was hardly a balance anymore. She supposed that balance had been teetering for as long as she could remember, perhaps since the Herington families' death. She herself was only young when the event happened. Since then, the Courts and their rulers had begun to withdraw into their own borders, before communication became almost non-existent.

The rogue guards were a whole other problem.

She vividly remembered slicing the hand off a man who had kept placing it where it did not belong, on a barmaid in the local tavern that she frequented with Krepth and Nem in Colkirk. Bearing the royal pin, the man lounged and demanded free mead of the innkeeper and grabbed the young girl's behind far too many times for Arii's liking. She could remember his howl of anguish and the thump of his hand as it hit the tavern floor. A riot broke out and she had had several Red Guards out on their arses.

Hell, that was a fun night.

If Lorch took his responsibilities seriously, she believed things would be a whole lot different. If what she had seen so far were any reflection, Lorch was a surprisingly kind person. She wondered what stopped him from speaking up and making change happen in the crumbling land around him. He seemed too kind, and perhaps that was making him easily malleable.

"All that go to Bonemire are murderers and common thieves," he said dismissively, bringing her back from her reverie.

Lorch placed a hand on her own and she almost jumped at the contact. They had covered so much ground, and she had been so distracted by her internal reflection that she had not noticed they were outside the royal stables.

"Care for a ride, Miss Clearwater?" he asked, opening the door to the stables.

Arii offered a small smile and nodded. "Alright, I guess there could be worse ways to spend a rest day."

Lorch's eyes wrinkled as he smiled, motioning for her to follow him to the stall where they had met for the second time.

Standing where she had been a little over a week ago, Day Dancer stomped her hoof and snorted a greeting. Arii took the horse's velvet muzzle in her hands, stroking and cooing softy. Lorch sidled up beside her, a look of surprise on his face. "It never ceases to amaze me how you let your guard down around a horse, my tough little warrior."

Arii threw him a look, and he laughed as he went to retrieve the saddle and riding gear. Lorch began to work, and Arii found herself surveying him, again surprised that he prepared the horse himself. He hefted the saddle onto Day Dancer's back with care, making sure not to catch her mane. He was lean, tall, and had the body of a dancer rather than that of a fighter like Elijah.

Leading the caramel mare by her bridle, they headed to the open space just clear of the stables.

Lorch turned to meet her gaze and his eyes twinkled, a sly smile curling his lips. He leaned towards her and she froze.

"Let me help you up," he breathed as he slid his hands around her waist. She knew it was not her imagination as Lorch paused, and they were suddenly eye to eye, nose to nose. His eyes flicked down to her lips, and she found herself holding still under his close observation. Lorch's eyes grew dark as they shared breath, his lips parting ever so slightly as he leaned closer. A shiver slid down her spine, and warmth pooled in her gut. She felt blood rise into her cheeks, and suddenly she felt a slither of anger.

A Fury does not blush.

A throat cleared just a few feet away, and Lorch paused inches from touching his lips to hers.

Elijah…

Lorch sighed and pulled away slowly.

"If I may, Your Highness…" Elijah drawled, leading a black stallion from the stalls. The man paused in front of Arii, and before she knew what he was doing, Elijah was sliding the daggers from her belt.

"Hey!"

"You will not be needing them on your ride," he said simply.

Arii's glare could have resembled daggers. At least she had her knife lodged firmly in her boot…

Elijah suddenly had *that* knife too.

"How the f–"

"Miss Clearwater, may I help you up?" called Lorch, all sign of their closeness a few moments ago wiped away. With a last glare at Elijah, she pushed passed him to the King. She could have sworn there was a small, mocking smile on the hooded man's lips as she passed.

Gods, he was infuriating.

"Of course." she said, allowing Lorch to help her on to Day Dancer's saddled back. Soon he was joining her, sitting snuggly behind and leaning his arms around her body to retrieve the reins. Arii thought it strange that he would not retrieve his own horse for their ride, but as he settled behind her and draped his arms around her to clutch the reigns – she quickly figured out why.

Beside them, Elijah mounted his own horse effortlessly. She was lightly disappointed that he was coming with them, but had she expected any different?

Clicking his tongue and nudging the mare's sides with his heels, Lorch moved Day Dancer to a gentle trot as they headed along a path into what looked like a small forest ahead.

It amazed Arii how big the castle grounds truly were. The golden castle and its grounds were situated on a small island, perched on the perfect lookout on the colossal waterfall, overlooking half the land to the sea beyond. At its back and beyond the forested grounds and gardens – a small town thrived.

Swaying as the horse moved, Arii felt the press of Lorch's body behind her. For the first time in a long while, she felt a cloud of content settle itself upon her.

The Three Fates would know by now that she was extending out her assignment in search of answers. Whatever was happening in the north would undoubtably affect them too. Soon she would have to return to them, convey her findings in more detail and discuss their thoughts on the issue. Despite their reputation, Arii trusted the three sisters. They had raised her for the majority of her life after all.

Even if that majority was bathed in blood.

Arii chewed her lip. She could use Lorch to get to Bonemire somehow. Convince him to set up some sort of expedition there.

As if he sensed the shift in her thoughts, Lorch brushed a stray lock of hair from her shoulder. His fingers brushed her neck and she felt tingles left behind on her skin.

"What is on your mind?" he said gently.

"How lovely the castle grounds are," she hedged quickly, peering over her shoulder at the King.

She met his bright blue eyes. They were fixed on her, before sliding away to survey the grounds beyond the horse's feet. Day Dancer's tail swished, and Elijah's stallion grunted close behind.

"I've been meaning to thank you, Miss Clearwater."

"What for?" The words were out before she had even thought about them.

Lorch smiled. "For saving my life yet again the other night."

Arii felt a fresh blush tinging her cheeks.

"My King, that was all Elijah's doing."

From behind them, the bodyguard huffed a short laugh. She hated to admit it, but it was true.

Lorch threw a glare Elijah's way before continuing. "Be that as it may, you aided him then and also against the Water Nymph breach."

Arii was silent, eyes on her hands as they clutched Day Dancer's golden mane. She was suddenly reminded of the golden thread of the Tapestry, safely tucked in her trunk in the barracks.

"I was doing my job," she said simply.

Lorch's finger brushed the back of her hand and she hoped he could not feel the heat radiating from her cheeks.

"Well, thank you."

The words were simple, but their weight had Arii's shoulders curling inward. Lorch did not seem to notice as he continued. "Devina Divine was a Fury, we all knew it, but she has frequented many of my parties in the past that her presence became normal."

Arii was again chewing her lip as Lorch said, "I believe she was sent to kill me that night. My father has said he thought there to be a Fury in the castle. Until the events of the other night – I did not believe him."

Arii could feel the heat rising from under her collar. Valdis was suspicious from the beginning. The man was far too cunning.

"Devina Divine is protected by the Three Fates, but should she come anywhere near the castle grounds again, there is an order for her head. She will not be feasting in my halls ever again."

Arii swallowed thickly. She detected a dark tone in the King's voice that almost resembled that of his father. Thanks to Devina, some of the suspicion of her own placement in the castle seemed to be diverted.

For the time being anyway.

Like a leaf floating downstream, the tone was gone as the horses began to pace down a small decline. Leaning back to better level the horse, she felt the warmth of his body and suddenly wished to press closer. Gods it felt good. She felt the little spark of unfulfilled need flicker within.

She doused the feeling quickly, shoving it down deep.

She could not be distracted with basic desires right now.

Especially not with the heavy weight of Elijah's gaze on the back of her head. Surely, he saw the King's unhidden affections, the way he meaningfully wrapped his arms around her, and lingered when they were close.

Despite what they had been through, Elijah still did not trust her. She was sure such a thing was near impossible to earn.

She did not need his trust anyway.

Soon they came to a small pool set in amongst some tall, weeping willow trees. A miniature waterfall fed the pool, the waters so crystal clear that Arii swore she could see the rock coated bottom. Leaves floated lazily down the small stream that was sure to connect to the body of water that the castle lived upon.

Lorch pulled gently on the reins, sweeping a hand towards the pool and a serene grassy spot by the water's edge.

"This is the crystal pool, somewhere I like to come to relax when the life of a King gets too much. I wanted to share it with you."

Arii surveyed the glittering water.

"It's beautiful," she said and meant it.

"And you have my permission to come here whenever you want. Elijah likes to come here often, right Elijah?" From beside them, the cloaked man huffed in annoyance, as if revealing any hint of personal information was painful. "Yes, Your Highness," he replied gruffly, only seeming to reply because his King wanted a confirmation. Had it been anyone else, she was sure the man would have remained silent.

Lorch slipped from the horse's back before turning to help Arii. She did not need his help of course but allowed the man to go through with the motions as she slid from Day Dancer's back and found her hands on Lorch's chest, her eyes fixed on his own. His hands remained on her hips for longer than what was probably necessary, and soon the two were parting as Elijah followed their lead.

Gods the cloaked man really knew how to bring the mood down.

She felt a tug of annoyance in her gut but brushed it away swiftly.

"It's perfect," she agreed and offered Lorch a smile. Why was he showing her such a personal place? The area felt intimate somehow – like being let into part of his personal chambers. This place… it was so different in comparison to other parts of the North. Here, there were no dirty streets, no dry crops, dangerous and uneven streets and dark, water deprived gardens. Here, there was wealth… so much wealth. It made her feel uneasy, causing her spine to straighten as she said, "Pendle once had pools like this, just beyond the town line and in the forest. Now, you'd be lucky to see an inch of water during the winter."

Lorch tilted his head her way, brows raised.

From behind them, Elijah paused and turned his head ever so slightly.

"Cannot say I have visited Pendle in… well, years actually," said Lorch, lifting a smooth stone and surveying it critically. Arii wondered how long it had been since he had visited any of the towns that made up his Kingdom. It was strange, despite what she had seen and learned of Lorch Kruel so far – she could see he was a caring person. Either he trusted that his father was doing the right thing for the Kingdom, or he in fact did not care – despite what his mother claimed.

She wondered if he had ever truly visited Pendle in his life.

Feeling an unease in the air, she thought it best to liven the mood by saying, "Well, if you don't mind dusty streets and shit mead – then by all means, visit Pendle."

"You judge a town by its liquor?" Lorch chuckled, lips quirking.

Arii placed a hand on her hip and tilted her head. "The time and effort put into a town's liquor says a lot about the town itself, I'll have you know."

The King chuckled, shaking his head. "I'd picked you for more of a sweet wine kind of lady."

"You have much to learn about me, Your Highness. Wine gives me a killer hangover. Mead though? Much friendlier the next morning."

Lorch smiled, before pacing to the water's edge and picking up another stone, tossing it in the air before catching it in his palm. He was silent for a time, and as she paused nearby – she saw him watching her from the corner of his eye.

He seemed to be working up to something.

Arii joined him slowly, and realised Elijah was hanging back at the horses. Had they brought her here to kill her? Slice her neck and dump her corpse in the pool? She would not put it past Elijah. Thoughts swirled in her head as Lorch glanced up at her, gazing through his thick lashes.

Gods he was handsome. If his face was the last thing she saw, she would not be entirely disappointed.

"May I put something to you, Miss Clearwater?" With a heavy pause, Lorch tossed the stone into the pool, before turning to her once more. Arii felt her tongue press against the roof of her mouth as she waited.

"I'd like you to move into a room in the castle," he said suddenly.

Arii's mouth popped open in a little 'o' of surprise. She was not expecting that. Then again, she was not sure what she had been expecting.

"I... Erm…"

Lorch approached, taking her hand gently.

Blood rose to her cheeks again.

Nyx's arse she had to stop blushing.

"I want you to begin training with Elijah, full time." He paused, running a thumb over the calloused skin of her palm. A palm accustomed to the weight of a dagger, and the warm kiss of fresh lifeblood. Definitely not used to the gentle caress of a young man's fingers. Her head tilted in Elijah's direction, wondering what he thought of this arrangement.

Elijah was tending to the horses, his back to them.

Deliberate, no doubt.

Her eyes slid back to Lorch, who was watching her now with an unreadable expression. What if she refused? Would he send her packing? Arii was sure that despite the gentleness she had seen in the King, Lorch Kruel was still used to getting his way.

"Alright," she agreed, before adding. "Your Highness. I would be honoured."

Lorch's smile lit his face in the shade of the trees.

Beneath his hood, Elijah's lips pulled into a frown.

03&80

Later that evening, Arii was escorted back to the recruit barracks by Elijah. After a few hours of sitting by the pool and nibbling on an assortment of fruit and cheese brought on Elijah's horse, Arii felt a serene tiredness lace her bones. She had learned a lot about the King that she was not expecting.

His favourite colour was green. He much preferred Winter to Summer (all the better to snuggle and keep warm beside a fire. That little bit of information had her fighting another stupid blush). That was odd as the North was a warm place constantly. He preferred reading a book to sparring in the training ring. And he enjoyed sweet wine over mead or beer.

"Pack your belongings and I'll show you to your rooms." said Elijah, his voice gruff. He stood to the side of the barrack doors, arms crossed over his chest.

She nodded and pressed into the barracks, soon greeted by a small sea of curious eyes.

"Well, where have you been?" called Tikkani, standing quickly and pointing a finger into Arii's chest. "Off gallivanting the castle grounds on your-" Tikkani's mouth slackened as Elijah moved into the doorway behind them, a heavy waiting shadow.

The entire room fell silent.

Arii then realised what it looked like as Tikkani's lips began to slide into a knowing smile, eyes narrowing and teeth flashing in a sly grin as the room began to fill with murmurs.

The recruits all began to whisper.

"You little hussy!"

"No, it's not what it looks like!"

"Sure sure!"

Suddenly Elijah spoke from the doorway. "I would not stoop so low."

The entire room fell silent, and someone exhaled a breathy *ohhhh.*

Arii slapped a hand to her face, before rounding on Elijah. "Would you mind waiting outside?" she hissed. His lips twitched before he turned and exited the room.

Wow, he *actually* listened to her!

Tikkani was inches from her face as she turned back around. "So how was it?" purred the elf. Emerson's loud sigh erupted from behind Tikkani, and the room burst into a flurry of voices once more.

"I was shown around the castle grounds, that is all." hissed Arii, feeling strangely defensive.

"And shown around the shadowy lord's *grounds* too, huh?"

giggled Tikkani.

"Argh, Gods!"

"Come on, spill!" she cried, almost sounding like an excited schoolgirl. Arii moved past her friends to her trunk, flicking open the latch and hauling open the lid with perhaps a tad too much force, pulling a few shirts hanging nearby and shoving them in.

"So good she's speechless!" exclaimed Tikkani.

Was Tikkani seriously implying that she had... slept with Elijah? The thought had her cheeks heating despite herself. She knew it did look odd – having been escorted back to the barracks by Elijah just after sundown. Arii was almost glad she was moving to the castle. But part of her would miss Tikkani's banter, Emerson's groans of disapproval and Quinn's raving about some cute serving maid who had eyed him in the kitchens.

Arii turned to face them, pausing before she said, "I've been asked to move to the castle, to train under Master Wolfe."

Quinn was the first to speak, Tikkani's eyes wide and matching her brother's. "You're jesting!"

"No, I'm not, King's orders," shrugged Arii as she packed her trunk. She could not help the tiny tinge of sadness in her voice. Quinn approached and placed a hand on her shoulder, a smile on his face.

"We all knew your talents were being wasted as a recruit, Arii."

Tikkani and Emerson's twin faces nodded over his shoulder in agreement.

"We are happy for you; your talents are needed elsewhere."

Arii swallowed thickly. "Thanks, I'll no doubt still have days of training with Commander Hawke. I'll see you all around."

Tikkani flew into Arii's arms, and the Fae for the second time in two days was floored.

Her arms slowly, awkwardly, lifted to embrace her new friend. She was not used to embraces.

Tikkani held her out at arm's length, her smile genuine. "Quinn's right, we have seen Master Wolfe's moves, you could learn a lot from him."

Huh, or he could learn from her…

Arii nodded and offered her friends a smile as she moved to lift her trunk. With a last look, she turned to join Elijah in the cooling night air.

They walked in silence to the castle and that silence was charged. Neither spoke though.

They entered the castle and Elijah took the lead, directing her to a room in the middle wing of the castle. Close enough to the royal quarters to get there as quick as possible should anything happen.

After a short time, Elijah's deep voice cut the silence as they paused at a door.

"This is your room."

The hall was lit with torches, the gold shimmering in the light. She hitched her trunk on her hip as he turned the golden doorknob and opened the door, stepping into the room.

It was warm, flames flickering in the golden hearth on the far side of the room. A large four poster bed with plush white down covers stood close to the fireplace. The window furnishings were a deep vermillion, the room simple yet richly adorned with gold finishes and dark mahogany furniture. A desk sat on the opposite wall to the bed, under a tall window. To the left was another door, she assumed to an adjoining bathing room. Lanterns were set around the room, giving it a warm golden glow.

This was by far the nicest lodging she had ever had.

Elijah motioned to the door. "My room is just down the hall, to your right."

Arii paced into the room as he spoke.

His comment from earlier still stung as she placed her trunk at the foot of her bed and turned to face him. Why his words hurt – she had not a clue. But for some reason, they had – and she was not sure she wanted him to get away with speaking that way. She felt the heat rising to her cheeks, the blood in her veins which had begun to sizzle all the way to the castle had finally boiled over.

"I thought you wouldn't wish to stoop so low as to tell me exactly where your rooms were located."

Elijah's lips pursed as Arii stormed towards him.

"Just because the King has ordered us to train together does not mean I trust you," he retorted darkly.

Arii's eyes narrowed as she stopped a foot from him, her hands resting on her hips, head tilting to glare up at him. Really, he was right not to trust her. She knew that. That did not stop her teeth from grinding. Why did he irk her so deeply?

"If we are to work together, you will just need to learn to trust me, then," she quipped. Trust meant she would have the chance to be alone with Lorch and maybe then she could finally cut the string of his life.

"Trust is earned, Miss Clearwater. So far you have done nothing to earn my trust."

Arii's brows rose, her expression incredulous. "I saved the King – twice!"

Elijah's teeth flashed in a half sneer as he said, "I think you forget that it was I who saved Lorch from the Fury assassin – not you."

Touché.

Anger bubbled in her gut, and her eyes narrowed as she leaned towards the bodyguard, lips twitching. "Well then, this little arrangement is going to be quite uncomfortable, don't you think?"

She swore he leaned closer as they stared each other down in a loaded battle of wills. Even as they glared at one another, Arii could not help but feel a snap of heat skitter between them. Her fingertips tingled with a sudden urge to grip his hood and rip it from his head, but she knew that doing that would earn her nothing but trouble. Despite how much she longed to strangle the man – she knew that earning his trust would definitely help her in her mission.

Wisely, Elijah turned from the room, but before exiting he turned to her. "Be ready at sunrise for your first day of official training. I do not take tardiness lightly, so you'd best be on time."

A growl ripped from Arii's throat as she slammed the door

behind him.

Prick.

She was going to make his life hell.

LAKHESIS
Melissa Kincaid

CHAPTER ELEVEN

Lakhesis turned to the room, her white hair fanning about her face as she addressed the small sea of attentive eyes before her. It was mid-afternoon at the School of Fate, and a young Arii found she was beginning to enjoy the gently-spoken sister's subterfuge classes.

During the months that had passed since her arrival at the school, she had learned so much that she felt her brain may just leak from her ears, not to mention the aches and pains from hours of intense physical training.

"To be an assassin you need to be a passing breeze, a hint in the darkness, an afterthought in one's mind," the woman said, golden eyes sweeping the room. "Stealth and subterfuge will be one of your most used skills. Some foes may be bigger, stronger than you – and the element of surprise can be the deciding factor in whether your target lives... or dies. Now that rule also applies to you, for not every assignment can be dealt with magic and brute strength alone."

Lakhesis' lips twitched as she motioned towards the window, grey skies filtering the room with dull light.

"There is only so much you can learn from textbooks about the art of stealth, so today will be a practical lesson." Slowly she reached a hand into her pocket, drawing out a single strand of glowing string. It cast a dim gold light; the fibres infused with a hint of magic. The class stared, some mouths opening in question as Lakhesis held the string taut between two fingers.

"As darkness falls tonight, you will be required to enter the town of Colkirk and hunt a target specified by the Tapestry. There will

only be one, and it will be up to you whether you choose to work together – or alone."

Arii snuck a glance toward the silver haired girl seated two chairs down from her, watching as Nem's hand lifted into the air before she asked, "How are we supposed to know who the target is?"

Lakhesis' eyebrows arched as she said, "Had you let me finish, Miss Rion, I would have told you what the Tapestry showed me. I will presume your quick tongue is simply eagerness to get started, hmm?"

Nem's head ducked slightly, her hand drifting down. Across the room a girl chuckled, her hair a deep shade of burgundy, her skin light and dusted with freckles. Lakhesis shot the girl a glare which had Devina snapping her lips shut.

"As you know, the Gods offer images as to who the target could be. What I saw was iron striking stone and a hot forge, sparks drifting over tired brown eyes. Long fingers curling around a woman's neck, those brown eyes watching the life drain from his victim's eyes before removing his soiled brown tunic and pants to have his way with the corpse. Your target is of middle age, and he wears a necklace of silver chain links to hide scars along his neck."

The students began to murmur as their teacher's words settled over them. Lakhesis spoke again, her voice rising.

"Be wary that you do not choose the wrong man, my sisters. Your target is nefarious, cunning, subtle and has been hiding his tracks for many years. The student to take him down – without disturbing the entire town – will be gifted with this."

As she spoke, Lakhesis lifted a shining silver dagger before her, causing the class to hush. The weapon was exquisite, the blade etched with intricate patterns that reminded Arii of the unreadable foreign languages in some of the books she had found in the library, the words fascinating to look at. The markings were beautiful, the blade serrated and deadly with a curving cross guard that ended in points that resembled dragon's teeth, the grip weaved with smelted copper. On the pommel, embedded in the silver tip, was a large gem of amethyst.

It was absolutely stunning.

Her classmates thought so too, if the sighs and gasps of awe were any indication. She almost swore Devina lifted a hand into the air as if to touch the blade.

"Go, prepare well and enter the town under the cover of darkness."

As the class prepared to be dismissed, Lakhesis said, "Oh and sisters... no killing of your classmates will be tolerated. May the Gods watch over you all."

They moved like shadows through the forest, cloaked and dressed in light leathers that allowed them to move without sound. Lakhesis had taught them how to move without snapping a twig under foot, how to breathe so that no mist gave away their position, and how to steady the thumping beat of their hearts in their ears to a gentle hum.

No distractions.

No mercy.

They would be the deliverers of justice tonight, justice for countless women who had been buried in undiscoverable graves by someone evil.

All of their training had been easy enough in theory, but tonight was the first real mission for five of them.

Stars glittered overhead, the moon hanging high, lighting their way like a big luminescent pearl.

As they entered the sleepy town, they kept to the shadows as they skipped along the outskirts. Arii tilted her head in the direction of her closest sister, seeing a slither of silver from beneath her hood.

They all paused, listening and breathing in the night air.

Livestock rustled in their pens, flickering lanterns casting dancing light across the muddy dirt road. Ahead, Arii heard the steady drum of a hammer on stone and saw the orange glow of forge fires.

The blacksmith.

Her eyes slid to the murmur of voices within the local tavern – shouts and sounds of merriment flooded to them through the night. Two of her sisters moved in the direction of the blacksmith, and Arii controlled a gentle breath between her teeth.

The blacksmith was the obvious choice – given Lakhesis' clues.

But that would be far too easy.

If she were a man who liked to pluck women and dash them into the night and murder them – she would not be working while a good deal of the town's men would be drinking in the tavern.

No, she would be scouting for her next victim where no-one would suspect.

Swiftly, Arii moved towards the tavern, following the scent of roasting meat and smoke. Using a nearby pile of chopped wood, she nimbly climbed up the side of the building, alighting on the thatched roof and swiftly making her way along the support beam to the raised section of the structure with an opening, allowing smoke from the cooking fires to escape.

Inching forward, she peeked – despite the acrid smoke and heat gusting against her face – into the tavern below.

People filled each chair within the room, the tables covered with food and drink. Voices rose to her ears, an onslaught of sound that had her wanting to back away.

She could do this.

She would do this.

Nose twitching, she ran her eyes over as many of the patrons as possible from her angle. How in Fythnar would she spot a subtle killer within the jumble of people, from above no less?

Her eyes narrowed as she surveyed each man, touching her tongue to her canines as she willed a pinch of magic forward. Her vision narrowed in, her senses heightening so fast she had to place a hand to the wood to steady herself against the onset of sight, smell and sound.

She saw a man stand, a flash of silver at his neck, and suddenly could not believe her luck. Adrenaline coursed through her body like a whip, her lips curling into a smile as the man placed his hand upon a serving maid's lower back, leaning forward to whisper in her ear.

The man was as Lakhesis had said – middle aged, with brown eyes. From what she could see of his face, she thought he was not an unattractive man – and realised that this surely aided him in passing a woman's defences, luring them into the dark and sating his devious desires. The thought had acid bubbling in her stomach as the maid giggled, placing a hand in the man's as he gently led her to the door.

Insides quivering with anticipation and nerves, Arii agilely slid down the roof, halting at the lip of an overhang and peering over to watch as the man draped his arm around the young woman's shoulders, their gentle laughter meeting her ears.

Arii's fingers touched the cool steel pommel at her hip, tongue dashing across her lips as she made her way off the roof and into the shadows, trailing in the couple's wake.

She had to be truly sure before she tried anything.

How would she do it? She had never killed someone before. Despite all of the textbooks she had read, all of the training and the portrayals of murder by the more established Furies – Arii still felt a settling of unease drift over her bones.

Pressing her back to the wall of a nearby cottage, her ears twitched to the sound of voices from within the stables nearby.

Then she heard a muffled scream.

It was all the motivation she needed, ducking into the stables and gracing the shadows like a flutter of dark smoke.

Her eyes fell on two forms as they struggled in the hay, the sounds of suppressed groans and ragged grunts spurring her on. Magic tickled her fingertips as she slid her fingers around the grip of her dagger, eyes fixed on the man's back as she stepped from the shadows.

Just as Nemesis fell from the timber trusses above and dropped upon her target's back.

The man yelled with surprise, his head flying and cracking against his attacker's face as he reared back. The silver haired Fury flew backwards, clutching her bloody nose with a colourful curse as the man spun, fist flying and teeth bared, smashing his fist into Nem's jaw. Her head snapped to the side as she dropped to the hay, the man's first victim swiftly fleeing as he flew upon his attacker.

Arii had a split-second moment where she wondered if she should stand back and let the other Fury fight her own way out of this mess. She watched as Nem's boots skidded on the dirty floor, her teeth baring and stained with blood as their man wrapped his hands around her neck and squeezed.

For months this girl had made Arii's time at the school far more uncomfortable than necessary, and for months had they shot each other angry glares and rotten curses across the training ring as they sparred.

The only thing they seemed to have in common was their growing dislike for Devina.

Nem had been hasty, had taken on their target with not a thought for the silence and swiftness that they had all been told to mind during training. As Nem struggled under the man's vice grip, Arii felt a strange fire begin to kindle in her chest.

No, she did not deserve to die on their first mission. She was a Fury, an assassin chosen by the Gods. She deserved to die with a weapon in her hand and a sardonic smile on her face, bathed in the blood of those she had sent to the depths of hell.

With flaming resolve, Arii flew forward and clutched the man's hair, jerking his head back and causing his attention to waver. She speared her blade towards his neck, but before the steel could slice flesh – he brought his elbow up to deflect her arm at the bicep.

Nem took that moment to slam her knee into the man's groin, and a strangled cry erupted from his lips as she followed with her boot to his chest, slamming him back in the dirt.

"He's mine!" hissed Nem as she flew to her feet, blood casting tracks down her lips and chin.

The man curled on to his side, groaning in pain as Arii growled under her breath. "Don't be a godsdamned fool, Nemesis! I was here first!"

"Nyx's arse you were!" the girl said as she stepped forward. Arii lifted her dagger, making a barrier between her sister and the man.

Nem's eyes slid to her and narrowed, her shoulders curled and quivering with anger. "You always have to be better, like you cannot bear anyone besting you!" the girl snarled.

"What in Nyx's name are you talking about?"

"As if you do not know! They're saying you're the Sister's favourite!"

Arii snorted a laugh. "You have got to be jesting, I have only been here for a few months – same as you! Whoever says that must be sleeping through our lessons."

Behind her, the man groaned once more.

Arii's violet eyes darted from their target, back to the ashen haired girl.

"I'm not sure what I have done to evoke your ire, but know that I only want to learn, to train, and to do as the Gods bid. I have no quarrel with you!"

Suddenly Nem was darted towards her, silver flashing so quickly that Arii did not have time to register the movement before pain was burning like starlit fire in her gut. The tip of Nem's blade broke through the barriers of her leathers and sank into her lower abdomen, causing Arii to twist and slam her elbow into Nem's face – before the girl could cause more damage.

Then the man was standing, his hands falling upon Nem's shoulders and slamming her against a nearby wall, his eyes wide and dancing with a strange sort of mad desire.

"I've never had an assassin before, young too," he hissed, his movements crazed as he threw Nem across the room like a doll.

Arii gasped as the man flew upon her, his hands at her chest – the smell of mead laced with dark liquorice battered against her senses. They dropped to the floor, her hands flying against his chest as she scrambled desperately into the pool of her magic, fingers groping the silver tendrils and clutching them in her fists. With a cry, she punched a burst of power into her palms, hitting the man square in the chest and sending him flying. He hit the hay, golden strands of dried grass dancing in the air.

Nem was back on her feet as the two young Furies stood side by side, both panting, both staring as the man struggled to his feet.

With a sideways glance, Arii shot a look of pleading Nem's way. If they did not cast this ludicrous feud aside – then this mission was surely going to fail. Her eyes met blue, and Arii saw a very subtle change within their depths.

"I don't want to fight with you any longer, Nem," she whispered, seeing the twitch in the girl's jaw as she swiped her sleeve along her bloody lips. "Look, I'll even give you the killing blow – if that makes you feel better."

Nem huffed, pausing as she slid her tongue over her teeth. After a few seconds, she finally ground out, "Fine."

Feeling a tiny sense of triumph – mixed with the faint lingering of pain in her stomach from the girl's blade – Arii offered her a grin. Nem's eyes lightened at the look, before Arii turned and dashed at the man.

As he got to his feet, she flew upon his back, hooking her legs around his torso and locking her arms around his neck, jerking them back as Nem drew her dagger.

Face twisting, Nem plunged her dagger into the man's chest, straight through his ribs and into his heart – just like they had been taught. The man jerked, eyes wide and mouth agape in shock.

Even with the steel in his heart, the man did not fall.

He moved forward, a low, unearthly sound leaking from his throat as his boots clapped against the dirt. Nem's eyes widened, and Arii felt anger spear through her veins.

He did not deserve to live. Men like him, men who preyed upon the weak deserved no mercy.

She would not give mercy.

Her blade was as swift as silver, sliding through the flesh and muscle of his throat, raining the hay with a shower of crimson. The man gurgled as he fell to his knees, and Nem stepped back nimbly as he fell face first into the muck.

"Once your thread is spun and measured..." whispered Arii, her eyes meeting Nem's as the girl lifted her chin.

"There is no escaping your final fate." Nem finished, breath drifting into the night air as the two girls stared at one another for a few heartbeats, faces unreadable.

Arii was first to speak, her voice gentle as she said.

"Let's go home, Nem."

⊱⊰

Nem sat with Arii within the golden castle in her new rooms, comfortably situated at the little table near the window as Arii's mind drifted over distant memories. The view beyond the glass was of the castle gardens, which at that moment were as dark as pitch.

Nem lifted a goblet of water to her lips, her eyes fixed on Arii across the small space. How Nem had known of her change of lodging in the golden behemoth so quickly, she had no idea.

"Training with Master Wolfe, hmm?"

Arii's eyes slid to her friend before narrowing. There was a strange tone in Nem's voice that she could not quite put her finger on.

"Mhmm," Arii hummed in confirmation, as if she could not bear to speak aloud.

Nem spoke, her voice nonchalant as she studied her friend. "There is something about that man that has shivers shooting down my spine." A pause. "And they aren't bad shivers," she said, a sly grin forming.

Arii stared. Could Nem feel the same weighted, heated and

charged air that lingered around the mysterious man like she could?

Clearing her throat, Arii swallowed before speaking.

"He definitely keeps things interesting," she hedged.

Nem's eyes shone with knowledge that Arii was not sure she was ready to discuss. Nemesis Rion knew her like no one else did. Their friendship spanned many years, the two only finding friendship after a complicated and heated beginning. It had taken time, but they had formed a tight bond during their training at the School of Fate. The only other person to know her better was Krepth.

She wondered what the sly fluff ball was up to.

Nem pulled her attention from her thoughts as she steered the conversation away from mysterious hooded figures.

"I have heard word of more sightings of carriages bearing the royal crests loading supplies in Amberbourne. A reliable source claims he saw Nexus Crystals inside one of the carriages."

This had Arii's brows rising.

That reliable source meaning Krepth.

"Nexus Crystals?" said Arii, brows furrowing.

"Hard to believe, I know." said Nem, nibbling a honey biscuit, her face thoughtful.

"Those crystals have not been seen since… well I'd like to say over a hundred years ago," mumbled Arii, worrying her bottom lip between her teeth in thought.

Nem nodded.

"Why now?"

With a shrug, her friend paused in her nibbling and her eyes met vivid purple. Arii had no need for her magical veil while sitting with Nem. Undulled, her skin was luminous in the moonlight, her purple eyes glimmering as half her face was bathed in golden candlelight, and the other lit with silver light. Nem read the slowly forming fire in Arii's eyes, and she inclined the biscuit in her direction as she said. "You're going to Amberbourne."

It was not a question. Nem knew the train of Arii's thoughts.

"Tonight." Arii confirmed, standing and heading to her dresser to snatch up her daggers.

☧

Nem offered to accompany her to Amberbourne, but Arii refused. She planned to slip into the town, break into one of the carriages and hopefully snatch a crystal for observation. Besides, she made quicker work on her own.

The moon hung high in the sky as Arii silently slipped from the castle, pulling the reins of a black gelding. She could have danced a jig through the castle gates unnoticed and felt a shiver of anger at how easy it was to slip through. Was Valdis posting blind men to the castle walls? Or were all available bodies being shipped to Bonemire?

She may have used a tiny dip of magic to aid her, but that was beside the point.

Swiftly and cloaked in shadows, her mount flew across the bridge heading east. With a little magic in the creature's legs, she would be in Amberbourne in half the time it took to get there with Commander Hawke's group. She had to make sure she was back before sunrise, lest she incur the wrath of Elijah Wolfe.

Her lips pulled in a sly grin.

Perhaps he would give her a tongue lashing?

Her toes curled in her boots of their own accord and she laughed into the wind as it whistled past, flinging her cloak out like wings in her wake. Gods it felt good to be flying across the stones, through the wind, her gelding sprinting like wolves were upon their heels. The fresh air filled her lungs as she tilted her head back.

The golden castle of Viridya was a clean, impressive place – but she had begun to feel trapped. A Fae feeling trapped was a bad thing, normally resulting in a mindless flail to escape their confines. She was used to going where she wanted – whenever she wanted. Any boundaries were of her own making.

Cool fingers of night air caressed her neck and cheeks, and she urged the horse on with a nudge of her heels as the pavestones below turned to a dirt road. The night was unusually calm, hardly a cloud in the sky. She did not need to draw upon magic to enhance her night vision – the moonlight lit her way like silver torchlight.

Her mount's hooves slammed the ground, dust rising in her wake as she entered the forest surrounding Amberbourne. Arii knew it would be wiser to not follow the road, and travel through the trees themselves instead. There could be thieves or bandits lying in wait. This would slow her down though, and she was limited for time.

She decided she would risk the road.

Her mount huffed as they sprinted, the trees thickening around them and bowing along the road as if to form an arch above her. It felt almost like the forest was warning her back, and a cloud began to drift across the moon.

It was at that moment an arrow whistled past her ear.

And then her mount was falling beneath her.

With a surprised animal scream, the gelding's front and neck slammed into the dirt, throwing her over board. She rolled and skidded on her feet, before flipping backwards to narrowly avoid another arrow. It lodged in the ground before her as she swiftly drew her daggers.

Crouched in the dirt, her lips curled to bare bloody teeth. Her face had met with the ground, and her bottom lip had split. Shadows emerged from the trees, flashes of steel and glints of arrow tips, aimed at her heart.

Bandits.

With a snarl, she stood and felt the cool press of a blade at her neck.

Absolutely-fucking-brilliant.

She had been too consumed with her destination that she thought the gods may just give her a sprinkle of luck this night.

It seemed she was wrong.

"What do we have here?" said a man, his cloak pulled back, revealing a bald head as he clicked his tongue and studied his prey.

"Lone traveller on the road?"

"Buzz off, flies. I have nothing of value on me. You would have been better to take my horse." Her eyes slid to the motionless mass a few feet away. "Pity you have the brains of a sewer rat," she spat, grinning through crimson lips.

The man did not look away, pressing closer and inspecting her face. "Don't always need coins, girl. Sometimes we be needin' entertainment. It's lonely out on the road."

She heard a smatter of laughter around her. At least a dozen men accompanied him.

Filthy bottom feeders. She would be sure to take off each of their manhoods while they watched.

"You're going to regret it if you touch me..." Her voice was low, gentle and deadly.

"Oh my! Scary little woman! You'll make for some interestin' sport. Greyson, bring me those leather straps you love so mu-"

Suddenly his speech was cut short as a dagger protruded from his throat. The blade was speared from the back, straight through to the front, the tip glittering ruby in the moonlight. Eyes wide, mouth opening and closing like a fish, the man began to topple. Grabbing his body, Arii quickly pulled him in front of her like a shield as a volley of arrows were let loose upon her. The man's body shuddered as the arrows made contact, and she shifted towards the trees.

Who had thrown the dagger?

Her question was soon answered. A dark figure leaped from the back of a thundering dark stallion, rolling across the dirt and arms spearing out to toss knives at the men surrounding her.

Thwack

A dagger hit one man between the eyes.

Thwack

A second buried in another's chest.

Arii knew exactly who her shadowed saviour was instantly. He moved like death on the wind, his sword a blur as he met the steel blade of one of the bandits.

Elijah.

Her eyes darted to a bandit as he drew an arrow from his quiver, shouts and grunts sounding all around them as he aimed his weapon at the new arrival. Unsure of how many bandits there were exactly, she decided best to fight until nothing moved. She sprinted at the bowman closing the space between them in the blink of an eye. Willing magic to coat her daggers, she spun and sheared her blade through the man's wrist, carving through bone and wood like soft butter.

Twisting, she threw the dagger at a man who was charging towards her, a battle cry erupting from his lips. *Thump.* The dagger embedded the man square in the ribs. Shooting forward, Arii placed her hand upon the man's back as he flew by, pushing herself to flip over his careening body. Eyes tracking the scene before her, Arii sprinted back towards her hooded saviour, adrenaline causing a sizzle to dance along her skin.

Elijah was carving through men like they were dummies in a training ring. To the backdrop of winking stars and a full moon, the bodyguard felled men with grace and fluidity unlike anything she had witnessed before. His cloak billowed out as he swirled, and she found the sight hauntingly beautiful.

Soon they were back to back, panting lightly.

"What the fu-"

"Where in the name of the gods were you going tonight?" He cut her off, his voice a snarl as Elijah kicked a man who charged at them – square in the chest. Arii slashed another man across his face with her dagger.

"None of your *godsdamned* business!"

Elijah drew his sword across one man's chest as he growled, "It *is* my business; you answer to me now!"

Their bodies danced around each other, two dark forms flashing with silver as they dipped and twisted, their movements fluid as lives ended all around them. When Elijah dipped, Arii's blade sliced the air where he had just been – gliding through leather and flesh.

Arii's head snapped back to Elijah as another man charged them, and as if they were of one mind, Elijah ducked and Arii pressed her back to his, using his solid mass to roll across him and strike the man down with an enchanted dagger to his face and chest, the blade sliding from chin to belly as easily as carving a turkey.

Arii panted and realised suddenly that there were no bandits left.

Reluctantly, she straightened, and her eyes met Elijah.

He stood, his breath clouding before the opening of his hood.

The cold air sizzled between them, and his voice was a low growl as he said, "Where did you learn to fight like that?"

"A woman never tells."

"I do not believe you to be a simple maidservant, you kill without hesitation or remorse!"

Behind her, a groan sounded as one of the bandits who had managed to survive the carnage began to rise. Arii's dagger twisted through her fingers, her body dipping – and her blade was suddenly lodged through the man's eye.

"Bad men who prey upon the weak do not deserve remorse," she hissed into the air.

The thump of the man's body hitting the dirt was the only sound in that moment. Elijah seemed to be staring, clouds drifting from his mouth.

"Keep your hooded nose out of my business!" Arii snarled.

Teeth slightly bared, Elijah was suddenly in her face. *Just* out of reach of seeing beneath his hood. "We are going back to the castle, *now*!"

"Fuck off!"

"You have the bloody temper of a Kryvern!" he bellowed at her.

"Oh yeah? Well, maybe under that hood you have the face of one!"

Elijah snarled and turned from her, dipping to retrieve his knives.

"Gods you are juvenile."

"And you're a fucking son of a-"

"Miss Clearwater, women *do not* speak that way."

"Shove it up your arse, Wolfe!"

With a dark chuckle, Elijah shoved past her to approach his stallion.

Arii hated to admit it, but for just a few minutes, they had made a formidable team. Where he moved, she moved in unison. Where their blades travelled, men fell as if breathing acid on the wind. Naught an opening was left undefended.

The bandits had not stood a chance.

Shooting a glance in the direction of Amberbourne, Arii knew there was no way she could slip away now, and there was no chance that Elijah would agree to come with her.

With a long, theatrically drawn-out sigh, Arii began to retrieve her weapons from the cooling corpses strewn around road.

Elijah was waiting by his horse, as still as stone, although she almost expected the man to be tapping his foot in agitation.

"The bodies?" she gestured to the dark shadows around them.

"I'll send for a crew as soon as we return to the castle," he said dismissively.

Slowly they began to head back to Viridya in silence.

After a few moments, he spoke. "What were you doing out here, Arii?"

She wiped the blood from her dagger on her cloak as they walked. Her name on his lips caused heat to slither down her spine. Gods, she was glad he was human and could not smell what it did to her body. Again, she was wondering how this mysterious man who made her blood boil with anger somehow managed to cause fire to coil in her belly. She dabbed at her split lip with the back of her sleeve and remained silent for a long moment.

Then she threw caution to the wind and decided to take another reckless chance this night. "I heard rumour of Nexus Crystals aboard supply wagons in Amberbourne. I wanted to see it for myself."

Elijah was silent beside her as they walked. She gazed at him, seeing a peek of his strong jaw, the dark stubble glinting in the moonlight. His lips were pulled in their usual, unimpressed line.

"The crystals have not been used nor seen in over-"

"One hundred years, I know."

"Why now?"

"Exactly my question, and the reason I was headed to Amberbourne before I was so rudely ambushed."

They walked in silence for a few minutes before he spoke again.

"What if it had been just that, a rumour? You could have been killed on the road." He tilted his head to examine her and was met with a stubborn stare.

"Well, emphasis on the *could* have been," he drawled.

Arii rolled her eyes.

After a while, the silence between them seemed to become less unbearable, less uncomfortable. The two cloaked figures soon entered the castle gates, and Arii was glad Elijah did not ask her how she had slipped past the guards, nor did he say anything as he unsaddled his stallion and bedded him down in the stables with feed and water.

Arii was surprised to see his strong, long fingered hand stroke the animal's snout tenderly. It was odd, this moment of gentleness. Up until now, she had seen Elijah as an uncaring, brutal shadow with not a kind feeling for anything.

Almost like herself.

She noticed his skin was dark with blood, now crusted in his fingernails, causing her to look down at her own hands. They were the same, the cuticles stained with dark red that was almost black. When her gaze lifted, Elijah was standing before her.

"Go and wash up and get a few hours' sleep before sunrise. You reek of blood."

She glared at him, feeling the comfortable silence wash away to be replaced with fury. Gods he truly got beneath her skin.

"Speak for yourself," she spat, turning on her heel to head towards the castle.

"I still expect you in the training ring at first light," he called after her.

"Unfortunately," she muttered and left his lone figure in the moonlight.

She realised later as she slid into the hot bath that she had not thanked him, even though she was still quite convinced she had not needed saving.

ରଙ୍କ

Training at sunrise was different to the other times Elijah and Arii had sparred.

It was as if something had begun to lift between them. The air remained filled with the crackle of sparks, but there was now an unexplained understanding. A new light had entered Arii's eyes as they clashed swords and parried each other's blows, seeming to work together rather than against each other.

Her move complemented his move.

His move made her dip into another.

Their bodies met, but always for a moment. Never long enough for her to glimpse under his hood.

He never let her get that close.

They bantered and insulted one another, both far too stubborn to admit that when working together they were almost unstoppable.

And so, they danced for hours, showered in the rays of a new day.

LORCH
KRUEL
Melissy Kincaid

CHAPTER TWELVE

Covered in sweat and feeling spent, Arii paced down the hall towards her rooms. Hair stuck to her neck with perspiration, her muscles ached and some actually throbbed with dull pain.

It was a good feeling, a feeling she missed.

Arii smiled to herself as she neared her rooms, silently pleased with Elijah's training today. Alright, she admitted that he drove her near to insanity with his barked orders and snide remarks, but he knew how to fight. She felt she could indeed learn from him if she allowed herself to listen.

"Miss Clearwater?"

Arii jerked to a halt, her eyes meeting Lorch's as he paced towards her. She felt the air shift around her and suddenly she realised that his expression was unfamiliar. Tense. Almost angry.

Oh *shit*.

He knew of her escape last night. Had Elijah tattled on her? Surely not.

Actually, she backtracked as her mind groaned.

Of course he would.

The King paused before her, his breath the only sound in the deserted hall.

She swallowed slowly.

"What were you thinking?" he hissed.

Argh gods here we go.

"Your Highness, if you'll let me explain." Suddenly he was before her, his sapphire eyes intense as he towered into her personal space. His hands gripped her shoulders, and she knew he was a

195

breath away from shaking her.

What in Nyx's name was his problem?

"You could have been killed, and for what? A bloody rumour?"

She felt confusion wash over her, before the heat of his fingers on her skin replaced her attention. He was close, so close that she could feel the vibrations of his anger, shaking his body in tiny tremors. She surveyed his face, saw the anger glittering and mixed with fear in his eyes, the way his jaw clenched with a little tick to the corner.

"I had to see for myself," she whispered in weak defence, pausing her inspection of his lips.

He was pausing too, his eyes fixed on her mouth now. Weeks of built-up tension seemed to gather at mass in the small space between them.

Lorch's eyes darkened.

His own lips parted, and he blew out a breath. A long, low and seemingly decided breath, his head tilting ever so slightly.

Then his lips met hers.

The kiss was hard, his lips claiming hers like they were starved.

Against all her better judgement, she found she was kissing him back.

Lorch shifted her to the wall, pressing her back to the flawless gold metal. She gasped as the cool material hit the exposed skin of her arms, her breath swallowed by his lips as he moved his hand to cup the nape of her neck, fingers sliding into her hair.

Her own hands were moving of their own accord, one gripping his back, the other twisted on his bicep. His arms were lean, strong and defined. He was not bulk and muscle like many of the soldiers of the castle, but that did not make him any less enticing. He wore a simple tunic, the first two buttons on his chest undone. The sleeves were pushed up, and she realised that in the moments before he had begun kissing her, he had looked flustered.

Flustered over *her*? Surely not.

His tongue slid across her lips and she swore she could hear panting.

With a sudden feeling of horror, she realised it was *her* who was panting.

Dark sapphire eyes held her in an iron grip as Lorch's lips left hers, and they curled into a slow, languid smile.

"You have no idea how long I've waited to do that," he sighed, his voice husky before pulling her to him again when she did not protest.

She had no idea how much she had wanted this until it was happening, too. Lorch pulled her against his chest, and she found one of her hands was tangled in his hair, his perfectly swept, thick copper-tinged hair. He smelled like sweet wine laced with a hint of vanilla and honey. His bath soap? He smelled clean, as if he had bathed not long ago.

His lips glided to her neck and she felt as if she were falling.

Gods, it had been too long since she had been with someone. Lorch's teeth grazed her skin, and she heard a low, breathy moan.

She realised that sound was hers, too.

Since when had she become a mewling little kitten? Had she not been swept up in the moment, she would have kicked herself. Warmth curled in her gut, and she felt a fire slowly being stoked in her core. Lorch's lips drifted up her neck to her earlobe, and she decided in that moment that she would beg like a little puppy if he decided to stop.

Gods and foreign feelings be damned.

She moaned, and his breath tickled her ear as he chuckled darkly.

"I didn't think you'd feel the same way…"

"I think that fact I have not pushed you away is proof enough of that," she whispered breathlessly.

His lips were on hers again, and she felt his hand at the front of her fighting leathers. He growled, nipping her bottom lip. "I have no idea how to remove this thing."

"I think it's best you don't, Lorch."

At that, he paused, his hand pressed against her breast. Her heart was thundering beneath his palm, a bird fluttering within the confines of her ribcage.

"It is not that I do not want you to…" she began gently.

Lorch pressed his forehead against hers, their breath mingled before them. "Apologies, Miss Clearwater. I…" he trailed off, panting and seemingly remembering himself within the fog of lust.

Her finger slipped between them and rested delicately against the bow of his lips. "Don't apologize. You are the King of the North – you can have whatever and whomever you want."

Lorch's eyes met hers, and they were like two endless pools in a raging sea. They say the eyes are a window to one's soul. She knew then that she saw a glimmer of his soul within – a shimmering of kindness, misunderstanding, and of someone who was lost, a flicker of light of someone who could perhaps bring about change.

And she was no longer sure she could be the cause of that light to fade.

Lorch's eyes drifted closed and he placed a hand on her cheek, the touch tender and soft. No one had ever touched her like this.

No one.

She had never allowed it, until now.

She realised she wanted him. More than she had wanted anything in a long time, but she was sure she smelled of sweat and leather. If one were to lay with a King, it could not be minutes after a heavy session of sparring in a training ring.

"You know, I can see purple in your eyes," Lorch said suddenly, causing her to freeze. His expression was light, no longer a hint of anger in the smooth lines of his face.

Her lips curled hesitantly and Lorch's lips met hers in a gentle kiss, the fire and hunger from earlier ebbing to flicking embers between them.

Lorch was first to pull away, albeit slowly. His lips hovered an inch from hers as he said, "Winter Solstice is in a week, there will be a large party to celebrate. It's a tradition my family has kept for years." He kissed her again, then paused. "I want you to attend, but not on guard duty."

Her hand was halfway up his arm, feeling the smooth, hot skin and taut muscles of his bicep when she paused.

"I want you to attend as my guest," he added.

She leaned back, and saw his eyes held a twinkle.

Her lips curled slightly into a smirk. "Scandalous."

"And what we are doing here is not?"

He had a point, but to parade amongst the people like she was one of them? That would take some convincing.

She felt unease, but the expression on his face wiped it away.

"It's fancy dress. Masks and all. You could keep your identity a secret," he persisted.

Well then, perhaps she could take the risk. A night of fun that did not involve blood and death? She was not sure she had ever experienced such a thing.

"Alright, I'll attend."

Lorch's eyes lit with fire and he kissed her again, the passion reigniting as he pressed her to the wall once more, one hand braced with fingers splayed against the metal beside her head. They remained tangled for a few more stolen moments, and the pit of fire that raged in her stomach was almost too much to bear.

Lorch spoke first after a few moments. "They'll be looking for me," he said, and she heard the tone of sadness in his voice. She too almost felt sad he had to go.

What was she becoming?

"You mean your constant shadow named Elijah will be looking for you," she pointed out. Lorch laughed against her lips.

"Yes." He smiled. "I will see you soon, Miss Clearwater." He stepped back from her, fixing his shirt and running a hand through his mussed hair. His cheeks were tinged pink and he looked breathless.

He looked divine.

Her tongue pressed against her elongated canines; the magic used to dull them dropping for just a moment as she used the pain to pull her mind from its desire induced haze. She could only wonder at what she looked like in that moment.

With a wink that had her heart fluttering, Lorch turned and swiftly paced down the hallway.

Arii watched his retreating back.

Nyx's arse she was in trouble.

It was then she caught her reflection in the golden wall across from her, and she noticed that the woman looking back at her was wide eyed, blushing and swollen lipped.

She looked thoroughly and utterly shocked.

The woman staring back at her was unfamiliar… a stranger.

A dark shadow began to emerge, and the woman's features slowly transformed, taking on their usual stoic expression – eyes narrowing to slits. She felt confusion, then anger. What was she doing? She had him alone, perfectly alone and she could have easily slid her dagger between his ribs, directly into his heart. It would have been completely and utterly silent.

Anger shivered down her body, replacing the warmth she had felt seconds ago with cold ice.

Arii stormed to her rooms, slamming the door behind her.

Cʒ8ಖ

Lips caressed her bare shoulder, and her head rolled to the side to allow them better access. Flames trailed along her skin where the lips went, fire ignited deep in her belly and her legs became jelly. His lips were soft, gentle, his nose caressing her earlobe. Teeth nipped the tip of her pointed ear and she felt the ground quake beneath her, and soon his lips met hers. They were hungry, needy, and devoured her whole. Her nails dug into the skin of his back as his weight pressed down on her. The pressure caused her body to sing – her mind whirling with unchecked desire.

She opened her mouth to his, and her canines pinched his full bottom lip. A light husky chuckle, a brush of fingertips on her lower back. Dark sapphire eyes shadowed with desire found hers, and King Lorch Kruel pulled her closer against his body, his breath laced with the smell of sweet wine as he whispered, "Have you come to kill me, little Fury?"

Arii's eyes snapped open as thunder boomed outside, awakening her from her light slumber. She never slept deeply, even the sound of a mouse in her heightened Fae hearing had her eyes snapping open and her hand reaching for the blade under her pillow.

Now, her brow was covered in sweat, and her lip ached as if she had almost pierced it with her canines during sleep.

A remnant of her incredible, thrilling dream.

She cursed the skies silently for her rude awakening.

Thunder boomed through the halls of the castle, as if the Gods were clashing in the skies above. Rain crashed against the windows relentlessly, the flash of lightning a strobe across the bedroom where Arii now lodged. The thunder boomed again, and she rolled over in the covers, the fire in the hearth nearby still crackling with smouldering embers, not quite enough to warm the room completely.

Unable to sleep after her heated dream, Arii sat up and pushed a hand through her sleep-mussed hair, before sliding from bed and dressing swiftly in loose pants and a white blouse, tucking in the shirt half-heartedly. She snatched a soft blue cloak from the hook by her door.

She felt like a mess.

Perhaps a walk around the cool castle halls would calm her boiling blood.

Exiting her rooms and nodding to the guards standing nearby, she slipped down the hall lit with an array of flaming sconces, their warm light warring with the silver flashing through the windows from the storm. As she walked, lifting the cloak about her shoulders, the light tap of her shoes was the only sound in the hall between the cracks of thunder and the distant hum of the waterfall.

Arii was not sure what brought her there, but without thought she was soon standing at the doors to the library. She felt a strange pull, like something had a hold within her chest and was luring her there with an invisible string.

She swallowed thickly, tongue wetting her lips as she pressed a hand against the door, feeling an unimaginable weight pushing in on her as her hearing seemed to dull.

There it was again, the taste of magic on her tongue, like a thin sheet of dissolving sugar candy on her tastebuds.

She pressed open the door and entered the library.

The glass dome encasing the room was lit with flashes of lightning, the stained glass which normally threw a rainbow of colours over the room now showered the place in glittering silver. The bookshelves were immaculate, the pool in the centre reflecting the storm above without a ripple. Slowly, her eyes were magnetised to a figure by the farthest window.

Oh by the Gods...

The figure turned to her slowly, his face in the shadow of his hood, having been staring out the window as she entered. Arii swallowed, her eyes narrowing as she closed the door behind her. That weight on her shoulders, pressing down on her very being, remained.

It always remained when Elijah was nearby.

He pushed from the wall, approaching her slowly, cape brushing the floor with a gentle *swish*. She noticed his sleeves were pushed up, revealing powerful forearms. One was marred with a set of jagged pink scars, standing out from his moonlit flesh. Remnants left by the Kryvern the night she saved the King, she recalled. Elijah stopped in front of her, towering, the air about him crackling with energy.

"Apologies..." he murmured, his voice like silk, and uncharacteristically gentle. She felt the familiar curl of her toes, moving of their own accord. As he began to slip past her, Arii paused him with a hand to his arm before she could stop herself. He was an absolute enigma to her, the King's shadow, who moved like death itself.

She had to know more about him.

She was insanely curious, and once she saw the way he had moved in a fight, the need to know more was only stoked like logs on a hot fire.

"Wait…" Arii murmured, her touch light. It met his skin, and she felt a crackle of power sizzle between them. Her eyes slowly lifted to his face, shadowed by the hood as she whispered, "Stay."

She let her hand slowly drop. Elijah was deathly still, no hint of expression on his lips. Finally, he spoke, tension thick in the air between them, his voice a ragged whisper. "If it pleases you, Miss Clearwater."

Arii broke the contact first, moving to the set of padded chairs and a small table by the window.

Elijah followed hesitantly.

She pulled the cloak tighter around her shoulders and watched as he slowly lowered himself to the settee across from her. His posture reminded her of a wary farmer, eyeing her as if she were a temperamental animal set to bolt at a sudden movement.

"I won't bite you, Elijah," she said lightly, hiding any evidence that hinted at the way this man made her feel. "Much, anyway," she finished, forcing lightness into her voice. Her eyes slid from his form to the window, watching the rain make tracks down the glass.

"I don't understand you…" said Elijah, sitting straight in the chair.

She wished he would just relax just a little.

"One minute you insist that you want to be left alone, the next you seek company. Something tells me you may have multiple personalities in that head of yours."

Arii's eyes shot to the hooded figure, and she saw his lips were twitching into a hint of a smile, a tiny dimple indenting his right cheek.

Well what do you know, the man can smile.

"Couldn't sleep?" Arii said, changing the subject.

Elijah's head tilted to the window. "No, I find it hard to sleep during thunderstorms."

She swore she heard an audible swallow, and she felt a curl of sympathy within her.

Now *that* feeling was odd.

Arii's lips twitched into a smirk as she forced the strange emotion back. "Why don't you ever remove your hood?" she grinned slowly, saving him from elaborating on his sleep problems further. "Is your face a sight that would scare the small children of the castle?" she joked half-heartedly before adding, "Or perhaps you are really a barbarian from the South Court?"

She was itching to see the man beneath the hood, no, she was *dying* to. Her fingers pressed against her lap, withholding the urge to just leap across the space and pull it from his head.

Something told her that if she attempted such a foolish thing, Elijah would not hesitate to run her through with his sword. She had seen with her own eyes the way he killed without hesitation.

Elijah paused before surprising her with an answer.

"I... feel most comfortable with it on." A hint of a smile again. It made her heart flutter strangely. "And I feel it has established me with an air of mystery – my unknown face is perfect for any assignments the King gives me."

She nodded in agreeance and offered him her own small smile.

"And how long have you worked for the King?" she asked, brows lifting curiously.

Elijah paused before answering, as if considering what information was best to disclose to her in that moment. "I grew up in the castle, since about the age of ten. I was adopted by a maid servant named Colleen. She is the closest thing I have to a mother."

"And what of your family before?"

"I do not remember much of my life before being taken in by Colleen," he said, and she believed him. She heard his voice drop an octave as he continued. "I was found in the forest when I was nine, I had lost my memory. My life prior to that is nothing but flickers of images and haze. Not enough to piece together my former life." He paused, as if wondering why his lips spilled history so easily to this woman. It was almost like he had forgotten he did not trust her. Perhaps he did not care for his own unknown history – what little he knew of himself would be of no importance to her.

He continued, "Lorch showed me kindness, and we have been friends ever since. To serve him is my greatest honour." His tone was resolute.

"Lorch… I mean King Lorch, is not the type of man I thought he would be," Arii admitted, picking at a piece of lint on her knee. "He is kind, albeit a cocky son of a-" She halted and glanced up to see Elijah's lips curled in a smile.

"Yes," he agreed. "My King is severely misunderstood. Under the mask of a spoiled bachelor, he is just a man seeking his true calling. What that is I do not know yet. I do not even think he knows himself."

"And to be a guard is your calling?" Arii felt a shift in the air, and another resonating clap of thunder crashed in the skies beyond. Elijah was silent for a time and she wondered if he had reached his daily quota of words. Arii watched a flash of light illuminate his form again – saw the tip of his nose tinge in silver.

He surprised her when he finally said gently, "To protect is my calling."

Arii surveyed his hidden face, eyes sliding over the marks left by the Kryvern on his arm. He had leapt in front of Lorch without hesitation and having gotten to know the man – albeit just a little – she realised that his words rang true.

With deliberate slowness she withdrew the dagger from her waist band, and she could feel Elijah's eyes on her hand. She placed the dagger on the table between them, her eyes lifting as a slow smirk gracing her lips.

"How about a game, Master Wolfe? I'll wager that I can lodge this dagger into the spine of a book on the farthest shelf, one on a specific title of your choosing."

When his head tilted to the dagger, Arii felt a sizzle of energy in the air between them again.

"If I land a hit, you must remove your hood."

She placed a finger on the hilt of the blade and flicked it, causing it to twirl on the wooden surface. Elijah's shadowed features gave nothing away as he leaned forward, elbows resting on his knees. She could practically see the fabric of his leathers straining over his muscles.

"And if you miss?" he asked, and she was surprised that he was going along with the little game.

Arii's eyes lifted slowly, staring at him through a thick veil of lashes.

"If I miss, I will kiss you."

It was then a boom of thunder rolled over the castle, feeling as if it were directly about the dome of the library. A flash of forked lightning snaked across the sky, spearing light across Elijah's hard jaw. The room was silent then, save the ever-distant rumble of the waterfall beyond.

"Deal."

Arii felt her palms begin to sweat.

Her palms *never* sweated.

To say she was surprised that the man was going along with this was an understatement. She was sure she would win, but she was also sure that kissing Elijah would not be the worst thing in the world if she somehow lost. If she could finally gaze upon the face under the hood, it was a risk worth taking.

Standing and snatching up the dagger, Arii moved to stand by the pool at the centre of the room. She shifted her feet, swirling the dagger in her hand. She heard the light sound of the chair moving back, then Elijah stood a few feet from her side, arms folded across his chest. His head tilted towards the bookshelves at the other end of the library and she knew he was choosing a title.

"The History of Castle Viridya," he said.

Nice, a title on the top shelf. Of course, he would choose one of the highest tomes, one which – if her aim was not true – would be a hard target.

Arii's eyes narrowed and she let some of her magic drop. Her dulled senses heightened, her eyes lightened and the veil on her sight lowered, offering perfect clarity. She inhaled deeply, before releasing the breath.

Her arm shot out and the dagger spiralled through the air, beginning to dip during its trajectory to the shelf. Her eyes narrowed, and thankfully the dagger stayed its course, soon embedded in the spine of a gold tome.

Arii straightened, glancing over at Elijah who remained silent. She paced to the shelves, retrieving the book with her dagger and lifting the book to show him the face. Pressed in gold lettering was *The History of Castle Viridya,* flashing for him to see.

A breath escaped Elijah's lips.

Placing the book with lodged blade on the table nearby, she shifted to stand in front of him, hands on her hips.

"Now, my end of the deal. I won fair and square." Her brows lifted as if she were expecting him to turn on their agreement.

Elijah looked tempted to point out that he was not sure it had been a victory earned with fairness. She wondered if he could possibly know anything about her abilities, but pushed the thought aside.

"If we are to train together, we need to have trust. You need to trust me enough to see your face, Elijah."

When he did not refuse nor move an inch, arms straight either side of his body, she moved closer and put her hands on the edges of his hood, then with painful slowness she lifted the fabric to reveal his face.

His hair was black and tinged with silver as lightning flashed above them, the hue matching the dark stubble on his strong jaw, a waving mass on the top of his head that curled at the nape of his neck and fell upon his forehead in thick waves. Unlike Lorch's perfectly swept hairstyle, Elijah's was dark and unruly, wavy strands reaching his eyes. His brows were thick and narrowed, his nose ever so slightly crooked as if it had once been broken. His cheeks and sharp jaw were dusted with a light layer of stubble, his face rugged and strong. Her gaze danced over his face, and his eyes made her pause her assessment of his handsome features.

They were like two molten pools of mercury, deep, clear and haunted. She noticed a darker ring of grey around the halo of his irises, two open windows to his mysterious soul within. Her breath hitched and she paused on his lips, full and slightly parted.

"Nice to finally see you…" she breathed.

Elijah's breath also seemed to release in a whisper, as if he had been holding it in as she surveyed his revealed features. Without a thought, they were mere inches apart, Arii having lifted onto her toes to get the hood over his head and resting on his broad shoulders. She could feel the heat radiating from his body at their closeness – feel the hum of strength inches away. It was not tension… no, what she felt was something wholly different. Curiosity, hesitation and a feeling of weight being lifted. They seemed to move with each other, in unison, just like when they fought together. Weaved from the same cloth, forged of the same fires.

She almost swore he inched closer, his chest expanding with a gentle inhale.

Her insides were a tempest, a barely controlled firestorm. She felt flame race through her veins, an overwhelming need to be closer, to have nothing left between them. Her fingers tingled, the compulsion to touch his face bordering on a nervous twitch. She swallowed audibly, lips parting with a small sigh.

Having finally seen his face, she felt something else was beginning to shift between them, a confusing slither entering the depths of her cold heart. Something between them had changed recently, and this moment seemed to seal that change.

He drove her crazy, pulled all of her strings and awoke a temper within her that she usually kept pushed deep, deep down. Why was it now that she longed to touch her fingers to his lips, followed by her own? She wanted to savour the moment, allow it to linger, take it slowly and explore every single storm-lit inch of him.

Confusion… she felt confusion mixed with the unfolding of

thunderstruck awe.

He was dark, brooding and beautiful.

The feeling was nothing like that of what she had felt with Lorch in the hallway. Her moment with Lorch was mindless, heat-filled and impatient.

This… this moment was something different.

Elijah's eyes were fixed on her lips now, their silver depths smouldering like melted iron embers in a hearth, and she felt the ghost of a touch of his fingers on her chin. His hand lifted, but hovered, as if afraid to close the distance.

"You…" he breathed, pausing before trying again. "You used magic to win our bet."

Her breath sucked in quickly. Had he seen her use magic? Or was he taking a stab in the dark? To guess at such a thing and accuse her without proof was dangerous. Had he voiced his suspicions to Lorch?

Magic was not something you spoke about openly in Viridya.

His voice did not hint at any anger, it was merely curious.

"And if I did?" she ventured.

Elijah's eyes studied hers, his expression unchanged save for a tiny crease between his brows. He was looking at her with what she believed was the same look of gentle wonder that was on her own face in that exact moment. Her reason for wonder was far more understandable than his own – he had seen her face many times.

"Who are you?" he whispered.

"I was raised in a circus; my act was the trapeze–"

"Who are you truly, Miss Clearwater?" he said, his tone hard but not unkind. A pause before he added, "Is Arii Clearwater your true name?"

She took her bottom lip in between her teeth. This conversation was becoming far too dangerous. Her mind was spinning, trying to formulate a believable answer to his question, but all the while wondering if she could somehow distract him from the direction his thoughts were taking. She felt that nagging tug between them pull tight again and as her eyes drifted to his, the two liquid silver pools fixed on her lip caught between her teeth.

Perhaps distraction would not be as hard to achieve as she thought.

For a single moment, her mind drifted and she realised the storm above them had stopped. Hesitantly, her hands rose to rest against his chest, feeling the strong, steady and quickening beat of his heart beneath her palms.

Their noses touched as their lips inched closer, her own heart hammering like a violent drum in her ribs. It thundered in her ears as her eyes dipped to his lips again. Featherlight, his fingers brushed her jawline, and she felt a sizzle of fire at his touch.

They inched closer, breath mingling…

Suddenly golden light bathed them as the door to the library opened and a maid began to enter. Arii and Elijah broke swiftly apart, like two teens caught behind the royal stables.

"Oh!" cried the maid, seeing the two and bowing apologetically. "My apologies, I was just here to attend to the library."

Arii was suddenly moving, the dagger retrieved from the book in a flash and placed back behind her cloak. She was slipping past the maid without preamble, dashing from the room before Elijah could see that her cheeks were tinged with scarlet.

Elijah remained where he was, a stunned expression on his features. "Colleen," he choked.

The maid's head snapped from watching the retreating woman to the King's bodyguard. "Elijah, how nice it is to see you without your covering. Oh, my boy, you need a haircut!" Bustling about the library, Colleen set to work as if she had not just walked into a room charged with static electricity.

Elijah stood fixed to the spot, reeling as Arii's violet eyes remained burned into his mind.

Then he tasted the lingering sheen of magic on his tongue.

CHAPTER THIRTEEN

Arii's eyes were fixed on Lorch's golden thread, the shimmering material now twined around the hilt of her dagger. Never in her years as a Fury had she ever felt like this, a raging inferno was slowly unfurling within her, a firestorm of foreign emotions that had her feeling like she was on the precipice of a cliff – a cliff that had either a sharp fall into soft clouds, or a bloody end on a jagged bed of rocks.

A mantra chanted in her head, words that had been said over and over as she grew up – as she trained under the heavy eyes of the Sisters of Fate.

Emotions are weakness.

Thoughts are as deadly as the blade you wield.

And love causes blindness.

Many of the strings pulled from the Tapestry of Life were that of bad men and women, people who the Gods saw as unfit for more time on the Earth. Arii's job as a Fury was to end those lives, ensuring the Fates' work was fulfilled. For weeks now, Arii wondered what Lorch Kruel had possibly done to incur the Gods' wrath, why his golden string had been the one pulled from the Tapestry. Having spent time with him, she struggled more and more to figure out what made him a bad person.

Perhaps for the first time, the Gods were wrong?

Arii balanced the dagger hilt on her finger, staring as the ends as they tilted like scales. The sharp, pointy end was Elijah, all deadly grace and sharp edges. The hilt was Lorch, all smooth and solid, balancing the sharp end perfectly. Her violet eyes were reflected back at her in the metal, and she saw in their depths a glimmer of anguish.

Was that what this feeling was? Anguish?

Or was it just simply confusion?

Maybe it was absolute, untamed, and inconceivable desire.

Emotions were so foreign to her that she was having trouble reining herself in, her anger at feeling so confused beginning to rise to the surface. An assassin was not meant to feel like this, was not mean to *feel* at all.

What she had always was her control – her focus.

Now that too was slipping through her fingers like sand.

Shortly after fleeing the library, Arii flew into her room and began to dress swiftly, preparing to attempt another escape from the castle. She could not do this any longer. She needed to clear her head, do something that did not involve either of the men. Preferably something with her hands. She swiftly braided her hair and slipped the dagger into her belt as someone knocked at her door.

Argh for the love of the Gods!

Was it Elijah? Or maybe it was Lorch?

She could not deal with seeing either of them at this moment.

"Go away!" she called, glaring at her reflection as her magic veil shimmered into place, dulling her features once more.

"Arii," came a female voice. Arii moved to the door, flinging it open. There stood Nem, and the look in her eyes told Arii that her friend knew something was wrong. Entering the room, Nem's stunning aqua eyes did not leave hers as she closed the door calmly behind her.

"What's wrong?"

Arii growled in response to her words, pacing to the window as dull light of the coming morning filtered through, then over to the fireplace.

Nem all the while watched her intently, silently. She was not the sort of person to force an answer, allowing her stoic silence to do the forcing for her. Much of the time it worked. Nemesis had an air about her that made secrets spill forth.

Arii was not sure she could let this particular secret spill though, even to her best friend.

"I just… I just need to get out of the castle, for a few hours." She paced like a caged animal, a jungle cat eager to break free and run. She felt as if she were drowning, the air in the room was too hot. She could not get enough air into her lungs. Nem was beside her in a flash, gripping her hands and forcing her to stop and look at her.

"Ariiaya, you do not have to tell me what is happening to you, nor what has you looking like you want to snap a few necks." Her silver hair shimmered in the firelight. "But I could feel the magic pulsing from your room, and if I could feel it, who knows who else can." She squeezed her hands firmly, then nodded resolutely. "Amberbourne. We will head to Amberbourne today. Perhaps a few pints of mead in the Tavern, and a little harmless brawl will let off some of your steam." The woman's head cocked to one side as she added, "Or perhaps a quick tumble in one of the taverns rooms with a young man, hmm?"

Arii's glare had Nem chuckling darkly.

"How is it you know my mind better than I know it myself?" sighed Arii weakly.

"Many years of suffering your company," Nem smirked. "Come."

Arii did not need to be asked twice as the two women slipped from her rooms, as silent as shadows.

⁂

As the morning's dull light turned golden, Elijah was not at all surprised that Arii did not show for training. Their nearness the night before had taken him aback, left him shaken inside. Confused and feeling a desire he had never felt before, there was a burning deep in his soul like a spark had just been flicked into a pile of dry tinder.

Sure, he had been with women before, quick flings to sate basic desires, but he had not seen any of them again, had not cared to.

This woman was different.

The way Arii Clearwater's temper flared whenever he spoke to her, the stubborn set of her jaw and the way her lips spat words like acid in such an unladylike manner had his blood boiling. There was a fire burning in her dark eyes, a fire that never seemed to dull. She was guarded and harsh – quickly pulling upon insults and profanities when she was uncomfortable within a situation. And the way she danced the dance of death in battle had him pausing. The languid and flawless way she ended lives around her was almost poetic.

In a way, she reminded him of himself.

She had barriers around her that resembled his own. He was torn between the desire to kick her arse and kiss her.

Just like they had been so close to doing last night.

In the silver light of the library, when he had stared into the two surprisingly deep violet pools of her eyes, he saw vulnerability there, and a glimmer of pain.

Along with a raging flame of desire.

He had smelled it in the air, heard the thundering of her heart like a bird stuck in a cage. He had held back, but not for fear of her rejection – he could sense that was not an issue – but for fear of what one kiss could lead to.

What one kiss could unleash within him.

He knew how Lorch felt about her, it was evident in his friend's eyes when he spoke about his saviour. He admired her, lusted for her, and Elijah was surprised he had not taken what he wanted already. He knew he would be the first to know. Lorch was not exactly secretive with him, he spewed his every thought like water from a fountain. It was not like his friend to hide things from him.

He did not hide behind a cloak like Elijah did.

Lorch knew more about Elijah than anyone else did, that was true, but Elijah could not bring himself to let his walls fall. He had been building them for years, brick by brick until he was surrounded by an impenetrable fortress.

Arii Clearwater was a hair's breadth from tearing it all down in one night.

And Elijah Wolfe had been close to letting her.

ೞ೮

The inside of the tavern was loud, rowdy, and filled with the sounds of men laughing and cursing. The smell of unwashed bodies, tobacco and hot roasting meat was almost too much for Arii's nose to handle. She needed this – this distraction from her own inner turmoil.

Why hold back? What reason had she to hold anything back, really? She could bed both men. They were best friends, feelings may get hurt, that was if those men cared enough when all was said and done. Who was to say they felt anything above desire for her? Who was to say that was all she felt for them? Perhaps breaking the tension and tumbling with them both would erase the strange, confusing storm of emotions brewing within her.

Arii touched the mug of mead to her lips and drank deeply, before gazing over the rim at her silver haired friend. Both women sat on a far table in the tavern, hooded and sitting in shadow. It was how they preferred to relax, a thin veil of magic making them inconspicuous to human eyes.

Nem was staring at her intently.

"Care now to tell me what's eating your arse, Violet Assassin?"

Arii placed her mug down, the amber liquid within sloshing close to the rim as she growled, "Fuck off."

Nem's lips split in a slow, languid smirk. "There she is," purred the Fury. "I thought for a little while you were lost to me and becoming… soft."

"Since when have I ever needed a reason to be pissed off, Nem?"

"That is true." Nem was silent for a moment, lifting her own mug to take a sip. Over Arii's shoulder, Nem saw a group of men dressed in Red Guard uniform who were beginning to overtake the riot of sound in the tavern, their laughter loud and fierce. She saw their hands groping maids as they passed, more than once. The barkeep's eyes were now landing on the group more often, his expression becoming dark. Nem assumed the young woman they were showing copious amount of attention could be the barkeep's daughter, or wife.

She hoped Arii had not noticed, her friend was not a fan of that sort of thing being forced upon a young woman in her presence. She had always been that way, making Nem think she had experienced something similarly unsavoury in her past. Nem knew more than most about Ariiaya Trillia, perhaps not as much as Krepth – but she was a close second.

One thing Arii had always kept veiled was her emotions.

The silver haired Fury knew that was thanks to years of intense training and brain washing by the Sisters of Fate – she too suppressed everything within herself.

Arii had always been a closed book, a tome needing deciphering ever since they had met. The woman was the pure definition of a Fury, emotionless and seemingly soulless.

Well, so Arii wanted everyone to believe.

Nem knew that she was far more complex than she would have anyone discover. Whatever was eating at her friend would soon be revealed, she just needed to be patient.

"Alright, I won't press it, but you know you can talk to me, Arii."

"I know, but I don't need to talk."

"Suit yourself."

The two women grew silent, drinking their mead and picking from their plate of cheese and finely sliced roast meat. Nem's eyes flicked to the rowdy table of soldiers often, surveying them before her eyes were back on Arii again. "Seen anyone you fancy?"

Arii's stomach coiled at the thought of sleeping with any of the patrons of this establishment.

None of them had brown locks tinged with copper, or sun kissed olive skin and the lean body of a dancer.

None of them were tall, dark haired and deadly with molten

silver eyes and sporting a body honed for war.

Gods she was in deep trouble.

One of the men at the rowdy table spoke, and if it were not for their Fae heightened hearing, the two Furies would not have heard the conversation one man was having with another.

"Jimmy said that his brother, Garvin, has not yet returned from Bonemire."

Mention of the fortress had Arii's ears perking.

"Mayhap he is still gettin' trained? Heard the place has had a mass intake of recruits lately. Lots of supply wagons, too."

"Wonder what they're preparing for? Ain't been no proper action since the last night them Fae royals were killed in the castle." One of the men snorted. "That boy King got the gig real easy, ey'? The last royal line killed in an unfortunate castle invasion. None left to take up the throne but the King's Hand, Valdis Kruel."

"Thank the Gods that them Fae bastards have been wiped out. I heard the Fae fed their servants to their pet dragons."

"I heard their magic was so strong it made them mad!"

"And it is said that it was their magic that created the filthy Shifters livin' in the Evergrave Forest."

"Shifters are a myth, you sod!" crowed another man.

"Nah ah! I seen one with me own eyes!" The man pointed a finger at his widened eyes, becoming all the more animated.

"Your own eyes are hazy with drink ninety nine percent of the time!" shot another.

"No, I'm serious! One moment there stood a woman then *poof-*" The man slammed down his mug, mead sloshing over the rim and splashing on the table. "-In her place stood a moon white fox!"

A crash sounded, and Arii found herself peering over her shoulder at a man who now had the serving girl on his lap, her tray of beverages strewn across the floor. The girl had a thinning veil of disgust on her face which she was trying to hide, but failing. The group of guards hooted and slammed their mugs against the tabletops, and Nem could feel the temperature of the already stifling room beginning to rise. She almost hoped the men would let the girl go.

"Come on now, little poppet, have you ever been with a guard of the royal army before?"

Nem took the thought back. He deserved what was about to get handed to him.

The girl squirmed, but that only spurred the man on. He grabbed her and tossed her onto the table, plates and mugs scattering as she screamed. The man pinned her with one hand, the other grabbed at the front of her blouse and was about to pull it open when a blade pressed between his legs.

The man became very, very still.

"Let her go, or I'll ensure you won't be able to show any more *poppets* what they're missing," hissed a voice behind him. The man inched his head to the cloaked figure, slowly raising his hands in surrender.

The serving girl fled, but Arii was not concerned with where she went. Her nostrils flared, lips pulled back over her elongated canines as they glinted in the firelight. She wanted blood.

"Who the fuck are you?" hissed the man, seeming to grow confidence even with a blade pressed against his genitals. Admirable, or perhaps just stupid. Arii's head cocked like she was inspecting a dung beetle under her boot.

"You can call me a cockblocker."

She slowly withdrew her dagger, and the man began to turn on her, the copious amount of liquor he had consumed leaving him seemingly untuned to how close to death he was.

"Do you often proposition the ladies of the tavern like this?" Arii asked casually. The man's expression began to twist as he realised it was a woman before him, as if the gentle lilt of her speech had not given her away.

He grinned savagely. "Oh aye, you'd prefer me to proposition you?" Arii could feel Nem a few feet behind her and saw the other guards at the table beginning to rise.

She licked her lips in anticipation.

The tavern had become silent soon after Arii's interference, and patrons began to slip out the door. It was as if they could feel the tension rising, the very air in the tavern becoming stifling.

Swiftly sheathing her dagger, she lifted a hand and touched her finger to his chest, removing her hood with her free hand. When her face was revealed, the man's expression twisted to delight.

"Well, hello there, little lady!"

Arii felt the tips of her fingers tingling, the hairs on her arms raising as adrenaline shivered through her veins.

A movement caught the corner of her eye as one of the men from the table grabbed the lip of Nem's hood, ripping it back from her head. Nem's azure eyes were fixed on Arii, and the Fury did not need to scowl to show her displeasure, it hung in the very air around her. The man brushed back Nem's silver hair, revealing her pointed ears.

"Looks like she has a friend!" the man hollered.

Arii's gaze slid to the barkeep, and their eyes met. Sweat beaded his brow, and he gently placed down the glass he had been drying with a rag. He nodded ever so slightly in reply to Arii's unspoken request, silently slipping away to the kitchens.

Arii turned and paced to the tavern door, flicking the metal latch shut with a resolute *click*, locking the door.

"I assume, by the way you have been handling the women in this humble establishment tonight, that you are unaware of how a lady *should* be treated."

Click, a second lock flicked down.

The men were no longer laughing.

"And I assume none, until now, have educated you in proper manners?"

Click, a third lock.

"What are you talkin' about? No little purple eyed elf *whore* can tell me who I can and can't grope or fuck!" barked the man, his tablemates mirroring similar looks of animosity on their faces.

Arii pinched the bridge of her nose, as if she were speaking to a child. Slowly she lifted her head to stare at the men, lip curling in disgust. "Either you apologise to the young lady you groped earlier and pay the Innkeeper for your meals, or I'm going to paint this room a pretty new shade of red with your blood and entrails."

All of the men began to draw their weapons in unison, looks of outrage replacing confusion on their faces. To the sing of metal leaving sheaths, Arii turned to front the group, boots sliding to brace on the dirty floorboards as she drew her daggers. Across the room, Nem mirrored her action.

"Suppose that means you need a lesson?" growled the assassin.

The man drew his sword, a snarl ripping from his lips.

"I'm gonna enjoy rutting your cooling corpse, elf bitch."

Arii's lips curled in a slow, sardonic smile. With that, the man rushed her with a yell, and the room erupted into utter, bloody chaos.

CB&CO

"So you see, my King, my family has not the coin to pay our taxes this month. The men, those who should be wearing the Kruel family crest with pride, instead wave it about like it is a substitute for payment."

A man was bowed before the dais in the throne room, head down as he spoke. His clothing was dirty, his boots having tracked mud on the immaculate marble floor. He looked like a gift left on the back doorstep by the resident housecat.

Nearby, more townspeople knelt on the marble, all bowing low. Arii's nose wrinkled as she stood guard by the door. The poor people were filthy, bruised and close to tears. The man's voice cracked as he spoke, yet he lifted his head to stare at Lorch with determination as he sat on his throne.

Today, the King was dressed in a vermillion-coloured tunic, stitched with gold and pinned with his family crest on his breast. His gold crown glittered in the filtered morning light as it streamed in through the cathedral windows above. To one side stood his father, dressed in his usual royal garb, his mother a foot away on her usual seat, dressed in a beautiful green gown. It was simple yet elegant. Commander Hawke stood on the lower floor, having seen the small group of people into the throne room.

As always, the shadow of Elijah lingered in close proximity to the King. Arii had not looked his way once since taking her post by the door, had hardly looked at Lorch either.

Having blown off some steam in the tavern the night before, the brawl seemed to bring her mind back into focus. Doing what she did best and what was familiar stilled the turmoil in her mind, even if it was just for a few bloody, adrenaline filled minutes. The guards had not stood a chance, but they had tried their hardest.

It was custom for the King to hear the grievances of the people every week, and after witnessing just a couple of these meetings now, Arii noticed a similarity in each wretched soul who stared up at the throne. His people were starving, they were unable to pay the high taxes set by the Crown and there were more Kryvern now threatening their livestock, more often than not wiping out entire pens of animals, leaving nothing but blood and remains. That was not mentioning the townspeople the beasts were picking off. Some approached his dais completely heartbroken, claiming a son had been snatched away, not seen in months. Arii wondered if the Kryverns were not the only problem – thinking back on what the Water Nymph had said the night of the full moon.

Perhaps someone was taking humans from the towns too, not just Nymphs from the lake.

Lastly, Red Guard troops were causing trouble in their taverns, taking food and drink without paying, and mishandling their women.

"That is unfortunate news to hear, Mr Spence. Please accept a waiver on your taxes for the month, to help ease the burden."

Valdis noticeably stiffened beside his son.

"T-Thank you, Your Excellence, thank you." With a bow, the man slowly rose and returned to his small group, exiting the room silently.

Lorch's mother straightened in her seat. "Would it not be beneficial to take this feedback and use it to apply discipline to your ranks, Your Highness? There seems to be a lack of respect fluttering over your men, perhaps it is time to make examples of these rogues?"

Lorch tilted his head to his mother. On his other side, Valdis' voice was a hiss.

"And have more men rebel, thinking us showing favour to the people over those taken into service of the Crown? That will make things worse."

Lynnera's chin rose. "So, we do nothing about it?"

Valdis' voice dripped with acid as he said. "We take those flaunting their authority and send them to Bonemire. Quietly."

"I believe it better to make public examples of them," said Lynnera, and the look her husband threw her was dark.

"I agree with Mother," said Lorch, looking then to his father. "It makes sense to make an example, so that others tempted to make trouble will hesitate to do so again."

At that moment, Commander Hawke turned to the dais and bowed.

"If I may speak, I have news from Amberbourne, my King."

Lorch glanced to Hawke and nodded before the man proceeded.

"It seems someone has already made an example of some of your rogue guards at the Amberbourne tavern last night."

Arii's blood ran cold.

"What?" barked Valdis.

Hawke cleared his throat before continuing. "A group of ten Red Guard soldiers attending the tavern last night were struck down." His eyes flicked across to Lynnera briefly, before returning to Valdis. "There are claims that they entered the premises and did not come back out."

"And you are sure they are dead?" said Lorch.

"It's said that some witnessed the Innkeeper scrubbing the walls of his tavern and mopping guts from his floors. It was a bloodbath."

Silence fell on the room, accompanied by Lynnera's gentle gasp.

Arii swore Elijah's hood inclined ever so slightly her way. She kept her expression unreadable, her eyes lifting to the dais where everyone stood. Well, she should have known that the news would travel back to the castle.

Maybe she should have shown some restraint and not have painted the walls red with the men's blood, but she had been angry.

Incredibly and stupidly angry.

She revelled as they begged for their lives, blood flecking her face and screams gracing her ears like a familiar song. She had given them a chance – a chance to swear they would never touch another unwilling woman again, but the whoresons had done no such thing. They were dirty, rotten pigs, it was true, but she felt like her self-control had slid away from her, much like it was beginning to when she was around Lorch and Elijah. She had always thought control was one of her strongest features. The solid steel walls she had spent years forming around her heart were beginning to be eaten away, and she was not sure how to handle it.

The tension was thick in the air, almost tangible enough that it could be cut with a knife.

Lorch was first to speak, his attention on the Commander.

"Perhaps it was someone from the South Court? Those Winter bastards are always looking for a fight."

"I do not think so, a brute Jero Vox may be, but stupid he is not. No one from the South has entered our borders in months."

"The West Court?"

"Kadec Brolikian is far too busy with his grand parties to be bothered with a small group of our soldiers, let alone crossing the border to us," said Hawke.

Lorch touched his index fingers to his lips, leaning forward and resting his elbows on his knees. "It has been months since we have even heard from the other Courts, perhaps years for some of them. Do we not have any allies there?"

His father barked a laugh. "Fae lovers, the lot of them. Ever since the tragic end of the Herington line, they no longer offer unison. You know this, son. I have struggled for years with the other Courts."

Arii was not surprised, who would want to deal with Valdis Kruel? He was rude, crude and a tyrant. He was probably the cause of the Court's division. Lorch on the other hand – she was sure the others would be more inclined to work with the North Court if they knew what he was truly like. Why hide behind a guise?

"We have friends in the East Court, do we not?" said Lynnera.

"Freya Bloom and her associates are by far the worst of the lot," answered Valdis, brows drawn. Lynnera's eyes fixed on her husband as he spoke, a frown curling her lips.

"But did we not have a good trade relationship with the East? The wood from the Evergrave forest fetches a fair price, which we secured for them. Surely they owe us that?"

"Bloom and her shifter tribe care naught for gold it seems, Wife."

Valdis's tone was dismissive, causing Arii's eyes to narrow ever so slightly. He treated his wife with such disdain, such disrespect as if her opinion did not matter. It was surprising that the man allowed her to attend the council in the first place. Something about Lynnera Kruel told Arii that the woman would not take no for an answer. How she endured to be married to the man, Arii had no clue. Let alone having borne him two children.

Valdis paced down the dais towards Commander Hawke. "Perhaps it is time to begin a fresh intake of recruits to Bonemire."

Lynnera stood then, her expression one of anger as she her husband quickly down the dais. "What in the Gods name for? Do we not have enough troops at the fortress already? Winter is on the horizon and the townspeople need their sons and daughters to help them though the coming months."

Valdis rounded on his wife, his face contorted in fury. "Whoever is deciding to pick off our troops may not stop at one group. Who is to say there is not a new rebellion gathering in the dark like rats to a carcass? If we let our guard down, we will end up just like the

Herington's – slaughtered in our beds!"

Lorch spoke then, following his mother.

"Perhaps we should discuss–"

"I think you are being hasty, Husband–" Lynnera began, speaking quickly and firmly, but was swiftly cut off with a cutting gesture to the air by Valdis.

"Commander Hawke, prepare for the intake. If you will all excuse us, I wish to speak to my *wife* in private."

Hawke hesitated, gazing in Lorch's direction, and pausing briefly on Lynnera, before straightening and bowing stiffly at the waist. "My Lord."

The Commander turned and paced towards Arii, and she could see the disapproval, rising in his expression. "Dismissed, Miss Clearwater," he said as he passed.

Her eyes lingered on the dais, a feeling of unease sweeping over her. She glanced in Elijah's direction and saw he was watching the tense exchange too, but what little of his face she could see was unreadable.

Before Arii turned to follow Hawke from the room, she saw the tense look on the older woman's face, her eyes narrowed and chin raised in defiance.

In the hall, Arii spoke quickly. "Commander, I don't feel we should–"

"Miss Clearwater, you were dismissed. Take the remainder of the night off." The Commander seemed distracted as he paused, his eyes taking on a faraway look. Although she had known the man for a short time, he had always had a keen look about him, a razor-sharp focus. He was distressed, but for what reason she was unsure. Was it the dead soldiers, the new recruit intake or the fact that Valdis wanted to speak to his wife alone, looking like he wanted to murder someone?

Well, the King's Hand always had that look about him, but tonight it was amplified.

Arii touched a hand to the man's arm and he seemed to focus on her. His brows pulled together, and he ran a hand through his salt flecked hair, his expression softening ever so slightly.

"Go to your rooms, Miss Clearwater, take this time to relax before we begin recruitment in a few days' time."

With a nod, the man turned on his heel and strode down the hall, his cloak fluttering behind him.

Just as Arii was preparing to head in the opposite direction, the doors to the room behind her opened and a figure entered the hall, closing the door softly behind him.

Elijah's intense silver eyes were fixed on her, his hood now pushed back slightly to reveal his face. Arii felt her breath hitch at the sight of him, at the sight of his dark brows narrowed and his strong jaw pulling his lips in a line. She had almost forgotten how incredibly handsome he was.

Elijah's head tilted, his expression radiating disapproval.

"Care to explain what happened in Amberbourne?"

How in all the Gods names did he-

"Or are you going to lie and say you had nothing to do with it?" he growled.

Her eyes narrowed and she smirked, waving a hand dismissively.

"And what makes you think I had anything to do with it?"

Elijah prowled towards her, pausing a foot away and glared down at her, his voice lowered to a hiss. "You do not deny it, and not to mention you did not attend training this morning."

Ah yes, training. In her haste to get as far away from the castle as possible after their near kiss in the library, she had forgotten about training at daybreak.

"So, you immediately assume I was the one slaughtering Red Guards in Amberbourne?" she hedged, forcing disdain into her voice.

Elijah leaned towards her, teeth slightly bared. The air crackled around them and she felt a familiar heat ignite in her veins at his close proximity.

"You make it hard to doubt." he growled, his voice turning velvet and dangerous.

She inched towards him, their noses close to touching as they stared each other down. His eyes tracked her face, assessing for a hint of a giveaway. She would be damned if she would admit anything to him. Her voice was gentle as she whispered, "What if they deserved it…"

"Be that as it may, who are you to mete out justice?"

"Perhaps it was their fate that night."

"And what do you know of fate?"

Arii's eyes glittered as she let her eyes drop to his lips… those perfectly shaped lips.

"I know plenty about fate."

His breath tickled her face, and Arii swore the temperature of the small space rose between them.

It was wrong, oh so wrong, but she wanted to kiss him – even now.

What was *wrong* with her?

He ignited something foreign within her, a fire that pulsed through veins, making her body wish to act of its own accord.

Elijah's brow arched comically as he said, "Are you one of the Fates in disguise?"

You could say that, in a way…

Suddenly the door behind them opened and Elijah straightened, the space between them yawning wide and becoming cold.

"Oh, apologies." said Lynnera gently, her voice cracking as she ducked her head and eagerly pressed past them. Arii peered over Elijah's broad shoulder to see the King's mother retreating down the hall. She could have sworn she saw the woman holding her cheek.

Odd…

The tension seemed to have been broken between them at the interruption, and Arii flicked her gaze to Elijah. He did the same, meeting her eyes after watching Lynnera's retreat.

"Don't think I won't question you again. We aren't done here."

"Perhaps you could question me in my rooms?" she purred.

"Grow up, Clearwater."

"Hah."

With a glare, he turned and left her in the hall without another word, leaving her staring after him.

ೞ

After her run in with Elijah, Arii glared down at her stomach which howled with sudden hunger. She headed to the kitchens for the possibility of a snack.

As she neared the room, her hearing picked up the sound of a sob, and she quickly headed in that direction. Pausing outside the entry to a room near the kitchens, she allowed her senses to reach out to the sound of hushed voices in the darkness.

Two figures stood by the far window of a guest room, a male and female. The male embraced the female, strong arms around her body as it shook with barely contained emotion.

"Lynn, you cannot allow him to continue to treat you this way."

"What would you have me do? Agree with him and suppress my opinion so that it slights his hand?"

"If that stops him from harming you, Gods yes." Hawke placed a hand on Lynnera's cheek tenderly, inspecting the dark bruise beginning to form on her pale skin. Their forms were tinged in moonlight as he held her close. Hawke lightly pushed the neckline of her gown, revealing another dark bruise marring her skin. His breath inhaled sharply.

This was not an embrace of friends, this was the embrace of lovers.

Hawke leaned in and brushed his lips over Lynnera's forehead, the caress feather light as if she were a delicate piece of porcelain that was close to breaking.

"It kills me to see your skin marred with bruises. I cannot stand by and let him harm you any longer…" He whispered; his tone laced with pain. Lynnera's eyes lifted to his, wide and fearful. "Hawke, no, he will kill you."

"If it means the slightest chance at ending his mistreatment of you, I will gladly face him."

"You are a brave old fool." Her tone was gentle, and her hand rested on his cheek. "But you cannot and should not. It is but a bruise. It will heal in a few days."

"It isn't just a bruise, Lynn, he may kill you one day if he loses his temper enough. He cannot treat you with such disrespect. He is cruel, he does not deserve you."

"I'm stronger than you think."

He chuckled softly in the dim light. "That I know. You are incredible and deserve far better. My offer still stands, Lynn."

There was a pause before Lynnera spoke. "You know I cannot leave them…"

"Please, just think about it." Insisted Hawke gently.

"He will hunt us down and take out his displeasure on the children."

"They can come with us, we will seek refuge with the West Court, I have friends there."

"I…" Lynnera fell silent, before whispering. "I will think on it, my love, I promise."

"Until then, please refrain from being the target of Valdis' ire. Gods Lynn, it took all my strength not to run him through today on the dais in front of Lorch."

"Oh Hawke."

His head dipped and they kissed in the moonlight. The moment was raw, sweet and Arii knew she had just stumbled upon something extremely dangerous.

The Commander and the King's Mother were in love.

With that knowledge, Arii slipped to the kitchens, teeth pinching her bottom lip in deep thought.

SYBELL
KRUEL
Melissa Kincaid

CHAPTER FOURTEEN

"Pull it tight, Ingrid. Tighter, if you please."

In the Princess' suite, Sybell stood in front of a full-length mirror, staring at her reflection with a scowl. Her handmaid, Ingrid, pulled at the strings of the bodice of her deep blue gown, before expertly tying them against her back. "Perfect," said Sybell, her breath light and airy. She turned then to face her maid.

Ingrid was a slight thing, her burgundy hair cut to her shoulders. The girl smiled timidly as Sybell stepped from the mirror and placed her hands on her hips.

"How do I look?"

"Resplendent." said the maid in response.

With a smile, Sybell stepped to the young woman and placed her hands either side of her face, before their lips met in a scorching kiss. They stood there for a few moments, enjoying their time alone before Sybell was called to attend a lunch with some lords and ladies. Gods, they were all so boring, droning on about the growing poverty of the towns in the land, and talking about how 'the crops are not as fruitful this year', the same as every time they visited.

Sybell leaned her forehead against Ingrid's, and the maid ran her hands down the Princess' arms in a comforting gesture.

"You could feign illness?"

"No, I used that excuse last time, remember?" she sighed.

"Mayhap it could be that time of the month?"

"You know it is not."

Ingrid frowned, caressing the Princess' cheek tenderly before leaning back to swipe a lock of golden hair from her face. "Will your mother try to marry you to one of the lords again?"

"I do not doubt it, she is becoming more… forceful about it of late. As if she *wants* me to move out of the castle."

"You are of the age now where marriage is expected," Ingrid pointed out.

"Do you *want* me to marry and leave?"

"Wherever you go, I go, you know this."

Sybell's frown was deep, causing Ingrid to dash a thumb over her lips. "You know I support you in whatever you set your mind to, Sybell, but I think I agree with your mother."

Sybell's lips popped open in surprise but she remained silent.

"Anyway, the Lord of Colkirk is rather dashing. It would not be all bad to be married to him, I'm sure. His estate overlooks the sea, imagine the lovely view."

The Princess took Ingrid's hand gently. "But you know it would all be a ruse."

Ingrid smiled gently, placing a kiss to Sybell's palm. "We do what we must for duty. You deserve a castle of your own, filled with riches and decadent cakes whenever you choose."

"You know me a bit too well."

"I know you the best."

The women embraced again, sharing a few more stolen kisses before Sybell sighed deeply, stepping from Ingrid to find her shoes. "I better not keep them waiting, the boring old fools."

"Good luck," said Ingrid, a small smile fluttering over her lips. With a reluctant glance, Sybell walked to the door and lifted her chin, her usual narrowed gaze and expression like she had eaten a lemon returned.

She closed the bedroom door behind her and paced down the hall towards the council chambers.

In a dark enclave nearby, eyes tracked the Princess' movements, hungry eyes that swept from her head to her toes. The shadow swept from one enclave to another, keeping pace but leaving distance between them. Teeth glimmered in a toothy smile as the creature melded into the shadow cast by a nearby pot plant.

Sybell paused at the doors to the council chamber, the murmured sounds of people talking within. Her shoulders dropped slightly, and the creature could smell she sweetness of the blood rising in the woman's cheeks. Sybell sighed and stood tall, fortifying her walls before entering the room and disappearing into the sounds within.

Tongue skimming its teeth, the shadow vibrated with anticipation. Soon.

Soon it would feast.

᚛ᚈ

"Is the Commander married?" asked Arii as she mucked the stalls with the other recruits. It had been some time since she had caught up with the trio, and even though the work was not what she would call *enjoyable*, nor was it necessary now that she was working with Elijah, but Arii decided to join them shortly after her training that morning. She was curious about what she had witnessed the night before, and hoped the recruits may be able to shed some light on the situation.

Tikkani paused as she speared a shovel into a fresh pile of horse dung. Her nose wrinkled with displeasure, and she tossed her hair over her shoulder before wiping her sleeve across her brow, her golden uptilted eyes narrowing.

"No, I do not believe so, why? Thinking of propositioning the Commander?" Her grin was wicked as she added, "He *is* handsome... for an old man."

Arii rolled her eyes. "No, you pixie eared fool. I was merely curious."

Tikkani chuckled and tossed the dung into a nearby crate. The gardeners would distribute the foul stuff over the gardens later. Tikkani grunted, spearing another mound before speaking.

"I did hear that he once had a relationship with the King's

Mother, back when they were younger and before she was married off to Valdis Kruel. Poor woman."

Well then, it seems a spark remained. If what Arii witnessed in the guest room was anything to go by. She felt sorry for the pair, and admired Lynnera's tenacity, as well as her sense of duty. She would rather bruises at the hand of her husband than to be silenced in her opinions.

Arii almost wondered why Lynnera had not learned to use a dagger, taking advantage of Hawke's skills, and use them to lodge the blade deep in that bastard's chest.

Arii would, but she was a cold-blooded killer.

Emerson joined the duo as Tikkani opened her mouth and cussed like a filthy sailor from Trader's Bay. Arii winced in sympathy as Emerson smacked his shovel against Tikkani's butt and she yelped, whirling on him.

"*Godsdammit* Emer!"

"What is with Valdis Kruel anyway? The man seems to have a constant thorn up his arse," said Arii, a grin plastering her face as they continued.

Emerson glanced to Arii as he speared the shovel into a pile of horse droppings. "I heard he wasn't treated well as a child." He frowned and lifted the full shovel. "Abused at the hands of his own father. I guess a childhood like that would leave a lasting impression. His father was said to be a real sadist – and he supported the old ways."

"Old ways?" enquired Arii, pausing.

"Yeah, you know – death to all magic users and all that kind of toss. There was a lot of fear back then, and Urther Kruel was the instigator of much of the murdering," Tikkani supplied.

"It's surprising, Lorch is nothing like his father," mused Arii.

Tikkani and Emerson exchanged a look and held it for a few moments, as if speaking to one another without words. Arii paused in her shovelling and stared as the two broke eye contact and continued their work.

"Okay, what was that?"

Emerson glanced her way. "What was what?" he hedged. At Arii's weighted, unblinking stare, the boy began to flounder. "I don't know what you're talking about, Arii."

Hmm, perhaps he was becoming immune to her glares.

"Come on, you two stare at each other like you're having a silent conversation. I've seen it at least five times now."

Tikkani paused in her work and propped up the shovel, leaning against it. "Fine, if you must know, we can speak to one another… with our minds." She gestured from her head to Emerson's. "Perks of being twins I guess, although I think Emerson would rather it was not so."

"You have no idea Arii, the constant dribble that inhabits her mind! Gods above!" groaned the boy.

"Hey, you don't exactly have a five-star show happening in your own head, you little shit."

"Shut up!"

The twins stared at one another for a long moment, eyes unblinking, and Arii did not have to guess that they were arguing telepathically.

"That's bloody awesome," she breathed.

The twins gazed her way and they seemed to become abashed at the same time.

"I guess it is kind of good sometimes," admitted Tikkani. "We can talk in private about anything, even when we are in a group of many."

Arii imagined the team they would make on a battlefield, looking out for each other's backs without giving away anything to the enemy. Fascinating. Until now she believed such a trait to be a myth, then again not many twins still existed.

"So, what were you saying before you revealed that little bit of information?" Arii asked, lifting a shovel load.

"Emerson seems to think you have a thing for the King," giggled Tikkani.

Arii paused halfway through flinging the dung into the crate. Her eyes darted to Emerson, and she swore she saw the boy's knees begin to quake.

"I did not! Tikkani said that, I swear."

Arii diverted her gaze to Tikkani, who was grinning mischievously. "Come on Arii, you've been spending an awful amount of time with him, after all. And Gods, he is one divine piece of man flesh."

"Argh, did you just say *man flesh*?" groaned Emerson.

Arii could feel her blood beginning to boil, but it was quickly simmering as she realised the twins were joking. She had to get a hold of herself. To react to little pokes like that would do more harm than good. Besides, she did not have *a thing* for the King.

That was preposterous.

"You talking about me?" came a voice from nearby. "I heard mention of divine man flesh," said Quinn, entering carrying two empty crates.

"Gods no!" replied Tikkani, flinging her shovel load of dung at Quinn. The boy screamed, dropping the crates and ducking quickly, narrowly avoiding a face full of crap.

He stood, eyes wide, before flipping a crude gesture the elf's way. Quinn huffed and retrieved the crates, setting them down near the others. He dusted hay from his messy locks and grabbed his own shovel.

"So, what'd I miss?"

"We were just discussing the lovely family occupying the castle currently," Tikkani replied.

"More friendliness at a funeral," Quinn chuckled, and glanced around quickly as if he expected Sybell Kruel to leap out of the nearby bushes and scowl at him.

"Do any of you know what the original royal family was like?" Arii asked, spearing a stack of hay with a pitchfork and distributing the golden strands across the floor.

"No idea, but I do know there are books still in the library about them. I'm surprised the Kruel family didn't have them removed,"

Emerson replied, wiping his brow. "I heard the Herington family were Fae."

Arii glanced up at Emerson. "Truly?"

"Yes, but it was said that the bloodline was so diluted that they hardly had a spark of the old magic left. There were no signs of the madness in Tyverus Herington, despite being a Fae and one of the last males, along with his two sons. It's incredibly sad what happened to them." Emerson frowned and continued to shovel hay.

"Do you think it's true that magic in Fae males leads to madness?" asked Tikkani.

Arii shrugged as she replied, "It's hard to know. All we have to go on are diluted manuscripts of history – as there are no male Fae left to ask."

Emerson nodded, "They say hundreds of years ago, there were many male Fae with incredible magic, magic that shook the land to its very core. The royal family in the North in particular fought on the backs of mighty dragons." Emerson lifted his hand and dipped and dove, spearing through the air. "The dragons were said to feed off the magic of their riders, making them incredibly strong. It also bonded them, riders to dragons. Without powerful magic though, the dragons could not survive. That is why there are none now, I guess. Powerful magic disappears, so do the dragons. As for the madness? I suppose with so much power there could be a little bit of madness." Emerson shrugged and gripped his shovel.

"The Herington's didn't have dragons, though, did they?" asked Quinn.

"No, the last dragons disappeared before Tyverus took the throne," said Emerson, digging his shovel into another stack.

"Gods I'd love to see a real live dragon," mused Tikkani wistfully, leaning her cheek against the handle of her shovel. Slowly her features twitched as she added, "But instead, we got stuck with those disgusting hybrids. Fuck, I hate Kryverns."

Emerson smacked his shovel against Tikkani's causing the end to slide out from beneath her and her stance to falter.

"You little dung beetle!" she hissed at her brother, righting herself.

Arii chewed her lip absentmindedly, deep in thought as the group continued their work in silence.

It had been twenty-two years since the night of the royal family's slaughter in this very castle. Five lives, along with loyal castle staff, had ended so violently that the Three Fates themselves avoided talking about the event. She wondered what they would be like if they lived today, what the land would be like under their reign.

What would their children be like?

Ghila, Brohem and Eliverus. Three young lives ended before they had truly begun, all because humans feared their potential magic and madness.

Later that evening, as she sat on her bed before a crackling hearth, something pressed at her mind, the shadow of a memory. Her fingers ran across Lorch's glimmering gold thread as she stared absentmindedly into the flames, watching the fire lick hungrily across the wood. The smell of the fire pulled at a memory as her eyes drifted shut, looping the golden thread through her fingers.

"I'll explain soon, little Violet. I promise," her mother gasped and continued their escape through the forest. Arii bounced on her mother's hip as they fled through the forest, the sounds of distant screams in their wake.

"Mama, please! Where is Papa? I want Papa!"

"Ariiaya, please my darling, keep your voice down."

"I want Papa!" she screamed again, wriggling like a worm in her mother's grasp.

"Arii, stop," begged her mother as they fled, stumbling on a log.

Suddenly an arrow whistled past her head and her mother cried out in alarm. Then, another and another whizzed past them as she ran, holding Arii tight to her chest.

Arii's eyes were wide, frightened as she saw the shadows of their pursuers over her mother's shoulder.

"Halt!" a male voice called in the distance.

Next thing Arii knew her mother was falling; hands were grabbing at them and Arii was screaming in terror. Hands clasped around her middle, and she felt as if the world were spinning.

"Let go of my daughter!" her mother hissed, and through her terror Arii saw she clutched a sizable rock in her hands. The woman brought the rock down on her pursuer's head with a sickening crack, and the man slumped against Arii's little form. Blood glittered against Arii's cheeks, crimson flecks dotting her eyelashes. The man was wearing armour but not a helmet, and he was not moving anymore. Quickly, her mother grabbed Arii, pulling her into a run.

"Mama, why are those men trying to get us?"

"My darling, please just keep running."

"Tell me Mama!"

Her mother was silent for a time as they ran, ducking below low hanging branches as they entered thicker forest.

"They got into the castle, my love, they have assassinated the King."

☙❧

Things only became more interesting after Arii's late night realisation.

Firstly, she had been there the night of the Herington family's murder, she was almost certain of it, lest her mind played tricks. She did not remember much of her time before growing up in Evergrave with her mother, and she was sure that the traumatising nature of the memories were hindering their clear recall.

Secondly, there were whispers of strange sounds coming from parts of the castle.

Arii's ears pricked as she helped herself to some sweetcakes and tea in the kitchens. Maids spoke in whispers to one another in the corner of the kitchen as they washed dishes.

Had Arii not had Fae hearing, she would have missed their hushed conversation entirely.

"Marg says she heard groans from the west wing the other night. I don' mean normal groans, ya know, I mean real strange inhuman sounds of something in pain."

"Was Marg gettin' into the wine again? She likes a little, you know," The maid pinched her fingers and made a motion of bringing a glass to her lips. "A bit too much."

"Nah, she said she was completely sober that night, truly."

"Hard to believe."

"I believe her, the look in her eyes showed no lies."

"I wonder what it could be," mused the woman as they scrubbed pots, then proceeded to gossip about things of no interest to Arii. She tuned out their voices before taking her haul back to her room.

Making her way down the golden halls, Arii balanced her tray on one hand and popped a little cake in her mouth with the other as she strode along. Feeling surprisingly light despite the servant's gossip and her own revelation, she was looking forward to sitting on her bed with her meal and a copy of *Recent Royal Histories* she had swiped from the library earlier that day. Determined now to learn more about the night the Herington family died, she hoped the book would shed a little bit of light.

"Oh, thank goodness!" a woman called as she ran towards her.

Arii suppressed a groan. "Oh for the love of-"

"Miss, you are a guard, are you not? Oh please, please come with me." The woman looked dishevelled and upset. Arii sighed, figuring it best she not hiss and shoo the woman away if she was supposed to be a guard. She placed her tray on a hallway table adorned with a vase of agapanthus and nodded to the woman.

"How can I be of assistance?"

The woman motioned for her to follow and Arii did as bid, following the woman as she opened the door to the crisp night air.

"I found something, Miss. I thought it best to alert a guard before disturbing His Highness. I… I do not know who it is, but I came out for some fresh air and found him just behind the geranium bushes. Oh, oh Gods."

Arii felt her hairs begin to stand on end. Something? Or someone? They paused by a thick garden bed of green shrubbery, and Arii's breath left her lungs in a whoosh. Poking out just visible of the bushes were a pair of feet.

The stench followed soon after. Arii's gag reflex rose swiftly but she stamped it down.

What the hell…

Arii spoke swiftly to the maid. "Thank you, Miss. Would you mind fetching Elijah, he's the-"

"The King's bodyguard, of course." The woman spun and fled back to the castle.

Arii watched her go, before she squatted by the body and surveyed what she could see in the darkness. The skin of the man's shoeless feet was as pale as chalk, leached of the warm glow of life, unwrinkled and dirty, his legs skinny and bony. As she glanced at the torso, she paused on the man's servant uniform, before fixing on his chest. His pale servant's tunic was ripped open and the skin from his chest to neck was torn to ribbons, exposing ribcage and muscle. His face was turned to the side, his mouth hanging slack and eyes rolled back into his skull.

This man, whoever he was, had died terribly, and Arii had a feeling this mutilation had been done while he was alive. She wondered how no one had heard his screams.

Perhaps he was the cause of the sounds Marg had heard?

Her scrutinization lingered on the man's skin around the wound on his chest, where the flesh seemed to glitter with tiny shards of crystal, as if something were infused with the very fibres of his skin. Arii's nose twitched as she noticed the man's ribcage was ruptured, and within the chest cavity…

"His heart is missing…"

His deep, smooth voice graced the air behind her. She stood slowly, glancing to her right as Elijah paused beside her, staring down at the corpse.

"What kind of creature would do this?" she whispered.

Elijah's hood was pushed back, his dark locks wavering in the light night breeze. His silver eyes were fixed on the body as he spoke. "Nothing I have ever witnessed."

They stood in silence, both minds whirling for an answer. Arii sneaked a glance at Elijah's strong profile, the hard lines of his face and noticed the crease between his brows.

"We should tell Lorch," she said gently.

"He is aware, he is gathering in the royal ballroom as we speak." Elijah's gaze met hers as he tilted his head. His eyes were like quicksilver, glittering in the moonlight.

"Come, we must attend."

∞

"I'm sure it was nothing but wolves. They occasionally enter the gardens in search of food."

Arii had to reign in her disbelief and an obvious eyeroll as Valdis paced the length of the long mahogany table where Lorch, Commander Hawke and a few other men of his personal council sat.

Was he consuming Crystal Ice, or was he just mad? Did he seriously expect wolves to have flayed the man's skin and ruptured his ribs, eating his heart in the process? Besides, how on Earth had the beasts entered the castle while it was locked up tight at night?

Lorch pinched the bridge of his nose between his thumb and forefinger, looking tired in the firelight. "Wolves? Father, that sounds insane."

"Perhaps a feud among the peasants? A blood debt unknown to us?"

Lorch's eyes lifted and his lips were set in a hard line. One of the councilmen spoke then, an older man with wispy white hair who looked to still be wearing his bed clothes. "Perhaps it was the same person who slaughtered our guards in the Amberbourne tavern? A message meant for us to decipher?"

"Preposterous, we are reading too far into this!" cried Valdis as he slammed a fist against the table. "Servants die all the time, it is nothing new."

Why was he so fixated on brushing the man's death under a rug?

Arii's gaze slid to Lorch and she found he was watching her, his blue eyes glimmering with concern. "What else can you tell me of the body, Miss Clearwater? You inspected it, did you not?"

She felt all eyes on her as she stood by the council chamber doors. Clearing her throat, she stepped forward. She felt Elijah's presence a foot away, a solid figure close by.

"I noticed his skin was tainted, seemingly with tiny shards of crystal."

That made the room pause with a heavy silence.

"Crystal, what kind of crystal?" said the white-haired man.

"The night was dark, perhaps your eyes tricked you?" snapped Valdis from across the room, his tone laced with condescension. "Mayhap his skin was wet with perspiration from his fight before death."

"I know what I saw," growled Arii, causing the room to silence again. Her chin lifted and she saw pure rage simmering in the man's eyes as they met, a muscle twitching in his jaw. The way Valdis looked at her was as if she were a roach under his boot.

Unblinking, they stared each other down in a silent battle of wills.

Lorch was quick to stand, his chair creaking across the marble behind him as he spoke quickly. "Leave me with Miss Clearwater, I wish to learn more of what she saw."

Valdis's mouth opened to protest, but Lorch's look was final. "Father, please."

His father's look was dark, but he complied with stiff bow and followed after the councilmen as they filtered from the chambers.

Lorch lifted a hand as Commander Hawke moved to follow. "Commander, I'd appreciate your input if you will stay for just a moment."

The older man paused and turned to face the King.

Lorch's cerulean eyes found Arii once again and flashes of their stolen kiss in the castle hallway fluttered across her mind's eye.

"The man's heart was missing, and his skin was littered with crystal?" Lorch continued, lifting a goblet to his lips.

"So it seemed, Your Grace."

Elijah spoke then as he approached the table. "Something about this feels… wrong." He paused and rested his hand on the pommel of his sword.

Lorch was nodding in agreeance, before his head inclined to Commander Hawke. "Commander, have our best healers survey the body and come to me tomorrow with a full report."

Commander Hawke nodded before bowing and turning from the room to fulfil his orders.

The King's eyes slid to Elijah and when he spoke, his voice was uncharacteristically low. Tired.

"Leave me with Miss Clearwater, Elijah. I will be along in a moment."

Elijah stiffened and before his protest could be voiced, Lorch raised a hand to silence him.

"Now," he ordered. The air in the room was heavy with sudden tension, and Arii found her fingernails had been biting into her palms since her stare off with Valdis.

Elijah bowed stiffly and slowly made his way from the room without another protest, but she knew he had been glaring at them with disapproval. The cloaked man paused by the King for a moment, and Arii heard the gentle whisper of Lorch's voice. "I trust her, Elijah."

Gods how foolish he was.

The door clicked behind Elijah, and Arii found she had been staring in his wake.

Lorch approached her, his eyes dark. "Are you alright? Seeing something like that would turn the stomach of a seasoned soldier."

Arii's eyes lifted to his as he paused before her. His head tilted ever so slightly as he surveyed her casual dress. She had not had the time to change between seeing the body and being summoned to the council chambers.

"I'm fine," she admitted.

Lorch's hand lifted, his thumb skimming her bottom lip. "Then why do you look like you are about to spit fire like a dragon?" His lips twitched in a small smile as colour rose to her cheeks at his touch.

Damn her body, giving her away so obviously.

"Your father, he…"

"Don't worry about what my father thinks."

"Do you not?"

Lorch chuckled low and ran his fingers along her jawline, causing flutters to ignite in her stomach like hundreds of tiny butterflies. His fingers snaked around her nape, and Arii's eyes drifted to his face, his expression so open that it caused her to pause. Slowly, her eyes dropped to his lips.

"Of course I do, but I believe he is wrong about the wolves. Something else is the cause of the man's death and I'm going to find out what it was," he said, his voice taking on a faraway quality, as if his mind lingered elsewhere.

He leaned in and she could smell the sweet smell of lavender and honey combined, with the faintest hint of cinnamon. Strange, that smell was new. His lips brushed hers, and she found she was holding her breath as the King's hand tightened at her nape. His tongue brushed the bow of her lips and she found them parting, allowing him to deepen the kiss.

She realised she was kissing him back, and with just as much simmering, barely held back passion, their tongues dancing gently. His hand slipped around her waist, resting on the dip of her lower back, fingers spreading and pressing her body closer to his.

He pulled away ever so slightly and spoke into the small distance between them, his breath warm on her face. "Why is it that I cannot get you out of my head, Miss Clearwater?" His voice was almost pained.

She swallowed and found herself staring at the smooth lines of his face, the clean-shaven ledges of his cheekbones and the thick crescents of his downturned eyelashes against his light olive skin as he sighed heavily. She knew that if he lingered to long, Elijah would soon come bursting through the doors to see what was halting them. She wondered if the bodyguard knew what was happening at that moment. If he did, she knew she would pay at training in the morning.

"I'm quite unforgettable," she said in answer, slightly breathless.

Lorch smiled and leaned back, studying her face. "That you are," he admitted, before grinning slowly. "You certainly aren't humble, are you?" he said, his lips pulling in a lopsided smile before stepping away.

"You don't become unforgettable by being humble," she said, a slow smirk spreading across her face.

"You're such a surprise, Miss Clearwater."

Oh, he had no idea.

The cool air in the space between them seemed to wash them both from their haze, and the King was soon pressing a kiss to the palm of her hand, eyes never leaving hers as he whispered a breathy, "Go get some sleep, Arii. We will talk on the morrow."

Arii.

He was beginning to throw formalities to the wind.

She was not sure how she felt about that.

As the King paced from the room, Arii felt a strange sensation eating at her stomach.

Later she realised it was sadness at his exit, and low, keening longing.

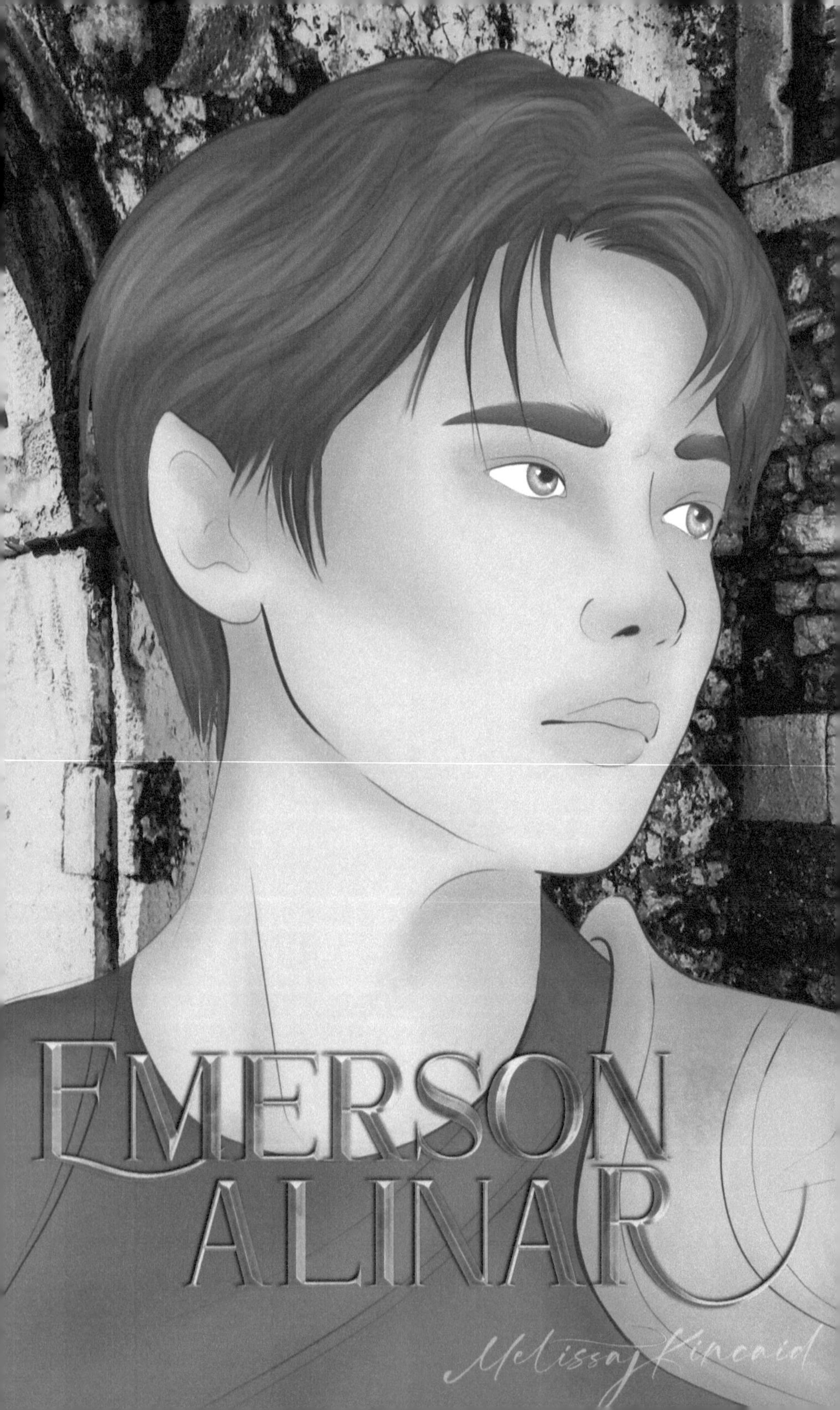

EMERSON
ALINAR
Melissa Kincaid

CHAPTER FIFTEEN

"Colkirk has the best mead you say? Well, you have not tried Mrs Mulvany's famous honey mead – best golden drop in the North I'd say! Come, they serve it in the tavern just around the corner," Lorch announced as they slipped down the main causeway amongst the bustling town of Viridya.

The town, connected to the castle grounds, was neat and spotless, the complete opposite to the dirty, rat infested towns making up the remainder of the North Court.

Visiting the town was something the King did monthly – ensuring he mingled with his loyal subjects. People bowed and sang praises his way as Lorch browsed their stalls, frequently complimenting the shopkeepers on their interesting wares and hoping their families were well.

Arii had been bold enough to ask why he did not frequent the other towns of his kingdom. Perhaps if he did so, he would see how much the people needed help. He had deflected her question, before moving on to how incredible the weather was – and had she been back to the pool since they were there last?

If she did not know any better, she would have thought he was avoiding her question altogether.

Well, she knew better.

Elijah and Arii trailed close behind as Lorch paused at a stall piled high with silks, the King's golden rings glittering on his outstretched hand as he fingered a billowing sheet of gossamer. As he conversed with the shopkeeper, Arii's head tilted to survey Elijah.

He had stopped, his cloaked hood angled towards a stall.

Arii's brows rose, wondering what had snagged the man's attention. Shifting to gaze around him, she noticed a little display laid out with rows and rows of little pots of paint and artists' tools. There was an incredible array of colours on display, from blues to yellows to oranges – some with matt finishes and some with hints of glitter mixed into the paint, setting off the rainbows of colours with sparkles in the sunlight.

The woman behind the counter smiled warmly, and Arii noticed her cheek was smeared with a streak of yellow paint. Her eyes were a warm brown – her skin a deep shade of brown and her dark hair pulled back into messy bun, the thick curls barely contained within the leather tie.

Arii's brows scrunched as her eyes darted up to Elijah's shadowed face.

"See any colours you like, My Lord?" the woman asked, her voice light and friendly. Despite the strange air around the hooded man, despite the fact she could not see her customer's face – it did not seem to deter the woman from offering her service. Her lips curled in a grin, a little space between her two front teeth appearing as she said, "We just received our shipment of hide canvases, they hold the colours far better once the paint dries – unlike the standard parchment." The woman angled her easel – showing them her artwork.

The canvass was covered in splatters of paint, no particular image to behold – but Arii could not help but stare at the random flurries of colour. They all worked so well together, the brush strokes haphazard and splotches of paint splattered like the woman had slit the throat of a unicorn – letting the rainbow lifeblood spray across the canvas like rain.

Of course, her mind would slide to violence.

"Can I put you down for some fresh canvas and paint, Master Wolfe? You always stop to look."

Arii's rows rose as the woman smiled at Elijah.

Strange, the shop owner acted as if Elijah was not a stranger to her.

Elijah hovered at the stall for a few moments more, before his deep, gentle voice drifted from the confines of his hood. "Thank you, Maggie – but not today."

Maggie nodded, busying herself in arranging some of the paint pots before her, seemingly nonplussed with his gentle rejection.

"Next time, then!"

As they continued on after Lorch, Arii whispered, "A painter, ay?"

Elijah remained silent, his boots barely making a sound. She knew he was surveying their surroundings for any signs of danger – any threat to the man before them. She was not expecting a reply, so when his voice drifted gently between them, she had to keep from glancing his way.

"I used to, but not for a long time."

"Do you visit the stall often? The clerk seems to know you."

His lips twitched before saying, "Sometimes I stop to see what new paints she had come up with. Maggie has a keen eye for colour."

It was strange, Arii did not see the harsh, brooding warrior as someone who would enjoy something as simple as painting. What would a man like Elijah hope to paint, anyway? There was a note to his voice that – had she not been so keenly aware of the tenor of his vocals – she would not have picked up. It was a tinge of sadness, a touch of longing for something he missed.

Arii risked a glance back at the art stall, watching as Maggie offered a wooden artists' palette to a browsing customer – her features bright in a smile.

Slowly, Arii's eyes drifted back to the cloaked man beside her, realising that she in fact still knew nothing about him. Simple things like what his favourite colour was, or how he enjoyed his coffee? Did he have a pinch of sugar with cream – or just straight black, bitter like the way he snapped at her in the training ring?

She was itching to know more.

So, as the afternoon sun dappled the market stalls as they cleared up for the night, Arii returned to the artist's stall, placing down a small bag of silver in front of the woman. Choosing a satchel of colours and a handful of supplies, along with a couple of canvas squares, Arii offered the woman a grin as she hefted the package into her arms and headed back to the castle.

There was a knock at his door that had Elijah pausing, his finger on a passage in the book he was reading. He placed it down, heading to the door, his brows drawn.

Opening the door, he paused, eyes dancing over empty air.

His eyes dropped to the floor, resting on a neatly packaged satchel of artist supplies, carefully bound in a ribbon of gold.

Elijah's brows shot up in a look of rare surprise as he cast his gaze down the hall both ways, wondering who had left the gift.

A gift? He *never* received gifts.

Hesitantly he dipped to lift the package, turning and pressing the door closed behind him with a gentle *click*.

Resting the parcel on his bed and stepping back, Elijah rubbed at his jaw, the look of surprise never leaving his face as his mind instantly danced to Arii. She had seen the way he had paused at the stall, his eyes catching on the beautiful array of paints and their assortment of colours. Could she have done this? He did not see her as the gift giving type.

Then again, he hardly knew her.

It had been so long since he had painted, so long since his hand had done anything but deliver violence and death. Art had once been an escape, something he enjoyed doing. Since his ascension to the King's bodyguard, he had not had the time – nor the drive – to pick up a brush and let his mind go.

He paused, noticing a little note tied to a gold string, the end curling around one of the thicker bristled brushes. Pinching the card, he flipped it to read the simple note scrawled in black ink. The writing was sloping and elegant, far neater than he expected of her.

I would like to see what those hands can do with a brush in them, brandishing paint instead of steel. Compose me a masterpiece.
Arii.

He imagined her face, eyes lightening with curiosity as she noticed his hesitation before the stall of art supplies, the gentle tilt of her head, her honey tipped hair sliding over her shoulders as she surveyed the arrangement of colourful paints. Sunlight had danced over her features, lighting her dark eyelashes with a tinge of gold as her lips twitched with a small smile.

That strange feeling began manifesting in his chest at the sight – at the hint of unveiled inquisitiveness that made her face soften.

Until her eyes met his, and the cool façade lifted like a mask once more.

He wanted so badly to trust her.

But around Lorch, he trusted no one.

Elijah stared at the note for a whole minute, his mind slowly slipping back to the gift.

Gods, she was so unexpected.

With a small smile, he began to unlace the golden ribbon.

⋐⋑

Arii was not sure why she was heading down the road, peering up at the hanging willows as dawn's light filtered through the leaves. She felt drawn to the pool, the peaceful place she had been introduced to by Lorch. That day felt so long ago.

The sun bounced off the crystal water that rippled gently, and she found her eyes sweeping the delicately swaying blades of grass as she paused.

When she saw his dark hair fluttering in the breeze, she did not feel surprise.

Arii paused a few paces away as Elijah touched a brush to the canvas resting on his knees, sitting on a blanket next to the array of paints she had purchased for him. He did not turn his head as he said, "You know, I have not held a brush in nine years."

She grinned. "I'll bet you're shit now, huh?"

His head tilted, silver eyes surveying her with a quirked brow, his expression lighter than she had been expecting.

"See for yourself."

She dipped to rest on her knees as she joined him on the blanket. Elijah angled the canvas, showing her the painting.

She felt her breath dash between her lips as her eyes glided over the almost perfect brush stroked image of the pool before them, the details intricate yet slightly abstract.

It was incredible.

"Holy hell," she whispered. "I take that back."

Her eyes drifted to Elijah, seeing his lips curling in the hint of a smile. Now if only he could paint *that*. His rare, hesitant smile – she would hang that over her mantelpiece like a prized possession.

Her hand reached out, hesitating a breath from his cheek as his eyes met hers, her fingertips hovering over a small smear of colour on his skin.

"You've got paint on your cheek," she whispered.

His expression changed then, an emotion she could not name fluttering over his face before becoming stoic once more, like a leaf falling to disturb the clear water before them – drifting out of sight and disappearing downstream.

Arii swallowed, gazing down and breaking the moment before the sudden tension between them became too much to handle.

"You're a master with blades, and now a master with a brush. Is there anything you can't do, Master Wolfe?" she said, her gaze sliding back to the canvas, before skipping to the rippling pool beyond. Birds darted over the water, catching bugs in the morning light as they dipped and dove.

Elijah gently placed the canvas down, and she swore she heard a deep exhale of breath – as if he had been holding it in.

"Well, I shouldn't admit to it but… I'm a rotten cook. Give me a rabbit to skin – but don't ask me to deliver anything spectacular."

Her eyes danced to him once more, surveying his silver eyes as he leaned back, hands splayed behind him and ankles crossing.

She had never seen him look so… relaxed.

It was a good look on him.

"Well, who expects you to cook when you have castle servants to do it for you?" she pointed out with a small smirk, watching as a breeze played with his dark hair.

"This is true," he agreed, his voice low and deep.

Oh, how far they had come. She had never thought they would be speaking in soft tones to one another, let alone sitting side by side on the banks of a tranquil, beautiful pool of water such as this.

There was no anger, no venom, no need to outmatch one another for once. Elijah lifted the canvas again, leaning to grasp a thin brush.

Arii leaned back, fingers splayed upon the warm blanket. Her head tilted, eyes fluttering closed as sunlight kissed her skin.

"What is your mother like? Colleen?" she asked softly, listening to the gentle swish of the brush against canvas. Elijah was silent for a few moments before speaking, his tone tinged with surprise.

"Colleen? She is a strong, gentle and kind woman. In all the years I have known her, never has she once raised her voice – even in anger."

When Arii's eyes opened, she saw that small smile once again twitching at the corner of his mouth. "She has always encouraged me to be the best person I can be, and not for a second has she ever doubted me. Of all people to have found me in the forest that day – I could not have asked for anyone better. She treats me like… like I'm her true born son. I have never felt anything but accepted by her."

Arii was surprised by his answer – and yet, she was not. Elijah spoke of his adopted mother with clear respect and admiration, and as her eyes danced from his face to the canvas, she felt a warmth bloom across her chest at his words. Despite what little she knew about the bodyguard, and despite his cool and withdrawn facade, one thing was obvious to her – he loved his family deeply.

"Your father?"

"Colleen's husband died a year before she found me."

"Oh, I'm so sorry." whispered Arii, surprised to feel a dash of sadness. Elijah inclined his head slightly, watching her for a few moments before continuing his work. "From what I have learned, he, Derek, died of Dragon Fever. They were married young, and Colleen speaks of him often. Even though I never met the man – I feel much of me has been moulded by his memory, living on through Colleen's undying love and admiration of him."

"And… do you ever think about your birth parents?"

Elijah dipped the tip of the brush into a pot of blue paint, his brows bunching as he considered her words. When he did not speak for a time, Arii felt perhaps she had overstepped. They were still almost strangers, after all. They may have found a soft middle ground – but that did not mean they trusted each other.

Finally, Elijah spoke, his voice a low whisper. "Sometimes…" he paused, before adding, "But I cannot remember their faces – so recalling who they were or what they were like is beyond my memory's clarity."

"That must be difficult," she said.

"Yes, but I have learned to accept it over time."

Arii tried to imagine what it was like – to have years and years of yourself lost beyond a hazy void – just out of reach. Again, she found herself wondering what could have happened to this hesitant, misunderstood man beside her, where he came from and *who* he truly was.

With a sigh, Elijah began to shift, packing up the paints and brushes as he said, "I appreciate the gift, Miss Clearwater. It was strangely thoughtful of you."

Her lips pursed as she retorted, "You think me incapable of giving gifts?"

Elijah's hands paused over his brushes, head tilting to look at her. "Well, yes. You do not seem the gift giving type. From what

I have seen so far, I believe all you'd give is the gift of death," he replied, his tone smooth and deadly serious. His silver eyes lifted, meeting hers. Arii's tongue pressed to the roof of her mouth, her brows climbing in a look of mock surprise. Oh, he knew her far better than she gave him credit for.

"Well, you're off my Winter Solstice gift list then, Wolfe."

His lips twitched in reply as he gathered the supplies. Slowly, she moved to help him, corking the top of a pot of mercury-coloured paint. She held the container up, watching as the light filtered through the glass – causing the paint to shimmer within.

"This one… This is my favourite." she whispered.

Elijah stood, eyeing her with an unreadable expression as she added, "It reminds me of your eyes."

He held out a hand to her.

After a small moment of hesitation, Arii placed her hand in his, the callouses of his fingers brushing her palm before firming his hold – pulling her to her feet.

Suddenly she was against his chest, her palms splayed as they both became still. Head up to gaze at him, her lips parted lightly.

She knew she should move, should step away, but she just could not bring herself to do so. His scent fluttered over her Fae senses, that annoying tug pinching at the middle of her chest once more.

"You know now of something I enjoy, it's only fair you divulge to me something of yours," he whispered, not making to move away either. His head tilted ever so slightly, eyes roaming her face as if he were trying to solve a puzzle.

Arii envisioned her blade as it slid through tender skin – the feel of warm blood as it skittered across her face and drenched her fingers. She imagined splitting the throat of someone sinister, making them smile from ear to ear.

Did she truly enjoy death? Or had it become all she really knew?

No… no, that was not true. Another thought came to mind.

She imagined her fingers skimming the smooth cover of a book, the smell of the paper, the feeling of excitement as she delved into a brand-new story – into a world far brighter, happier and better than her own. Holding a book reminded her of her father, as she perched upon his knee in his study, listening to the soothing cadence of his voice as he read to her. Images flickered across her mind – a shadow memory of her father's face, smooth, angular and strong, his hair as dark as decadent chocolate and eyes the colour of midnight.

He had sparked her love of reading, tending to it until it was a raging flame, her little hands eager to grasp the next tome and delve into another world. She once wished to place quill to paper and weave her own story – a story of dragons, magic, strong heroes, and fearless heroines, along with incredible foes. She had looked up at her father as she described her fantastical stories, grinning as she said, *"Don't worry, Da. Good always wins in my story, for evil will be driven away by magic, and love. Magic and love will always save the world from darkness... Right?"*

Oh, how wrong she had been.

Their land – their *home* had been plummeting into a blackening abyss for far longer than she had existed, plagued with fear that outweighing the good in the world. Uncertainty had created division... division had created fear... and then fear had begun to tear Fythnar apart.

And magic? Once a glittering, shining, spectacular force – now it was but a sigh upon the wind.

Despite the darkness, small stories of hope remained, inked into countless tomes nestled in libraries across the land. Stories of a land united, rich and prosperous. A shadow of pain bloomed across her chest at the thought of her father, at the rare feeling of grief she felt at his loss. She suddenly had the strange urge to be embraced, to press her face into a warm chest. It was not a feeling she was wholly unfamiliar with – but it was one she had buried deep in the confines of her black heart, even now.

Despite the time that had passed since her father's death, despite her suppression of emotion and the blood on her hands – she still felt that flutter in her stomach when faced with a wall full of unread books. No matter how much death she faced, no matter how much violence she witnessed, she was sure her love of books would remain until her very last breath.

In that moment, as she stared up into Elijah's eyes, she was reminded of that eagerness once more – to discover a new story…

His story.

They say not to judge a book by its cover – and she would fully admit that she had a bad habit of doing just that, reaching for the books with the most intricate and beautiful covers. She imagined Elijah as a dark, alluring and sturdy book with intricate silver detailing, just waiting to be held gently and opened slowly.

She had a feeling he would take time – *lots* of time to reveal the details of his chronicle. She imagined it as a carefully woven adventure, shrouded in thick, opaque mist. He had told her he had no memory of his past before being adopted.

Arii felt almost sheepish now, having judged Elijah so harshly in the beginning. As she stared into his deep, steel grey eyes – she noticed tiny dark flecks in amongst the silver.

"I do enjoy a bloody good book…" she whispered finally in response to his question, her hands pressing gently upon his chest. Beneath her palms she could feel the steady – albeit slightly quickening – thump of his heart.

A whole new look shimmered across Elijah's features. It surprised her just how expressive his face could be, and if he was anything like herself, then the expressions were involuntary. She imagined it to be a look of curiosity but was unsure as it faded just as quickly as it had appeared.

"It's strange…" he said, and she felt the gentle press of his palm against her lower back.

"What is?" she murmured, feeling her cheeks begin to flush under his unblinking gaze.

"I didn't think you'd be able to sit still long enough to absorb a book."

Her brows began to narrow, heat rising to her cheeks. "What is that supposed to mean?"

A tiny smirk, then that heart jerking dimple formed on his right cheek.

Oh.

Was he… *flirting* with her?

Like a fish out of water, she was unable to do anything but open her mouth for a moment.

"That's a little harsh, even for you," was all she could manage, eventually.

Brows rising, Elijah whispered. "Alright, prove it then. This is my first afternoon off in some time." His head tilted ever so slightly, his hair brushing across his forehead as he drawled, "Accompany me to the library? That is – unless you have somewhere else to be?"

Her heart fluttered in her chest.

This Elijah… this Elijah was new. She was not sure what to make of it – but she could see a haze of hesitation in his eyes despite his words.

She knew he had walls – heavy steel walls much like her own, wrapped tightly around his defences. It was evident in his movements, in his speech, and the way he hid behind the cloak. This… this was delving way passed his comfort zone, that she was sure of.

Question was… was she willing to let a tiny bit of her own defences slip in response?

Her fingers brushed the front of his tunic, delicately plucking at the buttons as she gathered her labyrinth of thoughts. Warmth warred against ice as a small storm began to ripple into existence in her stomach, years of suppression causing her insides to curl into a knot. Between them, warmth stirred. They were close, so close.

"I appreciate the offer – but…" she paused, biting her lip. She felt she were on the tip of unfamiliar territory once again, and as was her way – she felt the impulsive need to withdraw into herself. Her eyes lifted, meeting his as she rasped, "Tikkani needs me for this… thing."

Argh, it took everything within her not to cringe at just how pathetic she sounded.

Elijah huffed a small laugh, before being the first to step back – his expression nonplussed. He plucked the pot of paint from her grasp, placing it back in the satchel at their feet.

"Perhaps next time. We should get back," he said as she watched him pack in silence.

The moment had passed – whatever that moment had been, and she felt the absence of his warmth like a strike to the chest.

He straightened, casting his gaze over her and hitching the leather satchel upon his shoulder. "The Viridya library holds some incredible stories, ones I know are hard to find anywhere else. I'm sure Lorch would allow you free access anytime you like," he said gently.

As Elijah turned to stride away, Arii was left staring in his wake – uncharacteristically lost for words.

MelissaJKincaid

CHAPTER SIXTEEN

The events of the night she had escaped Viridya Castle with her mother plagued Arii's young mind in nightmares for weeks afterward, even after they had found haven in Evergrave with a small family of Shifters. Approaching the town, dirty and exhausted, the family took them in without hardly a thought. By this time, everyone in the continent knew of what had transpired in the castle, and what had befallen the royal family. Even now in the present, the memories seemed to slide back into the forefront of her mind unbidden.

"You gonna eat that?"

Arii gazed up from her barely-touched stew to the boy sitting across from her, his vivid green eyes fixed on the bowl clutched in her palms. The boy's hair was long, as dark as a raven's wings and as shaggy as a dog's coat.

"Um, no. I'm not hungry," said Arii, hesitantly offering the bowl to the boy. He was skinny and lanky, but she noticed that he ate as much as the grown men some nights.

Where in Fythnar did all that food go?

"Thanks!" the boy chirped, taking the offering, and digging in.

Arii watching him wolf down the stew with wide violet eyes.

"Arii, wash your hands and get ready for bed," said a gentle voice from a nearby hut.

Evergrave was a town of elaborately carved wooden homes nestled in amongst the thick, tall trees of the Evergrave Forest in the East Court of Fythnar. Many of the homes were carved into the impossibly large trunks of the ancient pine trees, accessible by winding wood staircases and pulley-operated elevator systems. It had taken Arii some time to get used to the height, often feeling woozy as she slowly made her way across the swaying bridges that joined the homes together in amongst the treetops. At first, she had refused to even be lifted in an elevator, only agreeing when her mother promised to shield her eyes the entire way up.

She was not terrified anymore, but that did not mean she would be swinging from the branches and flying across the bridges like the boy before her often did. She took the bridges and stairs with caution, her little face pursed with concern whenever she had to move from one home to another.

Now the boy was looking back at her, his teeth flashing in a toothy grin as he set down the empty bowl.

Shortly after they had been taken in, Arii had been approached by the boy, his cheerful grin and playful nature easing the confusion and fear within her. She was hesitant at first, but he persisted and soon the two children were playing together, becoming firm friends. Arii felt she had not smiled in weeks, but Krepth had a way about him that made her forget her worries – just for a little while.

"Don't forget, tomorrow I'm gonna show you the rock pools I told you about," he said, grinning and showing little sharp canines. The Shifters were so much like the Fae, only they did not have inhuman strength and speed, instead their magic gave them the ability to shift into an animal that resonated with their soul. Where Fae could conjure and use their magic in all sorts of ways – the Shifters could not save for a few with healing abilities.

Arii stood and dusted off her knees, giving the boy a smile. "Oh yes, I can't wait. Promise you'll show me how to skip rocks on the water, like you told me about."

Krepth gave her a gangly fingered salute as she turned and followed her mother into the little home they were occupying. It was not the biggest home in the treetop town, but it was warm and cosy. Windows had been cut into the walls, shielded with wavy glass that caused droplets of rain to run in random patterns. The room had a little kitchen, the benchtops and cupboards carved from the golden wood of the tree itself, fixed with a silver sink and taps.

A metal-hedged hearth was set into the wall with a carved flue running up and out, designed for cooking meals inside. There was a lot of wooden texture in the small space, but soft purple cushions on the carved sofa and the soft white down bed across from it helped offset the onslaught of wood. Intricately woven tapestries of forest animals hung around the room, making it more homely than cramped.

Candlelight flickered on the warm hued walls. At the hearth, her mother coughed loudly and Arii found herself glancing her way. "Mama, your cough is getting worse."

The woman turned and smiled at her daughter, raising a white handkerchief to her lips. "It's getting cooler now, my little violet. You know my cough gets worse when it grows cold."

Arii padded to the bed, nestling amongst the pillows and thick down coverlet. "I know, but it sounds worse today."

Her mother had a cough, and Arii knew that back when they lived in the castle, she had approached the healers in hopes of finding relief. Arii was too young to understand that her mother had been suffering for a long time with Dragon Fever, a slow painful disease that attacked the lungs and caused excruciating, burning pain in the chest and throat, akin to what it would be like to breathe fire. Despite healers working with magic and endless concoctions of herbs, Dragon Fever had no known cure.

Her mother approached with a mug of milk that she had warmed over the fire, sitting on the bed next to her daughter. "Always worrying, my little one. If you worry any more, you'll have permanent frown lines between your brows." She wiped a finger tenderly between the girl's eyes, smoothing the little creases there, causing her to giggle.

"I love you, Mama," she whispered, clutching the mug between her fingers and breathing in the hint of cinnamon her mother had

stirred in. She had always loved cinnamon.

"I love you too, my little violet," the woman whispered, tucking her handkerchief, stained with crimson blood under her pillow, away from the little girl's view.

"Drink, then sleep," she said, rising from the bed and moving to clear the kitchen. The girl drank her milk before sliding under the covers. Her eyes drifted closed, and she was soon sinking into a dreamless sleep.

Arii awoke next to her mother a few hours later, and immediately knew something was wrong. Her mother's breaths were shallow, her brow glittering with beads of sweat. Her skin, normally a gentle olive hue, was now the pallor of chalk.

Arii slowly placed a hand on her mother's cheek, the woman's own violet eyes red-rimmed and glassy. Arii felt her chest begin to constrict, her tongue too big for her mouth.

"M-Mama? Are you alright?" she forced out, her voice shaking.

Her mother coughed, but the sound was weak, a gentle groan escaping her pale lips.

Arii slid from the bed and ran, throwing open the door and sprinting as quickly as her little legs could carry her to Krepth's door, unfazed by the wobbly bridge separating their homes that would have normally caused her to pause and cross gingerly, clutching the hand ropes tight. She slammed her hands against the thick wooden door, tears pricking her eyes.

"Mrs Hallier? Krepth? Please, it is my mother, she's... she's unwell!"

The door opened quickly and a woman with long, jet black hair mussed from sleep stared down at her. "Ariiaya? What..."

"My mother!" It was all she could muster, a feeling of thick dread beginning to coil in her tiny belly.

The woman was swift, grabbing a cloak and throwing it across her shoulders before sweeping past the little girl. Arii was quickly following, her numb little body immune to the cool night. Through the slowly boiling panic in her mind, she heard Krepth's footsteps *behind her, his muffled yawn puffing mist into the night sky.*

"Arii?" he said, rubbing his eyes and following after them.

Mrs Hallier swept into their little home and dropped to her knees beside the bed, her fingers dancing over the rasping woman's forehead, then pressing to the pulse at her neck. Swiftly, the Shifter woman parted the front of her mother's tunic and pressed her hand, fingers splayed on her skin. Gentle, glowing light emanated from the Shifter's fingers as she whipped around and barked at her son. "Krepth, go get Freya, swiftly now!"

With a look of determination replacing sleepiness, Krepth straightened, and with a quick glance at Arii, spun and dashed into the night.

Sprinting across the little bridge, Krepth let his magic sweep through him, welcoming the change as his body flashed into that of a midnight wolf pup. Four legs were swifter than two.

Arii stood, fixed in the doorway of the room.

This tiny, wooden haven, nothing like the glorious and spacious rooms at the castle, had become a home – a place she shared with her mother and where she finally felt safe. The people, the strange placid people who took the forms of many different animals, had become her family.

But this place was nothing without her mother in it.

Her mother was her home.

Soon a long, delicate fingered hand gently lay on her shoulder as a tall, willowy woman entered. Her hair was as white as freshly fallen snow, her face long and delicately angled. Her eyes, lashed thickly with white, were as black as the night sky, flecked with tiny spots of silver.

Freya Bloom's eyes reminded Arii of laying in the fields surrounding the forest with Krepth, spotting constellations that resembled animals in the dark sky. Freya's gaze was heavy, as if that very night sky were pressing on her shoulders.

"Little one, we are going to try to help your mother. I need you to stay with Krepth, just beyond the doorway." Her voice was like

bells on the wind.

"But–"

"Come, Arii," said Krepth from behind her, and she felt a warm hand curl around hers.

Freya swiftly joined Mrs Hallier and then Arii saw the two women bent over her mother, their voices soft.

Freya Bloom was the Queen of the East Court and she was powerful. If anyone could help her mother, she could.

Arii let Krepth pull her out into the cool air, and almost flinched when the boy draped a small cloak around her shaking shoulders. She glanced up at the boy, his green eyes luminous in the flickering golden light of the cabin. His dark brows were pulled in concern. Without thinking, she lifted a hand and rubbed the spot between his brows with her thumb. Krepth's expression remained unusually serious, but softened ever so slightly. "She's going to be alright, Arii, you'll see."

Arii had come to love the boy. She did not have siblings, and Krepth was the closest thing she had to a brother. Her lips wobbled as she stared at her friend, biting her bottom lip to ease its trembling. "She's never been this bad, Krepth, ever."

The two children sat, and Krepth placed his arm around her shoulders, resting her head against his neck. He was a few inches taller, and she felt the warmth of his body. It was comforting, yet her mind was in the room with her mother. The pit of her stomach remained coiled, bubbling like a pot of stew, the hairs of her arms rising under the cloak, like she had a terrible chill.

It felt like an eternity before the door to her home opened, and Mrs Hallier entered the night. Her eyes were glassy, her cheeks flushed.

"Arii," she whispered. The girl flinched, having begun to slip into a light snooze on her friend's shoulder. She stood quickly, little hands balling. Krepth stood slowly beside her, completely and utterly silent.

"My darling..." she paused before continuing, "You can come

in now."

Arii swallowed thickly and inched past the woman as she moved to join her son. Everything around her turned to haze as Arii entered the cabin, her eyes going straight to where her mother lay. Freya was perched on the edge of the bed, before standing and turning to face her. The Shifter's eyes were pitch black – all trace of the silver flecks resembling stars were gone.

"Arii, come," she said gently.

Arii mechanically lifted her feet, one after another as she approached the Queen and stared down at her mother's still form.

"My darling, she is very weak. The Dragon's Fever has damaged her beyond repair, she is..." the woman paused. "She has not long left with us. I am so sorry, sweet child."

Arii's hearing began to fade, her little, delicately pointed ears rendered useless in that moment. She slowly made her way to her mother, her vision blurring as her eyes filled with tears. "Mama?"

The woman's head moved ever so slightly, her violet eyes finding her daughter. Arii swore her mother's eyes seemed to drift past her. "Come here, my little violet," she sighed, her voice barely audible.

Arii climbed upon the bed, slotting herself against her mother.

She smelled... strange.

Her skin which once smelled of roses and sweet sugar, now smelled musky and tainted.

"I'm sorry, my beautiful, strong little darling."

"S-Sorry?" Arii choked.

"Sorry that I cannot stay. You are so strong, my little violet fire. I know you will continue on when I am gone. Promise me you will live your life and bring change to those around you."

Arii gasped through the sobs beginning to form in her throat. "But, I can't... N-Not without you."

Her mother's laugh was a weak whisper. "You can do anything you set your mind to, my child. Already the children of the East Court respect you. You are strong, so much so that they believe that if you were a shifter, you'd take the form of a proud lioness."

Arii pressed her face into the damp skin of her mother's chest. "Don't go... I can't..." she wailed. She knew that when the Gods decided someone's time was up on the Earth, nothing could change their fate. That little fact had been ingrained into her from a young age.

"My legacy is you, Ariiaya. I know you will make me proud. Even if my body is not here to see it, my spirit certainly will." The girl lifted her head and stared at her mother's hazy eyes. Her mother's thumb whispered across Arii's brow, smoothing the lines there, before her hand gently fell to the bed.

"I love you, my little violet," she whispered as the light drifted from her eyes.

Arii stared, her mother's flawless face a blur before her. Her heart squeezed and her throat became impossibly tight as sobs began to wrack her little body.

"Mama?" she whispered.

But her mother's chest did not rise again.

"Mama?"

Pain tore through her. Great, heaving gasps began to shake from her lips, her skull began to throb.

Her mother's chest still did not rise.

"M-Mama?"

The coil in her stomach turned to stone, and her fingers tingled as she clutched her mother's tunic. The little girl shook, hoping beyond all hope that her mother's eyes would open again.

She sobbed, knowing in her heart that they never would.

Pain, pain was pressing in on her, the walls of the cabin threatened to swallow her whole. Hot tears cascaded down her cheeks, teeth sinking into her lip as she convulsed. The sound of a million humming bees began to swarm her senses, and her chest rose as her eyes snapped wide. She tasted something sweet, washing over her tongue and shooting down her throat. It was as if her head was being held underwater, and she was forgetting how to breathe.

Her mother was gone, and there was nothing she could do to get her back.

A pain unlike anything she had ever experienced ignited in her tiny chest, shattering something within her heart. She screamed as the pain flared out and exploded from her body, the shockwave rattling the pots and pans in the kitchen, shaking the glass windows.

Her world exploded into blinding sparks.

Awakening magic rocketed across the forest, causing the trees to shake and sleeping birds to flee their nests with cries of alarm.

The door flew open, and Freya was scooping the girl into her arms as Arii screamed.

She screamed for her lost mother, screamed for her lost father, and screamed to the Gods as the foreign feeling of magic erupted within her, sizzling her nerves and blinding her eyes with stars.

The Queen gripped her tightly as the little Fae girl's magic awoke that night, rattling the forest and no doubt awakening many just beyond their borders.

Freya knew that on the 'morrow, three women would enter the forest to claim little Ariiaya Trillia as their own, whipping her away to the shadowy school upon the western bluff of Fythnar.

As was the fate of all Fae who had magic awaken within them.

A fate Freya believed worse than death.

The grief Arii felt for the loss of her parents, the deep tearing anguish in her soul, was slowly replaced with shards of ice as she built an impenetrable wall of cold steel around her heart. If the many years spent training in the School of Fate had taught Arii anything, it was that emotion clouded judgement, and pain was naught but a feeling that could be pushed to the deepest reaches of the mind.

Now her solid walls were in threat of being slowly torn down by an unusual warm-hearted King and his wickedly deadly, silver eyed bodyguard.

How had Fythnar's most deadly assassin become entangled in a triangle of temptation and desire? Had the Three Fates known what they were sending her into, known that she would question everything she had been trained not to feel?

☙❧

Arii's brows creased as she stalked towards the training area, absolutely ready to hand Elijah's arse to him on a silver blade in the ring today. Her body was humming with confused frustration and coiled anger. She needed release, but absolutely refused to sate anything outside of the training ring.

Entering the training hall, she snatched a sword from the array of weapons and turned to face the ring, expecting to see the dark haired, hulking guard standing there.

Instead, she stared at Sybell Kruel.

"I dismissed Master Wolfe for a few hours," said the woman as she tightened the buckles on her boots, before straightening and adjusting the sleeves of her lightweight guard uniform.

Arii just stared, dumbstruck.

The golden-haired princess rested her hands on her hips and tapped her booted foot impatiently as she snipped, "Are we to train or not?"

"Erm, not."

Sybell's chocolate eyes narrowed at her tone.

Arii paused before adding. "No offence, Princess, but I wouldn't want to hurt you," she said as she began to place the sword back on the rack.

Suddenly a dagger flew over her shoulder, crashing against the rack and causing some of the weapons to fall. The clanging sound that rang out as steel met stone floor was almost deafening.

Arii slowly turned to face the Princess.

Sybell was breathing hard, her hand still hanging in mid-air from her sloppy throw of the dagger.

"I fucking order you to train with me, you *little bitch*!"

Oh, if only Arii was but a *little bitch*.

Lips pursing, Arii picked up one sword, then another and turned to the ring.

"Alright then," she said derisively, pacing forward and tossing one sword to the Princess.

Unbelievably, the woman caught it by the grip with two hands.

Arii's brows climbed on her forehead as Sybell moved into an extremely poor fighting stance.

"If I may ask, why do you wish to learn, Princess?" Arii flipped the sword in her hand as she spoke. "I would have thought you'd be too afraid of breaking a nail."

"I am sick of everyone telling me what I can and cannot do!"

The Princess' sword flew through the air, and Arii blocked it easily. Steel glimmered, aiming for her head. Arii blocked again. By the slow and untrained way the woman moved, Arii knew she had only handled a sword a handful of times.

"Isn't that part of being a Princess?" Arii said stiffly.

"Why does it have to be?" retorted Sybell.

Clang.

"Well, I guess it's just to be expected? Your life is not your own."

Clang.

"Exactly, it's vexatious!"

Clang.

"Ohh, big words, did you learn that in court?"

Sybell swiped at Arii's middle with a grunt of anger and the Fury chuckled as she half-heartedly blocked the woman's attempt with one hand on her sword.

"Look, Princess, I admire your tenacity, but you have guards to protect you. You don't need to learn how to fight."

With a frustrated cry, Sybell began an assault, her sword flinging through the air. Arii met her swings with hardly any effort, twisting away from her.

Gods, where was Elijah? She almost *wanted* to see his hulking, brooding form right now.

"Teach me, *godsdamnit*!" the Princess practically howled.

Arii paused, surveying the woman panting before her. Her

cheeks were flushed and red, blonde hair dishevelled and eyes puffy as if she had been crying not long ago. Her chest rose and fell, and she did not ease from her fighting stance. Well, if the Princess were not such a brat, maybe she would be more inclined to give in to her request.

"What about Master Wolfe?"

"Hah, he barely looks my way let alone speaks to me."

"Commander Hawke?"

"Refuses, constantly. Gives me a pained expression like I am asking him to hand over his first-born son."

"Maybe if you placed a please in your sentences every now and then, perhaps they would be more inclined?"

"I – I want to know how to defend myself."

"Defend yourself, or make an example of anyone who refuses you?"

The Princess huffed and waved the sword in front of her but remained silent as she seethed. Her gaze never left the Fury. In a strange way, Sybell reminded her of a couple of the younger assassins she had helped train at the School a few years ago. They had been angry, confused, and eager to spill some blood, having no idea why they had been taken from their families by three mysterious women. The School had been made up of predominantly women, as female Fae who displayed magic were far more common than male Fae with magic.

The new recruits needed stability and solidarity. Having a weapon and knowing how to use it was a starting point in their search to finding their purpose.

"Please."

Arii's reverie broke and her attention zeroed back to the woman. Had she just…

"Please," Sybell hissed again, her tone lightening ever so slightly.

If Arii's brows could continue rising on her forehead, they would have.

She studied the woman, before nodding. "Fine, as you asked so nicely."

Sybell blew out a breath, as if the word had pained her. She heaved in a sigh and lifted the sword again.

"Firstly, you are holding the sword wrong," Arii pointed out, pacing over to the woman. She tapped the pommel end of Sybell's sword with the tip of her blade. "Your hands are too close together; you need to grip it like this."

Arii lifted her sword and gripped the leather for her to see. "It gives you much sturdier handling and makes it less likely your sword can be flipped from your hands."

Sybell moved to mirror her.

"Good." Arii moved around her and tapped the back of the woman's leg with the flat of her sword. "Legs further apart…"

From the shadows, Hawke watched the women as they trained, his eyes smouldering with worry and his weathered features lined with exhaustion.

"I can think of many more preferable tutors for the Princess, honestly," Hawke glanced at Elijah as the man joined him in the shadows.

"She's so very stubborn," Hawke sighed and pinched the bridge of his nose. "Just like her mother."

"But she is also strong, just like her father."

Hawke paused at that and glanced at Elijah openly. Elijah stared back, his expression unreadable as Hawke replied with, "Or perhaps she is a sad, lost fool, just like her father too."

ELIJAH
WOLFE
Melissa Kincaid

Chapter Seventeen

She would not admit it to anyone, but Arii felt surprisingly proud of the Princess' eagerness to learn the art of combat. The young woman – despite not having a flicker of experience – had given it her all during their few hours of training. As they left the arena, Arii was nowhere close to winded or sated, but she felt a strange contentment drift over her. Unused to the feeling, she pressed it aside as she pulled shut the door to her room – weaving her damp hair into a quick braid before setting her sights down the golden hall.

With the remainder of her day, Arii decided to visit the castle library. She was determined to find out more about the Herington family history.

Pressing her palms upon the heavy mahogany doors, Arii entered the library. The room was bathed in afternoon light, amber tinged clouds drifting lazily beyond the domed glass ceiling. Her eyes drifted across the stunning room, noting that thankfully it was vacant. She thought the less people who knew what she was looking for, the better.

Pacing past the still pool, she headed towards the first row of shelves, skimming her fingertips along the leather-bound spines of different coloured books. Neat golden plaques labelled each section, and as she drifted along, she noted the various genres.

Fiction, Non-Fiction, Biography, Classic Literature, Horror and Mystery… the plaques and shelves seemed almost endless. Finally, she eyed the section she had been searching for.

History.

Arii paused at a stack near the rear of the room, passing her fingertips over the golden plaque as her eyes skimmed the spines, reading the titles. She plucked three books from the shelves and headed in the direction of a table by the window.

Dropping her haul onto the wood with a thump, Arii plopped onto the padded settee nearby and coughed as a plume of dust rose from the books. She waved a hand in front of her face, before leaning forward and brushing the fine veil of dust off the papers. Well, it seemed no one had picked these particular tomes in some time. She fanned them out before her, surveying the titles before focusing her attention on one with a dark leather cover, the least dusty. She turned it over, brows furrowing as she surveyed the cover – embossed with gold leaf.

The North: Past and Present.

Arii gently opened to the page of contents, and eagerly thumbed to the first chapter. The book was thick, and she could tell that it was a fairly recent publication. Strange… perhaps it had been added to the stacks recently and slid next to its dirty library mates. Judging by the dust on the other tomes, Arii guessed the history section was not visited often.

Leaning back into the padded settee and propping her feet upon the table, Arii settled into the quiet ambience – the gentle swish of turning paper and the constant hum of the distant waterfall beyond the only sounds.

The book contained a lot of what she already knew of the North's history, beginning two hundred and eighty years ago – the powerful Fae families who ruled upon each throne in the North, South, East and West, and the precarious yet short time across all four courts known as *The Time of Peace*. Her eyes roved an intricately decorated timeline of major events, and she surveyed the slow decline of the land. From the time of peace came *The Time of Divide*. Two hundred and twenty years ago, the rulers of the land began to see signs of unrest amongst their people. It began with small uprisings within the lowest notches of society – insignificant instances of crime that began to manifest into town square gatherings lead by outspoken individuals. Voices grew louder and fear began to bloom. Arii noticed that most of the unrest took place in the North, and all of that unrest was voiced by the humans. As the rulers upon the North throne grew stronger, so too did the uprisings. They warped from angry voices in a town square to violence and bloodshed. As she worked her way down to the main event of two hundred years ago, known as *The Time of Darkness*, Arii's eyes narrowed.

Humans began to rise up against the rulers of the Northern court, and slowly a strong population of Fae who lived amongst the humans became targets of violence and assassinations. Despite their strength and magic, the Fae became victims within their own homes. Neighbours turned against neighbours, servants against lords and the risings were swift.

Steadily the Fae race began to wane, and the violence reached its inky fingers towards castle Viridya. The ruling family began to fight amongst themselves. Some believed the humans deserved better treatment than they were receiving, and many did not.

Arii tapped her finger to her lip in contemplation.

What had the northern rulers done to raise such violence from their human subjects? She had read of similar uprisings in the other courts, leading to a steady decline of Fae. She had heard rumours of mistreatment of human slaves by some of the wealthier Fae, but so far she had found it hard to find evidence of such.

Her finger danced over a full-page illustration of a soaring, open mouthed dragon. The detail was impressive, sparkling magic flames swirling from its jaws, the spines of its back lit with sparks of lightening. She swore she could see the reflection of a burning city in its intelligent eyes. Finally, she noticed a hooded rider upon its back, nestled between the spikes of its shoulder blades – the figure's arm lifted and brandishing a flaming sword.

As she flipped back and forth between pages, scouring the dense paragraphs for further information, she noticed a peculiar section – pausing and running her finger along the dark ink.

Some said the Northern rulers had more magic than what was deemed to be 'balanced', and some even believed the ruler at the time, King Corvus Herington – the great grandfather of Tyverus Herington – had shown signs of madness. With the loss of his dragon – Lysander – during The Battle at Twilight one hundred and seventy years ago, the King of the North vowed that he would find enough dragons to bind all Fae in the North. This was the beginning of the end of the Fae.

She knew a little about *The Battle at Twilight*. The humans had amassed a significant army, and the first battle in many years had erupted on the vast expanse of space now known as The Wastes – just to the west of Viridya. Many lives had been lost – human, elf and Fae alike, bones scattered amongst the misty bogs that now resided there. A haunted place, a cursed place – shrouded with acrid mist that was said to drive people mad. The event had been the true beginning of the dark times they now faced.

Arii quirked a brow, quickly flipping to the forward of the book, surveying the small paragraph about the author. Thomas Clark, a human scholar, studied at the Great College of the West Court, who had then transferred to be a court scholar in the Northern Court.

Huh, human.

Arii wondered how diluted these notes had become after a few human lifecycles and considered grabbing another tome before she paused on a new chapter heading.

The Death of a Royal Line, a new Age of Men.

Feeling a rise in curiosity, Arii flipped the page just as a throat cleared behind her.

It was not often that she was caught unawares, and Arii felt as if her skin almost leaped off her bones as she slammed the tome shut and sprang from her place, whirling to see Elijah leaning against a nearby bookshelf, arms folded across his chest and hood firmly in place.

His lips held a hint of a smirk.

"Decided to take my advice with the library, Miss Clearwater?"

Heart thundering in her ears, she narrowed her gaze on the bodyguard as she hissed, "Elijah! Fuckin-"

"What are you reading?" he interrupted before the curse could fully form and burst from her lips, his head inclining towards the small stack of books. "Let me guess… thriller? Romance, perhaps?"

Romance?

Gods no.

"Do I look like the romance type?" she snapped, dipping to gather the stack.

Elijah's chuckle was low and deep. "I'd place my gold on a blood splattered horror – if your temper is anything to go by."

"Argh, what do you want, Elijah?"

Elijah's smile faded as he watched her slide the books back into their homes. "You did not attend training this morning."

Arii rolled her eyes dramatically before turning to face the man. "Uh huh, I had other commitments this morning."

"Other… commitments? You?"

Her lips pursed as she strode towards him, her hands resting upon her hips as she glared up at his shadowed face. "That's right."

She swore he leaned forward slightly as he growled, "You have one priority, one commitment and that – Miss Clearwater – is ensuring you are at your best to defend the King."

Gods, he made her blood boil. Or perhaps she was still jumpy from being interrupted.

Then she paused.

"Wait… I *was* in the training area this morning. Where the hell were *you*?!"

A small flash of teeth.

"I saw what you did for the Princess. Something tells me that kindness is not something you show often. Two acts of kindness in two days? Perhaps I haven't been harsh enough in the ring."

Her lips twitched. "Perhaps not. Maybe the implementation of leather straps and cuffs is required? A little… you know–"

"I never took you for a history buff," interrupted Elijah, flipping through the pages of one of the books she had selected.

She snatched the tome back, eyes shooting like daggers as she shoved it in its place. "Haven't you a king to watch over?" she said, brows high as Elijah leaned casually against the bookcase, closer now. His hood remained; half of his face cloaked in shadow as his lips curled in his usual hint of a smile.

"His Highness is in meetings all day. I was just on my way to return to him when I heard you humming. What were you hoping to find in those tomes?"

Wait, had she been humming? Well, she supposed it was a possibility… she had been quite absorbed in her reading material up until her rude interruption.

"Sometimes the best stories come from events of truth. The recruits were speaking of dragons earlier, I wanted to read more about them," she replied, leaning her shoulder against the bookcase, mirroring his stance. She added, "What do you know of the history of this land, Elijah?"

His smirk slowly dropped, bottom jaw sliding forward slightly as he pondered her words. "I'll admit, I know basic history of the North, but most of my time has been spent training as a soldier, Miss Clearwater. I guess you could say I prefer to make my own history, and not relive that of others. The past is the past."

"Be that as it may, do you not see the state of the land we live in? It has been this way for a long time – at some point in history some people made some bad choices that began the slow decline of Fythnar. Courts once united slowly turned against one another."

"The King is doing all he can to-"

"Bullshit."

The air slowly turned tense at her harsh word, and Arii straightened suddenly, hands balling to fists as her chin lifted. Was everyone in this castle so absorbed in its golden walls that they were unable to see what their land was becoming? She was not sure about the other courts, but the North was swiftly darting into ruin – and from what she has witnessed so far of Lorch and his royal advisers, none seemed to be doing anything about it. They just continued to hold their royal gatherings and splash money into places that did not need it.

Elijah straightened also, mouth drawn in a deep frown, a twitch ticking in his jaw. Slowly he leaned forward, and she could feel the heat of him as he growled, "You'll do well not to speak ill of our King in my presence, soldier."

"Oh, pull your head out of your arse, Elijah. Do you deny my words?"

"I am not blind to the blights of our land, but Lorch is looking for ways to bring the North back to its former glory."

"Its former glory involved magic, Elijah. Is Lorch willing to consider its return if it means things may get better?"

"You speak dangerous words, Miss Clearwater," the man hissed; his voice low and laced with carefully compressed anger. His head tilted slightly to the door, as if checking that there was no-one to overhear them.

She was not sure why, but she wanted to fight him. Her hackles were rising, her blood heating and her fingers tingled with the phantom tingle of magic. She knew she was treading dangerous ground, speaking about magic in the presence of someone who could hand her to the King for such talk. Elijah had the strength to put up a fair challenge – and she knew he had the best chance of putting her on her knees before the King.

Lorch would believe anything that came out of his bodyguard's mouth.

Ever so slowly, she leaned towards him, until they were sharing breath as she whispered, "When have you seen me shy from danger, Wolfe?"

The air became thick, charged between them. Anger, frustration – and something else she could not quite name – doused the air. She could smell it, the scent of his skin – the woodsy scent of pine and a deep mixture of leather and… male. Gods, even as they stared each other down, she could not help admitting that she wanted to touch him – even now. The insistent, annoying little tug formed between her breasts once more, drawing her to him like an irritable moth to a dark flame.

Unbelievable.

Then, before her eyes, she swore she saw the ghost of a smile, a hint of challenge in the barest flash of teeth.

"Master Wolfe, His Highness is ready for you to join him now," came a hesitant voice from the doorway. Elijah did not break her stare as he lifted a hand to the servant by the door, signalling he would be there soon.

At the soft click of the doors closing, Elijah's deep voice graced the static air between them.

"We aren't done talking about this."

"Until next we meet, then," she grinned slyly, tapping her fingers against the buckle of his leather tunic and turning from him. She had to get away from him – before she did something she would later regret.

As she breezed from the library, Elijah stared in her wake – his lips slowly dropping to a frown.

⊰⊱

She felt restless, shaky, itchy like eyes were watching her movements as she paced her bedroom that night. After her training session with Arii that day, Sybell had made her way to the castle feeling tired and surprisingly proud.

The strange, dark eyed woman had shown her a few simple moves, like how to stand and how to grip the sword. She had also gone on to show her the best points to strike to incapacitate a man if he had hold of her, and where to aim if she was being held against her will. It would all take practice, but she felt a glimmer of hope in her chest as she stared down at her hands.

One perfect rose-coloured nail was chipped, and for the first time Sybell did not care. She revelled in the imperfection, a little bit of proof that she could chip away at the expectations of being a Princess.

Now though, she had the unsettling feeling that she was being watched.

It was a feeling she felt most nights, particularly when she was alone and Ingrid was having a break for evening meal, or it was the middle of the night and the maid was sleeping in the room next door.

Sybell had forgone dinner that night, feeling a strange mix of excitement at the prospect of learning something that she wanted to learn so badly, and the fact that she was so exhausted she could feel it in her bones.

She had attempted sleep, but the feeling of being watched was still there, an ever-present shadow lingering over her shoulder.

She had shot up in her bed, sweaty and clammy skinned, deciding perhaps she was indeed hungry after all.

Slipping a cloak around her slim form, she headed silently from her rooms and headed for the kitchens, her feet barely making a sound on the marble floors.

Pressing into the spacious room and lighting some candles, she set about making herself a plate of fruit, cheese and cold meats, humming lightly to ease the feeling of aloneness that hung about her.

Perhaps she should have woken Ingrid, but the maid had been working all day and she thought it best to let her rest.

Her hand paused as she brought a grape to her mouth, eyes fixing on the shuddering darkness just beyond the light of the candles.

Had something just... moved?

Placing the grape back on her plate, Sybell moved to slide her hands under the plate when the candles around her suddenly snuffed out.

"H-Hello?" she said, but all that greeted her was silence.

Sybell fumbled in the dark, searching for a candle, a match, anything to light the darkness.

Her hands found a wet, inky texture, like cloth drenched in

Winter rain. She yelped, leaping back and hitting the table she had been preparing her food on moments ago.

The wet cloaked thing was suddenly upon her, and Sybell was screaming. As her mouth opened, she felt a cool gust of breath wash over her face. She smelled the reeking stench of carrion and death, just before she felt the strange sensation of falling. Her chest bowed as her back arched, feeling as if the very fibres of her being were being sucked up a black hole in the air above her. She felt sick to her core, all traces of happiness and light slowly sapped from her being, as if the thing were feeding on all that was good within her soul.

Her scream died in her throat as blazing red eyes winked open above her, and a half-moon of jagged white teeth appeared in a slow sardonic smile.

Eyes wide, Sybell attempted to scream again, but no sound broke from her gaping mouth.

Panic, pure and paralysing gripped her as a distorted laugh sounded from the thing above her.

Pain washed through her, her skin sizzled as if drenched in acid and the Princess tried to scream again, but her voice was lost to the void.

She was going to die, right here in the kitchens and she had not said goodbye to anyone, not Mother, not Father, not Lorch.

And not Ingrid.

Oh Ingrid.

Candlelight split the darkness as the kitchen door flew open and the sound of boots broke through her pain filled haze. Her eyes slid to the door, every nerve ending and every muscle locked in a silent battle, and Sybell saw the broad-shouldered silhouette of a man, his hair laced with silver as he drew a sword and shouted her name.

Whatever the thing was, it lost its grip and screeched, fleeing into the shadows.

Sybell slumped on the table as if she had just been dropped, her prone form boneless.

Commander Hawke flew into the kitchen, his sword clattering

to the floor as he rushed to the Princess, curling an arm around her torso, his other hand pulling her face to his as he inspected her deathly pale skin.

"Sybell!" he barked, his voice hinting hysteria as his head dipped to her chest in search of a heartbeat. When a weak thrum beat beneath his ear, a sound like a pained gasp left Hawke's lips and he held her to him as a guard ran into the kitchens.

Hawke lifted Sybell into his arms and cradled her like a child. The Princess' pale form was limp as the he hitched her head to rest against his chest, his dark eyes darting to the soldier as he said, "Notify the healers that the Princess has been attacked by a Reaper."

⋘⋙

"A Reaper?" Lorch breathed in confusion as he sat by Sybell's bedside. Mild morning light filtered through the windows of the Princess' rooms, highlighting the russet in the King's perfectly swept hairstyle. "What, by the Gods, is a Reaper?"

"Something I thought no longer existed," said Hawke, his gaze hardly leaving the Princess' sleeping form as her chest rose and fell lightly.

He had been scared, more scared than he had felt in a very long time. Seeing Sybell's pale, boneless form arched on the kitchen table, the terrifying shadowy *thing* perched with its jaws hovering over her body, inky black arms curling like a spider around her, sucking the very essence from her being – Hawke swore he had never felt so afraid in his fifty-two years.

He had almost lost her.

"What was it doing in the castle?" asked Elijah from the far right of the room, his cloaked form hovering by the window.

"Or a better question, why does it exist?"

Hawke speared a hand through his hair in frustration. From her place by the door, Arii could see the Commander looked beyond exhausted. The Princess' discovery seemed to affect him worse than she thought, as if the girl was perhaps more important to him than Arii realised.

Lynnera sat on the opposite side of the bed to Lorch, her hand clutching Sybell's as her thumb dew circles on the back of the girl's pale hand. The King's mother looked like she would be sick.

Hawke spoke after a short silence. "A Reaper is said to be drawn to powerful magic. It is incredibly strange that one was in the land at all." He paused. "Magic strong enough to draw such a creature is rare these days – nothing or no one with such power should exist." Hawke ran a hand down his beard in agitation as he paced the room like a caged animal.

"It's lucky you got there when you did, Commander. Thank you for saving my sister," said Lorch, his tone heavy with gratitude.

The King stood, before looking at Elijah and then Arii. "Someone else must have seen or heard this creature around the castle grounds. Commander, would a Reaper cause the damage seen on the servant found in the gardens a few days ago?"

Hawke paused; his brows pulled together. "No, taking out the heart is not characteristic of a Reaper. They feed on life essence, and strong emotion. Normally they would target a being with powerful magic but perhaps Sybell was in the wrong place at the wrong time…" He paused. "The creature may have been lurking the castle in search of someone else."

Arii's mind was coasting over each person she had met in the castle. So far, she was stumped at who could have drawn the Reaper, no one she could think of had displayed any sign of immense magic. Something tickled at the back of her mind then, as if a thought were wading from the far reaches of her mind before it was interrupted by Lorch's voice.

"Commander, I want you to ensure all of your soldiers keep a keen look out for anything suspicious, and if they see anything, even a *hint* of something strange – I don't care how minor, you make sure they report it immediately," he ordered.

The Commander's face was drawn and tired, but the order

seemed to give him a new sense of direction as he bowed low then took a last lingering glance at Lynnera and Sybell before sweeping from the room.

Lorch turned to his mother, his tone soft. "Mother, watch over Sybell while she rests. She will need to see a familiar face when she wakes. I'm going to find this creature, and I'm going to make sure it cannot harm anyone else in our home."

Arii was surprised to hear a tone of steel in the King's voice that she had not heard before. The time she had spent in Lorch's presence never hinted that the young man had an ounce of steel in his body, but now she could hear a dangerous, determined edge to his speech that had her brows rising. Sure, Sybell was a bitch, but Arii supposed no one deserved their essence sucked out like honey to a bee.

"Elijah, Miss Clearwater, if you'll come with me, I want to relay what has happened to my sister at the council. Maybe one of the old coots knows more about this Reaper." Lorch nodded to the two guards before sweeping for the door.

Elijah paused by Lynnera's side and placed a gentle hand on her shoulder, before following the King, sweeping past Arii and exiting the room.

Arii took a few extra moments, her eyes fixed on Sybell's sleeping form. She looked so small, so fragile. When she spoke, her voice was gently laced with cold calm.

"We will find the creature, Mrs Kruel, and believe me when I say we will make sure it pays."

Lynnera gazed up at the woman, reading the quiet determination on her face as she replied, "I have no doubt you will, Miss Clearwater."

૦ૐ૪૦

Masculine hands slid around the woman's small waist as he pulled her body against him roughly, breathing raggedly as two bodies twined in the privacy of an unused room. The woman's breath hitched as the man's teeth dragged across the sensitive skin of her neck, dark hair rolling from her shoulder as she tipped her head to the side. The man with copper hair tangled his hands in her hair, their lips clashing in heated passion.

"Had I known I would receive this welcome; I would have visited sooner…" purred Klotho as a sigh graced her blood red lips, her hands gliding up the man's chest and into his shirt. "It's too bad we could not speak like this when you visited the School."

Valdis' lips paused their ascension of the Fate's neck as he spoke against her skin, his voice deep and husky with lust. "Did you bring what I asked?"

"Oh yes, just a small few to avoid any suspicion. Won't you tell me what you need the crystals for? We are on the same side, you and I…"

Valdis' hand took hold of her hair and yanked roughly, her head pulled back to allow him better access to the skin of her neck as he growled. "When you answer my question, I shall answer yours."

"Ah, about your son and the Tapestry of Life," she answered.

"Indeed. Tell me why you sent a Fury to kill my son."

"You know the visions granted by the Gods are mere glimpses of images – my sisters and I put the pieces together and determine who the target could be."

She paused as Valdis' head dipped lower to the front of her parted blouse. His free hand pulled open the material, exposing her breasts to him. Hungrily, he took one nipple in his mouth and sucked, causing a moan to erupt from the Fate's lips.

"All of the images alluded to your son," she gasped, panting.

"But there was something within the images that I did not disclose to my sisters," she continued.

This caused Valdis to pause in his task, stormy blue eyes lifting to meet hers. She ran her hand down the side of his face, tracing the scar that marred him, her eyes hooded as a smile played on her lips.

"The Gods showed me an image of magic. Pure, spiralling,

untamed magic. Unless your son is a Fae, which I doubt, I believe the Gods may know of the existence of a male Fae magician, the first in over two hundred years."

Valdis' eyes glittered in the dim light of the room as he surveyed the woman. "You do not lie."

"I never lie," said Klotho dryly. "I merely… withhold little bits of information."

"And you did not tell this to your sisters?"

"No, I promised this sort of information to you, my love. I always keep my word."

Valdis' lips met hers again, swallowing her breathy sigh as he pressed her body against his, their movements barely containing their lust. They paused only briefly in their exploration of one another to speak.

"A tell for a tell, Valdis. Why the Nexus Crystals to Bonemire?"

Valdis had opened his mouth to speak when the door to the room opened, causing his head to snap up as a servant entered the room carrying freshly washed sheets.

Klotho spun around, black hair whirling about her like a curtain as the maid made a sound of alarm, dropping the sheets to the floor and staring with wide eyes.

"Oh Gods, my apologies!" stammered Ingrid, her bright burgundy hair haloed in the doorway by the hall lamps. Before she could turn and flee, Klotho lifted a hand and balled it to a fist as the air crackled with magic, causing the girl to halt mid turn as if frozen in ice.

Klotho sighed and righted her blouse as Valdis passed her, heading for the maid. "Well, this won't do, we cannot have word of our little–" she waved her hand in the air, "–displays of affection fluttering across the entire castle."

Valdis surveyed the maid, her eyes wide and frightened as they stared back at him. His harsh, ragged face was drawn in a frown, eyes narrowed. "She is my daughter's handmaid."

"So, get your daughter a new maid."

Valdis sighed and turned to the Fate. "Fine, I will take her to the dungeons myself and decide what to do with her later. The council is waiting, Klotho, as is your Emissary."

Klotho sauntered past Valdis, giving him a smoky stare. "We will continue this later, then," she purred, passing into the hall.

Valdis watched her leave, before turning and hauling Ingrid in the direction of the dungeons.

⚬

"You focus too much on offense, Miss Clearwater."

Arii's brows narrowed as she stared at Elijah, the hood of his cloak pushed back as they sparred in the training arena. His silver eyes watched every tiny move she made like an eagle watching prey, his lips drawn in his usual disapproving frown.

The Elijah from the pool? That hint of a smile in the library? That Elijah was long gone.

Gods if he just smiled – a full lipped smile, not just the hint of teeth or the tilt of his lips that she had seen before, she imagined his handsome face would light the room like a fire in the darkness. She would not admit it, but she longed to see more of the smile she had glimpsed in by the pool, and in the library the night she had revealed his face and they had almost kissed.

Pausing, Elijah ran a hand over his dark stubbled chin.

"You press your offense with anger and ferocity. If you held back and allowed your opponent the thought of an advantage, you would end him much quicker, and use much less energy."

"Who made you the King of combat?" she snarked, easing her stance as they drew near to ending their training for the morning.

Elijah sighed loudly, and Arii found herself beginning to grin. Only she seemed to get a rise out of the stoic soldier, and it amused her. Elijah, on the other hand, looked like he wanted to wrap his strong calloused hands around her neck and strangle her.

"Years more experience on the battlefield, Miss Clearwater," he ground out.

Arii chuckled, slamming her boot on the edge of a nearby fallen sword, causing it to flip before her hand shot out and snatched it from the air.

Just like every other day, their training had gone well, their skills so smooth and similar that they practically danced in the ring. Commander Hawke was silent most of the time, only adding his opinion in some cases where he believed there could be improvement. Elijah kept his hood down most days, but today it was about his shoulders, his black hair falling around his face in unruly waves, some strands sticking to his forehead and neck with perspiration. There was something about the man standing with little beads of sweat tracking down his neck that caused something to rise to the surface within her, an annoying little beast of lust that was rearing its head far too often lately.

Really, Arii was mesmerised by Elijah's battle prowess, bringing to the front of her mind the question she was beginning to obsess over knowing the answer to.

Who was he?

On the sidelines, Commander Hawke fixed Quinn's grip on the hilt of a dagger. Tikkani and Emerson were nearby, clashing training swords in a practice duel. The twins danced and slashed with surprising speed. Tikkani ducked Emerson's attack, neither recruit landing any blows as they moved, seemingly reading each other's moves a split second before making them.

If Arii had not known about the twin's telepathic abilities, she would have watched the duel with confused wonder. Pitted against enemies, their gifts could be a colossal advantage. Against each other through? Not so suitable.

The look Tikkani shot her way multiple times during the training caused Arii to growl, her friend's eyebrows raised and waggling as the elf nodded in Elijah's direction.

Gods.

She supposed the recruits were not familiar with Elijah's face, and now that it had been revealed, Arii was sure to get a fair amount of shit from Tikkani about how dark and handsome the man was.

Like she did not know that already. Elijah was a mystery wrapped up in the form of a tall, rugged, battle hardened god of war.

And she was determined to figure him out.

"Lady Kruel, what a surprise to see you here."

Arii turned to the sound of Commander's Hawke's surprised voice, expecting to see Sybell up and about. She assumed the Princess would still be resting and recovering, but when the King's mother entered the training room with her face drawn, Arii paused with her sword hovering in mid-air.

"Commander, I was hoping to speak with you a moment?" Her voice was laced with concern. Arii shot a quick glance at Elijah, seeing his attention was on the woman also.

Hawke instructed Quinn to join the other recruits before turning to Lynnera. When she spoke, her voice was low and had it not been for her keen Fae hearing, Arii would not have noted the carefully veiled panic in the woman's voice.

"Have you seen Ingrid? The slight girl with red hair, Sybell's handmaiden?"

Hawke's hands twitched as if he were holding back from taking her hands in his own, seeing her fingers shaking.

"No, is everything alright?" he said gently.

"Sybell is asking for her maid, but I cannot locate her anywhere. The castle staff have not seen her since last night. It is awfully strange for her not to be close by, especially since Sybell's ordeal," Lynnera paused, wetting her lips before continuing. "Sybell is becoming… increasingly upset."

"She is awake?"

"Yes – but she is still very tired…"

Arii's eyes slid from their exchange to Elijah once more and was surprised to see his heavy gaze fixed directly on her, glittering with suspicion.

Did he suspect she could hear their conversation from where

they stood, where a normal human or elf would be out of earshot?

Arii arranged her stance and lifted her free hand in a beckoning gesture, a sly grin splitting her lips.

"Shall we continue?"

ೞ80

Moonlight showered the golden castle causing the shimmering metal facade to appear almost silver in the night. Two figures clung to the overheads outside the Princess' rooms, their forms shrouded in shadows as they watched the moonlit silhouette of the girl as she slept. Arii's violet eyes reflected momentarily in the moonlight as she shot her gaze quickly to the silver haired Fury beside her. They had been lying in wait now for hours, and so far there had been no signs of the Reaper.

"Are you sure it will return?" whispered Arii as piercing blue eyes met hers, reflecting like a fox's in the dim light.

"It is said that when a Reaper tastes its prey, it will hunt them until either it drains the soul from its victim, or it is repelled away with strong magic."

"The attack on Sybell was obviously a 'in the wrong place at the wrong time' kind of situation… I have not felt any strong magic in the castle… have you?" said Arii, watching Nem in the moonlight. If there had indeed been strong magic in the castle – strong enough to draw a Reaper, she would have felt it, surely. So far what had drawn the creature was but a mystery, a mystery she catalogued into the back of her mind to figure out later.

"No, I can't say I have. I believe we are the only users of magic in the castle currently." Nem's brows narrowed as she dipped her hand into the pocket of her pants.

"Well, the shadowy piece of Kryvern shit better show soon, my legs and arse are falling asleep," sighed Arii as she shifted uncomfortably on her perch.

The silver of Nem's hair peeked from the cover of her hood as she inclined her head, her nose twitching as her lips curled back. "Well, you have your wish, it's nearby."

Arii felt a shiver of anticipation shoot down her spine as her eyes speared to the window. The plan was simple – wait for the creature to appear for round two with the Princess, then send it back to whatever hell hole it had crawled out of.

"Remember, a Reaper cannot technically be killed, we must banish it with magic. Our magic combined with this should do the trick." Nem lifted her hands and uncurled her fingers, revealing a small chunk of crudely cut crystal in the palm of her hand. It glowed with a strange inner blue fire, as if power contained within the stone was bouncing around, looking for a crack in its prison.

Arii stared, wide-eyed. "Nexus Crystal? No fucking wa-"

Nem lifted a finger to her lips. "Shh, it's here."

Nem placed the crystal in her cloak before shifting to land nimbly on the balcony of the Princess' rooms, Arii following close behind. Pressing open the window, the two figures slid silently inside as an inky black mass shifted above the Princess' bed. The creature's existence was heavy in the room, a chill sweeping the air. Frost coalesced on the windows – ice fingers skittering along the windowpanes.

Nem was swift, acting quickly lest the creature sense their presence. The Fury thrust out her hand, the Nexus Crystal throwing flickering blue light across the room.

Arii threw her magic out, encasing the room in a thin veil and ensuring anyone near would not hear, before darting past Nem to perch on the bed between the Princess and the creature. Snapping out an open-handed palm between them, she threw out her magic again in a rippling blue shield.

The Reaper screamed and whipped its head, a terrifying screech tearing from its widening jaws, its glowing vermillion eyes flashing as it recoiled from the Nexus Crystal's radiating power. Nem's teeth bared as she lifted her free hand against the one holding the crystal, shoving her own magic into the spell.

"Leave here, beast!"

The creature screeched, an inhuman, terrifying sound that grated down Arii's senses like Nem's silver nails on a chalkboard. As planned, Arii added a second hand and threw more magic against the shimmering blue bubble created by Nem that now enveloped the writhing creature. It thrashed in a whipping flurry of darkness, clawing at the shield and screaming with fury. The Reaper howled and slammed against their barrier, its shadow claws slashing and cleaving as it tried to find a way out.

Blue light bounced about the walls, reflecting off the golden accents of the room and giving the place an underwater effect. Had Arii had the time to look, she would have thought it beautiful in a cool, mystical way.

"If you banish me-" called the thing as it thrashed, jaws snapping. "Then you will allow a power unchecked to be unleashed upon this land." The creature screeched and Arii could feel her magic beginning to wain as she threw it all into the spell.

What was it talking about?

She saw through the whipping darkness that Nem's face was beginning pale. Their magic was not an endless well – it had its limits and they were fast approaching the bottom. She could feel sweat blooming on her forehead and neck, her teeth clenching in a snarl.

With one last cry, Nem pushed the crystal closer and the creature howled, shadow claws clutching at its head as it coiled as if in horrible pain.

"Be gone, you filth!"

The Reaper screeched as it writhed, and with a drawn-out scream the thing imploded within itself, withering into a pop of inky black mist.

As soon as the last whisps of shadow receded, Nem dropped the crystal to the floor and stumbled back as if burned, their hard breathing the only sound in the now dark room. Arii lowered her hands, eyeing the dormant crystal on the plush floor rug, now looking like nothing more than a clear glass paperweight. The magic within was no more.

From behind Arii on the bed, a gasp sounded.

Head whipping around, Arii saw Sybell pressed against the head of her bed, eyes wide and fixed on the two women at the foot.

Oh, bloody hell.

"You said she'd been given a sleeping draught?" hissed Arii as she shot a look at Nem.

The silver haired woman shook her head, her glossy bob whipping from side to side. "I slipped it into her tea, she must not have drunk it all."

"W-What in all the Gods–" choked Sybell, eyes darting between them. "You… you are Fae?"

Arii swiped a hand down her face and she groaned.

Nyx's arse they were in trouble.

There was no telling how much the Princess had seen, but by the ashen look of pure shock of her face Arii knew she had most definitely seen their use of magic to banish the Reaper.

Only Fae had magic like that, and those few Fae that were left were taken in by the Fates and turned into assassins… into Fury.

"You are both Fae! I knew there was something about you, but Fae assassins?" Sybell's eyes hardened and her jaw set in a stubborn frown.

Arii turned to face the girl and tilted her head, like a cat surveying a mouse. For a moment, she considered silencing the girl with a quick hand to the mouth and a knife across her slender throat, but before she could action the thought the Princess lifted her hands into the air.

"I won't tell anyone."

Arii's brows shot up at this.

"I'm serious, I won't tell."

"How can we trust you will not breathe a word to anyone, Princess?" murmured Nem from over Arii's shoulder. She knew that the Fury was having the same thought process as she had. They could not allow their cover to be blown, not now.

Sybell's eyes darkened as her face remained serious, not a flicker of untruth upon her expression. If Arii had learned anything about the Princess, it was that the girl did not lie. Every single snide thing she said came straight and unfiltered from her brain to her mouth.

"I swear it on the Gods. You saved my life, and for that I am in your debt – assassins or no. Look, I do not know why you are here, and honestly I do not care."

Arii blew a breath through her lips and glanced to Nem over her shoulder. The woman's stare answered her silent question; if the Fury had decided to end the Princess' life, she would be dead already.

"Fine," sighed Arii, eyes returning to Sybell. "But if you breathe a word, utter a single thing to anyone that alludes to what we are..." Arii leaned forward, her pointed canines flashing as she bared her teeth in a warning smile, "I will gut you, letting you watch as your entrails paint these ridiculously expensive royal rugs in red. Trust me, death by disembowelment is incredibly painful and a very slow, excruciating experience. Or so I have witnessed – if the screams are anything to go by."

Sybell swallowed audibly, her throat working as she stared at the two sets of glittering eyes before her. "I swear it on my own life," she said, her voice resolute.

Ariiaya knew she spoke true.

Everyone knew that Sybell Kruel loved no-one more than herself.

CB&CO

"So, the Reaper is… gone? How?"

Lorch stood, hands braced and splayed on the council table, his eyes fixed on Elijah as the man stood a few paces away. Cloaked in his hood, Elijah folded his arms across his broad chest and paused before speaking again.

"There have been no signs of the thing over the last two nights.

Dare I say after attacking the Princess, it may have realised there was no magic here and fled."

Lorch sighed heavily, his shoulders slumped, as if he had just blown a gust of tension from his lungs.

"I hope you are right, Elijah. Only the Gods know what the thing was doing here. Have you found any other clues as to why it was here?"

Elijah shook his head gently. "No, Your Highness. I stood by Sybell's door and checked on her throughout the night."

"Could it be waiting? No doubt it knows we are aware of its presence by now."

Elijah repeated the shake of his head. "No, Commander Hawke believes if the creature was to return it would be immediately during the first nightfall."

He would not admit that he had felt something, something simmering upon the air and coating his tongue with sweetness on the first night he checked on Sybell's rooms. After entering, the room was silent and the girl slept in her bed, no signs of disturbance. He had paused, surveying every inch of the room with his silver stare.

He could have sworn…

"I'm glad, Elijah. Gods, I haven't been able to sleep since the ordeal. My sister is a spoiled brat but no one deserves their soul sucked through their skin by a shadow demon." He rubbed his eyes and Elijah frowned.

"Perhaps you should rest, Lorch. You're exhausted."

Lorch knew that when Elijah addressed him by his name, he was pulling the concerned friend card. With a sigh, Lorch straightened and smiled at his companion. "You're such a mother hen, Elijah. I'm fine. I was actually just about to visit Miss Clearwater and see if she wanted to picnic by the waterhole again."

Elijah stiffened. "Lorch."

"Oh come on, Elijah. Arii has been around long enough that we can allow her a thread of trust, right?"

Elijah's entire face did not need to be visible for Lorch to see that his hackles were rising. Lorch moved towards him but paused a few feet away. "You still do not trust her?"

"Around you? Not at all."

"Why?"

Elijah's top lip twitched. "Do you remember why you assigned me to be your personal guard, Lorch?"

Lorch groaned, but Elijah barrelled on.

"Because I would always tell you what you *needed* to hear – not what you wanted to hear. All of the snivelling, grovelling councilmen and courtiers that scuttle about your feet would sell their own mother to have the opportunity to line their pockets with your gold or spend one night in your bed."

Lorch's mouth opened, but Elijah was not done. "You've always trusted my judgement, why not now?"

The King rubbed the back of his neck, looking for a moment like a young boy being scolded.

"There's something about her, Eli. I just can't-"

His eyes lifted and his brows narrowed. "I just can't stay away. It's like something is pulling me to her and I can't stop it, it's like an invisible cord."

"Of course you can stop it. Post her to an assignment outside the castle. She's talented, and that talent is not being fully utilised here."

"It's almost like you want her to go away."

"Precisely," growled Elijah.

Lorch grunted in frustration, taking a step forward. "What is your problem, Elijah? Arii is talented in battle, and I trust her! She has saved my life twice, why would she do so if she were here for anything else but to serve the Crown?"

Elijah's arms dropped to his sides as Lorch moved closer, and the two men sized each other up. The guard was half a head taller than his friend, their builds completely different but at that moment the same anger radiated from them both.

Lorch lifted a finger and poked it in the centre of Elijah's broad chest. "You feel the same way!"

There was a weighted pause before Elijah spoke, his deep voice low and dangerous. "Don't be ridiculous."

Lorch's brows shot up as a look of mock horror fluttered across his features.

"Gods, you feel the same pull to her! You always do this, Elijah. As soon as something strange, something exciting and new happens to you, you withdraw into yourself and close your walls. It was the same with-"

Elijah's lips twitched, but he did not bare his teeth fully. The air sizzled around them and Lorch swore he heard a clap of thunder in the distance, far beyond the castle.

"Don't you dare say her name."

Lorch had hit a nerve, and he knew it. The King pressed his finger harder into Elijah's chest, as if he knew the man would not lay a finger on him.

Of course, he was right.

Elijah would not touch a russet hair on his head even if the King was raining blows to his face.

"Clera."

Elijah whipped the hood from his head, and the two men were nose to nose then, both breathing heavily with anger. Elijah was practically vibrating with suppressed rage.

Clera Citera, the woman who had woven him around her finger with her beauty and charms, and after a night of passion – attempted to kill him while he slept, all for some jewels and gold.

Elijah could still see her face, frozen in shock above him as the light ebbed from her eyes, his dagger lodged in her neck. He still had the scar from her blade on his abdomen, a reminder of why he had not let anyone that close ever since. His silver eyes flared, a sound like a growl ripping from his throat as Elijah stepped back from the King, seemingly remembering himself after a few breaths.

When he spoke again, his voice was a hoarse whisper.

"That was a long time ago…"

"But it still affects you, Elijah. It doesn't take a magician to see that."

Elijah was the first to break their stare, grunting with frustration as he turned from Lorch and paced a few feet away.

"It's not as if I'm completely useless, Elijah. I know how to defend myself; you saw to that."

Lorch had no idea, had not seen how the woman moved during a fight, had not seen how she danced like death gave her wings, felling trained men and beasts alike. Never had he been matched by anyone in the ring, let alone a female. There was also the minor detail that the woman could use magic. It was terrifying, truly awe inspiring and it scared him.

What scared him most was the hot fire she brought to parts of him that had been dormant for years.

"Arii is not Clera," Lorch called from behind him as Elijah spun and paced to the door.

"I cannot take any chances…" Elijah growled as he paced from the room, ending the conversation with the slam of the heavy mahogany door.

KREPTH
HALLIER
Melissa Kincaid

CHAPTER EIGHTEEN

The dungeon was freezing, the floor ice cold stone beneath her as Ingrid Polaris curled on the thin mattress, the only thing in the tiny cell besides a pot and small basin of stagnant water.

What she had witnessed in the castle days ago was becoming a distant memory, confusion causing her mind to fog as she tried to recall what she had seen.

The woman in the arms of the King's Hand was definitely not his wife, and they were not merely speaking to one another in private. They had been embraced as if they were lovers.

Ingrid's body had stiffened as if clenched in an invisible hand of ice, and the girl knew who the raven-haired female was almost immediately as magic caused her body to freeze.

She was one of the Sisters of Fate, a weaver of the Tapestry of Life.

How long had this affair been going on? And what was she doing in the castle?

Ingrid had not meant to stumble into the room, she had been gathering clean supplies to take to Sybell, itching to sit by her bedside and ensure she was resting. Since the attack by the Reaper, they had not had the chance to speak about her ordeal. She had not had the chance to hold her, had not had the chance to kiss the worry lines either side of the Princess' lips. Last she had seen, the Princess was awake but pale and with haunted glassy eyes.

Thank the Gods she was alive.

The lock in the cell door cranked, and the heavy door swung open on squeaky hinges as Valdis Kruel appeared.

Ingrid gazed up, her eyes red rimmed and puffy from crying, her skin pink and scattered with gooseflesh from the cold. The handmaid uniform was not incredibly thin, but it did not protect her from the biting cold of the stone room.

Valdis paused in the doorway, his face in shadow as he spoke.

"This is… unfortunate."

If his words were meant to be sympathetic, his voice surely was not. Ingrid felt the hairs rise on her arms as he entered the cell, the flames from the wall sconces of the hall flickering with minimal light.

Valdis crouched before her, moonlight filtering dimly over his rugged face. The deep, jagged fissure of a scar was more prominent on the right side, reaching from his brow and running down over his cheek to end at his jawline.

When her gaze settled on his eyes, she inhaled a swift breath. Two blue pools stared at her, and she swore within their depths she saw a hint of sadness.

"Lord Kruel, what I saw… between yourself and that woman, I swear to the Gods I will not breathe a word to anyone."

Valdis rested his arms on his knees, a hand lifting to swipe through his hair in a gesture Ingrid had seen King Lorch make many times before. As he lifted his head to watch her again, she saw a flash of silver in his hand.

A dagger.

"Unfortunate that you had to see that, Miss Polaris. Unfortunate for you, but your misfortune is my gain."

Her blood ran cold as she began to inch away from him, his hard face watching her with naught a flicker of emotion.

"W-What do you mean?"

Valdis lifted the dagger, scrutinising the blade as it reflected the moonlight. "I was going to wait until I returned to Bonemire before I could test a theory, but thanks to Sister Klotho I am able to have my answers here tonight."

The sound that escaped her lips was a low, keening moan.

"Nooo… Please. I'll do anything, anything you wish. P-Please…"

His eyes found her again, and Ingrid knew at that in that moment she was about to die. There was no sympathy, no empathy in their dark depths.

Oh Gods, Sybell. She had not had the chance to say goodbye.

The dagger was swift, the steel swiping across her throat and the girl coughed, her hands flying up to clutch her neck. Blood oozed through her fingers as she emitted a strained gurgle, her eyes wide and staring.

Valdis watched; his expression impassive as he studied the girl. Her mouth opened and closed, eyes beginning to dart as she slumped back against the stone wall.

"The others… they did not survive." He paused, lifting a chunk of glittering, glowing blue crystal in his palm as the girl gasped and coughed, her skin becoming pale as her lifeblood drizzled through her fingers.

"Merely ingesting the crystal in shavings was not enough to grant the power of the magic contained within the Nexus Crystal, neither was consuming it in larger pieces. Many of the experiments become sick and violent." He paused again, eyeing her. "In high doses they began to lose themselves, but some began to show signs of retaining the slightest signs of magic in their bodies."

Ingrid gurgled again, beginning to slide down the wall, her eyes rolling back in her skull.

"Their minds though, their minds were lost to the madness. They were incoherent, fixated on causing death, mindless with rage." He studied the girl as her struggling began to cease. Blood bloomed in a slow-moving pool around her, staining the floor.

Valdis, his boots just out of reach of the pool of blood, continued to speak, his low voice gracing now deaf ears.

"The Nexus Crystal. It teems with magic, pulsing with energy as if it has its very own heartbeat. That had me thinking… What if the crystal were to replace a heart?"

Valdis spoke as if the room were his audience, as if the girl laying close to death at his feet were part of a casual conversation. "Of course, no one can live without their heart, and many times had we attempted to place the crystal within the heart of a live host. Countless hosts died, none surviving."

His eyes glittered, transfixed on the crude, glowing quarts-like crystal in his palm and the blue glow washed over his wide eyes.

"But, what if the crystal itself acted as the host's heart? Replacing the organ completely within a still warm body."

Swiftly, Valdis' body shot forward as he speared the dagger into the girl's chest with a sickening *crunch*, before jerking the dagger savagely.

"I guess there is only one way to find out…"

⊰⊱

"Your father will kill us if he finds out," grinned the young man as his fingers twined with those of his lover.

The moon was high, stars an endless sprawl of diamonds in the inky blanket as his head tilted back, against silver-lit blades of grass.

They were naked, the two of them. Skin pebbled with gooseflesh and sweat, golden hair swept into a messy thatch, the man's fingers danced over his partner's palm, before sliding his dark green gaze to the void above.

Tonight had been a significant step in their relationship and they knew that their lives would only become far more complicated because of their feelings for one another.

They would not approve.

Or… his father would not approve.

But they did not care. If tonight was their last, then they would welcome it with open arms.

Surveying the sky, he pointed at a constellation of stars bunched together within a hazy band of light.

"It's strange, where I come from, you can't see that particular

family of stars. What are they called?"

The golden-haired man inched forward and placed his lips to a quivering, pale-skinned bicep.

"Valdis?"

Valdis tilted his head, his young face unmarred, copper hair swept in the same messy manner as his lover and blue eyes luminous in the starlight.

"Dragon's Breath, they call it Dragon's Breath," he replied, face unchanging as he whispered, "Are you cold, Micah?"

Micah shook his head, his gentle smile never leaving his face as he sat up and stretched languidly.

"No, but we should get back before anyone sees we are missing."

Valdis sighed, following Micah's lead as they dressed in the clothes they had left strewn across the grass.

Their friendship had been a long one, and despite Valdis' flaws, Micah had persisted in being his friend anyway. Slowly their friendship blossomed to something more, and for a long while Valdis had tried to dismiss the feelings warming inside him.

Micah had become a soft escape from his father, for when they were together, he could almost forget the feeling of his father's blows to his body – almost forget the heavy, terrible weight of his father's words on his mind.

You are not good enough.

You are weak.

You will never amount to anything in this life.

His father was a curse of a man, but his words held a truth that Valdis could not ignore. He felt weak, and he did not feel anywhere good enough.

But when he was with Micah – none of it mattered. Not his duty, not what he was set to inherit – despite his father's acidic words.

Despite it all, Valdis had the overwhelming need to impress his father, to make him proud. He knew Micah hated that he felt this way, but Micah did not know what it was like to have a powerful, influential parent.

A wealthy merchant with a steady following, Urther Kruel was a hard and unforgiving man. He was ancient in his beliefs and would never approve of his son's love for another man.

Everyday a violent tug of war raged within Valdis' heart. It left a bitter feeling of sadness and shame.

But then he saw Micah's face, and storm clouds parted to reveal blue sky.

Cool fingers tugged at his hand as Micah brought Valdis' thoughts back, and the young men began heading back towards the substantial building atop the hill behind them. With a small smile, Valdis and Micah shared a quick kiss under the torchlight before breaking apart.

Valdis let their hands drop as they alighted the back steps to his father's estate. Micah pressed against the heavy mahogany doors, straightening his scholar's uniform as they entered quietly.

Then they heard the sound of a woman's scream.

Sharing a quick, startled glance, Valdis and Micah flew down the hall, following the now audible thumping sounds of struggle – coming from his father's study.

Slamming into the room, Valdis froze in the doorway.

Blood.

So... much... blood.

It coated the walls, puddled on the floor, beaded against the glass of the window looking out over the estate grounds – vermillion rubies in the moonlight.

On the floor was his mother.

And above her glassy eyed corpse was his father, mad eyed and shaking.

"Father!" called Valdis, taking a step into the room. "What in the Gods' name have you done?"

Urther's head snapped up, his eyes widening as his thick bearded jowls quivered, gold buttons shimmering in the candlelight upon his expensive tunic.

"She deserved it. She was one of them. One of them." The man

breathed, hands shaking around a ruby hilted knife.

One of them.

When his father spoke this way, Valdis knew he was referring to the beings they hated above all else.

The Fae.

Valdis tasted sweetness on his tongue, mixed with the copper tang of blood.

Magic.

But... his mother was human, not Fae.

Valdis held up his hands pleadingly as the smell of alcohol asserted itself in the thick air. His father was prone to fits of rage, induced by alcohol and drugs and often Valdis and his mother were on the receiving end of his dissolution – until the effects wore off.

"Father, you are letting the madness win. Put the weapon down," he pleaded, moving towards him slowly.

"You don't understand, they're coming for me, for all of us! Magic is whispering madness in their minds. Magic is madness! Magic is death!"

"Father, please."

Suddenly in the darkness just beyond his father the shadows rippled.

And then, a figure emerged from the black.

Draped in black leather, the figure was slim yet tall, hooded in shadow.

Female.

Valdis suddenly knew what had come for his father.

His fate had been decided.

His string pulled taut.

Ready to be cut.

Micah pushed into the room behind them, and Valdis' head turned just as the man's mouth opened to scream.

Magic flared through the air, a hot crackling whip of electricity that slammed Valdis to the floor and sent Micah flying against the wall.

With a mere flick of the assassin's wrist, his lover was pinned there – eyes wide and terrified, hands scrabbling at his throat as if invisible fingers choked his windpipe.

Valdis' boots seemed to be melted to the floorboards, palms stuck to the wood like glue. Straining, rage flickered to life as the woman – the Fae woman – gripped Urther's throat.

Urther spun to face the assassin, the knife slicing through the air. She slapped the weapon from his hand, and Valdis swore he heard bone snap as his father grunted in pain before being thrown to the floor. Pooled blood sprayed as his father's back hit the wood, and the assassin poised above him, elongated canines glaring in a snarl from beneath her cover.

Valdis' eyes slid from Micah, to his mother, then to his father as the man struggled.

"No!" Valdis yelled, struggling against invisible bonds. "You are unnatural! Evil!" Deep down, Valdis believed this to be true. Magic brought nothing but fear to his heart, his father's words thundering in his mind as he delivered blow after blow.

Swallowing against bile and sugar, Valdis watched as the assassin tilted her head, strands of golden hair slithering from the confines of her hood, blue eyes glowing against skin of alabaster, elongated canines revealed in a half moon smirk.

"Once your thread of life is spun and measured, young lord, there is no escaping your final fate," the woman whispered, her face wiping of all expression as her hand hovered over his father's chest, nails sharp as talons.

"Too bad your son and his lover had to see this, Urther Kruel. But no longer shall the Gods watch your reign of death upon our land. Your actions unbalance Fythnar and plunge us all into chaos."

Valdis tried to rise, his muscles straining against invisible bonds. He did not wish for his father to die, despite his abuse, despite everything he had done to him over his eighteen years.

In a strange, twisted way – Valdis admired his father's strength and steely determination to stand up for his beliefs, even if they were said to be dipped in darkness. As he watched now, he knew what his father preached was true – magic brought nothing but pain as the woman's hand speared into his father's chest.

Her fist emerged, dripping with blood, fingers curled around Urther's heart.

Valdis had not realised he was yelling, wailing at a pitch so high he hardly recognised his own voice.

Then something dashed past and Valdis felt his heart lurch as Micah ran at the assassin. His friend was swift, slamming against the woman during her momentary distraction. They fell to the floor, a flurry of limbs and blood.

Valdis was fixed to the spot as the assassin's hand flew up, slamming against Micah's chest. Bright light burst forth, their bodies engulfed in blue flame as magic snapped in the air.

Then, Micah fell.

His back hit the floor, smooth features frozen in a look of gentle shock.

His eyes slowly glazing.

Chest still as stone.

Valdis stared into lifeless green eyes, eyes that had held a sparkle of mischief and love.

Just beyond his vision, the woman's face contorted in a strange expression, and if Valdis had not been slowly consumed by heart-tearing grief, he would have seen the brief look of sorrow she gave.

Swiftly, she placed a simple line of thread upon Urther's hollowed chest, before slipping out the open window and into the night.

Valdis choked against the remnants of magic, his arms quaking as he crawled to Micah's still form.

His fingernails caking in congealing blood, he scooped Micah into his arms, rocking back and forth as he gazed upon the face of his love.

No, no, no, no.

He could not be gone.

Just like that, with just a small shock of magic, the light of his life's heart ceased to beat.

Magic was madness.

Valdis pressed his forehead to Micah's, pain stabbing at his insides.

Magic only brought death.

He had believed it before, but now – now he believed it with absolute clarity.

His father had been right.

Micah was dead because of magic.

Darkness coalesced within his heart, thick black tendrils of ice sprawling like fingers across his soul.

From that night, Valdis made a vow as he bellowed to the Gods, his heart shattering like fallen crystal.

He swore to end magic... no matter the cost.

໖ઌ

Lifting the clear crystal to the moonlight, Krepth studied the thing with narrowed green eyes. His jaw slid forward as he brought the empty Nexus Crystal to his nose and sniffed.

"I wonder if I were to lick it, would it taste sweet like that which magic leaves on one's tongue? Or like a rock…"

Arii snorted a laugh as she said, "Go ahead, try it."

"Trust you to sniff the thing like a mongrel, Krepth," Nem commented as they loitered in the shadows of the castle on the dragon landing. The constant rumble of the waterfall was the best cover for their conversation. Nem leaned casually against the cool golden wall, her oceanic eyes luminous in the moonlight as she studied the Shifter.

Krepth's eyes slid to the silver haired Fury, smirking. "You have no idea what I smell on you, Silver Moon, forest leaves and… is that jasmine? Delicious. What would you taste, like I wonder?"

Nem rolled her eyes. "Do not even *think* about licking me."

"Surely I can *think* about it, but you never truly know until you try."

"Try it, and you'll lose your tongue, dog."

Krepth huffed a laugh as Arii gestured at the crystal. "The Reaper was drawn to someone here in the castle, someone with powerful magic. So far, I have not seen anyone with such power but that does not mean it is not here."

Krepth's head tilted to Arii, his dark hair flicking into his eyes as he rubbed a hand across his smooth jaw. "And you haven't sensed anything?"

"No… nothing significant… but there have been hints of magic in the castle. Nothing to draw a Reaper's presence."

"The Princess?"

"Pure human. In the wrong place at the wrong time."

A canine tugged at her bottom lip as Arii retrieved the crystal from Krepth's palm, staring into the now dormant thing as if it held the answers.

"I can't help but notice the King is still breathing."

Arii's head snapped up to two sets of eyes watching her. Immediately, her hackles began to rise. Krepth lifted his hands before his long-term friend could tear his head off. "I'm presuming there is a good reason, Arii? It's not like you to flounder on an assignment."

Her violet eyes were fixed on her friends as she thought through her answer carefully. They were just that, her friends, and had been for a long time, but they still answered to the Three Fates, and what she told them could either land them all in bloody water or cause them to turn her in to the Sisters for punishment.

How was she supposed to admit to her friends that she was beginning to doubt fate? The very thing she had believed basically all her life, especially since her initiation into the school. Everyone had their fate and it was inescapable. The Furies just… sped up the process for those chosen by the Gods.

"I have hit a few, shall we say, hurdles."

Krepth's brows shot up.

"Hurdles in the shape and form of a tall, dark and handsome bodyguard to the King?" drawled Nemesis.

"Not only that, I feel something else is at work here, as if something is being… prepared," said Arii.

"Arii, what are you talking about?" snapped Krepth.

"The Kryverns, the missing creatures from the lake, the heartless corpse on the castle grounds and now the Reaper? All of these things are pointing towards a disturbance, something that I don't think this Kingdom is ready for. The land is divided, the Courts have never been so disjointed," she explained, beginning to pace.

Krepth tapped his lips with a forefinger, studying the dark-haired Fury with keen, assessing eyes. "I think our little Violet Assassin is right. Nothing this exciting has happened since… well, since before the last powerful Fae magicians were hunted to the point of extinction. With powerful magic came all sorts of strange and wonderful beings, but back then the Courts were united and balanced with magic."

"You mean to say that killing the male Fae magicians has… unbalanced Fythnar?"

Krepth shrugged. "I believe so."

"What about the other Courts, what do you know of them and their leaders?"

"Not much," Krepth admitted, his forest green eyes glimmering. "Hard to believe, I know, but the other Courts very much keep to themselves, it has been that way since King Herington's death. As for my own Court, Freya Bloom still does not recognise the boy King as the true ruler of the Fythnar. My guess is that the others will be like-minded."

"The boy flounders with the courtiers and passes on his duties to anyone who is willing to do them for him. He is naive and has no thoughts to rule the Kingdom properly, leaving the job to his father – who mind you hardly seems any better," said Nem.

"The people of the North Court's lands are starving, it's true. They lock themselves up in their golden castle and invite only those with the right coin and status to enter, leaving everyone else in the dirt as feed for the Kryverns," Krepth speared a hand through his hair, mussing the short locks and causing them to stand on end.

Arii kept her expression carefully neutral, but she knew there was more to Lorch Kruel than they realised. Over the weeks she had kept in his presence, she noticed more and more how his father took control of all royal matters. Lorch had become used to it, perhaps trusting his father was doing the right thing, but she believed if he knew the true extent of the land's devastation he would be incredibly concerned, and perhaps do something about it.

Surely, he would.

Arii had never liked Valdis Kruel, felt a tremoring dark energy in his presence, and the uncomfortable feeling that something was off about him. It was not just that he was a stone-faced hard-arse who had probably only smiled a handful of times in his life, or the fact he beat the mother of his children. Arii felt as if the very air lingering about him was tainted and wrong.

"What if... the Fates were incorrect in deciphering the message from the Gods? What if... King Lorch is not my true target?" said Arii gently.

Both Krepth and Nem were staring at her now, open and unabashed.

"What the hell are you saying, Ariiaya?" hissed Nem, kicking back from her lean against the golden wall.

Arii could feel the rippling waves of disbelief from her friends as she folded her arms across her chest stubbornly, not allowing their glares to sway her as she asked, "Has it ever happened before?"

Krepth spoke then, his voice low and careful. "If it has, it has never come to light. I'm willing to hear your reasoning, Arii. I've known you for a long time and I know that you would not question fate lightly."

Arii's violet eyes met emerald, and her voice was stern yet gentle. "Lorch is not evil, nor cruel. I was waiting to see signs of why the Gods would want him ended, yet those things elude me. Which has me wonder if perhaps my target could be someone close to him."

"You said the Sisters saw a crown and the throne covered in blood before they announced your assignment. To me, that signifies a royal death, or that of someone sitting upon the throne. The boy is upon the throne, is he not?"

Arii growled with frustration as her eyes lifted to the moon hanging in the night sky, the silver light bathing her face. Krepth's hand rested on her shoulder and she gazed his way. His face was soft, the usual smirk replaced with a look of seriousness that took her back to their nights around the fire as children.

"If you think something more is at work here, Arii, I believe you."

Arii felt her throat tighten with emotion that was so foreign to her, emotion she had been taught so long to suppress deep within.

"I'll feed some reports to the Fates, distract them as much as possible before they begin to get impatient. But as soon as you see a flicker of something – you report it to me immediately, alright?"

Arii nodded and watched as Nem's expression softened also. The silver haired Fury spoke, and Arii realised that she had never done anything to deserve friends like these, yet fate had handed them to her.

Suddenly the trio stiffened as something caused the air to ripple around them, all of their heads twisting to the castle behind them.

Arii spoke, her voice a breathy whisper. "Did you feel that?"

Nem's eyes were wide and Krepth's brows were drawn.

"Magic," he barked, and the three friends lifted their hoods and headed for the castle.

∞

The ripple of magic that disturbed the air would not have awoken anyone else in the castle, lest they were attuned to magic, and aside from the Furies and the Shifter there was not anyone else who would have felt the tremor.

Arii led Krepth and Nem into the castle halls as they followed the pull, leading them to a heavy locked door in the east wing of the castle that she had seen before. Krepth deftly picked the lock, and as the door opened, they found themselves at the top of stairs fading into darkness. Glaring down into the inky void, Krepth was first to speak.

"I vote for *not* going down there first."

Nem shot him a sly sideways look. "Is the big bad wolf afraid of the dark?"

"Cut it out, you two," Arii pressed forward first, brushing past them and entering the dark stairwell. It took a few moments, but her vision began to clear as her pupils drank in the darkness. She could hear her friends behind her as they slowly made their way down the stairs. The pull of the magic was much stronger now.

As they came to the bottom, the three paused, heads tilting up and eyes widening.

The cavern was colossal, the ceiling glittering with stalactites hanging like spiked crystals, moisture dripping to the polished stone floor below. Scattered pools of aqua water reflected the ceiling above as if they were seeing double and the ceiling sparkled as if encrusted with millions of tiny diamonds. The walls were rough and winking with the same texture.

Directly ahead was a large cave opening, the stalactites seeming like teeth in the maw of a dragon as the crashing thunder of the waterfall boomed beyond. Sprinkles of water coated the walls with a seemingly permanent film of water. The space looked as if it could house a family of dragons. Perhaps hundreds of years ago it was used for that exact purpose.

That was when Arii realised that they were in a cave behind the waterfall, within the bowels of Viridya Castle.

"Nyx's tits!" cried Krepth in awe as they gaped at the impressive, raggedly raw cave before them. None of them could have believed such a natural, untouched place could exist under such a perfectly built castle of gold.

A groan sounded, and their attention flew to a form slumped to the far right of the room. Hands clutching her skull, a woman curled into a ball as if in pain, a strangled groan sounding again, her back to the trio.

Arii glanced at Nem and then Krepth before stepping towards the woman.

Had she been the cause of the small ripple in magic?

Arii felt the hairs begin to rise on her arms and her hand hovered over the dagger on her hip as the girl moaned long and low.

"Hey." said Arii, her voice stern but gentle. "What are you doing down here?"

The red-haired girl slowly turned, and Arii heard Nem's sharp intake of breath and Krepth's muttered curse.

The girl's throat was sliced and gaping like a second mouth, the front of her servant's uniform almost black with drenched blood, and her chest... her chest was ravaged, skin hanging like ribbons to reveal a black pit where her heart *should* have been.

Instead, the hole in her chest glowed with a faint blue light, pulsing as if a heart still lay within. Arii knew that what beat within was not a heart at all. No, the girl should be dead. Having assessed her wounds quickly, it was obvious.

The girl clutched her skull and groaned, low and long and keening, her cries laced with a despair so horrendous Arii wondered how she could even move.

Then the girl began to scream.

"Kiiiilll meeee!" she wailed, her hands clutching at her chest, eyes almost entirely consumed with black, only a hint of white still visible.

Arii felt another pulse of magic from the girl, and the feeling reminded her of the night with the Reaper as they used the power of the Nexus Crystal to dispel the creature.

"What happened to you?" Arii whispered, loud enough for the girl to hear as she inched closer, hand raised and placating. The girl dragged her hands down her cheeks, nails leaving bloody gashes in her skin.

"No… Nooo… Kill me!" she moaned in agony. "I'm not meant to be!"

"What in the Gods happened to her? I can feel… I can feel magic pulsing from within her. But she is human." Nem's eyes were fixed and narrowed on the girl. "She should not be… alive right now."

Arii was not sure *alive* was the correct word for what they were witnessing in that moment.

As Arii inched closer, the girl's head suddenly snapped up and her wholly black eyes widened. She jerked, her lips pulling back from bloody teeth. All signs of the pained girl begging for death moments ago were suddenly gone, and the thing began to rise to its feet.

Its movements were jerky, as if not in full control of the body. A guttural, inhuman growl ripped from its lips.

Whatever this thing was, it was no longer a human girl.

This was something wholly different, completely and utterly unnatural.

"Oh fu–"

With an animal scream, the thing launched itself with inhuman speed straight at Arii, colliding with the Fury and causing the trio to scatter.

Arii's hand flew for her dagger, the other shoved against the thing's neck as its teeth snapped mere inches away from her face like a rabid dog. Steel speared and embedded into its side as Arii stabbed at the thing, but it continued to attack as if unable to feel anything. Arii stabbed blindly as its hands – nails in jagged points as if filed crudely from clawing the cave walls – scraped her chest and neck.

Next thing Arii knew, Nem had the thing around its waist, lifting as it shrieked and clawed at the air in a blind fit of rage. The thing moved like lightning, twisting in Nem's arms and slamming its head into the Fury's nose. Nem stumbled back and let it go, blood spurting from her nose as the thing screamed and leaped upon her.

Arii was already running, colliding with the body before it could sink its teeth into Nem's throat.

The thing skidded across the stone floor, before coming to a stop in a flailing heap.

It was then that a roar reverberated through the cavern, causing the stalactites to rattle above them.

Scales glittered with water as it climbed through the cave mouth and the side of the waterfall, the Kryvern's glowing vermillion eyes were fixed on them as lips rippled over serrated iron fangs. The beast's eyes swept the maid, now standing up jerkily, as if it were nothing, before passing onto the others. Iron nails clicked on the stone floor as it assessed the room, chest rumbling.

Nem swiped at her bleeding nose as Arii shot a look her way.

What was a Kryvern doing down here? More importantly, when had Kryvern learned to swim?

As far as she knew, the animals were far too dense to remain buoyant on the surface of the lake, and normally shied away from deep bodies of water. It seemed the castle fortifications were becoming so low on the royal family's agenda that a beast as large as a Kryvern could slip through unnoticed.

Before Arii could ponder on the thought some more, the beast roared and started forward, before coming face to face with a massive black wolf.

Krepth stood his ground between the beast and his friends, his wolf fangs bared in a grimace of rage.

Arii stood and screamed, "Krepth, NO!"

The wolf lunged just as the girl's animated corpse flew at them again, and the room erupted into a flurry of roars, inhuman screams and vicious sounds of animal attack.

Arii dodged the flying body, dagger flashing and slicing through her tunic and across her stomach as she spun and sprinted for the Kryvern and the wolf. "Nem, deal with the girl!"

"Oh yeah, sure!" bellowed Nem as she flew at the corpse, grabbing its head and cracking it against her knee with a sickening *crunch*. The body began to crumple, before its hands shot out and pulled Nem's boot from beneath her. The Fury fell, but not before kicking a foot out and slamming it into the thing's gut. No blow Nemesis landed seemed to register as it attacked blindly, and no stab to its body seemed to slow the animated corpse down.

"And how the *fuck* do I do that?" Nem bellowed as the body gnashed its teeth and screamed with untamed rage.

Krepth's teeth were latched on the soft skin of the Kryvern's jugular as the beast threw its head back, flinging the wolf's body from side to side as it tried to shake him loose. Krepth's wolf was only a quarter the size of the Kryvern, and Arii knew that if she were not quick enough, the beast would have its claws in him at any moment. She snapped her hand out and shot a burst of magic at the cavern ceiling, causing some of the spiked stalactites to come loose.

It was at that moment that the Kryvern whipped its head to the side and dislodged the wolf, flinging the black form across the room as the glittering spikes on the ceiling broke free, falling and smashing into the beast's thick scales, causing a momentary distraction.

That was Arii's opening.

She launched herself upon the creature's back, flipped her dagger and tried to lodge the steel in the beast's cranium. The Kryvern jerked and her balance faltered, her dagger glancing off its thick scales and flying from her grip to clatter on the stone floor.

The beast twisted wildly and bellowed, its tail whipping past Krepth as he attempted to launch at it again, but the appendage caught him in the chest and sent him flying into the cavern wall.

Arii held on to the protruding spine from the beast's back, hand wrapped around her second dagger as her eyes narrowed on the flailing animal's neck again.

Nearby, Nem's palm flashed out as she shot a burst of magic at the girl's body, causing it to slam against the stone wall with a vicious crash, slumping to the floor. She spared a few precious moments to make sure it did not move, before turning and sprinting to Arii and the Kryvern.

The silver haired Fury threw a blast of magic at the beast's face, causing its head to snap to the side and scales to clatter against the floor like stones as the magic tore through to flesh. It stopped and screeched at its new target.

Arii took that moment of distraction and shot forward, bringing the second dagger into the back of the beasts' skull with a cry. It jerked beneath her as she leaped from its tumbling form, rolling across the floor before turning to watch as the Kryvern fell like a sack of bones.

Beside them, Krepth limped to their side with a low growl, remaining in his wolf form.

Arii felt a wave of gratitude that the two of them were alright.

"Well, I'm believing you more and more, there is *definitely* something amiss here," panted Nem as she wiped at her nose with the sleeve of her cloak.

Krepth huffed beside them in agreeance.

Arii nodded and glanced to where the dead girl lay crumpled only a few moments ago, and she froze.

The slumped form was nowhere to be seen.

"Um, guys… Where did she go?"

The only passage was the one they had entered through, which lead back up to the castle.

Oh flaming hell…

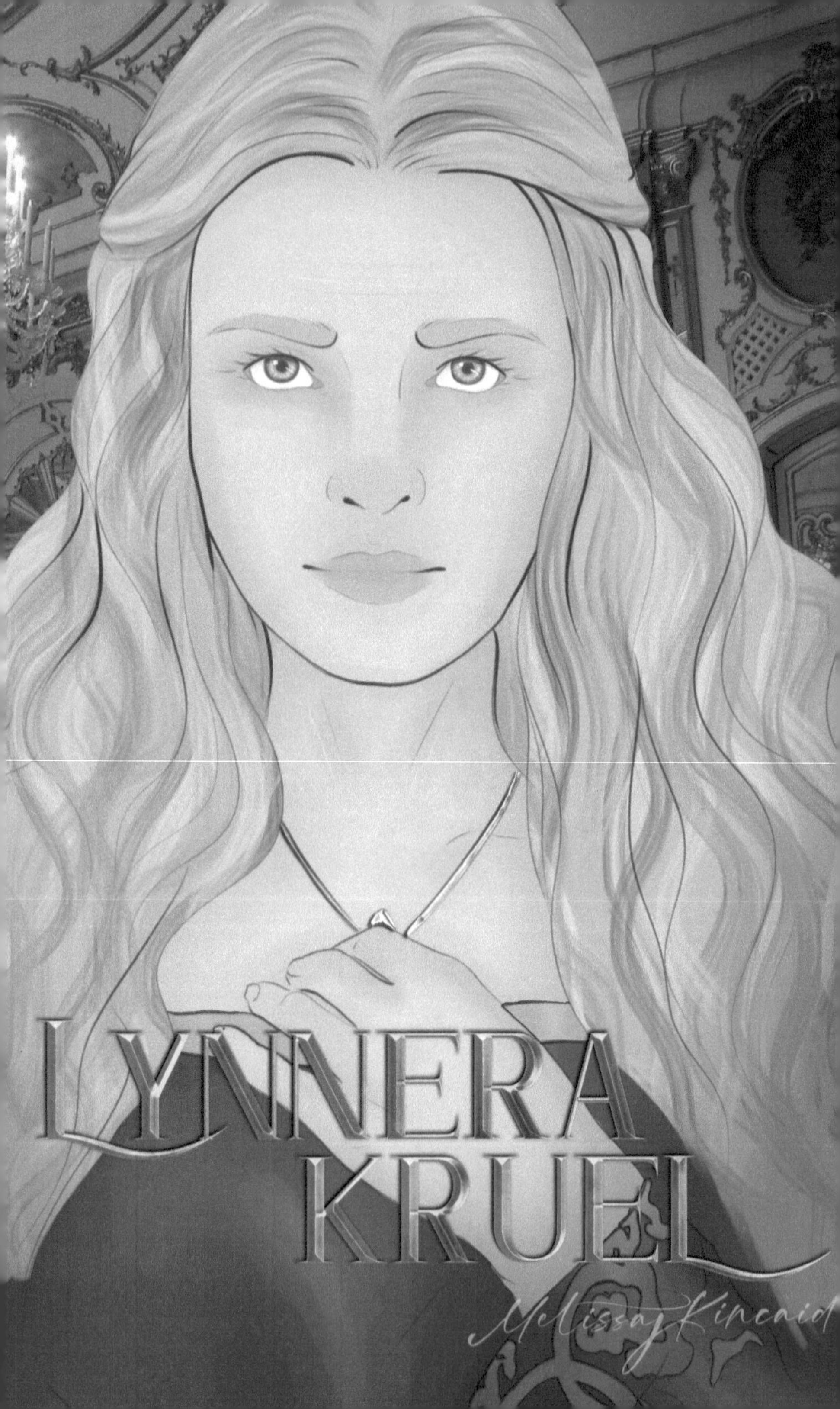

LYNNERA
KRUEL
MelissaJKincaid

CHAPTER NINETEEN

Arii, Nem and Krepth flew up the stairs to the sounds of distant screaming. The animated corpse was loose in the castle, and they had no idea how to stop it. The thing was obviously already dead, only brought to life by the pulsing magic inside its chest, acting like a living heart, as well as giving it incredible speed and taking away the feeling of physical pain.

How could you kill something that was already dead?

As they ran through the castle hall, Arii called to Krepth. "You need to go and notify Freya of what you have seen here. You cannot be found on the castle grounds."

Krepth, now in his human form, had a look of anguish on his handsome face.

"We will send for you as soon as we know how to stop it. Who knows if there are more in existence" Arii's face scrunched when her friend hesitated. "Something tells me this one isn't the first and won't be the last."

So, this was what the body in the castle garden was supposed to become. An animated corpse. But for what cause, and who was doing this to innocent human servants?

Krepth shot Arii a look, passing them to flee the castle halls before the entire building awoke. Arii and Nem raced down the hall, following the pull of the magic and the sound of an inhuman scream.

Another, more human, scream followed and Arii knew it was Princess Sybell.

They burst into the Princess' chambers to see her standing before the hearth, brandishing a poker. She pointed it at the jerking form of the red-haired girl, her face screwed up in pure agony.

"Ingrid? Oh Gods, Ingrid!" Tears streamed down her face as her eyes met Arii's across the room.

"What happened to her?" she wailed as the corpse jerked its head to the side, seeming to hesitate before the Princess.

Ingrid's once gentle eyes were large pools of dead black as she studied the girl brandishing the poker.

"Ingrid!" cried Sybell, eyes red and swimming with tears. "Ingrid, I looked for you everywhere. My Gods…" Her hand pressed against her mouth as her eyes took in the ravaged body.

It was then that a tall, cloaked figure entered the room, brandishing a sword.

Arii's eyes darted to Elijah as he jerked to a halt in the doorway, silver eyes swiftly taking in the scene.

The corpse whirled, nostrils flaring and teeth baring in a feral snarl. Elijah went rigid as it lunged at him, the heart of crystal within her chest flaring as if his presence awoke a new spurt of energy.

It lunged in a frenzy to reach the bodyguard but collided with Arii, sending their two bodies crashing to the floor.

Nem flew to Sybell as the Princess wailed, putting her body between the girl and the creature.

It slammed Arii's skull against the floor. Stars burst before her eyes as the back of her head collided with stone, and the animated corpse lunged from her to Elijah.

It hit him in a wild flurry of arms, hands clasping his head as its teeth sank into his neck. Elijah grunted, grabbed the body's hair, and yanked it free of his flesh, punching a hand to its chest so it stumbled back.

Arii rolled onto her stomach, eyes wide as Elijah pressed a hand to his neck before pulling it away, fingers tipped with blood. Her stomach rolled as she felt bile rise in her throat.

He had been bitten.

For all they knew, the curse could be transmitted by bite. If what this was could be a curse. They could not rule it out.

The corpse screamed, teeth red with blood as it lunged at him again.

Elijah's sword was swift and without hesitation as the steel slid through flesh and bone, severing its head from the shoulders.

The body dropped like a stone, the head rolling across the floor to rest beside his feet. Elijah dropped to his knees before it, sword clattering to the floor soon after. His eyes were fixed on the servant's head, red hair fanned out against the warm wooden floor, his expression drawn with sadness, brows pulled into a grimace.

Arii slowly stood, the back of her skull throbbing as she made her way to the guard, pausing before him before kneeling too. Her hands clasped his cheeks, angling his head to survey the wound.

His silver eyes lifted, their deep, haunted depths swirling and complex as they met hers.

"I guess decapitation is the answer to stopping it, then," said Nem gently as Sybell cried in her arms, the girl's head pressed into the Fury's shoulder. If it were any other time, Arii would have laughed at the fact that Nem was allowing a human to seek comfort in her arms.

Arii's fingers touched to the wound as Elijah watched her in silence, his eyes fixed on her face. She was surprised he was allowing her to touch him, but then her mind slid back to their time in the library, his breath on her face as their lips inched closer, electricity sparking between them.

"We need to monitor you, just to make sure whatever that thing was – it cannot pass on its affliction by bite."

Nem spoke from the hearth. "I do not think that is how it was made. The thing inside the afflicted girl's chest was a Nexus Crystal. Its magic gave life to the corpse."

Elijah frowned, now hard as ice as he began to rise. Arii followed.

"Something sinister is happening here and we need to figure out who or what is behind this before anyone else shows up like that… thing."

"Thing? That was Ingrid!" wailed Sybell, her eyes red rimmed as she pushed from Nemesis. "Someone did this to her! And now…" The Princess choked, her words halted by a terrible sob.

"We found her in the cavern under the castle," said Arii, her eyes sliding to Elijah as she felt his heavy gaze. Hopefully, he would not ask what they were doing under the castle late at night, but she knew that he would – and she hoped he would wait until they were no longer in Sybell's rooms.

"We must call a meeting with the King and tell him everything we have learned," Elijah finally said, his tone flat but gentle as his eyes found Sybell. "Princess, I will have someone gather Ingrid's remains so that you can have a proper burial."

Sybell sobbed as she pressed her hands to her face. Arii had never seen so much emotion from the girl before and wondered why a mere maidservant's death brought forth such anguish.

"I'm… truly sorry Princess," said Arii, her voice devoid of any mocking.

The maid, she had not deserved her fate.

No one deserved that.

Arii meant every word as they moved to tend to their wounds before facing the King.

 C3&80

Nem offered to stay with the Princess for a short time before agreeing to meet with the King to report on what had happened.

Arii gently wiped the blood from the bite on Elijah's neck as they stood in the healing ward, studying the shallow crescent of human teeth dotting his skin. It seemed to be healing already, the broken skin scabbing with dry blood – the corpse's blunt human teeth had not been able to tear a chunk of his flesh, and for that she was grateful.

Arii's eyes inched to Elijah's face as she worked, seeing his brows drawn and his silver gaze fixed anywhere but on her. The vulnerability she had seen in the library was long gone, the sharp lines of his face hard and distant as if in deep thought. Pressing a thin square of gauze to the cleaned wound, Arii's fingers brushed a lock of his dark hair from his neck.

His hand shot up and grabbed her wrist with the swiftness of a striking snake.

Elijah sat on the edge of a medical bed, Arii close enough to tend his wound. His head turned and his eyes met hers, her own wide with surprise. She felt the air sizzle between them as his frown deepened.

"Have you something against your neck being touched?" she forced out, feeling that strange warmth in her stomach return under his gaze. Elijah was silent a short time, his iron-like grip on her wrist not letting up.

"I have something against *all* of me being touched," he said, his voice a deep rumble. There was a dangerous glint in his eyes, and it was not lost on her that his chest had begun to rise and fall just as shallowly as hers had.

Arii's throat worked as she swallowed, a small smile tugging at her lips. "I'm trying to help you, Elijah."

His silver eyes softened ever so slightly then, as if a layer of his own carefully composed defences had hesitantly slipped. "My apologies…" he said gently.

What had happened to this man that just a simple brush of his neck had his hackles rising? His hand loosened its grip, fingers sliding across her skin as it dropped to his lap once more. Warmth pooled in her belly at his brief, gentle touch, and she quickly finished pressing the gauze down.

Arii stepped back from him, surveying her handiwork.

"The wound is not deep, it'll heal quickly."

If only she could have used a tiny bit of magic to help heal his wound to prevent a scar, but then her cover could be blown. The thought of a scar marring the smooth skin of his neck had her feeling uneasy.

So strange what emotions these men were dredging through the ice of her heart.

Elijah stood then, rolling his neck gingerly before gazing down at her. "Thank you," he said, and she felt he meant it.

He moved towards her and she stiffened as his hand brushed back the neckline of her tunic, revealing the light scratches there. His fingertips lightly brushed her flesh, and she felt fire ignite within her core.

Oh Gods.

All from a tiny brush of his fingertips.

"What of your own wounds?" His eyes surveyed her, roving over her neck and down her body. Every part of her that his mercury gaze touched seemed to flare with fire.

"Merely scratches," she whispered, all too aware of his fingers on the skin of her collarbone. Something seemed to shift between them, and Elijah moved closer. His tall, solid form was so large in comparison to hers, his breath hitched as his thumb swept over the shallow scratches.

"You heal quickly…" he murmured.

She looked up at him, his eyes now fixed to the creamy skin of her neck and collarbone.

The moment almost felt… intimate. The adrenaline of the events in the Princess' rooms had long gone, leaving them with an aftermath of confusion and fatigue. It was a biproduct, this strange feeling between them, from the stress of seeing and being attacked by an animated corpse…

Right?

Arii's lips parted, and Elijah's eyes swept to them, their depths darkening with something… desire?

No, the bodyguard surely did not feel desire for her.

Perhaps it was disgust?

But if it was disgust, why was he standing so close that their bodies almost touched? So close that if he were to lean his head down, their lips would collide without hardly an effort of movement.

If it was disgust, he would not be surveying her face with a look of intense curiosity.

"Elijah…"

His name on her lips seemed to break whatever trance he was in, and the man's eyes lightened, his face taking on its usual hard expression as he moved away from her, fingers falling away from her tunic.

As they fell, she saw tiny fleck of purple paint on his fingers.

"Come, we should get to the throne room," he said, his voice rough as if he had not spoken in hours.

Arii watched his broad back as he lifted his hood and swept from the room. The fire still remained, smouldering, warping – flickering deep within her core as she swallowed. She remained where she was for a few long moments, pinching at the strange feelings and gingerly pocketing them back behind her crumbling defences.

Before too long, Arii sighed deeply, gathering herself to follow Elijah from the infirmary.

Ↄⴲↄ

By the time their meeting in the throne room ended, Arii could not stop the feeling of bone deep fatigue flooding through her body. Nothing but the thought of falling upon the soft down covers of her bed filled her mind as she trudged tiredly to her rooms. Once there, she did not take the time to undress – instead falling face first onto the bed, quickly drifting into oblivion as soon as her head slammed against the pillow.

Before long, a world began to form before her eyes. Her feet dashed through the inky darkness, cutting through the water and creating swirling flurries of bioluminescence around her boots. Stars littered the midnight void above, hanging in the air before her as she waded through the shadow dream.

"Not again," Arii groaned.

Last time she was here a mirror of herself had torn out her heart, claiming she did not need the beating, bleeding muscle.

This time, there was not one figure standing a few feet away.

No, there were many.

Some were tall, some were short, and some were an average height, ranging from rotund to slim. None were the same, except all were faceless, their features blurred beyond recognition.

Star-speckled mist danced around her feet, gliding across her path. It was cold, almost bitingly so, and Arii felt the strange sensation of unfamiliar dread blooming in her chest.

Her nose twitched, eyes narrowing as one of the figures moved. Her hand flew to her hip, fingers curling around the hilt of her dagger.

The way the figure moved… it was not right.

Arms jerking, feet moving like they had no joints – wooden and stiff. Head lolling to the side, hands raising to their dark chest.

Arii felt weight on her shoulders, invisible hands pressing her down as mist drifted past. Her teeth clenched, jaw twitching as she watched the bodies jerking her way – faces blurred.

Afflicted, they were afflicted, just like Ingrid – Arii was sure of it. Blue light dashed across the space between them, watery light ricocheting off the starlit pool at their feet.

Muscles coiling, stomach tightening in knots, Arii prepared herself to fight, teeth baring in the beginnings of a snarl. The bodies moved, flickering beacons in the dark as the hairs on the back of her neck stood on end. Anguished moans drifted across the mist, wails of despair so deep she felt them to the depths of her soul.

Her soul, the dark depths that felt nothing – suddenly flared with sympathy. Yet, she felt a fire enter her limbs as awareness narrowed her vision.

Fight, she had to fight.

"Run, Ariiaya."

Head jerking to the side as a gentle voice sounded beside her, Arii's eyes widened in shock at the figure as it shuddered into existence.

It was almost like looking into a mirror, only this time, the woman beside her had creases on the corners of her eyes, and smile lines around her mouth. Dark chestnut hair waved around her strong face, her lips curving into a familiar smile,

Then Arii saw eyes of luminous violet.

Replicas of her own.

"M-Mother?" Arii whispered.

Her mother's eyes softened, before fire ignited within their purple depths as she gripped her daughter's shoulders. She was naught a few years older than Arii, and her touch felt realer than real. Arii felt her insides melting, liquifying with grief.

"My Violet Fire, you must run!"

"But-"

Her mother's head twisted to the blackness behind them, the sounds of feet disturbing the water becoming clearer.

"You must get to him!" her mother growled, voice laced with severity, fingers digging in deep. "Do you understand?"

Following her mother's gaze, Arii spied a figure in the distance, in the opposite direction to the slowly growing mass of afflicted bodies. A dark silhouette against a sky tinged purple and blue, misted galaxies glittered around a broad-shouldered, masculine body.

Who was he?

Eyes darting to her mother – her face so much like her own, Arii felt doubt tugging at her heart. Her eyes slid to the figures of the moving corpses, mere metres away now. "I can't run, mother. A Fury does not run."

"You *must*, Ariiaya. You must get to him; he is our last hope!"

Shaking her now, her mother pushed her roughly towards the figure as Arii objected.

"But who is he?"

The wails grew closer, the sounds turning to snarls.

"Go!"

Her mother whirled, hair fanning around her as she drew a knife. Boots fixed to the spot, Arii looked towards the shadowy figure, seeming impossibly far away.

"Is he... is he Father? Is Father here?"

"Ariiaya Trillia, you have potential to do good within you. You have a chance to make a difference, a chance to save this world from darkness." Her mother's hand flew to grip Arii's fingers, her violet eyes bright with love. "You will change the path of destiny. It is your fate."

Her fate?

Arii had never really given much thought to her own fate, truth told. She was content to drift along, doing as the Gods bid. She had always thought it was her fate to die at the end of a blade, smiling through teeth stained with blood, her heart a war drum within her chest as her veins danced with adrenaline.

This star-streaked dream was farfetched, a trick of the mind. The strange, whirlwind of emotions and thoughts she had been experiencing over the last few weeks had her losing trust in her own mind – in her own heart.

Her mother's fingers squeezed hers, bringing her thoughts back. Amethyst eyes softening, her mother's expression turned tender as she whispered, "I am so proud of you, my Violet Fire."

Proud? She had nothing to be proud of. Arii was a killer, an emotionless shell who cared not for anything.

Her mind brought forth the faces of her friends, and she suddenly felt her knees weaken.

If she did not care for anything, then why did she hope with such intensity that none of those figures ahead of them were the faces she had grown to love – despite all she had been moulded to believe in, and how hard she tried?

"GO!"

With a final squeeze, her mother pushed her back in the direction of the figure and twirled to face the oncoming undead storm.

Arii felt a phantom pain spear her chest. With a cry of anguish, she spun on her heel and began to run, water splashing as she sprinted away from her mother.

Screams sounded in her wake, horrible cries of anger as Arii gritted her teeth and glanced over her shoulder. Her mother was gone, consumed by a rising wave of writhing, violent undead bodies. There were hundreds now, flailing forms with flashing eyes and bared teeth, screaming and wailing and the earth seemed to quake under her feet. Eyes widening, she twisted and sheathed her dagger at her hip, working her arms as she pushed all of her energy into her legs, eyes fixed on the figure in the distance.

The midnight sky above flared as lightning snapped in the distance. Thunder boomed, followed by a rush of air, causing the endless pool around her to ripple and whirl – reflective stars dancing across the tide. Lightning strobed across the horizon, illuminating the shadow dream in flashes of white light followed by a deafening boom.

Still, the figure ahead did not move.

"Father!" she called as the voices grew near – the gnashing of teeth so close she was almost afraid to look back. Suddenly the length of space between her and the figure began to fall away, dropping like she was sprinting towards the edge of a waterfall. Water fell like ink into an abyss, a bottomless oblivion with no end.

Still, the figure stood motionless, on the edge of a glittering cliff of stars.

Between them was a slowly widening, mist sprinkled chasm of space.

No... NO!

As her boots slammed against the water, droplets coating her arms, her cheeks, drenching her leathers – Arii realised she could not stop. Not because of the ravenous sea of undead in pursuit behind her, fingers reaching for her clothing and hair. No, if what her mother said was true – then there was a darkness on the horizon that she would have to face, one that she could not turn her back on.

It was a feeling to being on the edge of a new emotion, an uncertainty that she was not ready for it, or felt she was not worthy of feeling. Arii knew that what was coming was going to be far more complicated than what she was ready to accept.

Fire snapped from her chest, spearing through to her fingertips as her palms crackled with sparks. Once again, she was closing in on a waterfall of brimming emotions, facing the prospect of an unknown ending at the bottom.

With crystalline clarity, Arii felt her heart reinforce, closing over with battle hardened steel.

She *had* to jump.

She had to let go and *leap*.

As the reflective pool beneath her feet began to run short, her muscles bunched before rocketing her forward like a spring, the solidarity below falling away into nothingness as she made the leap. Stars caressed her cheeks, glittering spheres of water dashing against her lashes as she flew across the void, her world nothing but a floating realm of mist and stars as she reached out her hand, fingers splaying towards the figure.

It was her father… it had to be.

He could help her. He could offer her clarity in this world of darkness and confusion.

But… her father was dead. Her mother too.

Tears glittered from the corners of her eyes as she drifted, closer and closer to the faceless figure.

Thunder boomed like a drum, lightning forking across the dreamworld in strobes of blue, alighting the figure's form in ultramarine as a robed hand lifted into the air, as if he were reaching out to her, too.

As she drew near and their hands reached across the sparkling, magic filled darkness – Arii felt warmth spear across her chest.

Her heart kicked a beat.

And their fingertips touched.

As her dream world exploded into a swirling, enraged cataclysm of sparks.

ଓଞ

Sybell cried in her mother's arms as the woman stroked her golden hair. She had hardly slept, eyes marred with bruises of fatigue, their deep chocolate depths glassy and red. Ingrid's body had been taken and the remnants of her destruction swept away as if the girl had never been. Her black, inhuman eyes were burned into Sybell's mind, staring at her every time she closed her eyes.

Oh Ingrid. Who had done such a terrible thing to you?

"My darling, I am so sorry about Ingrid," her mother crooned sadly as the girl leaned back and wiped at her eyes.

Commander Hawke stood in the room, his face drawn with sympathy and anger. He had headed straight back to the Princess' rooms as soon as the meeting in the throne room was over, unable to stand still the entire time, itching to making sure Sybell was alright. He had not slept a wink, had not allowed himself to.

Lynnera gazed up at the man, lines deep on her tired face.

It killed him to see her so stricken with grief. The grief though was not for the handmaiden, but for her daughter's heartache.

To see Sybell so overcome with heart-splitting sadness also had him feeling cleaved in two. She was always so strong, so... angry and distant. To see the girl so grieved over a handmaiden had him wondering if all that had been a ruse to bury her true feelings deep within. To protect herself from feeling exactly what she now felt.

"We will find out what happened, Princess, I promise you that. Your maid's death will not be in vain."

Sybell shot a gaze to the Commander, seeing his haggard face pulled in concern. She hiccupped, before speaking. "She wasn't just a maid, she was my friend. My..." Her voice trailed away and her face contorted in grief once more. "If only I had known how to protect her, knew how to fight. I could have stopped whatever did this."

Hawke's brows pulled and he spoke gently. "Knowing how to use a sword would likely not have prevented what happened to Miss Polaris."

Sybell's head whipped to him, grief replaced with fury. "How could you know?!" she shrieked, as Lynnera clutched her hands and murmured gently for the girl to hush. Sybell stood then, facing the Commander and baring her teeth.

"Why do you refuse to teach me? Had I known how to-"

"Knowing how to fight will only give you confidence to seek danger."

"No! You just don't want me to know how to defend myself, otherwise I would not need you!"

"Princess," he said gently, pleading.

"Why do you even care! Why worry about what I do? It's not as if you are my father!" she screamed.

Hawke flinched, and the air in the room seemed to cool suddenly as Sybell studied the man's strange reaction. Her lips twitched, and her eyes darted from Hawke to her mother. Her mother's expression had the girl falling back on the bed, as if her legs could no longer support her weight.

Lynnera spoke so softly that the girl almost did not hear her. "Sybell, we… I…"

She did not need them to speak as the puzzle pieces clicked into place within her. Not a single part of her appearance reflected that of Valdis Kruel, her golden spun hair was a reflection of her mother, but her eyes. Deep dark chocolate, unlike either of her parents, who had deep blue.

The Commander had always treated her with caution and kindness, his eyes always aflame with concern at everything she had ever done.

Eyes the same shade as her own.

"You're my father," she whispered into the silence.

Hawke swallowed audibly. "Sybell, you were not meant to know. Never meant to find out."

Lynnera stood and approached the Commander, her hand lacing with his own. Sybell watched the two exchange a heavy glance, a glance she had never seen her mother and Valdis share. Her mother turned to face her, and the lines of her face smoothed, as if the touch drew out all of her woes.

Her mother looked… happy. She was hesitant, but not because she held the Commander's hand. She was afraid of how her daughter would react.

"We wanted to tell you, but…"

Sybell was silent, watching the exchange between her mother and the Commander.

No, not just the Commander… her true father.

Something within her clicked into place as she stood. Perhaps it was the loss of her closest friend and lover, perhaps her heart yearned for a family she had never truly known, but Sybell approached her parents and slowly walked into their arms.

"It does not matter…" she whispered into the dim candlelight.

For just a fleeting moment, Sybell felt her worries disappear as hesitant arms wrapped around her.

Just for a little while, she let the weight leave her shoulders.

Just for a little while she was not a Princess, but just a daughter, in the arms of her parents.

CHAPTER TWENTY

Standing before the full-length mirror, Arii stared at her unfamiliar refection.

It was the night of the Winter Solstice, the night Lorch had asked her to attend the extravagant party held every year in the castle.

After what felt like hours arguing the day before in the throne room about the cause of the affliction on Ingrid Polaris, and who could have done such a thing to the girl, Arii and Elijah realised that Lorch's mind could not be swayed. The party would go ahead, albeit with additional guards posted around the castle. Arii had argued that she should remain on duty, but the King insisted she take the night off. After heated discussion, Lorch determined that whoever was doing this was already on the castle grounds and called for them all to be extra vigilant when surveying the patrons and staff of the castle tonight.

Elijah would remain on duty, causing Arii to wonder if the man was given much time off. What would Elijah do with time to himself? She imagined him sitting by the pool once more, hands and arms dashed with rainbow splotches of paint, his hair drifting over his silver eyes in a cool afternoon breeze.

The little dimple on his cheek as that hesitant smile curled his lips.

Thoughts pinched at the edge of her mind as she recalled her strange dream from last night, and the hooded man whom she was so desperate to reach. Until now she believed it had been her father. But Arii suddenly found her mind drifting to Elijah. Could it be that he was the man in her dream? Could there be something about him that was far more important than she knew? He was still an enigma, a carefully shrouded shadow. Perhaps there was more to the man than even he knew himself.

As if her thoughts drew the devil, Elijah entered her suite after a brief knock, causing her to whirl and clutch the dress she was wearing to save it from slipping.

"Nyx's arse Elijah, what if I had been halfway through getting dressed?" she snapped as the man paused in the doorway. He did not seem the shy type, and when her eyes met his, she saw she was right about that.

His expression was one that she had not seen before. He seemed fixed to the spot as his eyes slid over her body, unashamed and unabashed as he studied her.

She wore a gown that clung to her lithe form, hugging her curves in all the right places, running straight to flare lightly past her hips and fall to the floor like water. The material was like liquid silver, rippling in the dim golden light from the windows, the strapless bodice featuring intricate patterns like the vines on the castle walls, light mesh in places to show a hint of skin beneath. She had never worn such a gown before – actually, she had never been to a Royal Ball such as this in her life. The dress was from Lorch, of course, the note accompanying the golden box in which it arrived said that this dress reminded him of the silver daggers she loved so much.

Her eyes had been expertly lined with kohl and a dusting of silver paint applied to her eyelids, causing a hint of purple from her irises to be brought through the magically-dulled blue. Her thick tresses fell in heat-curled waves down her shoulders, the tips lightening to gold just below her breasts.

Elijah's breath whooshed from his lungs as he stared, and it was only when Arii's brows narrowed and her free hand lifted to wave his gaze back to her face that he seemed to snap out of it.

"Seeing as you're here, help me get the back of this thing done up, would you?"

With a moment of hesitation, Elijah slowly moved to her, his gait almost that of a stalking wolf. She felt the now familiar tug at her chest, the pool of warmth in her stomach as he paused before her. She turned to the mirror, watching his reflection over her shoulder as his hands lifted to the zip of her bodice.

"This entire party is a load of bullshit," she said, causing his fingers to pause on her gown. His silver eyes met hers in the mirror, and she saw his cheeks were ever so slightly tinged with pink.

"I understand the King's thought process. Perhaps whoever is behind the affliction on Ingrid may be drawn to a crowd of unknown, drunken party goers." His fingers brushed the skin of the small of her back and she felt her heart kick a beat. The zip glided up, perhaps a little more slowly than necessary, as if he was scared it might catch on her skin.

Or he was prolonging their closeness.

Her eyes found his again in the mirror as he looked up, head tilted slightly as the zip reached the top.

"You look… exquisite," he whispered hoarsely.

Slowly Arii turned to him, and he did not back away as she thought he would, the dress brushing his legs as she stared up at him. Chests almost touching, she wondered what it would be like to be in his broad, incredibly strong arms, skin to skin and nothing between them.

Gods, she was getting in too deep. Far, far too deep.

Blood rushed to her cheeks, and she bit her lip, brows narrowing. Never had she felt like a blushing maid under the gaze of a man before. But the look in his eyes at that moment had warmth shooting to her core, almost toppling her over.

She studied him, clad in a uniform made entirely of black leather and cloth, the hints of steel dyed to match his dark attire. It brought out the silver colour of his eyes, two liquid pools of swirling mystery.

They fluttered over her face and slowly – oh so slowly – his hand lifted to brush the line between her drawn brows.

That tiny gesture and what it meant to her was almost her undoing.

She held everything back as a flood of desire crashed through her, causing her to close her eyes against the sudden wave of feeling.

"Perhaps tonight you can afford to let your hair down, just for a short time." His voice was a deep, gentle melody. Thick lashes swept her cheeks as she exhaled, his fingers tracing her jawline to pause at her lips. It was as if he knew she had never allowed emotion to pierce her, never allowed herself to feel like a normal… woman.

"And perhaps smile for once?" he added gently.

He was telling her to smile? Coming from the man who hardly ever hinted at his emotions – his face a stoic façade of stone – this was almost laughable.

Arii's eyes drifted open, the dark pools of violet glimmering as she murmured, "Perhaps I'll find you for a dance? Maybe you could let your hood down for a night." His lips twitched in response as she added, "I imagine you would be an incredible dancer, if how you fight is any indication."

"Well, actually…"

She poked a finger into his chest as she exclaimed softly, "No! You can't dance?"

A quirk of his brow and a slight tilt of his head to the side was her only answer.

"Well, we will make quite the entertainment – I can't either," she said, grinning. "Two fish out of water."

"My excuse is lack of practice… you? I imagine it's like in the training ring – all offense and no discipline."

Her hand snapped to playfully shove him, but the move was pointless. Elijah did not budge, her palm slapping against his solid chest.

"And dancing takes a level of discipline – just like in the ring, which as I've said, *you* lack." He cut off her quickly formulating curse as she moved to playfully whack him upside the head – but her wrist was suddenly caught in a vice-like grip.

They paused, staring at one another for a few silent moments.

The air began to heat, and Arii felt the steady staccato of Elijah's heart beneath the palm that remained on his chest, her eyes widening as realisation dawned at what she was about to do.

He had said just yesterday that he did not like to be touched.

"Elijah, I'm sorry – I was only jesting."

Her eyes met silver, and instead of seeing anger there, she saw something else.

A glimmer of hesitation, yet there was a sparkle of amusement.

His thumb stroked over her wrist, skimming her quickly rising pulse as he whispered, "You don't need to apologise. I knew what I was getting myself into."

She swallowed thickly as his eyes danced from her face, along her bare shoulder and up… up along her arm to her hand – held firmly in his. Voices sounded in the halls beyond, and Arii was dimly aware of the sounds of the castle grounds outside her window – bustling with activity and arriving guests.

They stood in the gentle afternoon light, the rays dancing along their joined hands. Slowly, Elijah's fingers brushed down her forearm, and they both watched as gooseflesh rose in the wake of his touch on her skin.

Gods, her body was going to give her away.

With deliberate slowness, she dared to let her hand drift to his face, fingers hesitantly skimming the stubble of his jaw – adventuring lightly to his neck, pausing a few fingers from where Ingrid's bite had healed in a white crescent moon upon his skin.

She heard his inhale of breath, saw the gentle flutter of his eyelashes as mercury disappeared behind closed lids, thick lashes brushing his cheeks.

Holy mother of darkness.

She knew it was wrong… oh so *wrong*.

But she wanted him.

Wanted him more than anything she had ever wanted before.

In that moment, she did not care for anything anymore.

Her assignment, the Kryverns, the afflicted, the Nexus Crystals. In the small, yet heavily charged moment – she wished to be someone else. Not an assassin, not a killer suppressed of emotion, not a deliverer of fate.

She wished to be just… Arii.

They were so close that she could smell him – pine and sandalwood mixed with an unfamiliar scent that was just… him. She felt the heat of his breath as he exhaled, their faces a mere inch apart now as she whispered, barely audible, "The party is probably starting."

He swallowed, his eyelids lifted a fraction.

"Then you shouldn't be late…"

She wished for just a few more moments, almost begged the gods for more time. But, as her hand slowly fell from his neck, she felt a featherlight touch on her chin as Elijah's breath brushed over her lips.

Oh… so… close.

It was like a kiss from a butterfly's wings – fleeting and gone before she could fully register the touch.

Elijah stepped back, breaking the moment.

"Don't worry," he said, the corner of his lips twitching in the hint of a smile, and she longed to see him give a smile that was free and uncaring. His eyes had darkened like storm clouds over the Dragon's Teeth mountains.

"I'll be watching over you. Have some fun tonight."

Incredible, was Elijah Wolfe truly telling her to have *fun*?

Perhaps Ingrid's bite had dislodged something in his brain.

Or perhaps the words were lightly veiled as a threat.

Her brain was so muddled that she could not think straight.

With that, he swept from the room, leaving Arii to struggle with the inferno of raging emotions within her.

കൃജ

The throne room of Viridya Castle was crowded with bodies as people danced, drank and conversed under the twinkling chandeliers of candlelight. The room looked ethereal, adorned with garlands of glittering holly leaves, tables spread with hundreds of tealights and incredible arrays of food. Roast lambs sliced delicately, colourful vegetables and steaming pots of herbed gravy, accompanied with arrays of cakes and delectable finger sweets. Pine trees had been brought into the space and placed in the corners of the room, decorated with sparkling baubles and glitter, causing everything to reflect the light flickering across the room.

Arii paused in the doorway, her simple silver mask fixed with diamond-encrusted clips to her hair, covering the top half of her face. The entire room seemed to pause and turn to face her, and she felt her spine straighten under the weight of hundreds of eyes. In that moment she was incredibly grateful for the mask as she lifted her chin and entered the room.

She searched for a familiar face, and sure enough her eyes landed on a woman with silver hair shimmering to her chin. Arii made her way to Nemesis, and the woman's lips curled in a smile.

"Well, well," purred the Fury, her aqua eyes striking even behind her mask of black velvet. Nemesis wore a velour gown as black as the night sky, encrusted with tiny sequins which glimmered in the candlelight.

"Well yourself," said Arii, gesturing at her outfit. "You could kill a man with heart palpitations just by looking at you, Nem."

"Let's not shy away from the fact that practically every eye is on you tonight. Where did you get that dress?"

Arii cleared her throat, dipping to snatch a crystal goblet of sweet wine before her eyes surveyed the party. "The King," she answered simply.

"Of course."

Arii's eyes found Lorch on the dais, Elijah a few feet away and cloaked in shadow. Her mind slipped to the feeling of his lips bushing hers, his warm fingers gliding down her arm. She suppressed a shudder of longing.

"We'll need to be alert in this crowd."

Arii's eyes slid to Nem and she nodded in agreeance.

"Should you see anything at all, send a small burst of magic and I'll find you."

"Same to you," said Nem, before the two women parted to mingle in the crowds.

Music thrummed through the hall, the melody reverberating off the high ceiling and creating a crush of bodies in the centre on the dancefloor. People danced and laughed, pressing together as the music reached an exciting crescendo. Despite herself, Arii felt the urge to tap her toes as the dancers thumped their heels in time with the music.

Her eyes slid across the scene as she surveyed it for anything odd. She may have been given the night off, but Arii could not let the habit slide. She found the dais once more, lingering for just a few moments on Elijah before skipping to Lynnera, who was conversing with Hawke as he stood vigil nearby. The woman's face had healed, a slight tinge of purple still evident under her eye – and Arii could tell that makeup had been used to cover it.

Nearby, Valdis stood. His own eyes swept the party, expression unreadable.

Then, they paused on her.

She felt a shiver of disgust dance down her spine, recalling his insistence that the body in the courtyard was simply an attack by wolves. And then his quiet, angry glare as they discussed the affliction on Ingrid.

It was strange. Every time his eyes rested on her, she felt like there was flickering hatred in their oceanic depths – a fire of resentment that she could not quite understand.

He had been unusually quiet when Lorch insisted they let the party go ahead.

As always, she felt uneasy and queasy in his presence. Not many men did that to her.

After an hour, Arii was surprised that the King had not sought her out yet. He had merely caught her gaze a few times from his perch on the throne, smiling as he lifted a goblet as if to salute her.

She had offered a smile back but found herself caught speaking to people she had never met, and graciously dodging offers of dances from countless young men who worked up the courage to approach her. A few times she sought reprieve with Tikkani and Emerson, off to the side as the two elves watched over the proceedings.

So far, nothing seemed amiss.

After catching the twins up on the events of the following night, they had become sombre and took their guard posts particularly seriously after that. Their eyes scanned each party patron, Tikkani's usual glitter of mischief non-existent.

"Anything?" Arii said as she picked at the food on a table nearby.

Tikkani shook her head gently.

"No, nothing out of the ordinary, besides you in that gown – Gods above, girl!"

Arii rolled her eyes and grinned. There it was. She could not help herself, and Arii found that the girl's easy banter was a balm in an otherwise awkward situation.

"I'm guessing Quinn has not seen you yet, he may just forget Devina Divine," muttered Emerson from the opposite side of the table. Arii waggled her eyebrows at the boy, and his cheeks flushed scarlet.

"Go and enjoy yourself, Arii. We have your back," said Tikkani, and Arii believed her. The last month had solidified a bond between them all, even though she spent more time training with Elijah. She found the days where the group mucked the stalls, ran the castle grounds and broke their fast on the dragon landing were some of the best moments of her time there. She slowly found a sense of ease, a sense she had not felt with anyone aside from Nemesis and Krepth.

She knew it was dangerous – becoming attached.

Attachment meant weakness, and a Fury could not afford to have weakness.

Arii moved from her friends and pushed into the throng of bodies, eyes sweeping faces for anything out of the ordinary.

Like water, the crowd began to part before her, and she soon found herself pausing before the King.

He stood in the middle of the dancefloor, adorned in a fine suit of cream laced with gold thread, his crown perched on his head. He wore a mask of simple white, the edges framed with stitched gold filigree.

Lorch smirked as he motioned for her to join him, his oceanic eyes glittering with mirth. Arii's eyes flicked across the people standing either side of them, looks of disbelief and jealously mixed with awe. She lifted her chin and approached, her hand sliding into his as the music began again, a gentle tempo that had couples coming together to sway.

Lorch pulled her to him, his other hand slipping around her waist as they slid into a gentle waltz.

"Gods, I thought you'd look beautiful tonight Miss Clearwater, but I severely underestimated how much." His voice was smooth as honey as she glanced up at him, his eyes fixed on her face.

She felt blood rise to her cheeks under his unabashed stare.

"Thank you, Your Highness," she said, her hand resting on his bicep as they gently swayed in time with the music. He pulled her close, their chests touching as they twirled.

His head dipped to rest against her temple, and she felt the tension she had been holding slowly melt away. He seemed to have that effect on her, stoking a gentle flame and making a warm heat glide through her body, easing her muscles and causing her to become comfortable.

Far too comfortable.

"I've been thinking about the girl, and what you witnessed in the caverns. I am going to find out who did this, Arii. And when I do… They'll wish they never set foot in my castle."

Arii paused, glancing up at him. The tone in his voice was like steel, a harshness she had not expected. What had happened to Ingrid perhaps rattled him harder than she had thought.

"But for tonight, let us enjoy the festivities. It is Winter Solstice after all, a day to eat, drink and be merry."

Arii's teeth clenched as the King brushed recent events aside, like dust under a heavy royal rug. She guessed she should not be surprised, Lorch was known to leave the hard work to others, but she did sense genuine concern radiating from him as he squeezed her hand.

Sharing a dance and some wine for one night would not hinder them from getting to the bottom of what happened. Perhaps the party would yield results. Arii hoped Elijah was watching for unusual signs during the party rather than her dance with the King, but something told her that he was sure to be keeping his eye on them.

Did it matter what he thought, truly? Yes, they had a strange, sizzling attraction forming but the King's bodyguard was still a mystery to her. Besides, he did not trust her, and he had made that clear plenty of times, despite his sweet words prior to the party. She knew Elijah still had his walls up tight – what she had seen was a small slip in the defences.

It did not mean anything.

A strange feeling of melancholy wrapped her heart.

The music upped in tempo, and Lorch swept her into a deep dip, causing her to yelp in surprise. She could toss blades like darts at a board, slice through men's necks like butter and leap nimbly from rooftop to rooftop, but that did not mean she could dance.

In actual fact, Ariiaya Trillia was a fish out of water then it came to the art of a dancefloor.

Lorch pulled her up smoothly from the dip, holding her body against his as he grinned down at her with a look of smug satisfaction. Arii's lips pursed and he chuckled.

"Don't tell me you cannot dance!"

Argh, was it that obvious?

She bit her lip and her eyes darted away. "Perhaps dance isn't my strong suit," she whispered. This only seemed to spur him on as the music rose in tempo, and Lorch showed her the steps to what was called the *Royal Jig*.

Left hands up and pressed together, left foot kicked out then back in, before partners spun while keeping their hands together and eyes locked. Then, repeat with the right hand and foot. After a couple of rounds, Arii picked it up quickly and was surprised to feel the blooming of a laugh. The dance became fast paced, and the entire floor of people became a twirling, glittering sea of vibrant colours as elaborately designed masks and outfits added to the dazzling kaleidoscope of hues.

For the first time in what seemed her entire life, Ariiaya the heartless assassin was having fun. Actual mindless fun. There was no duty, there was no impending doom looming over the castle, just sweet, gratuitous fun.

She grinned as her eyes met Lorch's, their expressions mirrored behind their masks, his eyes glittering as they twirled in time to the music. His fingers laced with hers as the beat began to level, and she found she was staring at him as their bodies slowly spun, coming together in the middle of the dancefloor. In that moment, the people around them dissipated as her attention was squared solely on the handsome man before her, his lopsided smile slowly gracing his lips as they came together under a canopy of glittering gold.

His eyes hooded, and she felt his hand slide to her waist once again, settling on the small of her back.

"Gods, you're breathtaking…" the King whispered as they swayed, bringing their twined fingers up to his lips before gliding them over her knuckle. His breath was warm, tinged with faint traces of sweet wine. Not for one moment did their gazes part, and she felt almost lost in their oceanic depths.

Her damned cheeks flushed with scarlet again. Was this how Emerson felt every time she made him feel uncomfortable?

No… No, she did not feel uncomfortable. She felt… warm, dare she say, fuzzy inside. Hell, if Nem heard what was happening in her mind right now, the woman would not let her live it down.

"You aren't so bad yourself," she said, unable to look away.

"It's stifling in here, what do you say we get some air?"

Oh gods, yes please.

"That would be fantastic," she agreed as Lorch led her from the crowded dancefloor to the balcony doors.

The cool air was like caressing fingers across her heated skin as they pushed into the night, and she tilted her head back in pleasure, a small smile on her lips. The cool, damp air felt like heaven after the roasting throne room. The covered balcony, of polished marble, had a stunning view of half the castle grounds. The other half was the dark, glittering stretch of The Sapphire Depths. Rain was beginning to ease into a light sprinkle, and the moon peaked from behind clouds in the night sky, reflecting silver across the vast body of water. The night air was biting, and as the thought crossed her mind – a cloth blanket draped over her shoulders.

Lorch.

He smiled and led her to the railing, turning to lean on the polished marble, surveying her expression. "It's cold out tonight, I didn't want you to catch a chill, so blankets are available at every balcony doorway."

"Incredible foresight you have, or do you do this with all of your dates?"

"On a date, are we?"

She chomped down on her lip.

"No, I–"

Lorch lifted a hand to brush a bead of rain from her cheek, his head tilting gently. "I know what you mean, Arii. I would say no but I'd be lying if I said I didn't prepare my parties according to how I'd hope the night would play out."

His eyes glittered behind his mask.

"And how do you hope this night will play out?" she asked carefully.

Lorch picked up on her tone and moved to stand beside her as his eyes took in the breathtaking view before them. "That is completely up to you, Miss Clearwater."

She could feel the heat of him beside her as their arms brushed. How did *she* want this night to play out?

She felt on the cusp of the royal waterfall, staring down into the churning white depths as she struggled within herself. Could she take a leap of faith and plummet into the unknown waters below?

Lorch inched behind her, his hand hesitantly sliding up her arm. Her skin rose with gooseflesh at his touch, and she slowly turned to face him. She felt the railing press against the small of her back as Lorch rested his other hand on the railing behind her.

She heard his breath catch as his hand moved to her cheek, drawing warmth along her jawline. "Anything you do not wish to do, Arii, I will not make you."

Surprise flickered across her features.

He was the King of Fythnar, used to getting everything he wanted, *whoever* he wanted, and she had no doubt by now that he wanted her.

Yet he hesitated, allowing her to make the choice as to where they were headed, showing a decency so unlike that of what he was rumoured to possess. Arii was still seeing those rumours stamped as false.

Her own hand gently tugged his mask from his face. He did not stop her as she let it clatter to the marble, and she removed her own soon after, adding it to his on the wet floor.

She made her decision and knew exactly where this night was to end, in the arms of this gentle, misunderstood young King.

Her lips met his, and that was the only signal of approval Lorch needed. His hand slid around to the nape of her neck and he deepened their kiss, his body pressing against hers as he pinned her against the railing. She felt warmth erupt in her chest, a pleasant feeling of heat as her hand tangled in his hair, the other clutching his back. Her fingers glanced over the crown, the cool metal against her fingertips causing her to pause.

Lorch broke the kiss and gazed at her, his blue eyes mirroring the depths housing the Water Nymphs beyond.

"Crown," she said with a smile, and he grinned back.

"Damn thing, so uncomfortable after wearing it for hours on end. Alas, I cannot take it off until in the privacy of my chambers."

He dipped his head to her neck, placing gentle kisses up to the sensitive skin just beneath her earlobe. Her toes curled in her slippers. Gods, he had no idea what that did to her. If he were Fae, he would be sure to smell her arousal by now.

Thankfully, he was not Fae, but she could not help the small sound that escaped her lips.

Lorch grinned against her neck. "Like that?" he purred, placing another kiss to the spot, causing her to roll her head to the side and a small moan to escape her lips.

"Gods yes," she whispered hoarsely.

Raindrops glittered against his lashes as he moved to face her, his eyes hooded and dark now.

"If there is anything you do not wish me to do-"

Arii placed a finger against his lips before he could continue.

"You'd know with steel to your nether regions, Lorch. You may be the King but you are still a man."

Lorch chuckled and nipped at her bottom lip. "Of course, my little trapeze artist. I do not doubt it."

She felt the press of steel at her inner thigh, the cool metal reassuring against her skin. She was a guard; protection always came first.

Lorch dipped to retrieve their masks, flicking water from them and handing hers back.

"Shall we find somewhere… warm?" he ventured, his breath misting against her neck.

With a nod, Arii smiled and took his hand.

ᘓᘔ

Elijah watched as Arii and Lorch returned from their time on the balcony, grabbing glasses of sweet wine and laughing while holding hands. Lorch had no idea what gossip this would begin, the courtiers would have a feeding frenzy as tales of a new mistress to the King fluttered about the kingdom.

Something within him coiled at the idea, his eyes narrowing in on their joined hands.

What was it to him who his friend chose to bed?

Perhaps it was because he still did not fully trust the woman, or perhaps it was the pull he felt between himself and Miss Clearwater.

Was Lorch correct in saying he felt the very same pull to her as what he felt? It was like an invisible thread wrapping around his heart and tugging on his chest. She was beautiful, he had known that the moment he had seen her fell the beast at Lorch's birthday celebration. Since he had come to know her as a cocky, fire tongued woman who radiated confidence, but also he saw vulnerability in her dark eyes. He believed her to be far deeper than she allowed everyone to see – or allowed herself to feel. He found himself wondering about her past.

What had caused her to build such walls of stone around her heart?

Elijah watched with arms across his chest as Lorch tugged Arii from the room, headed in the direction of his chambers.

Trust… He had to have trust.

He hoped the hours of training had sunk into the young man's head and trusted that if something were to happen then Lorch would know how to defend himself. Elijah let out a low breath as they disappeared, and he felt something crawling up within him.

He supposed the feeling may have been sadness, but he did not allow it to rise to the surface as he turned and stalked from the throne room.

MelissaKincai

CHAPTER TWENTY-ONE

Lorch's breath whooshed from his lungs as his back hit solid metal, fingers tangled in her dark tresses as Arii pressed him against the wall of his personal suite. Their tongues danced, and fingers grasped at each other's clothing as she tore open the front of his tunic. Far from Arii's mind was the worry of damaging the expensive piece of clothing.

She gazed down at his lean chest and stomach, her eyes slowly tracking back up to his face.

Lorch's eyes met hers, and what she saw had her pausing.

They were dark like the deepest churning seas.

His lips began to twitch in a grin as she pressed her lips to his collarbone. A groan escaped him as he brought her lips to his again, shrugging out of his tunic and letting it fall to the floor. Swiftly he set his crown on the side table to his right, the gold shimmering in the moonlight. Gently he turned her body around, proceeding to slide down the zip on her bodice. He paused, his head dropping to place a gentle kiss upon her shoulder.

Arii was reminded of how she stood with Elijah mere hours ago, his fingers gliding against the skin of her back. Her skin pimpled with gooseflesh as her head rolled to the side, a silent sigh passing her lips.

What she was feeling now with Lorch seemed wholly different to what she felt in Elijah's presence. With Elijah, it was as if she were inching around a dangerous animal, her skin prickling with electricity and a strange thrill of danger. With Lorch, she felt warmth with a fluttering of excited butterflies in her stomach.

This feeling though was strange and new, something she had never allowed herself to feel, having only overheard it described by giddy barmaids in dark taverns.

Why was it now that as the King turned her to face him, did she feel she could allow a little of her walls to come down?

Her gown fell and pooled at her feel like molten lead, and she was suddenly standing half-dressed before him. As his eyes soaked up her body, his smile faded as something completely different washed over his features.

Awe.

Then his brows knitted in confusion.

She knew then that he saw the scars that marred her alabaster skin, little reminders from her past bathed in the moonlight. She had refused to heal them completely with magic, reminders of her life upon the pages of her own book. Each scar held a tale, and short of inking her own novel – this was the only way she felt her stories could be told.

In flesh, in blood, in defects upon her skin.

She was far from perfect.

She was far from human.

She was a Fae.

A Fury.

Under his flickering gaze, Arii felt stronger than she had felt in a long time. His eyes jumped to her hip, and she felt a moment of pause.

Lorch's eyes fell on the dagger strapped to her thigh.

With deliberate slowness, she unstrapped the clasp on the leather strap, before placing the dagger on the nightstand beside his crown. Lorch did not move, fixed to the spot as his eyes tracked her movements.

Was he afraid? Had he forgotten for just a moment that she was a soldier first, and a lady second? When her eyes met his once more, there was fire there that she was not sure she understood.

"Gods, you're like the goddess Nyx herself sent in the form of a woman, here to end my life," he blew out a breath and whispered hoarsely, "You are incredibly sexy."

Arii almost laughed at how close to the truth he had come.

She kept the amusement from her face as she sauntered towards him, her strides confident and hips swaying. Perhaps he was used to meek women? She was anything but meek, in truth. She imagined that was why he was drawn to her.

No, she was not like other women.

Oh, how easy it would be now to end him at this moment. She was right where she wanted to be naught a month ago – no guards and no one to stop her. So much had happened since her arrival, and the events they had witnessed in the short time had changed her perception of him.

Lorch's eyes searched hers, hunting for any sign of hesitation within their dark depths.

They met with smouldering purple fire.

Outside, a resounding boom of thunder sounded, and a flash of silver lightning tore across the room.

Were the Gods sending her a sign? Perhaps they were stomping their feet in frustration as Lorch's back hit the mattress, the Fury straddled atop him as they kissed with abandon. Their lips searched each other's skin as if a drug laced their very flesh and they were feeding an addiction.

Lorch kissed her scars, his breath causing goosebumps as her teeth caught her bottom lip, stifling a moan. Flipping them so that he was upon her, leaning back to survey her beneath him with dark eyes.

"Where did you get this?" he panted, a thumb passing over a puckered scar just below her breast.

"Sword point after beating a man at a game of cards. He was a sore loser," she sighed as he dipped his head and kissed the scar.

The way he looked at her scars had her heart fluttering. He looked at them as if they were stories on the page of a tome, eager to learn their origins. There was naught a hint of disgust in his eyes, and she was surprised to feel that she had expected it from him.

He chuckled breathlessly as his finger traced a small, thin scar on her abdomen.

"And this?"

Arii paused as she formulated a story for that particular scar, but all she could muster was the truth.

"My best friend gave me that scar… Well, that was before I found out she wasn't a complete and total bitch."

Lorch's brows rose at that. "She sounds delightful. Why do I find it hard to imagine anyone tougher than you?"

Arii grinned and flipped the King onto his back, straddling his thighs as she smirked down at him.

"Oh yes, she'd chew ore and spit out nails… She even scares *me*."

Arii imagined Nem's face glaring at her at that moment and suppressed an internal shudder. The woman would find out about this, she always did find out about things eventually. It was if the silver haired Fury had a sixth sense.

"That's hard to believe, you don't seem to be afraid of anything," said Lorch, brushing a lock of hair over her shoulder before leaning up and skimming his lips along her collarbone. "Perhaps I'll meet her someday…" he continued, words trailing away upon her skin. As his hand laced in her hair once more, pulling her to him, her lips crashed against his and she knew they were done talking.

Thunder shook the windows and caused her dagger to rattle against his golden crown on the nightstand.

Arii pressed all thought from her mind and just allowed herself to feel the physical pleasure, to drown in the warmth of his body and the flutter of his uncalloused hands over her skin. The scent of him filled her senses, vanilla and honey with a dash of cinnamon.

Everywhere on their bodies they could touch, they did, exploring every inch of one another in the flickering firelight as the flames in the hearth slowly dimmed to smouldering embers.

As his fingers laced with hers on the mattress and their bodies melded in the moonlight, Ariiaya Trillia, the emotionless Fae assassin allowed her carefully constructed walls of ice to crumble and fall – just for one night.

Perhaps she was not so different from those other women after all.

ᎧᏠ

The next morning, Arii slipped from the bed covers and ran a hand over her recovering lips, still slightly swollen from the King's kisses during the night.

She paused, seeing a small pile of clothing folded neatly on the settee across from the bed. A maid must have left the pile of clothing while they slept, having known the King had a visitor. Her eyes drifted to Lorch on the bed, a hand resting on his stomach as his chest rose and fell gently in sleep, his head tilted to the side, the lower half of his body covered by the sheets. Well, the maid must have carefully chosen their chance to bring the clothing. They had spent most of the night lost in each other, their bodies coming together with more stamina than she had thought the King capable of.

Her body felt languid, relaxed.

Strangely, *almost* sated.

During their coupling, her beast had hardly risen its head – remaining firmly asleep despite the ripples of pleasure Lorch had wrung from her body. During the time between while they recovered, skin coated in sweat and chests rising and falling, they had talked in hushed voices.

Arii learned that Lorch deeply cared for his sister and mother, and in an odd way he admired his *bastard* of a father. Another testament to the gold lacing of his heart. She supposed if it were not for his mother, Lorch Kruel would be far closer to resembling his father in personality, not just in looks like he did now.

Last night… what they had shared. She did not regret it. Not at all.

As her fingers brushed her lips, she envisioned flashes of memory.

Lorch's eyes lifting to meet hers as he dipped his head between her legs – their gazes unbreaking.

His hand clutching her hip as they lay side by side, legs entwined and his low sigh against the crook of her neck, the brush of his sweat drenched brow against her own.

The way he looked beneath her – glistening and golden – as she sat upon him and moaned her pleasure to the Gods in the heavens above as her body exploded with stars, shattering like delicate glass.

Yet, her beast had not stirred.

She felt a flicker of regret at leaving Lorch while he slept, but she knew Elijah was going to be waiting for her in the ring for their morning spar.

She dressed swiftly, sliding the dagger against her hip and under the band of the simple cloth pants, tossing her mussed hair into a quick braid.

Arii glanced down at Lorch once more, his face smooth in sleep. Her heart squeezed, and she realised that she had entered this room last night with the intention of sating a burning need within her, nothing more.

Now, she was leaving having learned far more about herself than she expected. She knew deep down she was not heartless, no matter the years of training and suppression of her emotions. Lorch stirred something within her, and at first, she thought it had been simple lust, something that could be sated within his chambers.

What she had not expected was that she suddenly did not want to leave. She wished to remain, folded in his embrace as he pressed his lips to her brow, the way they had lain tangled together a few hours ago.

She was changing, and she was not sure that what was happening to her could be undone.

What this meant for her future moving forward, she had no clue. She had always been like a Kryvern at a gate, unthinking of consequences and just living in the now, with no thought for her future. She figured fate knew what was in store for her, and whatever that was she would face with open arms.

She had been moulded to never think or question fate.

Suddenly, she was dangerously close to doing both of those things.

Silently she slipped from the room, gently pulling the door closed as she turned towards her rooms, eager to change before training.

That was when she suddenly came face to face with Valdis Kruel.

Cool steel shackles snapped over her wrists before she could think, and the man's lips curled back in a feral smirk. Her chest constricted and her mouth snapped open, her magic fleeing her body in a sudden, violent rush.

No, not steel.

Iron.

Valdis' deep, drawling voice whispered against her ear as arms seized her from all sides. Red Guard soldiers, she realised through the haze.

"You have a date with Bonemire, little Fury," he purred, before something struck the back of her skull and her vision plunged into darkness.

಍⁊

Eyes flickered open, blinking back a haze of fog as Arii awoke to the sound of horses' hooves crunching on gravel. Her back pressed against hard wood, her head pounded as if she had consumed more than a few tankards of sweet wine the night before. She groaned, then spat blood onto the floor of the carriage, right onto the polished boots of a Red Guard soldier sitting across from her.

The man's face twisted as his head snapped up, meeting dark purple eyes and a slow, bloody smirk.

"You Fae bitch," the guard snarled, shooting forward and cracking a gauntleted hand across her face, snapping her head to the side.

Stars burst before her eyes as Arii rolled her jaw, her head turning back to glare at the soldier, before proceeding to spit fresh blood onto the floor by his boots once more. The man jerked up but was held back by a second soldier before he could strike the Fury again.

"Blair, it isn't worth it. Valdis wants her alive."

The man grunted and shrugged off his companion, dropping back onto the bench seat reluctantly. His eyes did not leave the woman though.

Bonemire, they were taking her to Bonemire.

How had Valdis found out that she was a Fury? Her mind worked quickly, grasping at the fragments of memory, at anything that could help solve the puzzle.

The carriage jerked to a stop, causing the fragments of her mind to scatter like the stones beneath the horse's hooves. The doors flew open as the guards moved to grab her arms, dragging her roughly from the transport.

She did not fight them, but oh how she wished she could.

Her body felt weak without her magic, limbs trembling and fluid like a newborn deer. She stumbled and the guards flanked her sides, dragging her towards the fortress.

Her head tilted up, eyes wide as the behemoth structure loomed over them, the opening into the grounds beyond yawned wide, ready to swallow them whole. The walls were dark grey and made of thick stone, a startling contrast to the shimmering golden castle they had left behind.

The structure loomed, solid and dark, parts of the stone chipped away as if by past onslaughts. Two towers stood either side of the square fortress, another two peaking in the distance, sentries to the inner ward and structure below. Soldiers paced inside them, keeping watch over all.

As they passed through to the gatehouse, Arii's eyes darted to the platforms above as the guards paused to watch while she was brought into the inner ward.

Ahead, her vision stilled on Valdis, standing in his perfect Red Guard uniform, lips curled and eyes narrowed to slits. Her stomach churned, bile rising as the guards threw her to the mud before the Hand of the King.

"Welcome to Bonemire," he announced, lifting his arms in theatrical welcome as all eyes now rested on them. He stared down at the woman in the mud, his expression unchanging, surveying the dirt coating her legs and hands, the blood caked on her lips as they curled back over her teeth.

"What do you want with me?" she hissed.

This only seemed to stoke the fire as Valdis laughed darkly.

"I knew it was only a matter of time before you would let your guard down and slide into bed with my son," he sneered. "The perfect opportunity to catch you unawares, for you see, I am in need of you." He flicked his hand in her direction, as if she were naught but a sewer rat. "Well, your body anyway."

Cold hard dread doused her rage.

"How did you-"

"How did I discover you were a Fury assassin? Well, it isn't what you know – but perhaps *who* you know."

Swallowing her rage, she glared at the man as he motioned to the soldiers.

"Take her to the cells," barked Valdis, and hands grabbed her again. His blue eyes, so much like his son's, watched as they passed and she struggled to walk proudly upright.

Perhaps the gods were indeed upset with her, causing her to question if her decisions leading up to that point had twisted the string of her own fate, and not for the better.

০৪৪০

Iron manacles rubbed against her wrists, the flesh so raw from her struggles that it had begun to cut into her skin. Arii's eyes squeezed shut as she reached inwards, grasping for a flicker, a single ember of her magic.

She felt nothing, as if she was a shell of her former self.

A wail left her, unable to accept that she was completely and utterly alone. The brief fleeing of her magic after the Kryvern's claws cleaved her skin had nothing on this. Now she felt weak and shaky, the feeling of hopelessness weighing heavily, part of her soul torn from her and tossed far away.

Arii's mind slid back to the fuzzy details of her capture. Valdis had hinted that someone had given her cover away, but who?

Her head rested on the solid stone wall, her mouth gaping as she sucked in a deep breath. The cells in the depths of Bonemire smelled of faeces and rot, the walls gouged in places as if something with claws had been housed here at some point and had marked the walls with its fury.

Her arms rested before her as the fight slowly ebbed from her body.

She wondered why they did not fix her with chains to the wall but supposed the iron on her skin was doing the job of keeping her pliant. It was only when her magic was gone completely that she realised how much she relied on it. How much a part of her the magic was.

Was this what it was like to be human?

She swallowed, her throat bone dry and her lips cracked.

The lock in the cell door creaked before the door opened and a soldier entered. He held a small bucket of water, the liquid sloshing against the sides as he placed it on the floor before her. Never had she heard a sweeter sound at that moment as she shot forward and clasped the bucket. When the metal sizzled against her fingertips, she cried out and let it fall, water gushing over the cold stone floor.

The bucket was made of iron.

White hot rage shearing through her like lightning.

Fucking bastards.

Arii launched herself at the guard, her iron shackles looping over the man's head before he could blink, yanking the chain against his neck as he choked out a sound of alarm. She leapt upon his back as they crashed to the floor and with what little strength she had left, Arii pulled the chain against the man's windpipe, her face contorted in pure animal rage. The man rasped as his face turned blue, his legs kicking wildly as his hands scraped feebly against the iron links around his throat.

Suddenly hands seized her and she was screaming, limbs shooting out as two more soldiers swarmed her. Her foot connected with the gut of one man and he stumbled back, hitting the wall. The other soldier seized her waist and threw her to the floor so violently that the breath left her lungs and pain rocketed up her spine.

The man who had thrown her down loomed over her, his sword pressing against her neck as she gasped for breath. From beside her she heard the soldier she had nearly choked to death gasping and cursing with words so vile she would have blushed had she been a mere maiden.

"Do you kiss your mother with that mouth?" she choked out, and the man's boot connected with her face. Blood exploded from her lips, splattering across the dreary granite walls.

"You little Fae slut!" he roared and prepared to boot her again, but the second soldier halted him with a hand.

"No! Lord Valdis wants this one relatively unharmed–" he jerked his chin as the woman groaned on the floor "–unfortunately. She needs to be conscious for what he has planned."

"Lucky me," she spat as the soldiers hefted her up and out of the cell.

Arii slumped as they dragged her through the freezing cold halls of the fortress, the walls lit with flaming torches. There was not a flicker of royal extravagance here. The exposed stone with the raw flickering firelight created an eerie feel, the floors stained with what could only be dried blood.

As they passed lines of cells, Arii swore she could hear the sounds of others within, groaning and pleading to be released. A hand shot out from within one of the cells, reaching for them and clutching the air wildly as the thing inside moaned and screamed.

Arii was immediately reminded of Ingrid Polaris, her black eyes devoid of all humanity as she launched herself at them with no other intent but to kill.

Was that what they were doing here? Experimenting on people with the Nexus Crystals? What was the purpose of it, what had Valdis to gain by creating that… thing?

Ingrid had been consumed with the need to maim and kill, mindless; except when the girl had hesitated before Sybell. Had she had a flicker of remembrance for the Princess from her former life, like a flicker of sunlight through the darkness in her dead mind?

As they dragged her through another courtyard, Arii's eyes widened in horror.

Kryverns, there were tens of them.

All were caged, some were awake and watching her with blood red eyes, some dozed against the bars. Some fought, crashing against their prisons and bellowing with animal rage. Iron lined the tables adjacent to them, iron shaped into claws and teeth. Littering the yard were piles of glimmering Nexus Crystals, in wooden crates and on tables. Some of the dormant crystals were tossed carelessly to the floor and swept into corners.

Where had they found so many crystals, powered with magic? Her mind flicked over possible magic wielders who could have lent their power to the crystals.

Apart from what few Fae still existed within the School of Fate, Arii could think of no one else.

Was someone working with Valdis to power up the stones? Or was the power being *taken*, and not given.

Nexus Crystals did not just flare to life of their own accord – someone had to charge them up, lending their magic to the stones.

Three men dressed in white cloth and splattered with blood worked on a sleeping beast, sawing off its claws to replace them with new iron ones. She saw bodies on tables as the same cream clothed men stabbed daggers into their chests, and some were in the process of shoving heart sized crystals within their splayed ribs.

She saw humans, and elves, and Nymphs. All milky white in death, all wide eyed and slack mouthed – gazes to the starry sky they would never see with living eyes again.

Arii jerked forward and vomited across the stones, much to the dismay of her escorts.

Her jailers soon threw her to the floor of a large room, her knees hitting the stone first, hands flying out to prevent her face from colliding with the floor. Arii jerked her head up to see Valdis, standing before an array of tables, his face set in the smirk she had seen earlier.

"Leave us," he barked at the soldiers, who bowed and quickly swept from the room. Arii leaned back on her haunches, eyes tracking the man as he turned to one of the tables and began to mull over the instruments on top. From her place on the floor, she could not see what was up there, but she was not stupid.

He was choosing his device of torture.

"Why?" she said to his back, her voice stronger than she had expected it to be.

Valdis glanced over his shoulder, his copper hair tinged like fire in the flickering torchlight. His ugly scar stood out predominantly as he turned to face her.

"Why?" he echoed, as he lifted a nasty looking knife and held it to the lamplight. "That's a good question. The feeling you have within you right now is the reason why."

He stepped towards her and she felt panic bubble within her, acidic and powerful.

Fear.

She had not felt fear such as this in an awfully long time.

The man crouched down to her level, his eyes dark with intent. "Fear, helplessness… powerlessness. That very feeling you have within you at this moment without your precious *magic* is the reason why I do this."

She still did not understand, her brows narrowing in confusion.

Then slowly it dawned upon her and Valdis watched her reaction. The way he spat the word *magic* had her piecing things together.

She remembered what Tikkani had said as they mucked the stalls, seemingly weeks ago. It was said that Valdis Kruel has been badly abused as a child, his father a powerful merchant who had not risen in the ranks by being a gentleman. He had been a sick bastard who had influenced his son to walk in his own twisted footsteps. A man who had hated magic and had been an instigator in the rebellion against the Fae.

"That feeling is what it is to be human, Miss Clearwater. Or shall I call you Miss Trillia?" he sneered. "Always in fear of those who with the flick of a wrist could snap our necks or stop our hearts with the clench of a fist. To be human is to be weak, and you have no idea what that is like."

Arii swallowed, her throat working on nothing but dust.

Something told her that the burning hatred she could see in his dark blue eyes had not just manifested from his father's influence, but from something more. Something had happened in his past that tipped him over an edge, and as much as Arii wished to know the details of that event – she also wished she never found out.

So, Valdis Kruel wanted to wipe out magic?

Such a thing was not possible.

"How does killing innocent people and tearing out their hearts help you conquer fear? Wiping out magic is impossible, and even that will not sever the divide between our races," she rasped.

Valdis placed the tip of the blade against her neck, just below her chin. His eyes roved her face, before resting on her lips. The feeling of his assessing eyes had her choking down vomit once more.

"I do not wish to wipe out magic… No, I need it for what I have planned," he paused. "The hosts are reacting as expected to their new hearts, but the magic awakening them from death makes them savage and unmanageable." Valdis pressed the dagger tip deeper and Arii's lips curled back. "Soon I will have enough to raise an army, the likes of which this land has never seen before. I just need a way to control them." He clucked his tongue and tilted his head. "I feel close to a solution, so close I can taste it."

"You allowed one of your experiments to run loose in the castle, and it was incredibly close to attacking your own daughter!"

"Ah, the handmaid. An unfortunate oversight on my part – I had not expected her to come back so quickly. I guess I have you and your friends to thank for bringing the success of her reanimation to my attention."

"You are sick!" Arii barked in disgust.

Valdis' lips spread in a sardonic smile in response.

She did not cower, did not flinch before him. White hot rage boiled in her gut, sizzling through her veins. Even without her magic, she was still a Fae.

She was a Fury.

She was The Violet Assassin.

With a swiftness Valdis was not expecting, Arii's hands jerked up and using the shackles she swiped the blade away, the dagger leaving a small hot line of fire on her neck. Her head shot forward, connected with the man's nose and causing a sickening *crack*. Valdis's head snapped back and then Arii was leaping upon him, but not fast enough to prevent his leg flying up and booting her in the chest.

She flew back, hitting the ground a few feet away. Her jaw clacked together as the back of her skull smacked the floor.

Gods, if she did not have a concussion after this, she would be heavily surprised.

That was if she survived this place.

She was so weak, so sure now that she had just used the last of her reserves of strength.

Valdis' hands were in her hair as he lifted her up by the strands. Pain shot down her spine as she cried out, then he threw her across the room so that she skidded along the stone floor only be stopped by a wall. She struggled to rise as the iron manacles clattered against the stone, then hands were upon the front of her filthy tunic as Valdis hauled her to a sitting position. Through the blur of her vison, she saw his face contorted in rage, blood tracking down from his nose and dripping down his chin.

"Oh, I am going to enjoy this, and all that is going to come as I tear down each and every scrap of this land. Nothing will stop me until everything is eliminated, and I am all that remains." Madness glinted in his eyes, and Arii felt fear pierce her soul.

"I will take back what magic stole from me. You see, I am on the cusp of something extraordinary." Valdis lifted the blade again, and she saw that on the end of the hilt, encrusted in the iron head was a glowing orb of Nexus Crystal.

Valdis levelled the knife at her chest, and Arii did not have time to brace.

The dagger of iron punched through her ribs and hot fiery pain unlike anything she had ever felt erupted from her flesh as the iron seared her skin, her insides. Magic flared, blue light erupting and lighting the stone, flashing across a despicable array of iron weapons hanging on the walls around them. She felt electricity surge across her skin, the sweet coat of magic shoved its way down her throat as she gagged, refusing to scream as Valdis continued his torture.

The blade twisted, and darkness speared around her vision.

Pain – pain unlike anything she had ever felt before, ignited her body in flames. Her mind was a whirlwind of pain, fury, fear and regret as the fire consumed her body, her mind, her soul.

Arii slammed her mouth shut and refused to scream, teeth biting into her bottom lip until she tasted her own blood. She refused to give him what he wanted, refused to lay bare what she had hidden for so long.

Weakness.

She could not allow him to have that satisfaction.

As the night drew on, she refused to scream.

She would not give him the satisfaction of seeing her pain.

No matter the agony, never would she yield.

CHAPTER TWENTY-TWO

Lorch had awoken with a smile, his hand sliding across the covers to seek warm skin. Instead, his fingertips grazed only cool sheets.

Empty.

Slowly he sat up and gazed around the room, before spearing his hand through his hair. He could still taste her on his lips.

Arii.

Where was she?

He gazed out the window and noticed a hint of morning blue sky.

"Of course, training," he muttered to no-one in particular as he moved to get changed. He felt light, happy and dare he say sated – for now.

His night with her had been perhaps the best he had ever experienced. She was confident, stronger than he was used to, so sure of what she liked. Her eyes were purple fire, a shade he had never noticed before, and as he had kissed her scars, he had seen something unreadable flicker over her normally stoic features. The entire night he felt she had allowed a little of her walls to crumble, and he was sure he had seen the true Arii beneath.

Fiercely passionate, a woman who he was sure would die for those she loved. That love would be carefully earned, and he was sure once that it was – she would love hard.

Striding from his rooms, he was suddenly faced with Elijah. The man was standing a few feet from his door, hood lifted and mouth set in a frown.

Shit.

"Good morning Elijah," Lorch said merrily and went to brush past him, but Elijah lifted a hand to stop him.

Oh yes, they had not made up after their little argument a few nights ago. Knowing Elijah, it was still a shadow on his mind. When the hooded man spoke, Lorch felt the warm happiness of his Winter Solstice night flush from his body like a cold sweat.

"Have you seen Miss Clearwater?"

Lorch stopped, brows rising. "What, she wasn't at training?"

Elijah shook his head ever so slightly. Lorch felt his heart begin to pace.

"Erm," he offered Elijah his trademark lopsided grin. "I have not seen her since last night."

The air in the hall seemed to become thick.

"Perhaps she is in the kitchens?" offered Lorch gently.

He knew she would not be in the kitchens.

Where was she?

"If you see her, tell her that for not attending training she is expected to run the castle grounds ten times."

Lorch made a face as Elijah spun and stalked from the hallway, his cloak flapping in his wake.

He could not help feeling that something was wrong, very wrong.

ର⊛ର

"Miss Rion, thank you for seeing me."

Nem watched Elijah carefully, unsure as to why he had requested her presence. She could feel something radiating from him, his body seemed to hum with pent up energy as he paced the small room like a caged wolf. She felt he were holding a tight leash on himself, and that leash was close to snapping.

"Of course, how can I be of assistance?"

The bodyguard paused, lifting his hands to slowly pull back his hood. Nem looked up at him from the settee, silver hair brushing her cheek as she surveyed his newly unveiled features. Fingers curling around the handle of a cup of tea, Nem averted her eyes to the amber liquid as Elijah spoke.

"It's Arii. I have not seen her in two days."

Nem paused, the cup touching her lips. She lowered the cup to the saucer on the table before her.

"Arii?" she echoed.

Elijah paused and his arms folded across his chest. "She did not show for training yesterday, nor did she show this morning. I can…" Elijah grunted and glanced away, his jaw set as he ground out his next words as if they pained him.

"I can no longer… sense her."

That had the woman's silver brows shooting up high on her forehead.

Sense her?

Nem paused and allowed her magic to flare out carefully. She did not do it often for fear of being caught, but now she sensed an array of bodies occupying the castle.

None of them were her best friend.

Nem stood then, her striking eyes fixed on the bodyguard.

"Where could she be?"

Elijah strode to the nearby window, gazing down at the courtyard below. His eyes tracked the castle servants as they scurried about, performing their daily tasks. When Arii had not arrived for training, and when Lorch had been alone when he had approached the King's rooms, Elijah knew something was wrong. Seeking Nemesis out was not his first thought, but he had noticed the women spoke quite often, and after some time put the pieces together. They knew each other, and it was likely they were friends. His voice was low, careful, as if fearing them being overheard.

"A small party of carriages left the morning after the party, Valdis Kruel with them. They were bound for Bonemire."

Nem's body went rigid.

"And you think Ariiaya is with them?"

Elijah turned to her. His face showed no hint of expression, but he had noticed the slip from Nem's tongue.

Arii's true name.

He catalogued it for later. If the silver haired woman's reaction had been different, he would have headed to Bonemire alone, whether she had agreed to come with him or not.

"Guests leaving after any festivities here in Viridya are thoroughly searched. None of the guards stationed around the castle exits report seeing her leave," Elijah said

The woman nodded and folded her arms across her chest. "What would you have me do?" she asked, her expression morphing to steely resolve.

Elijah turned to face her fully as he said, "We must go there, under the cover of darkness. Tonight."

꒰꒱

The stone was cool beneath her cheek. Everywhere the floor touched her soothed her tired, aching muscles.

Arii had endured hours of endless torture, how long, she did not know. Her skin had been sliced, before the magic stitched her back up again, her insides seemingly set on fire before magic was used to heal her wounds, ready for the next round. Her mind had blanked after the first hour, darkness pulling her into its inky embrace, so she did not need to feel the horrendous, soul shattering pain.

It was easy, plunging herself into a part of her mind that felt nothing, as if welcoming home a long-lost friend. She had done it before – vision turning inward to a place where she no longer felt the outside world.

This pain though, it was unlike anything she had ever experienced, as if the magic in Valdis' iron dagger set every nerve alight with acid. The crystal set into it was slowly killing her every time he fixed her to the solid wooden table in his room of torture. She saw his face hovering above her, teeth glinting in a sardonic smile.

It reminded her of the Reaper – the creature that had set itself upon Sybell back in the castle.

Now, all she could focus on was the cool stone beneath her cheek.

Her eyes slid slowly to the window, seeing the glittering of stars beyond the barriers. The blink of her lashes was slow, but they did not leave the tiny lights as she lay in her own vomit and bodily fluids.

Her body was covered with cuts and bruises, parts of her skin bubbling with burned flesh. Her face was marred with a bloody lip, her left eye so savagely beaten that her lids had swollen shut.

That was the external damage.

Internally, she felt as if she had fallen into a pit of broken glass.

Why Valdis had not killed her yet, she had no clue. He was obviously trying to get a result from his experiment. What that was, she drew a blank.

The iron manacles remained around her wrists; their weight seemed pin her to the stone floor. She twitched, testing her limbs ever so slightly, her muscles bunched as her brain forced them to move.

She sat up, leaning against the wall, remaining in view of the night sky beyond the window.

Had Lorch reacted badly to her slipping from his chambers without waking him? Had Elijah noticed her absence at training? She wondered if they were both angry at her at that moment, imagining Lorch's gentle frown and Elijah's thrumming disapproval.

At some point, someone had tipped water down her throat. Probably to ensure she did not die of thirst. Her tunic was soaked with dark liquid, a mixture of her own blood, water and vomit.

Gods, she reeked. How long had she been here?

Her vision blurred as she again sought the stars, her entire being wishing that the next time Valdis tortured her, her soul would flee her body in search of the next life. Her body would give out before her mind did, she knew that. With a strange wave of emotion, she hoped she would see her mother, waiting to greet her at the edge of a rainbow celestial clearing with open arms.

Her throat clogged as a small sound escaped her.

No. No, if she let go, she would be turned into one of those mindless *things*. She could not allow that to happen, nor could she allow it to happen to anyone she knew or cared about.

And she cared. Oh gods, she *cared*.

She cared about what could happen to thousands of innocent people, and to those she had grown to love.

Love. It was unfamiliar… foreign… strange…

Her heart squeezed in her chest, her teeth baring as a new kind of pain sought its way into her cold heart. And like always, she flailed with shaky fingers – trying desperately to push the feelings back within the stone confines of her carefully moulded defences. She understood why the Sisters of Fate trained all of their Furies to suppress emotion – locking their hearts against feeling. Feelings opened her to pain – a different sort of pain that had her feeling bare and exposed.

Yet – it also filled her with a fire of determination, and purpose.

She imagined the faces of those she cared about. Krepth, Nem, the recruits. Lorch. And then a last face danced before her eyes, silver eyes gentle yet flickering with hesitation.

Elijah.

Oh, how she cared for them all.

She cared about the strings of their fate – cared with a ferocity that brought forth sparks to her blood.

The emotions cascading through her – they made her feel almost like the magic had never left her body. Tingles danced along her fingertips, a phantom glitter of feeling gliding along her nerves. She lifted a hand, shakily turning it to gaze at her open palm.

Then, before her watery eyes, the tiniest hint of a spark snapped upon her skin.

One tiny spark of magic.

There was a sound at her door, and her heart began to thunder as she feared who was about to enter the room. Thoughts of emotions fled, leaving her pressed against the stone wall.

Were they returning to take her to Valdis again? Already?

The door opened slowly, and Arii blinked as a cloaked figure entered the cell, followed by a second figure. They moved like silent shadows, and Arii felt her world spin beneath her as a familiar voice whispered from the darkness.

"Well, this place is all kinds of brilliant shades of fucked up," whispered Nemesis.

Arii almost cried with relief.

The second shadow swept towards her as Nem pressed the door closed without a sound. Arii found her eyes fixed on two silver pools as Elijah gently wrapped his arms around her, his dark face drawn with a look she had never seen before.

Concern. He was concerned for her.

As he studied her, she felt his body begin to hum with suppressed rage. His eyes were like quicksilver in the dark as Nem slid beside him, her lips uttering a curse as she touched a finger to the iron manacles shackling Arii's wrists. Her hand retreated just as quickly.

"Iron," she whispered with dread.

Arii was almost about to tell her to shut her mouth lest Elijah ask why iron was a concern, but their heads both lifted to sounds outside the cell.

"We need to move, now," ground out Elijah as he lifted her against his broad, solid chest as if she weighed next to nothing.

Her eyes were fixed on his face, wide and unblinking – as if he were some sort of mirage in a desert. She supposed she was probably delusional from the torture.

Was her mind conjuring up this as another form of torment?

Her fingers lifted, brushing his jaw as if to prove to herself that he was indeed real. In response, Elijah's head tilted slightly, eyes lowering to fix on hers as Arii's hand dropped back to her chest.

"You're real." she whispered; her voice pathetic even to her own ears.

Gods how far she had fallen.

Elijah's eyes held hers, his expression softening ever so slightly, the little crease never leaving the space between his drawn brows. Her eyes catalogued his face to memory, seeing it now like she were in a dream. Her memory of him, the memory that had kept her grounded, dimmed in comparison to seeing his face now.

"We are getting you out of here, Ariiaya."

Ariiaya.

Ah, he knew her true name.

Through the haze of her mind, she noted to find out how he had come across that knowledge later. If they survived their escape, of course.

Nem's fingers flew through the air as she weaved a thin veil of magic around them. It would not make them invisible to the eyes, but it would help them escape if they remained in the shadows.

There were a lot of shadows in Bonemire.

The trio swept through the halls, keeping to the darker areas and surveying around corners before continuing when the space was clear. Distant groans and screams sounded every now and then, the sounds more spaced out during the dead of night.

Nem's hand shot out, halting their escape for a moment as a shadow began to inch its way around a corner they were headed. Their backs hit the stone, and Arii heard Nem's sharp inhale of breath.

If they were discovered, she knew it would be incredibly difficult to escape.

Nem drew her dagger as the shadow elongated across the space beside them as its maker drew closer. They could not afford to alert anyone – if one guard saw them, the entire keep would surely know shortly after.

The soldier came into view, and Nem's movements were swift and savage. She grabbed the man's shoulders, pulling him back before her blade was sliding across his neck. She dropped him to the floor and pulled his twitching body back to lean against the wall, his mouth working in a silent scream as his eyes rolled wide.

Leaving the man twitching in the darkness, they hurried on,

keeping to the outskirts as they entered the courtyard containing the caged Kryverns and experiments. In the flickering torchlight, they could see that many of the animals slept.

Nem's eyes danced over the scene, noting the array of humans, elves and even Water Nymphs – their scales glittering with blood, their chests open to the night.

Thank the gods for the tiny mercy of the beasts sleeping.

Nem lead the way as Elijah followed, moving on swift, sure feet as they ducked behind crates of crystals. They were quick to move on, the blue light from the stones sending shadows across the courtyard as they passed.

One of the cages rattled as they crept past, and Nem's hand flew out once more in warning.

Blood red eyes flickered open, nostrils flaring as they froze in front of the cage of a Kryvern. Its head began to rise, eyes blinking as if still waking from sleep. Elijah's voice was a guttural whisper as the beast's lips rippled with the beginnings of a growl.

"Nemesis," he said in warning as jaws began to part, hot breath causing their cloaks to flap around them.

Nem's hand flew out, through the bars and onto the beast's muzzle, palm slapping against solid black scales. She threw magic into her hand and prayed to the Gods that what she was about to try did not backfire. Blue light flashed momentarily as she forced her magic into the beast's skull, directly into its brain.

Blood red eyes dimmed and slid shut as the Kryvern's head slowly dropped, rippling jowls softening as she put it back to sleep. As its head rested on the floor, Elijah's breath whooshed from his lips silently.

"Impressive," he whispered, meeting Nem's small, triumphant smirk.

"I can't believe that worked," she whispered back.

They continued on, clearing the area to head into the inner ward of the fortress. They paused as they surveyed the main doors into the structure.

Firmly closed.

Elijah's eyes slid to Nem, and with a small nod, the Fury slipped into the shadows.

Elijah stepped into a dark enclave, setting Arii down while he waited for Nem to open the doors, hopefully undetected. His muscles bunched, ready to spring into action if this went badly.

Arii grimaced, her swollen eye darting to find his face. Elijah placed his palm against her cheek, his hand practically hovering for fear of hurting her. In the short time he had known her, he had become used to her sassy, bold and strong demeanour. To see her so broken physically, it took his breath away. Even now as their eyes met in the dim light, he saw dim, flickering fire in their purple depths.

He knew that even the worst torture could not douse the fire in those eyes. It had been there from the moment she had knelt before the King at his birthday celebration and every time they had exchanged threats in the castle halls, or when they sparred in the training ring. There was a fire in her that he could not help but be drawn to, no matter how hard he tried.

"You look like shit," was all he could manage, and her lips curled in a smirk that ended in a pained grimace.

"I may need to borrow your hood," she croaked in reply.

"Hah." Elijah's laugh was half hearted, before his expression became serious once more. "We are going to get you out of here, you have my word."

Arii lifted her hand to rest on his own as it continued to cup her cheek. Her touch was cool against his warm skin, nails skimming his knuckles as her eyes drifted shut. Her head tilted against his palm, her lips parting with a tiny sigh that had Elijah's creased brows softening.

Elijah promised himself that he would do anything to see her safe again, see her unharmed and fighting with the ferocity and fire he had come to admire.

When their gazes met once more, Arii felt a heavy weight press upon her chest, and at the same moment – felt she may just drift away upon the storm clouds in his eyes.

She realised then that it was not gravity keeping her there at that moment.

It was him.

Elijah.

She felt as if he *was* her gravity, keeping her to the Earth.

His face was all she could see, the taut pull of his lips, the unexpected softness in his eyes.

Oh, how things had changed in the last few days.

She could not imagine anyone better to have come to save her. She imagined Elijah and Nem would be a force to be reckoned with.

Above, the gates creaked and began to open. Elijah deftly scooped her up once more, her entire body protesting with burning hot pain, and she bit back a scream. She would not undo how far they had come.

Nem leaped and landed with a subtle thud a few feet away, wiping a blood coated dagger on her sleeve as they made their way through the gates, swiftly melding into the darkness beyond.

૦૩৪૦

Once out of range of any eyes upon the fortress walls of Bonemire, Elijah began lifting Arii onto the back of his black steed while Nem untethered her own horse. When she groaned in pain, he immediately paused.

"No," Arii groaned, and it took a moment for Elijah to understand that she was struggling to be released from his grip.

"You cannot stand let alone mount a horse on your own," he said firmly as she groaned again.

Nem lead her dappled brown mare over to them.

"N-no, you cannot take me… back to Viridya," Arii ground out.

Nem paused and her eyes met Elijah's. "She's right, as soon as they figure she is missing, the castle is the first place they will look."

She paused. "We need to take her to the Sisters."

Elijah's brows narrowed in confusion, and Nem's lips curled. "The Three Fates," she elaborated.

Well *hell*, if Elijah was not already suspicious of who Arii truly was, this was surely going to reveal it to him.

Elijah gently set her down at the feet of his horse as Nem placed her hands on her friend's shoulders. Light flared as she attempted to heal some of her wounds, but her magic was almost spent. Between keeping up the veil and making the Kryvern sleep, she found her pool was depleted.

Warmth flooded Arii's muscles, seeping into her bones. She could feel some of her internal hurts slowly disappear as Nem leaned back into a crouch, heaving a sigh. "We should get moving. I can take her from here."

"I will come with you." Elijah's voice was like the steel of his sword, hard and sharply edged.

Nem hesitated, before her head snapped to the man, her eyes luminous in the dark. "Absolutely not."

"And why not?"

"Because it will look awfully suspicious if Valdis returns and his son's personal bodyguard is nowhere to be seen."

"I will leave before the sun rises." He paused. "Having only been gone for one night, that will not be seen as overly suspicious," he reasoned, his tone firm.

"And could you return to the castle before the sun rises?"

"Caviar here is the fastest horse in the stables. He will get me back before sunrise."

"Caviar?" laughed Arii between them. Elijah's eyes dropped to see her grimace, a hint of her flippant attitude leaking through her pain. He huffed just as the dark horse behind them snorted. "I did not name him…" Elijah muttered, as if offended.

When his eyes lifted to them once more, the silver haired Fury's arms were crossed upon her chest, chin lifted stubbornly, and eyes narrowed. Nem was assessing the man carefully, her face not at all looking convinced, but slowly her expression softened.

"Fine, but we must go *now*."

What she had seen between them in Bonemire was not but a fleeting moment. Nem had felt the fire between her friend and the man, seen the tender way the guard handled her. Ariiaya did not need tender handling, not really – the Fae needed a strong partner to move with her, bring out the fiercely passionate woman Nem knew her to be inside.

Elijah had not needed to come to the fortress, he had not needed to put his life on the line to save a Fae. He had, though – and Nem knew that if she had not come with him, then he would have come alone.

Whatever Arii was part of in that castle, Nem had a feeling she was in deep. Things were slowly making sense, her hesitation and fixation on finding out about the Kryvern with iron claws. It was safe to say now that they knew what was transpiring, and it was not good.

With a swift nod, Elijah helped Arii up onto Caviar's back, mounting the horse shortly after her. Even though she was still burning on the inside with aches and pains, Arii was incredibly aware of the solid form at her back as his arms came around her, clutching the reins.

Despite herself, she found her body leaning back into him, her head resting against his bicep as her eyes drifted closed.

She swore she heard a soft intake of breath before she drifted into a fitful sleep.

VALDIS
KRUEL

CHAPTER TWENTY-THREE

Arii's eyes slowly opened, her vision blurring before gradually coming into focus as consciousness took over, her sluggish brain catching up with what she saw.

Moonlight dusted the grey sheets of the cot where she lay, streaming through the windows and gently lighting the small room. There was a hearth, the logs within crackling with flames. The room was warm, and she could smell the smoke lingering in the air.

Her eyes slid across the room, seeing the familiar imperfect stone walls, the smattering of vines as they crawled through a breach in the wall and spread across the stone. There was a damp, salty smell in the air, a constant reminder of their proximity to the ocean.

The School of Fate.

Her lungs expanded as she breathed in deep, taking in the familiar scents of her home. The crumbling structure perched upon the bluff was nothing in comparison to the glittering gold castle of Viridya, but the old building had its own kind of strange, ancient charm. It was old, run down and half falling apart, but it was home.

She felt tingling in her fingers, her lungs expanding again as a feeling of lightness washed over her.

Magic.

It simmered through her veins, like liquid starlight. With a small sigh, she welcomed the feeling with wide open arms.

Feeling like part of her soul had clicked back into place, Arii's lips twitched with a smile, before her eyes slowly rested on a cloaked figure, sitting beside her bed.

His dark hair was bathed in silver light, his body leaning forward and arms resting on his knees. Elijah's dark, brooding face was angled, his brilliant mercury eyes fixed entirely on her.

She felt that familiar weight of his gaze upon her, that hot sizzle down her spine and the rising of the hairs on her arms. At first, she had thought it was her magic reacting to the man, but after seeing him in Bonemire when her magic had been stripped – Arii knew the feeling was far deeper, something within her very soul.

"Do you often watch women while they sleep?" she said by way of greeting, her lips parting in a wide yawn as she hesitantly stretched.

"Not often do I find myself rescuing women from Bonemire," he replied, his voice deep and soft in the silent room.

Arii rubbed her eyes, before pausing at the lightness of her arms. She lifted her hands in front of her, almost crying in relief as she realised the iron manacles had been removed. All that remained was lightly irritated pink skin around her wrists. Her eyes found his once more.

"You saved me. How… How did you know where I was?"

Elijah paused before speaking. "When you did not appear for training the morning after Winter Solstice, I presumed it was due to the copious amounts of wine and mead you consumed during the night." He tilted his head, surveying her.

Argh, he *had* been watching.

Elijah did not mention that he had first looked for her in the company of the King, deciding it best that that detail was left untold. "But when you did not show the second day, I grew suspicious."

She offered a weak smile. "You thought I was off slicing up bandits on the road again?"

Elijah shook his head briefly. "No – something felt… off. I could no longer sense you."

Sense her? Strange…

"When I approached Nemesis, she confirmed my suspicions that you were no longer in the castle. The fact that a procession had left headed for Bonemire was not unusual, but I placed the pieces together."

Arii's eyes remained fixed on the hard lines of his face, the shadows flickering over his features from the flames of the fire in the hearth. The stubble upon his cheeks and chin seemed darker… thicker.

She thanked the Gods then that he was so observant. She was absolutely positive that she would not have been able to escape Bonemire on her own. He had saved her life.

"You endured something unimaginable in the fortress, your injuries were complex and strange." He surveyed her, eyes flicking over her face as if she were a puzzle to solve. "The healers said you had injuries that looked to have been weeks old on the outside, but when they delved deeper…" He paused. "The tissue of your injuries looked to have been damaged hours before."

Arii swallowed.

"Look, Elijah I – I don't know how far your loyalties run when it comes to Valdis Kruel–"

"I serve Lorch, not Valdis. He may be the King's Hand – but my loyalties ultimately lie with the King, and no other…"

When Arii remained silent, Elijah hand began to twitch her way – but stopped, as if he had thought better of it.

"What did he do to you?" he asked softly. Had Arii not known Elijah, she would not have heard the hint of suppressed anger in his deep voice, coating the tone of concern.

"He…" Her eyes lifted to his after a slight pause. "He experimented on me, using iron and Nexus Crystal. He seems to think there is a way to control those *things* – there are more of them, many more Elijah. I'm unsure if he got the answers he sought before you found me…" Her voice trailed off and a phantom bloom of pain speared across her chest, as if her mind were fighting against the memories.

When Elijah remained silent, she wondered if he could see the pain she was trying so hard to hide. Her eyes dropped to her pink wrists, her hands resting on the sheets in front of her and their location in that moment dawned on her. Her features were unveiled, her eyes vivid violet and skin luminous, and they were in the place where they trained young Fae to become assassins.

"We have to talk," she said, her eyes reluctantly sliding back to Elijah.

As she thought, his gaze was still fixed on her, and she felt the familiar thrum of something in the air when she was around him.

"Indeed, we do," he agreed, his tone unreadable.

Arii swallowed thickly, watching him in silence for just a moment before speaking. She felt he was waiting for her to speak first, and she was almost unsure of where to begin when Elijah spoke.

"You're one of the Fae."

It was not a question. More like a statement. She nodded in answer.

"So, your strength, your battle prowess – you learned it all here?"

Another nod as she took her bottom lip between her teeth. She was waiting for an explosion, for him to yell and scream at her in anger of this revelation, for keeping the truth from him.

Elijah did no such thing, proceeding to stare at her thoughtfully in the firelight.

"And I'm presuming you are a Fury, one of the assassins trained here by the Sisters of Fate." He had been quick to piece it all together. She had known Elijah was no simpleton, he had a mind as sharp as the sword he carried at his hip.

"Yes, all correct," she said, noticing his eyes were on her lips then, watching as her bottom lip popped from between her teeth.

Why was it that his intense gaze had her feeling almost… self-conscious?

She *never* felt self-conscious.

Her hand lifted to her face, feeling that her swollen eye was healed, and her split lip was gone.

Elijah's eyes tracked her hand before they met hers.

"Why were you sent to Viridya, Ariiaya? Why hide under the guise of a mere servant girl, and endure the training and guard duty?"

Arii felt she was treading dangerous waters. She could not tell him the true reason for her undercover operation in the castle. He may have saved her life, but she knew him well enough to know that as soon as the truth spilled from her lips, his sword would be through her heart before she could blink. She saw the metal glint at his hip, as if to emphasize the thought.

"Perhaps I simply admired the King?" she hedged, shrugging her shoulders.

Elijah's lips twitched. "I guess that is likely. Lorch does seem to have a way with women. I would not be surprised if he worked his magic on you."

Elijah now knew what she was, what she was capable of. The irony of his choice of words was not lost on her.

Arii huffed at this, her hand clutching the sheets as she glanced down once more. She remembered the feel of Lorch's body against her own, skin on skin as their bodies melded as one on the night of Winter Solstice. Her fingers gripping the sheets reminded her of his hands tangled in hers upon the white bedcovers as warm pleasure bloomed through her body.

"That he did…" she whispered absentmindedly.

Elijah shifted in her peripheral vision, and the air in the room suddenly felt cold. Her eyes lifted to him, and she was not expecting the glint of silver anger in his eyes.

"You and Lorch…" He did not finish, but his meaning was clear.

Her hackles began to rise at his tone, her eyes narrowing into slits.

"What is it to you if we spent the night together?" she snapped.

Elijah was standing then, the wooden chair skidding back as he went rigid, his hands balled to fists at his sides.

"He… He is the King! And you're a-"

His mouth gaped as sudden realisation dawned upon him.

"You were sent there to kill him."

Another non-question.

Arii sat up straight in the bed, her own hands balling.

"Yes, alright, yes! That is why I was there." She threw back the sheets covering her as Elijah turned and headed for the door.

"But I didn't!" she yelled at his back as her bare feet slapped the stone floor.

Elijah paused before the door, his body so rigid she wondered if his spine would snap. Suddenly he was whirling, his face twisted with fury as he stalked towards her.

She barrelled on, a strange sense of fear coiling in her gut. Not of *him*, but at how close he was to *leaving*. Had her mind not been so preoccupied at the thought of his near departure and the strange feelings it dredged up, she would have slapped herself again at the fissure forming in her defences.

"I couldn't do it, I…"

He was before her then, tension radiating from his body in tsunami waves, his face inches from her own. Her shoulders began to quake under his shadow, her nails biting into her palms.

"I would rather fight the strings of fate than harm a hair on his head. On *either* of your heads," she whispered hoarsely, her voice thick with emotion.

Elijah's eyes flicked across her face, and when his expression did not change, her voice dropped to barely a whisper.

"A Fury is not meant to feel what I have been feeling over the last few weeks. We are not meant to question fate, and we sure as *hell* aren't meant to develop… feelings." Upon the last word – her voice cracked.

Elijah's eyes softened ever so slightly and his face began to change.

She laid herself bare to him then. Her eyes dropped to his boots, as if she could not bear to look at his face as the words spilled forth.

"But after getting to know you both, I have done just that. I have questioned everything! Everything I have ever been taught, everything I have been trained not to *feel*." Her voice began to rise, and she felt the air crackle with electricity.

Elijah was silent as he towered over her.

Tears pricked in her eyes, real *godsdamn* tears and she could not stop them. Her walls – her carefully constructed walls were crumbling around her and she could not stop the dam threatening to burst forth from her heart. She recalled the warmth in their silver depths as his head inclined towards his painting – a dimple appearing on his cheek as she praised his talents by the shimmering pool. She remembered his face as he gazed down at her on the floor of the cell, his arms coming around her as he lifted her to his chest.

His eyes as they swept over her damaged face.

Concern, anger, thinly veiled fury behind a cover of storm clouds.

It caused her vision to swim as she finally said, "And I would not change a single moment, nor do I have a single regret. Yes, I was sent to the castle with orders to kill, but I would not have done anything differently," she swallowed before whispering, "I do not regret questioning fate."

Fingers touched her chin, then hesitantly her jaw – gently bringing her face up. Elijah's hand slid to cup her cheek, and through the swimming of tears in her eyes she saw he was watching her with an intensity that she did not have the words to describe. His face was wiped of anger, replaced with a look similar to the first time she had uncovered his face in the library, the first time she had seen his incredible features and silver eyes. It was awe, as if he were seeing her for the first time, his eyes shimmering with an intensity she was not sure she was ready for. She supposed he was seeing a part of her unveiled which she had never allowed anyone to see before – a part of her which was always there but hidden so deep she had believed it gone.

Hesitantly he leaned in, his lips brushed hers with the tenderness of butterfly wings. She felt as if her legs would give out, her entire being having been torn asunder over the last two days, not just physically but mentally. He was her anchor in that moment, the only thing keeping her from drifting away.

What had kept her clinging to sanity during Valdis' torture was not only thoughts of her friends – Krepth and Nemesis, people she had known for half her life, but those she had discovered over the last month. Tikkani's crude humour, Emerson's blushing cheeks and Quinn's cheeky grin. She had envisioned her night spent with Lorch, his easy smile and the unexpected gentleness he was not truly known for.

Then there was Elijah, the dark and mysterious man whose eyes mirrored a haunting inside him that she had not had the chance to discover. Nor had she the chance to help erase the hazy pain in his eyes, the pain she knew he felt within his soul. As he had looked down at her in Bonemire, she had seen that exact feeling mirrored in his eyes, a flame of determination to end her suffering, flickering like the beginning of a firestorm.

Now, that firestorm was making its way through her veins, igniting something within her chest. As Elijah's lips slanted across her own, a little more forcefully this time, she felt it rage into an inferno.

Despite everything she had done, despite what she was and how he no doubt viewed her kind, he kissed her. Kissed her with a tenderness that curled her toes and snatched her breath from her lungs. His hands slid around her waist, her own sliding around his neck and burying in his thick hair as he lifted her up, his grip surprisingly firm despite her fragile state a few hours ago.

Thank the Gods for the healing power of magic.

Her legs wrapped around his waist as their kiss deepened. He tasted of the forests around Evergrave, of pine and woodsmoke.

He tasted of home.

Gently, Elijah lay her on the bed, his body following to cover hers, the cool buckles of his uniform pressing against the skin of her abdomen as her loose tunic rose with their movements.

Fire, it burned her from the inside out.

She heard the clatter of his sword as it hit the floor, so consumed with him that she had not noticed him removing the weapon. Their kisses became deeper, less hesitant and more desperate. Hungry, heated. They hardly broke apart as her hands flew to the front of his uniform and using just a flicker of magic, she popped the buckles and clips of his leather tunic.

He paused, their fervent breaths melding as his lips hovered above hers. She had begun to push the tunic over his broad shoulders when he whispered, "Arii, wait."

She stopped to meet his eyes. She waited – partly because he had asked but also because she was suddenly breathless. Then she inhaled sharply as her gaze danced down and caught sight of his body.

Elijah's torso was perfectly sculpted, his arms and chest solid with hardened muscle. His body was a canvas of battle scars, healed to little ridges. On his chest was a light dusting of dark hair, and trailing lower she saw a puckered scar on his lower abdomen.

Stories upon his flesh, just like her own.

She wanted to ask him for their stories, learn how he received each one, but now was not the time. Her eyes lifted to his, and she expected to see a frown.

Instead, his face held a surprisingly hesitant look – lips pursed, and brows drawn. "You were close to death only a few hours ago, perhaps we should stop," he whispered.

Gods, she did not want to stop. Fire was pooling in her core, and she wanted so badly to sate the intense desire now rocketing through her body. His eyes were dark silver pools, his body thrumming as if it were taking all his immense strength to hold back. It pressed against hers, his thighs aligned with her own and she knew he felt exactly as she did in that moment.

Elijah Wolfe, seemingly the master of self-control, was quivering on the edge of the same cliff as herself, mere steps from freefall.

Her eyes flicked across his face, seeking any other signs of uncertainty, but was met with a look of dark smouldering silver.

Decided, her hands gently pushed the tunic over the bunched muscles of his shoulders, watching as she leaned forward and pressed her lips to his shoulder, before brushing her canines against the thrumming pulse at the base of his thick neck, the beast rising and rippling beneath her skin.

"I don't want to stop," she breathed against his earlobe.

"Ariiaya…" he whispered hoarsely, her name a prayer and a curse. A slow smile curled her lips, igniting her blood with sparks.

Swiftly he removed his leather tunic and rested against her again, his weight causing her body to sing. She had not known that such intense, soul-altering desire such as this even existed. Her time with Lorch had been gentle and sweet, a moment she did not regret, nor would she forget.

This though, this feeling with Elijah was bordering on primal. Despite wishing to have his skin against hers, she felt the strange need to prolong the moment, wring every little sound and feeling she could from him – and she wanted to hear her name as a whisper on his lips a thousand times more.

He was magnificent, every inch of him moulded from years of intense training. The Fae within her was clawing, keening to be released.

No holding back.

No suppression of her true nature.

She did not wish to hold back any longer, the feelings thundering forth like a raging, whipping storm. Fae loved with a fierce intensely, almost to the point of obsession. Until now she had never felt what she had only heard described in textbooks in the Fate's library, and by those who had been lucky enough to have the feeling themselves.

A Fury was not meant to have such intense feelings.

The man above her was tugging at the untamed part of her that normally lay dormant. Now it was throwing itself against her walls, desperate to reveal her bare soul under his heavy silver gaze.

She wanted to give him what little she had.

All the emotional turmoil she had experienced in the last week had her almost suffering whiplash. One moment she wished to drive her blade through his chest – the next she wanted to make love to him until the mountains shook with their ecstasy.

His lips crashed against hers, his body radiated heat, thrumming with desire that matched her own. Her hands slid around to his back, to muscles which felt as if they were made from steel beneath his skin. Her fingertips skimmed lower.

Then she felt them.

Large, violently raised scars upon his back.

Sucking in a startled breath, Arii's fingers traced the imperfection, the large ridges of impossibly long puckered flesh that ran from the middle of his back, down to just below the belt of his breeches.

Elijah turned impossibly still above her, his lips hovering over hers as his breath fluttered across her face.

"Wh… What happened to you?" she whispered, inhaling her horror, unable to hide the tremor in her voice. Her hand traced the other side of his back, feeling similar violent scars.

His voice was soft, deep as he whispered, "I… I am unsure. I have had them for as long as I can remember. My memory of my past is hazy at best."

He did not remember anything before Colleen had found him in the woods near Amberbourne. She swallowed and continued to trace his scars, her fingertips feather light, causing him to shudder above her.

"Show them to me," she exhaled, her voice but a whisper.

Hesitantly, Elijah pulled back from her, and the expression on his face was almost… pained.

"Please," she said, her purple eyes glittering in the moonlight. "You don't have to hide your scars from me, Elijah."

He watched her for what felt like an eternity before he moved from her and stood beside the bed. She followed, sliding to stand before him as he watched her, his chest rising and falling quickly from their breathless kisses. The moon bathed his broad chest in pale light, casting shadow across his clenched jaw and hard muscles.

Slowly he turned his back to her, and the breath left her lungs at the sight of him in the mixing of moonlight and golden torchlight.

Three thick puckered tears marred the perfection of his skin, running from mid-back to just below his belt. They looked old but were still raised upon the skin as if they had been left upon him only a few months ago. No steel could have done this, no manmade weapon in existence that she could think of.

She wanted to bellow at the Gods for allowing such a horrible thing to happen to him, to mar such a perfect canvas of skin. The event that left such things on his body must have been incredibly traumatic, the pain excruciating. He had endured something truly macabre, and the haunted look in his eyes that she had witnessed seemed all the more warranted.

Slowly she brushed her fingers over the skin, tracing the ridges from pointed tip to the thicker parts of the tears.

They looked like the claw marks that riddled her jail cell in Bonemire…

Elijah's shoulders shuddered and his head tilted back. Arii leaned in, pressing a kiss to the first scar, and then the second.

Beyond the old castle, waves crashed against the bluff, and she swore she heard thunder boom far offshore.

Little did Arii know, Elijah had never allowed anyone to touch him like this, to see the full extent of his ravaged, marred skin.

Perhaps she was not the only one changing tonight.

As soon as she placed a kiss upon the last scar, Elijah turned to face her, expression unreadable.

"Gods, you are so… unexpected." he whispered. His eyes danced over her face, and she wondered how he could look upon her with such rapt awe.

"Forgive me, Elijah… I never meant for any of this to happen."

His head tilted as his expression changed to confusion.

She continued, gesturing between them. "I'm an assassin – not meant to feel, not meant to think. Everything I have been through this last month has shattered years of training. I'm…"

Elijah's fingers lifted to her lips, his other hand slid around her waist as he said, "You're apologising for feeling emotion?" When she swallowed and glanced away, his fingers pinched her chin, bringing her gaze back to him. "Never apologise for how you feel. It is part of being…" he paused, brows narrowing.

"Human?" she finished, lips parting with a low breath. "I'm not human, Elijah."

He blinked slowly, eyes roving her face. "Perhaps Fae can feel with an intensity that surpasses that of human emotion. You have all just forgotten how…"

She smiled at that, before his lips were on hers again in a far softer, far tender kiss that had her heart fluttering and her toes curling. His kiss was almost hesitant. His fingers traced her jawline, then the shell of her ear. For a warrior, his touch was so incredibly gentle. He had seen her in action, he knew she did not need delicate treatment like a maiden – and yet, he handled her like she was made of glass.

For just a moment, she felt herself believing that his words could indeed be true.

Gods in the skies above, she had become totally and utterly tangled up in something she swore would never touch her ice-cold heart. The muscle was thundering in her chest, adrenaline coursing through her body as if she were about to stride onto a battlefield.

She needed him like the breath in her lungs.

"I'll kill whatever did that to you…" she breathed, palms pressing against his chest – needing to feel his solid heartbeat – needing to know that he was truly here before her and not a mirage. The deep reverberation of his dark chuckle rumbled beneath her fingers, his lips brushing the tip of her ear, then her neck. His lips met hers again, the tug drawing upon her heart more forcefully now. Her nails pressed into his flesh, and she felt his hand splay on her lower back, pressing her against him.

A knock sounded at the door and Arii stifled a groan of frustration.

Were they destined to be constantly interrupted?

Their foreheads touched, and Elijah sighed deeply. Her hand curled over his as it cupped her cheek, their eyes closed and breaths combining as they stood in heated silence. Their heavy breathing was the only sound between them, and she wondered if he could hear the steady staccato of her heart, the air thick and humming with energy and desire. She could smell it – taste it upon the salt flecked air.

Elijah moved from her reluctantly, eyes fixed on her before breaking away and dipping to retrieve his tunic.

He was pulling it over his shoulders and buckling the front when Nem entered the room.

The Fury paused, a look of suspicion on her face as her gaze slid from Arii – swollen lipped beside the cot – to Elijah.

"I'd get your arse back to Viridya before your absence becomes truly suspicious," she said to him.

Silver hair flashed, and she was gone just as quickly as she had appeared.

A long, shuddering breath escaped Arii's lips.

What an absolute mood kill.

"She is right," Elijah said, his voice hoarse. He wanted to finish this just as much as she did, but she knew that now was not the time.

Now was not *their* time.

She felt her heart squeeze with anguish.

He must have noticed the look in her eyes, for his expression softened in the moonlight. "I dare say we will finish this later, but I do not know when I will see you again. I must return to Viridya and warn the King."

He was right, and the longer they spent together now, the further the darkness within the depths of Bonemire would spread. Arii's throat constricted, but she shoved some of her fire to the surface.

"Perhaps I will come find you, we aren't done talking, Wolfe." Her voice came out far stronger than how she felt inside. She had always been so strong, so sure.

Now, she wanted to clutch the man and not let him go.

The thought was so foreign to her that she paused, biting her bottom lip.

His lips curled at her words, and she was almost knocked over by the beauty of his half-smile. Gently, his hand slid around her waist, drawing her body against his once more for a deep, passionate kiss.

Not wanting the moment to end, her hands slid into his hair again, curling in the dark mass.

Elijah's mouth dropped to her neck, and she took a swift intake of breath as her palms brushed the top of his ears – just as his teeth grazed her flesh.

His ears were delicately pointed.

His teeth against her skin, canines elongated.

Had they been before? Her mind was suddenly hazy.

As if in a dream, his hand passed her cheek, fingers threading in her hair – but not before she saw evidence of burns on his palms. In her pained daze during their escape from Bonemire, she now recalled Elijah attempting to pull the manacles from her wrists just after they had found her, burning his hands in the process.

As they parted and Elijah retrieved his sword, Arii could only hear the buzzing of bees in her ears. She forced a smile through the weight and revelation as he lifted his hood, glancing at her one last time before sweeping from the room.

His unbelievable strength, his deadly swiftness, the way the air seemed to become heavy around him as if his emotion were a tangible thing.

Her heart almost stopped as puzzle pieces slid together.

Elijah was a Fae.

ɔʒ8ʋ

"I guess we should be grateful for the King's personal guard for returning you to us in one piece, Violet Assassin. Grateful so we can kill you ourselves!"

Klotho's face was a careful mask of fury, her tone underlined with disapproval.

Arii kneeled before the dais, the Tapestry of Life glimmering behind their ornately carved chairs, looming over them as if to bear witness to her damnation. She kept her head bowed, the thick locks of her hair hanging like two curtains over her shoulders.

"Forgive me," she muttered.

What else could she say? Sorry, Sisters, I think I am developing feelings? Feelings you have spent the last eighteen years ensuring I should never, ever feel?

Lakhesis' voice sounded from the dais, the cadence soft and calm unlike her sister. "Now sisters, I'm sure she has a very good explanation."

Etropos added quickly, her voice high pitched. "Of course! Why else would the King not be dead right now?"

Arii's eyes lifted to the Sisters, three sets of golden eyes upon her. She slowly stood, her chin rising as she fixed her gaze on them.

"I believe my target was incorrectly identified," she paused as the three sets of eyes began to dart amongst one another at her words. When none of their faces showed any expression, Arii felt the hairs on the back of her neck begin to stand, cold rage seeping into her bones as she growled, "You are not surprised."

Lakhesis spoke first. "Sometimes the Gods provide… murky hints as to who they decide. It is possible that our visions may have been misconstrued." She looked almost troubled, her fingers tapping against her lips.

Klotho's face was hard, but her tone softened ever so slightly. "It is rare, but not unheard of. We trust you have not come to this assessment lightly?"

Arii's nod was swift. The less she had to tell them about the finer details of her time in the castle, the better.

"Nemesis would have filled you in on what we witnessed in Bonemire, and the events leading up to my capture. Valdis Kruel is using Nexus Crystals to reanimate the dead in a bid to forge an army. He seems to believe using the crystals will somehow allow him to take the entire Kingdom by force, the other Courts included."

Arii had never seen all three Sisters of Fate speechless before, their faces shocked and angry.

"I would say impossible, but I believe you would not lie about this, Ariiaya," said Etropos before adding, "If what you say is true, then a darkness is about to fall upon Fythnar the likes of which has never been seen before. If Valdis finds a way to control this… army of undead, I fear our small force of Fury assassins will be no match." Her face was drawn, her hand flying to press against her temples as she paced the dais.

"How has he powered the crystals, with magic being so scarce?" said Lakhesis. Her eyes met Etropos'.

"Perhaps this could explain the reason why all male Fae have been slowly wiped from existence. Valdis and those before him have ensured that when this army was finally risen, there would be no-one powerful enough to stop them."

As the Sisters tossed around theories, Arii could not help but notice how quiet Klotho was. The dark-haired beauty was watching the Tapestry, her lips set in a line.

"I have a… feeling, but I need some more information before I can draw a conclusion." Arii moved a few steps toward the dais. "What do you all know of the night the royal family was killed in Viridya Castle?"

Lakhesis' brows rose in surprise of the sudden turn of conversation. "What has that to do with Bonemire?"

"The royal family – the Heringtons. How did they die?" Arii persisted, ignoring her question.

Lakhesis' lips pursed before she answered, "It is said it was a band of rebel forces, intent on stealing from the castle. The royal family and their subjects were but collateral damage. I heard those rebels allowed Kryverns to infiltrate the castle, it was a bloodbath. Some seem to believe that it was not just rebels looking to steal gold, but a revolution from within the royal ranks themselves."

A cold chill slithered down her spine as Etropos continued for her sister, her voice light as it delivered the sickening story. "The humans began to fear the Herington sons had magic. Those poor children were slaughtered in their beds on the night of Winter

Solstice," she paused, her eyes troubled. "If the stories are true, one of the sons survived the initial attack – the youngest son, Eliverus, but he was said to have been mauled to death by a Kryvern in the aftermath." Etropos' tongue clucked with pity.

"I need to return to the castle," Arii suddenly said, spinning on her heel. The Sisters watched as she headed for the doors. Klotho spoke from the dais, causing Arii to pause in the doorway.

"Guard your heart, Violet Assassin. You are going to need all of your strength for what is to come. May the Gods watch over you."

Klotho's words sunk to the core of her, far deeper than they would have a few months ago.

ETROPOS
Melissa Kincaid

CHAPTER TWENTY-FOUR

Arii's hands flew over the buckles of her horse's saddle, securing straps with deft fingers. She had donned her fighting leathers, strapped her daggers to her hips and ensured she had enough steel on her person to take on a small army. How she was going to get into the castle unseen, she was not sure. She thought it best to move now and think later.

"Do you not think you should rest just a little longer?"

Arii peered over her shoulder to see Nem, leaning against the stone wall of the stables, expression unreadable.

"I need to get back," Arii said simply.

Nem pushed away from the wall, to stop just a foot away. "It's about him, isn't it?" A pause. "Elijah."

Arii worked in silence, feeling her friend's eyes on her back.

When the silver haired Fury did not budge, Arii turned to face her. "What is about to be unleased from Bonemire will hit Viridya castle first. I can't let that happen, Nem. They must be warned."

Nem's brows narrowed. "But Elijah would have already warned them. He might be dead now for all we know, if Valdis noticed your disappearance first. They could all be dead."

Arii's heart jerked and her pain must have shown in her face, because Nem's eyes widened and her expression turned to surprise. She had had a feeling, but Arii's reaction to her crude words iced the sweetcake.

"You're in love with him… *Nyx's tits!* You're in love with *both* of them!"

Silver flashed, and Nem's back hit the wall with a violent thud as

Arii's dagger hovered over the woman's heart. Violet eyes ablaze, teeth bared in a feral snarl, Arii pressed the metal into her best friend's tunic.

"A Fury does not feel love!" Arii bellowed, her calm composure slipping and her reaction telling Nem the truth far better than if she had admitted it in words. Arii's hands trembled, the fingers curled around the dagger quivered and the blade began to lower. Her eyes were fixed on Nem's, their depths mirroring confusion and pain.

"We are not *supposed* to love, Ariiaya. That does not mean we cannot."

As much as Arii wanted to deny it, as much as she wished it were not true, Arii knew that her heart was cracking in two.

Nem's voice was gentle, but firm. "Only you know your heart, Arii. Follow it and it will lead you true. I know it's against everything we have been taught – but if you feel you must go, then I will not stop you."

The dagger lowered slowly; the two Assassins' eyes locking as Arii stepped back.

"Go, and for the love of the Gods, do not die," Nem said, inching her head in the direction of Viridya.

Arii sheathed her dagger, swiftly mounting her horse as it stamped its hooves in preparation, flanks twitching with adrenaline. Her eyes slid to her best friend, their depth dark as her expression softened.

"Thank you, Nem."

"In what world could an assassin be a hero?" Nem laughed darkly.

Arii flashed a small smirk at her friend. "I'll let you know when I see you next," she called as the horse reared, shooting forward and flying through the castle gates and in the direction of Viridya, moving as if Kryverns were snapping at their heels.

ଓଃ

Arii pushed her mount to breaking point, flying across the land at a breakneck pace, the earth moving beneath in a blur. Her mount was breathing heavily as the golden castle peaked over the rise, and once within distance of the bridge, she led her horse into the trees and out of sight. Sliding from the mount's back, she lifted her hood and headed towards the castle, her steps swift and intent.

Guards lingered before the castle gates, heads lifting as she approached. After a quick assessment of her face, one man motioned to another upon the wall, and soon the gates were opening for her. Luckily after her time training on the grounds, the guards knew her well enough to allow her swift entry.

There was no sign of an attack, no sign of distress as she slipped into the castle halls, heading swiftly for the throne room. It was late afternoon – the sun was just beginning to slip behind the mountain peaks, bathing the land in brilliant shades of apricot. The light filtered through the windows, making the golden lining of the walls shimmer.

It was odd, now that she was back within the warm hued halls, she realised how much she had missed the golden goliath of a structure. The distant hum of the waterfall was a sound she had become used to.

As she closed in on the throne room, her keen Fae hearing picked up the murmur of voices within. She paused, throwing her back against the wall and veiling herself in magic just as the door opened and a small group of soldiers exited.

A guard meeting? She supposed they were assigning more guards to the King and his family. Well, that was what she hoped. As the men marched down the hall towards the barracks, she closed her eyes, her senses flaring out tentatively to survey the throne room. She felt her breath release as she felt only one presence. Humming, and heavy.

Elijah.

Swiftly she slipped into the room and closed the doors gently behind her. Elijah was leaning over the sturdy mahogany table where the King often took his meals, a map spread over the surface, his fingers splayed across the parchment. As she stepped forward, he removed the hood from his head, sighing deeply. She paused, surveying his broad shoulders, the mass of dark hair on his head, the pointed ears she knew he hid underneath. No wonder he had allowed his hair to grow, had hid under the hood of his uniform for so long, building a mysterious persona that hid his face from everyone.

Elijah turned to her, his silver eyes widening with surprise.

She almost wept at seeing him unharmed. She had braced herself to find the castle in ruins, the people she had come to know – come to love, nothing but mindless husks of their former selves.

"Arii?" he whispered.

She stepped towards him, feeling the air sizzle with a familiar energy. Her eyes drifted closed, her lips parting as breath blew from her lungs. She thanked the Gods that Lorch was not in the room for what she was about to say.

"The night you received those scars on your back, what do you remember?" she said gently, and Elijah stiffened.

"Nothing, I've told you this."

"What is the earliest thing you can remember, before you came to live in the castle?" she urged, taking a step forward.

Elijah's keen eyes tracked her step, and his eyes flew back up to meet hers. He missed nothing. His expression was instantly guarded.

"Colleen's face when she found me in the forest between Viridya and Amberbourne – Arii, what are you doing here?"

She ignored him and stepped closer, hands up and palms towards him, the pink skin of her wrists visible to his gaze.

"Do you not feel like you are different, Elijah? Your speed, your strength – faster and far stronger than any human or elf."

Elijah's voice dropped an octave as he spoke. "Stop."

The air hummed between them as she inched closer.

In the beginning, she had believed it merely to be a product of his mysterious presence, the feeling of being in proximity of a powerfully trained bodyguard. She had also thought it were a strange sort of air of attraction, a tether drawing her to him, invisible strings of fate pulling them to one another. Now she realised it was far more than that.

"And your canines?" She opened her mouth, pressing fingers to her own elongated two teeth. "Do they not resemble mine?"

"That's enough," he bit, voice laced with cool anger.

Now she was before him and he had not moved a muscle. She gazed up into his eyes, noticing the chocolate tinge in his dark locks as the afternoon sun bathed his hair.

Sweetness coated her tongue like honey.

"Can you not taste it, the strange sensation on your tongue? Can you not feel the roiling of something beneath your skin? I know you can feel it, it is how you found us the night Ingrid attacked Sybell in her rooms."

"No..." he whispered then, moving from her and pacing a few steps away to the middle of the room. Golden light streamed in the cathedral windows, blanketing the colossal room in hues of red and orange. Arii remained where she stood, watching as Elijah shook his head in denial.

"Arii, you don't know what you're saying."

"I have never been so sure, Elijah. You may not know, but I do. I know who you are..."

Elijah's silver gaze met hers, and she saw the darkness of thunderclouds rolling behind his eyes. The fog hazing his mind, the doors firmly locking memory just out of his reach was slowly cracking open. Her voice was soft, but it seemed to echo about the room as she finally said it.

"Eliverus Herington."

Dead silence, before a boom of thunder sounded in the distance.

Odd, there had not been any signs of a storm minutes ago.

"No."

Elijah's voice was low, guttural, barely a whisper, the syllable laced with something Arii could not understand. She stepped forward, watching as Elijah's shoulders began to shake, his entire body humming, hands balling at his sides.

Power, untapped and unbidden, pressed in upon the room. The air was so thick with it, Arii almost felt she was wading through water.

Magic.

This magic though was unlike anything she had ever witnessed or felt before. It was as if the air was becoming harder to breathe.

"You have been suppressing your magic for over twenty years, Eliverus."

Elijah whirled on her then, his face twisted in agony.

"Don't call me that!" he bellowed, the cords of his neck straining as he pressed his hands to his temples, the rolling boom of thunder sounding closer now. "That's not who I am, I'm-"

"I can feel it, taste it in the very air of this room. Your magic is brimming, churning, and straining against the very fibres of your being. You cannot suppress it much longer, or it will kill you."

Gods, it was killing *her* to see him in so much pain, pain from the truth as memories slid from the darkness of his mind. Elijah made a sound like a groan of anguish as Arii stepped forward. Her face slowly morphed to mirror the sympathy she felt – her eyes glistened with unshed tears.

She had to do this, had to tell him the truth of what she had pieced together.

"It was the iron – the iron in the claws of the Kryvern that left those scars on your flesh. It must have suppressed your awakening, keeping it within you and that may have resulted in your amnesia. You survived the night your family was slaughtered. Elijah, you're the last of the Herington bloodline, the true heir to the throne of Fythnar."

"No, no I'm not... I'm not some lost Fae prince!"

"Gods, the Reaper! Your magic drew the Reaper to the castle when it attacked Sybell," she whispered, eyes widening as realisation dawned.

Elijah groaned again as he said, "Gods, it isn't true."

The cathedral windows shuddered above, and Arii's head snapped up to the sound. The golden chandeliers swayed as flashes of lightening strobed beyond the towering windows.

She barrelled on, feeling every muscle in her body tense as power rippled through the room. "You could be the last hope we have to stop what is about to be unleashed from Bonemire, Elijah. You're the only surviving male Fae magic wielder."

Another shudder, the goblets rattling as one fell on the nearby table, spilling wine across the dark wood, causing a shadow to bloom across the map of the continent.

Perhaps an omen for what was to come.

Elijah suddenly jerked, hands flying to grasp at his tunic as she felt a snap of magic on the air. Her breath inhaled sharply, the air in the room rapidly thinning. The floor rumbled beneath them, as if something were threatening to break through the surface.

His expression of agony told her that he knew what she said was true, the memories were flooding back with such intensity that he was losing grip of his magic, loosing grip of himself. He had kept his magic on such a tight leash for so long, kept it buried inside himself, wondering what he truly was but knowing he could not allow anyone to see.

It was pressing upon them, pressing against her chest as if she were being gripped in a vice, and Arii knew they were seconds away from a cataclysm.

Elijah's eyes were wide and glazed as their depths began to glow with blue light. The air about them snapped with energy, and Arii saw her hair begin to rise as if invisible fingers tugged at the strands.

Arii let her feelings show, her eyes pleading as thunder boomed above them. Elijah's face was a crystal clear picture of anguish.

"Let me help you," she whispered desperately.

Then, the doors to the throne room flew open, the wood crashing against the stone walls with a resounding crack. Valdis entered the throne room, flanked by five soldiers of the Red Guard.

Arii spun, facing the man. As his eyes surveyed the scene, she saw rage twist his features into a look of pure fury.

"You!" he snarled.

Thunder boomed again and silver light streaked the cathedral windows, the glass within rattling as the entire castle seemed to shake. The guards gasped in alarm, steadying themselves as Valdis stepped further into the room.

Arii's pulse thrummed in her ears at the sight of the cause of her torture, the man who had almost shattered her body, her mind and soul. She had never known hate so acidic as it washed over her, making her fingers itch and shoot to the dagger at her hip.

Her hand paused above the hilt as Lorch pushed into the room behind his father.

Arii's heart hitched as the King stopped, his expression one of confusion, and then when his eyes slid over her and Elijah, it changed to something unreadable. She saw the beginnings of pain flicker across his face.

"Arii?" he said, stepping forward. "What is going on?" His eyes darted over her pure unveiled features, her luminous skin, her vivid purple eyes and to her pointed ears as her hair levitated around her.

"Lorch," Arii whispered, hands rising to the daggers on her belt as the earth quaked beneath them. "I can explain…"

Lorch's brows scrunched, his chin lifting ever so slightly as he surveyed her with apprehension in his eyes. Then there was the tiniest shutter in his blue eyes. He shifted, his hand gently rising in a clenched fist.

A flash of glowing gold.

She noticed then with a slow dawning horror that it was her golden thread from the Tapestry of Life, laced over his clenched knuckle, touching his skin with warm gold light.

No, he could not find out – not like this.

Before she could explain, Lorch's eyes widened and darted over her shoulder, and the hairs on the back of her neck stood on end.

Behind her, Elijah groaned, and as Arii turned to him upon the dais, the rumbling of the waterfall beneath them slowly faded before it just…

…stopped.

It was as if the world outside the castle had suddenly fallen completely and utterly silent. Arii felt as if her ears had been covered with pillows – as if someone had just ripped hearing away from her senses.

She watched, eyes widening as Elijah dropped to his knees, his hands flying up to clutch at his skull as he yelled in pain.

Something snapped in the air, as if a final tether came free…

And the colossal glass cathedral windows above the throne imploded.

⋘⋙

Her magic flared just as the crackling force hit, palm snapping out to erect a swift shield of magic in front of her as the room exploded into a glittering, electrified whirlwind of untamed power.

She glanced back to see Lorch's eyes widen in sudden realisation, and the momentary distraction had her magic ripped from her palm and the breath smashed from her lungs. Her body was lifted and thrown across the room as her vision blacked out.

Moments later, Arii's head lifted from the cool marble floor, her vision blurring then slowly coming into focus. The guards, Valdis and Lorch had all been thrown across the room too. Her ears rang, her movements disorientated as her hearing slowly returned amongst the shrill squealing of her burst eardrums.

Blinking slowly as if in a dream, she glanced to where Lorch lay flat on his back, a line of blood trickling from his ears. Her hand gently wiped at her own ears, coming away red.

Her eyes darted to the dais, where Elijah remained knelt with his head bowed. Movement drew her eyes to the side, and she saw Valdis had recovered far quicker than anyone else. He was rising on shaky legs, unsheathing his sword and heading in the direction of the dais.

No.

Elijah!

Arii felt as if she were wading through thick oil, her movements sluggish as she rose, boots slipping on shards of glass. Her muscles bunched and she sprinted for the dais, her hearing returning with the sound of Valdis's enraged roar.

His sword came down, aimed for Elijah's head.

Her boots skidded again on the glass, her daggers shooting out to intercept the sword. Steel clashed and her arms shuddered at the impact, her crossed daggers stopping his sword in its tracks.

Valdis's face was twisted with rage, his lips peeled back in a snarl. He leaned forward, so close that she could see the whites of his wide eyes, the tiny cuts scattered across his skin from the glass, blood trickling down from his ears. "I should have killed you when I had the chance."

"You are going to wish you had done far worse," she sneered back, pushing her energy into her legs and thrusting herself forward. Valdis was shoved back, sword jerking to the side before he brought it back down upon her with an enraged yell. Her blades flew, deflecting the steel as they broke into a swift dance of sword against daggers.

Valdis was quick, but they were both still slightly disorientated and she had to admit he was keeping up with her far better than she thought him able.

Arii spun, dagger narrowly missing his arm as Valdis jerked to the side, before swinging the sword savagely at her thigh. Blocking just in time, Arii slid steel on steel until the blade of his sword met with the cross guard of her dagger, using it as leverage to twist his sword away, making an opening for her to attack.

Her blade sang through the space, slashing across the man's gut before she sheathed her dagger in one swift movement, spinning in a pirouette before slamming her palm into his chest. With a cry of anger, she threw a punch of magic into her palm, causing the man to fly back with force and crash to the marble floor below.

When Valdis' sword skidded across the floor and the man did not rise, Arii spun to Elijah. They did not have long.

She sprinted to him to clutch at his face, raising it up.

His silver eyes met hers, swimming with a look so pained, so haunted that it stole her breath away.

It was then that Ariiaya Trillia made her choice.

"We have to go – now!" she whispered urgently.

When Elijah did not move, she growled a curse and grabbed his arm, sliding underneath to help lift him. She was strong, but not strong enough to carry him completely.

"Eliverus!" she yelled, jerking his bulk against her, and attempting to rise.

He seemed to respond then, slowly rising with her help. He was in shock, she knew that. When she was a young girl and her magic awoke, the feeling was as if something had exploded within her, like a supernova within her soul. That was from roughly a decade of stored magic in the body of a child.

Elijah had just allowed over *twenty years* of pent-up magic to break free, magic that he had held suppressed the entire time, magic he had never learned how to control.

She could feel his trembling, the static radiating from his body as he shuddered. They moved from the room, stepping over the bodies of the guards.

Arii stole a glance at Lorch, his prone form laying sprawled on the glittering marble floor.

She felt pain unlike that inflicted upon her in Bonemire. This was something else entirely – the beginnings of her heart's severing.

She wanted to take him with them, but that was impossible. She could feel her heart breaking, a fissure splitting it in two and she stifled a sob.

Overhead, alarm bells began to toll.

The entire castle would be on alert now.

They stumbled down the castle hall, gold a blur either side of them as they ran. Ahead, two guards entered the space with weapons drawn. Arii drew one dagger after another then cocked her arm back before letting the steel fly. The metal buried itself in one man's chest, the second spearing through another's jugular.

Another soldier appeared, sword drawing before Arii threw a burst of magic, causing the man to fly back into the wall with a sickening crash. She grunted, still bearing some of Elijah's weight as they passed, her hand flying out to grab the dagger lodged in the guard's chest.

They could not escape through the castle gates; they would surely be overrun. If Elijah fought alongside her, they would stand a chance. She knew he was too far gone at that moment to be of any assistance.

She could think of only one way out of the castle. He was not going to like it, and there was a chance they may die anyway. Arii figured it was a risk she was willing to take. Valdis would not kill them quickly should they be caught. Elijah's very existence meant overwhelming danger – and hope. Hope that could cease all of Valdis's plans in Bonemire.

The waterfall rumbled as they stumbled on to the Dragon Landing, light mist coating their leathers as she dragged Elijah onto the flat expanse of stone. The Sapphire Depths beyond shimmered, the dark depths a blue blanket beneath a twilight sky of purple, blue and gold.

"We cannot allow you any further."

Arii stopped dead as a familiar voice sounded ahead.

Standing with weapons drawn, donned in full guard uniform – stood Tikkani, Emerson and Quinn.

No, no, no.

Arii grunted under Elijah's weight, her eyes spearing to the three recruits. "Let us pass," she said, her tone laced with stone and non-negotiable.

"What the *fucking* hell is going on, Arii?" snapped Tikkani, and Arii was almost surprised to see Emerson hardly flinch at the curse.

The boy stood, sword lifted but she could tell it was half hearted. He was unsure.

Above them the bells tolled again. Her eyes danced over the trio, Tikkani's look of anger, Emerson's pain and Quinn's drawn, unsure face. Three faces she could not bear to hurt.

"I don't have time to explain. Let us pass," she growled, stepping forward. When the three did not budge, Arii's face twisted into a look of pain and fury.

"I swear to the Gods, I will kill you all if you do not let us pass – now!"

The fissure in her heart threatened to break further.

Please, do not make me do it. Please, Gods!

Tikkani shot a brief look at Emerson, and then Quinn. It was Quinn who lowered his sword first. Emerson slowly followed, then Tikkani's voice whispered, "Go."

Arii did not have time to thank them. She hauled Elijah past them, heading for the peak of the landing. Quinn cried suddenly. "Wait… where are you going?!"

Arii peered over her shoulder, eyes of amethyst shimmering as her lips curled, a ghost of her usual roguish grin alighting her features.

"Tell them we fell."

Hold on Elijah, she thought.

With that, the woman clutched the man at her side and shot a prayer up to the Gods as they tipped over the stone barricade–

And fell.

Fell and disappeared into the white mist of the raging waterfall below.

EPILOGUE

Moments before he had followed the commotion to the throne room, Lorch had paused in the doorway of Arii's rooms, hoping to find a clue as to where she had gone. Elijah had remained stubbornly silent the morning after her disappearance, prompting Lorch to lead his own search.

Arii's rooms had been immaculate – not a piece of furniture out of place. What had drawn his attention to the slightly weathered chest at the foot of her bed, he was not sure. But as he neared it and spied the faintest hint of gold light filtering from the keylock, Lorch had not expected to find the luminous, magical thread inside.

He knew what it meant, everyone in Fythnar did.

The pieces had fallen together as he stared at her in the throne room some time later. Her eyes were a vivid purple, her skin luminous. Somehow, her features were sharper as her hair whipped about her face, her ears narrowed to delicate points which he had not noticed before.

Magic flamed from her palm, and Lorch felt several realisations spear his heart just as the flare rocketed out from the dais.

First, Elijah had magic. Impossibly powerful and untamed.

Second, Arii was a Fae, and he had been falling in love with her.

Then his body flew back from the force of the blast, his skull hitting marble and causing his vision to snap to black.

What felt like moments later, he was being woken by a firm shake to his shoulder.

"Lorch."

His eyes opened slowly, before blinking rapidly. He felt as if cotton lined his eardrums and he could taste blood on his tongue. Hesitantly, Lorch stared up at the man who had woken him.

Valdis rested on his haunches and watched him silently, eyes narrowed and face flecked with tiny lacerations. Lorch remembered his father had been at the forefront, before Elijah… It had been Elijah who had made the room explode with magic, had it not? As he stole a glance past his father's shoulder, he saw the throne room in complete disarray.

The chairs on the dais had been toppled, the table upturned and the beautiful windows – they were a shell rimmed with broken glass. The floor glittered with shards of all sizes.

Elijah had done this.

How? How had he hidden magic for so long and no one had known?

He had been by the King's side for so long, a constant protection and faithful servant to the Crown. Lorch swallowed thickly then noticed a dark red stain on the belly of his father's tunic.

"You're hurt," he choked out.

"The Fury bitch nicked me before escaping with the Fae traitor." His father's tone was laced with acid. Lorch felt as though strength would never return, his muscles refusing to obey.

"Get yourself looked over by the healers, then we must organise as many men as possible to form search parties. Wherever they have gone, we must find them." Valdis motioned to the dais, where Lorch now noticed blood on the marble. "They have injuries, which may aid us in catching up to them, but we must act quickly."

Lorch felt numb. His body, his mind, his heart. His entire being was completely and utterly devoid of emotion.

As guards escorted him to the medical ward, he felt as if the golden halls around him were a blur within a dream. Two healers fluttered about as they poked and prodded him for signs of injury but Lorch knew that apart from bruises and a few shallow cuts, physically he was fine.

It was the damage within that they could not see, damage to his heart, slowly manifesting into a raw flicker of anger.

Had it all been a lie? What he had shared with Arii in the month since his birthday celebration? He felt he had partially thawed the walls of her stoic demeanour – her guarded face began to soften as he allowed her closer. She was not like the many women he had tangled with before – he found himself chasing her. As the King, he had never had to make the effort before. She was fierce and harsh, but he saw something in her – a tiny flicker of her soul behind her large dark blue eyes.

No... not dark blue – violet like the amethyst stones lining his crown. Violet like the skies above the castle just as the sun dropped behind the mountains.

He figured then that she had dimmed her looks with magic.

He remembered the feel of her soft skin beneath his fingers as he traced her scars... her gentle moan as they came together in his bedchambers. Had his mind not been so drugged by her, perhaps he would have put things together far sooner.

Gods, he had been such a fool.

If she were indeed an assassin, why had she not ended him? She had plenty of chances, plenty of times they were alone where she could have slipped a blade into his heart.

But she had not.

Perhaps he was not her target? Perhaps it had been Elijah all along, and she had used him to slide into his best friend's defences too.

Fire began to rise in the King's chest.

"Leave me," he snapped at the healers, and they exited swiftly at his command.

As the door closed behind them, Lorch stood from the cot and paced to the window. Moonlight now blanketed the courtyard below, highlighting a mad scurry of soldiers as they prepared small groups for search parties.

Elijah. His best friend, his protector, the one person with whom he felt he could be himself – was a Fae. Thinking back about their lives growing up, things were beginning to make sense – Elijah's withdrawn nature, his memory loss resulting in him unable to tell Lorch where he had lived before the castle, his insistence on his cloaked garb. He had been hiding – and Lorch was unsure if he had even known himself what he truly was.

Elijah had always had a weighted feel about him, the very air around him charged with energy. Lorch had figured it was just his nature – a result of the battles, the intense training… the countless lives he had taken in the name of the Crown.

Now he realised it was far more than that.

The door to the medical room opened, and his father entered. Valdis pushed the door closed before striding to his son. Lorch's gaze met his father's, and what Valdis saw there made his face harden – but not with his usual look, Lorch realised. It was a look of determination.

"I don't understand how we harboured a user of such immense magic, and for so long. How could we not have known?" Lorch said.

Valdis's brows narrowed. "Elijah Wolfe took us all for fools, my son," he paused, before speaking again. "We have reason to believe that he is in fact the last remaining son of the Herington bloodline."

Lorch's eyes widened.

"What?"

"Eliverus Herington, the rightful heir to *your* throne, my son. He appears to have survived the Kryvern said to have mauled him to death twenty years ago."

When Lorch did not speak, his father stepped forward. "That is why it is imperative we locate him and the Violet Assassin quickly. If word spreads to the other Courts, they will rise up in support of Eliverus. They have been waiting for an opportunity such as this, I feel it in my bones." Valdis' tone had begun to rise, as if he were suppressing something – excitement perhaps.

Pain laced Lorch's chest, seizing his heart in a fist. He bellowed in anger and smashed his hand across the table nearby, sending a glass of water across the room to crash in shards on the floor. Lorch dropped to his knees, clutching his hair.

Rage and pain, so potent he could taste it, shuddered through his body like shockwaves.

Valdis almost looked startled; Lorch was not known for outbursts of rage. He had always been so calm, so uncaring of anything to do with the Crown. It had made Valdis' overarching control so easy.

Slowly his expression changed to something else.

"You're angry, son – I can see that. This woman meant more to you than you care to admit – Elijah too. They betrayed you, betrayed the Crown." He knelt before his son on the floor, his hand resting on one shuddering shoulder. Lorch's head was bowed, his breaths choked and ragged as Valdis slid a hand into his own pocket.

"I have a plan, a plan that will ensure our grasp of the throne is secure, and all threats will be wiped away."

He produced a glowing shard of ragged Nexus Crystal.

Lorch's eyes lifted to the blue glow, then widened.

"My methods have been… well let us say not everyone would agree with them. But I am on the cusp of a breakthrough that will soon make us invincible. No one will question your place on the throne when I am done."

Lorch stared at the severe scar on his father's face, the spark of cold determination in the eyes that mirrored his own. He saw something else there, something shifting within the blue depths that he had only seen glimpses of before.

Madness.

In that moment though, his own heart was torn asunder, shattering like the glass windows above his throne room. He had been too gentle, too blind to see what was happening right beside him. Perhaps he had been too consumed by the fancy glitter of court life and all the perks which came with the job of being King.

It had allowed him to be used, to be stomped on and tossed aside.

No longer.

Lorch's hand lifted to rest on top of the glowing stone.

Its flickering light danced over his features as he whispered in a voice so resolute he almost believed it was not his own.

"Show me everything."

FROM THE AUTHOR

My story has passed through a few hands before landing in yours, so I have some people to thank who helped shape my debut novel into something incredibly special.

To my husband, Greg – I could not have written *Love, Blood & Fury* without your unwavering and unending support. Thank you for your patience with me, and for putting up with my hours and hours of silent treatment as I blasted music in my earphones and delved deep into my world while commandeering your work laptop. I also appreciate your help with my publishing timeline and setting out a clear plan to ensure I kept my release date in sight. I love you so much, and you are undoubtedly the gravity holding me to this Earth.

To my parents, Lynne, Allan and Carolyn – You all helped shape my love of reading from an early age, and most of all you have shaped me to be the person I am today. My fondness for reading is your doing, and without your encouragement I never would have taken this leap to publish something that is truly my own. You have all been so incredibly supportive, and I know you are all my biggest fans. I love you all immeasurably.

To my draft readers! Alisha – your intense enthusiasm from the moment I voiced my plans to you, up until the moment you finally had my draft in your hands has been a shining light on this whole journey. Thank you for picking up those hilarious typos, and for your suggestions on some key scenes.

Kate – you were the first to finish my book and the first to suggest so many great ideas that, as you will see, I took on board. Those ideas helped make *Love, Blood & Fury* even better, and for that I am incredibly grateful to you. Thank you from the bottom of my heart.

Marie, Tamara and Jennie – thank you for cheering me on and taking the time to have a read through my story. I hope you enjoyed reading it as much as I did writing it.

To Kalynne Vorster (Kalynne_Art on Instagram), who illustrated the three images of Arii, Lorch and Elijah – you took what was in my head and brought them to life on paper. You are severely talented, and I am incredibly grateful for your work. I am so excited to feature them in this book, and I know my readers will love the beautiful pieces as much as I do.

To my incredible editor, Carolyn Gilpin, I cannot thank you enough for your time and efforts with my manuscript. Thank you for pointing out some plot holes that I would not have noticed, along with your honesty, enthusiasm and positive feedback on my story. Your expertise has helped smooth out my work considerably and even though the readers would not see the difference – I surely can. I am so grateful to you!

To my son, Elijah, who will have just been born by the time this book was released, hopefully you inherit a bit of my love of books in the future, and I hope one day you can read this and be proud of your mum.

Lastly, to you – the reader. The fact that you are reading this right now means you made it to the end of my first novel. There are not many words to convey how truly humbled I am that you have my book in your hands right now. Whether you loved it, enjoyed it somewhat or thought it was not quite your cup of tea – just know that I am grateful that you gave *Love, Blood & Fury* a chance.

As I mentioned before, this is my first book. *Ever.* I am not a professional writer by any means, and what I have learned has all been from reading loads of books of similar genre. Those who know me will know how much of a major bookworm I am, and how much I adore books! (Not necessarily good ones, mind you. Like Arii, I too shamefully judge books by their covers!) The story of Arii, Elijah and Lorch has been in the back of my mind for a long time. The general plot, their names, their appearances and their personalities have all been stuck up in my brain for ages, just waiting for me to put pen to paper and bring them to life. I'm not going to lie and say that this process was easy – it wasn't! I was scared – very scared – of how my book may be perceived, and if it would be liked at all. I had no idea how to make a story flow, but with the help of some writing apps, a bunch of incredible friends and an editor, I was finally able to get the story of *Love, Blood & Fury* together.

My ultimate goal was to write a story that I myself would enjoy, something I would happily pop on my overly full bookshelf along with all of my favourite books. If I were to give any advice at all to aid you if you were thinking of writing your own novel, it would simply be: Don't think – just write!

There is a lot left to come for Arii, Elijah, Lorch and the gang, and I hope you will continue to follow their journey when I release book two in the not-too-distant future.

Finally, from the deepest depths of my heart, thank you for your support.

See you in book two!

THE
Strings of Fate
SERIES

STRINGS OF FATE BOOK ONE
LOVE, BLOOD & FURY
MELISSA J. KINCAID

STRINGS OF FATE BOOK TWO
MAGIC, MIDNIGHT & STARLIGHT
MELISSA J. KINCAID

STRINGS OF FATE BOOK THREE
FIRE, FURY & CHAOS
MELISSA J. KINCAID

Spin-off
STRINGS OF FATE BOOK FOUR
AFTER the FURY
MELISSA J. KINCAID

Melissa J. L. Kincaid is a fantasy author from Melbourne, Australia, who has a passion for creating worlds filled with magic, adventure, and heart. Known for her rich world-building and strong female leads, her stories often weave together forbidden love, powerful magic, and epic battles, a blend that draws in fans of both fantasy and romance.

Melissa took the plunge into self-publishing in 2021 with her debut novel, *Love, Blood & Fury*. She went on to release *Magic, Midnight & Starlight*, before bringing the trilogy to a breathtaking close in 2024 with *Fire, Fury & Chaos*. Not yet ready to leave the world behind, she returned in 2025 with *After the Fury*, a spin-off that invites readers back into the realm they had come to love.

With a background in graphic design, Melissa brings her creativity full circle by designing her own covers and book interiors, ensuring every detail matches the vision of her stories.

When she isn't writing, illustrating or curled up with a fantasy book, Melissa enjoys exploring the outdoors with her husband, Greg, and their son, Elijah Gregory, often camping under the stars.

www.**lotsoflovecreations**.com.au

 /melissa.j.kincaid

 #melissa.j.kincaid.author

 @melissa.j.kincaid.author

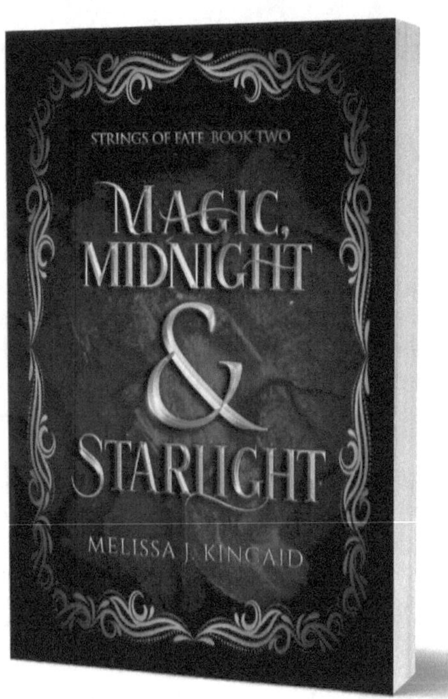

The heart-stopping second book in the thrilling *Strings of Fate* series - an exhilarating romantic fantasy set in a hazardous world of magic and adventure where stakes are high, love is a war of many hearts, and fate is never truly set in stone.

Did you enjoy the story?

PLEASE LEAVE
a Review!

KALYNNE ART

goodreads

fable

THE STORYGRAPH

Reviews help independent authors like me reach more readers. Every review means a lot!

Scan the code to go to Goodreads.